RIDER OF RO...

THE IRON GATES

By S.J.A. Turney

First Edition

For Ciprian and Leo, both of whom, for me, bring Rome and Romania together

I would like to thank Rod Walker, the cavalryman on the book's cover for permission to use his image for Maximus, and for his enthusiasm and support. Huge thanks also to Ciprian Dobra, Centurion of Legio XIII Gemina in Alba Iulia, and to Leo Bacica, a long-time good friend and lover of Roman fiction, both these men being inordinately clever, conversant with Rome, and sons of Romania. I would like to thank the wonderful Leni McCormick, who has been instrumental in so many of my novels reaching print, and the fab Gordon Doherty, my long-time collaborator and friend. And then last, but far from least, my amazing wife Tracey, so still, incredibly, puts up with me. All of these people helped read, test and shape this book in its final format. Thank you, and mulțumesc, all!

Cover cavalryman photograph courtesy of Michelle Walker, also with thanks.

All internal maps are copyright the author of this work.

Published in this format 2024 by Mulcahy Books

Copyright - S.J.A. Turney

First Edition

The author asserts the moral right under the Copyright, Designs and Patents Act 1988 to be identified as the author of this work.

All Rights reserved. No part of this publication may be reproduced, stored in a retrieval system or transmitted, in any form or by any means without the prior consent of the author, nor be otherwise circulated in any form of binding or cover other than that which it is published and without a similar condition being imposed on the subsequent purchaser.

By the same author:

The Praetorian Series

The Great Game (2015)
The Price of Treason (2015)
Eagles of Dacia (2017)
Lions of Rome (2018)
The Cleansing Fire (2020)
Blades of Antioch (2021)
The Nemesis Blade (2024)

The Marius' Mules Series

I: The Invasion of Gaul (2009)
II: The Belgae (2010)
III: Gallia Invicta (2011)
IV: Conspiracy of Eagles (2012)
V: Hades Gate (2013)
VI: Caesar's Vow (2014)
VII: The Great Revolt (2014)
VIII: Sons of Taranis (2015)
IX: Pax Gallica (2016)
X: Fields of Mars (2017)
XI: Tides of War (2018)
XII: Sands of Egypt (2019)
XIII: Civil War (2020)
XIV: The Last Battle (2021)
XV: The Ides of March (2023)

The Ottoman Cycle

The Thief's Tale (2013)
The Priest's Tale (2013)
The Assassin's Tale (2014)
The Pasha's Tale (2015)

Wolves of Odin

Blood Feud (2021)
The Bear of Byzantium (2022)
Iron and gold (2022)
Wolves around the throne (2023)
Loki unbound (2024)

Rise of Emperors (with Gordon Doherty)

Sons of Rome (2020)
Masters of Rome (2021)
Gods of Rome (2021)

The Agricola series (as Simon Turney)

Invader (2024)
Warrior (2025)

The Damned Emperors (as Simon Turney)

Caligula (2018)
Commodus (2019)
Domitian (2022)
Caracalla (2023)

Tales of the Empire

Interregnum (2009)
Ironroot (2010)
Dark Empress (2011)
Insurgency (2016)
Emperor's Bane (2016)
Invasion (2017)
Jade Empire (2017)

Standalone Roman novels (as Simon Turney)

Para Bellum (2023)
Terra Incognita (2024)

The Templar Series

Daughter of War (2018)
The Last Emir (2018)
City of God (2019)
The Winter Knight (2019)
The Crescent and the Cross (2020)
The Last Crusade (2021)

The Legion Series (Childrens' books)

Crocodile Legion (2016)
Pirate Legion (2017)

Non-fiction:

Agricola (2022)
The Roman Auxiliary Units of Britain (2024)

Compilations, Novellas & Other works:

Tales of Ancient Rome vol. 1 (2011)
A Year of Ravens (2015)
A Song of War (2016)
Rubicon (2019)
Vengeance (2020)

*For more information visit www.simonturney.com
or follow Simon on:
Facebook Simon Turney Author aka SJATurney (@sjaturney)
Twitter @SJATurney
Instagram simonturney_aka_sjaturney*

Maps

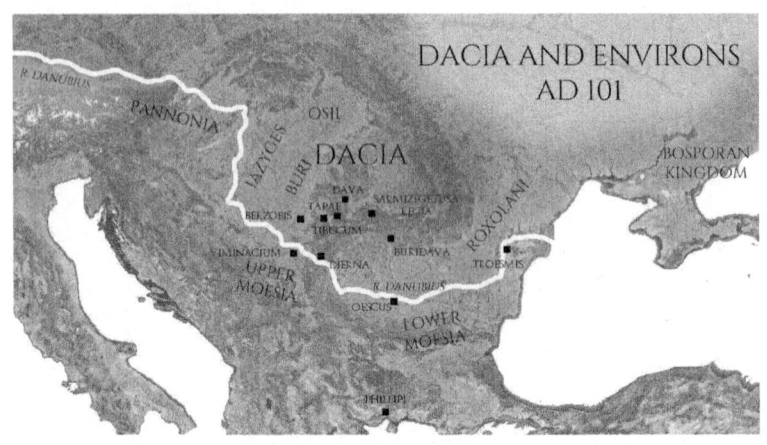
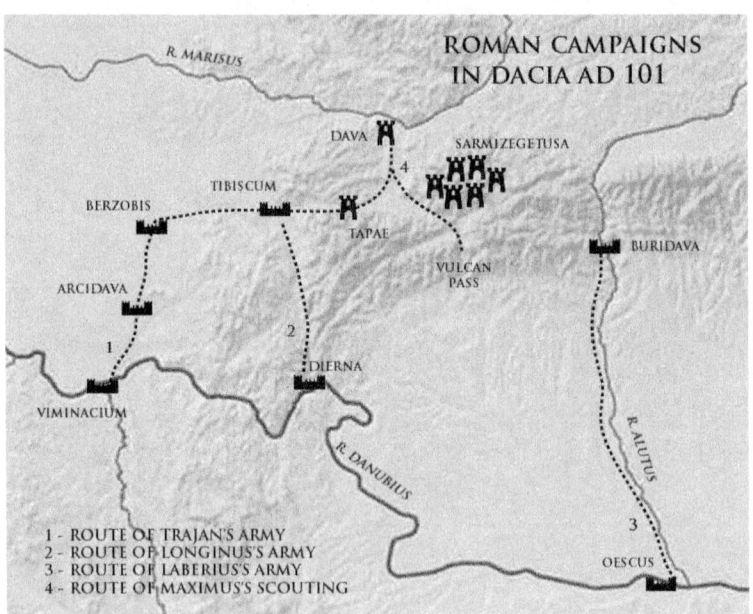

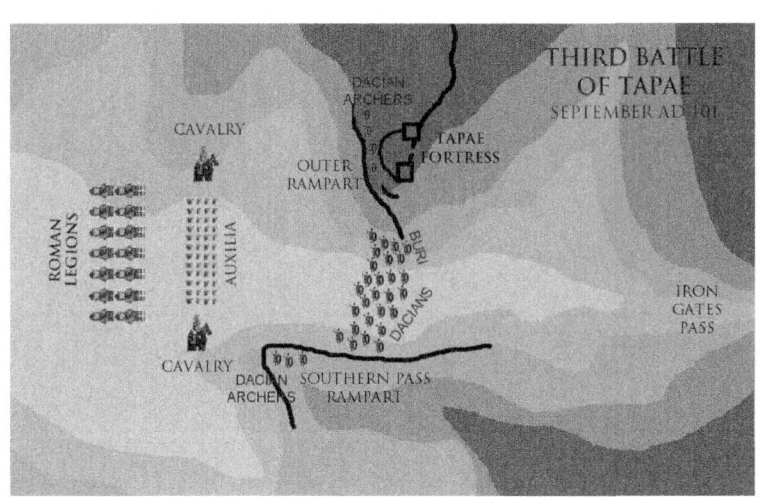

"After spending some time in Rome he made a campaign against the Dacians; for he took into account their past deeds and was grieved at the amount of money they were receiving annually, and he also observed that their power and their pride were increasing. Decebalus, learning of his advance, became frightened, since he well knew that on the former occasion it was not the Romans that he had conquered, but Domitian, whereas now he would be fighting against both Romans and Trajan, the emperor."

Cassius Dio: Roman History 68:6

Chapter One

Thirteen years ago, a hundred miles northeast of the Roman border.

Tiberius Claudius Maximus shifted in the saddle, the leather horns digging slightly into the chain shirt at his midriff as he leaned forward to look left and right with just a little difficulty. A full turma of cavalry, formed of selected men drawn from the horse contingent of four different legions, sat ready, just as tense as Tiberius, each waiting on a single command from the man in their midst, the new commander of the Danubius army, Lucius Tettius Julianus, governor of Moesia and de facto legatus of the Fourth Flavia Felix.

The equipment Tiberius wore and carried was uncomfortable, as yet unfamiliar and not worn-in, for his transfer from the cavalry of the Fourth to the proconsul's singulares, his personal bodyguard, had only been effective as of two days previously.

Back in camp yesterday morning, he had given up his shield with the green painted linen and the golden wreath and thunderbolts, and taken up this hexagonal red one with the golden Capricorn favoured by the new governor of Moesia. And he had given up his white tunic, though with a little more relief, for the red one of the proconsul's guard. He'd bought a new sword for the occasion from one of the better merchants among the camp followers, since the one he'd been using since first signing up was nicked and slightly pitted, and it looked good against his bodyguard's red cloak. The new chain shirt he'd been issued was still shedding tiny filings and felt stiff. But the real discomfort came from the helmet. Gone was his comfortable bronze bowl with its embossed cheek-plates, replaced by this ornate monstrosity, gilded with divine images, sporting a plume that looked like a volcano spewing slightly hairy lava high into the air, and, worst of all, with a silvered face plate that probably looked ferocious and disconcerting to the enemy, but felt claustrophobic from within, and cut visibility by around seventy-five percent.

But these discomforts would iron themselves out in time, and they were a weight that had to be borne, since it was worth it for the honour of serving among the singulares, not to mention the other fringe benefits. A tent he shared with only three other men, among the officers, riding at the head of the army, where the dust had not yet been kicked up by thousands of feet and hooves, the favours of the lovely girls in the inevitable civilian mob that followed the army on the move, and, best of all, the marked rise in pay.

And today it seemed likely that all he would have to do to *earn* that pay was to sit in his saddle and look dangerous, for no one would come near the commander at the rear of the army.

Today was pay-back.

Today was revenge for the fallen.

Today, Tapae would become a name spoken with triumph rather than humility.

Just a glance across the tree-studded slopes before them brought it all flooding back. More than a year ago: blood, steel, screams and death. The army of Cornelius Fuscus, including a much more bright and positive Tiberius Claudius Maximus among its horsemen, had crossed the Danube on a pontoon bridge and force-marched into Dacian lands, only to be led into a trap, here at Tapae, and butchered. Nine legions had entered the narrow valley at Tapae, and though all nine had managed to limp away, they had lost more than half their number in that meat-grinder, along with a score of standards, including one belonging to Domitian's Praetorians. Fuscus himself, the army's commander, had been cut down among the men. It had been a disaster. The Dacians had jeered as the

Romans fled the scene, every man intent simply on surviving the day.

This time, though, was different. They had come to this place deliberately today, prepared for a fight. No surprise attack, no panic, no routing. And Julianus was no Fuscus, enthusiastic and careless. Julianus was a hard man, a soul of granite and a mind like a knife blade.

And that, as much as anything else, was why they would win at Tapae this time.

The Dacians were spread out before them, in unruly mobs, just as they had been a year ago, although on that occasion, they had emerged from the trees suddenly, attacking an army unprepared for battle. This time, the legions and their auxiliary support were deployed and well-prepared. The Dacians had emerged slowly, forming up, those wicked blades of theirs glinting in the sunlight. There was no hint of a uniform among them, each man garbed as he cared to be, each man sporting a shield with his own favoured design, if he could afford one, and a strange, ornate helmet if funds allowed. Each man there among them, bearded and grizzled, carried a spear, or a long sword, or a hatchet, or a brutal falx, a two-handed weapon with a long blade that curved forward, almost into a hook, which the Romans had learned a year ago to their peril could cleave through shields like a knife through butter and punch a hole in helmet and skull together.

But they were only perhaps two thirds of the enemy force. Just like last time, the archers and slingers would still be among the trees, on the higher slopes, ready to pound down on the advancing Romans, brutalising them before they could even meet a Dacian face to face.

They were going to be sorely disappointed today.

And sore, in fact.

His musing evaporated as a few feet away the proconsul raised and lowered a hand, and horns honked and whistles blew shrill, officers bellowing orders as standards dipped and swooped, directing their men.

Revenge had begun.

The legions started to move at the front, the heaviest men with their segmented plate armour and great rectangular shields formed into lines like a mobile wall, gradually closing on the enemy, hundreds of steel points jutting out, ready to bite into flesh. Behind them came the rest of the legionaries, mostly clad in chain, ready to cast their pila over the heads of the heavy footmen at the front before drawing their own swords and joining in.

To each side, and following up behind the legions came smaller numbers of auxiliary infantry, lightly armoured and ready, with spears and swords, and on the flanks and at the rear: the horse, ready to move out and engage any enemy they saw detached from the mass, and vulnerable, or to flense and mop up any who fled the slaughter that was about to happen.

Sure enough, within a dozen heartbeats, as the legions and auxilia came within reach of the Dacians, the missiles began to fly, arrows and bullets whipping down from the heights, some striking trees, many falling upon the legions, who were ready this time, shields coming up into a roof at a single command, prepared to defend themselves. Of course, in forming a roof against the missiles, they opened themselves up to disaster at the front in a few moments when they met the enemy warriors, but that was not a problem. They would not have to hold off the missiles for long.

The arrows and bullets stopped coming from both sides at much the same time, accompanied by honking native horns and screams and cries of panic and despair.

The rest of the army had engaged.

Last time, Fuscus had led his entire force into the valley of the Iron Gates, and they had fallen prey to a vicious and wily enemy, any survivor counting himself lucky to have got away.

This time, Julianus had turned the tables and sprung the trap on the Dacians instead. The army had departed their camp at the site they'd named Acmonia this morning, once the ever-vigilant scouts had confirmed they were being watched. The main force, mostly legionary and cavalry, had advanced at dawn along the valley in much the same way they had a year earlier, albeit ready for a fight, with much pomp and splendour. Horns blowing, drums banging, legions glittering and gleaming, horses thundering.

Of course, those same scouts had been at work during the previous night, and when they'd been sure the Dacians were *not* watching, two forces had left the column, quietly and without fanfare, in the dark. Each had been led by scouts familiar with the terrain, yet Roman to the core, and had consisted of light infantry auxiliaries, fast moving and adaptable. They'd been halfway to Tapae when the legions had taken down the tents and marched on, watched by Dacians who, as always, paid attention to the gleaming legions and failed to note the diminished number of auxiliaries.

They were very much learning to regret that now as those same two columns of auxilia came pouring down from the mountains on the Dacian flanks, where they'd been in position for over an hour, awaiting the signal. The archers and slingers among the enemy had managed one volley each at the legions advancing below, and then been thrown into a sudden, defensive panic as the auxilia hit them from behind on both sides of the field, swords and spears out, tearing into the undefended missile troops like wolves at a sheep banquet.

The arrows and bullets stopped coming in an instant as the poor bastards suddenly found themselves fighting for their lives against a savage and far superior foe on the hillsides. Aware of the plan, the beleaguered legions in the valley below suddenly dropped their defensive roof as fast as they'd raised it, setting shields into position for infantry combat, and broke into a run at a shrill blast of centurions' whistles.

Maximus watched with a sense of appreciation at the sheer scale of what they'd done. Julianus had used the Dacians' own tactics against them, turning what could have been a disaster into a bloody triumph. The legions hit the Dacians in the valley, and the work began.

Men drove forward, their shields up in lines, swords stabbing like some grisly machine.

They ran into trouble here and there, as Maximus knew they would, indeed as the *entire army* knew that they would, for many among them had fought here before. The terrain favoured the brutal guerilla tactics of the Dacians, rather than the ordered battles of Rome. Shield walls could not hold as they passed small thickets and individual trees, as they scrambled over rocky shelves and scree slopes, for in this Hades that led to the Iron Gates, the only flat and open ground was ten men wide at the base of the valley. The Dacians, on the other hand, who did not hold to formations, who fought as individual warriors, or small warbands at the best, whose strength lay not in fighting beside their compatriots, but in finding a Roman and putting a falx vertically through six feet of meat, were fine among the trees.

This was the part of the battle that could not be anticipated.

No matter what plans they had come up with, or Julianus had considered, once the legions were among the trees, it would come down to grit, determination, skill and strength. That, of course, was why Julianus had so concentrated on removing the Dacians' early advantages, so that the legions were still in good shape and good fighting spirit by the time they were in the trees. It had worked, and Maximus could see that, even as the butchery went on. The ratio of killing changed now, in the woods, from the overwhelming slaughter the legions had practised initially, to a much more even abrading of numbers as men died with screams and welters of blood on both sides amid the trees. But the legions would continue to have the edge this time, without the enemy archers having picked off a third of their number before sword met shield, without each Roman fighting their own panic that they'd been ambushed. Now, the legions were determined, and deadly.

If, apparently, not deadly enough.

'See how we have an issue to resolve?' Tettius Julianus suddenly said, throwing out a finger, whose direction was followed by every rider among his singulares.

'Sir?' asked the decurion who led the guard.

'The Fourth. They are struggling. By sheer chance, or the malicious will of gods, they have been given the worst terrain. They fight on a slope, and they struggle, for each man's friend is a foot higher or lower to either side, and they cannot hold a shield formation, no matter how hard they try. And they are foolish, in a way, to try at all. They should be mimicking their enemy, fighting as sole killers, now. Trying to maintain their formations will see them destroyed.'

'Signaller,' the decurion shouted, 'sound the call for melee for the Fourth'.

'Belay that order,' Julianus countered, the signaller removing the horn's mouthpiece from his lips only just as he'd raised it.

'Sir? They're in trouble. You said they should be fighting like individuals.'

'But if you give them the call, and they are not expecting it, they will try and reform or pull back, and then that whole wing will collapse in chaos. They must try and maintain what they are doing until they can change safely, and gradually.'

'And how can that be guaranteed, sir?'

'By being told personally. Give the signal for your unit to move, and the one for my cavalry reserve, too. We go to the aid of the Fourth, to put them back in order. They are brave men, and they deserve a chance.'

Maximus glowed. This man put the soldiers fighting for him higher than his own safety. He was riding in to deal with the matter himself, not sending some tribune or prefect. Of course, some of that may be that Julianus was currently serving as legatus of the Fourth, too, but still, a commander's care for his men was paramount.

His heart lurched for a moment, as he realised that this meant he was charging down into the fray, as well. It was not that he was afraid of the fight – far from it – but he had fought on this field once before, during that dreadful day a year ago, and the shade of that battle hung over every head who recognised the terrain. He was aware that he might be unmanned during this, not by the fear of battle itself, but by the remembrance of that dreadful day, and the knowledge that today could so easily repeat the disaster.

But Julianus would not let that happen. The man was making sure, even at risk to his own flesh. The proconsul pulled a glorious, probably unblooded, sword from his belt and gripped it tight. As they started riding down towards the struggle, the man who governed Moesia, chosen by Domitian himself, gave the men at each side a fierce grin. 'You are my singulares, my bodyguard. I know it is your sworn duty to protect me. But in what comes now, the best way to protect me is to kill Dacians. If I live through this and we lose, the emperor will have me fall on my sword, and I'd rather die on the end of a Dacian falx than my own blade, so any man who shirks the fight to save me will find himself beaten if I survive. Kill Dacians and win Tapae for me, and I will see every man here rewarded.'

Glorious.

Maximus felt a thrill run through him that he'd never felt in battle. Julianus would not have to worry about *him*, that was for sure.

They raced along the valley, hooves thundering, swords out, for each of them was armed with spatha and not spear, given their close protection duty. Ahead, Maximus could see the legions, swarming between the trees, struggling to push back the Dacians, while elsewhere the Romans were ascendant, hammering their foes. There was another thrill at work, as well as that of serving alongside such a powerful commander, in his personal guard. That was, it was his legion to whose rescue they raced. His tent-mates, his old decurion, that drunken knob Blaesus who still owed him seven sestertii from dice, every man in that endangered legion was one of their own.

They rode on, ever closer, as the struggle of the missile troops against the auxilia raged to both sides, the main battle ahead, and Maximus was certain that at any moment the proconsul would shout, and the reserve cavalry would race past them and into the fray. His heart thundered as the man remained silent, for that meant that Julianus was holding true to his word. He intended to race to the Fourth's rescue personally, and he expected every man on the field to fight, including himself.

They were careful, selective. The cavalry horns called to warn their infantry counterparts they were coming, and the legionaries moved appropriately, making way to allow riders into their midst wherever they were in the most trouble. Here and there they had been forced to leave gaps due to the terrain, or said terrain had been poor enough that they were struggling to use it. The horses moved into those gaps. Again, Maximus was impressed, for horses were really no better on scree and rocky shelves than men, but Julianus was determined and, given that he was tackling them without complaint, the other riders followed suit.

He had no choice. Moments later, he was fighting at Tapae... again. He was swinging a sword from the back of a horse... again. He was struggling against Dacians for his very life... again.

With the spectre of a defeat on this very hillside hanging over him, his sword rose clean, fell, rose bloody, fell again, each time biting into the flesh of a native of these lands, a warrior of Decebalus, their hungry, violent nature radiating from them across the pass.

Battering a man down with his shield even as he swung in for the kill with his sword, Maximus heard the rider on his right cry a warning, and turned just in time to see the falx coming. He knew the power, the danger, the sheer horribleness of the Dacians' pet weapon, and he knew as he saw it swooping his way that it presaged not only death, but in the most agonising way, sheared in half by the wicked razor edge.

Only a decade of horsemanship, both civilian and then military, saved his life. His knees pressed, pulled, directed his horse urgently left even as his heels kicked it to move. He and Celeris had fought together in the field for four years now, and man and horse worked as a perfect team. Without even needing to voice the command, or use his hands, the horse reacted to his urging and pushed its way left, even though that meant barging into another fight that was going on. The falx failed to take the life of either Maximus or his horse, thanks to their combined skill, but he was given a hefty slash across the leg, right above the kneecap, to remember his lucky escape.

Normally, like all men, he would cry out in pain at the wound, but when in the thick of battle, he'd found that there was an odd numbness – an unwillingness even to register pain – that overrode the senses, something given to man by Mars, to allow them to fight on, even as they bled out. He thanked the lord of war as he swung out and dispatched his would-be killer, and then parried another man until he could look about and take stock.

He half expected Julianus to be on the ground, mortally wounded, a repeat of that day a year ago when Fuscus had lain in the scrubby grass and rock, a Dacian arrow jutting from his liver as he desperately tried to speak around gobbets of blood, telling his adjutant where his will was to be found, as he'd changed it that day. In actual fact, when Maximus found the proconsul, he was only *more* impressed, for Julianus was engaged man-to-man with a Dacian, and was fighting like a Titan. Even as he saw this, he noted three of his fellow singulares register their master's peril, almost break off their own fight to help him, then remember their orders and return to their own struggles.

'To your left,' someone shouted, and Maximus, like any man with a will to survive, immediately assumed the caller meant him, and turned. As it happened, this time he was right, and he was just in time to throw his shield up to stop a falx that would otherwise have split him in half. Instead, the wicked curved blade did precisely that to his shield, treating the bronze edging as though it were cheese, scraping and grating around the boss that protected his hand. Even as he lunged out with his sword and stabbed the man, he shook the ruined shield from his other arm and searched out the next opponent.

Looking about, he suddenly realised that he was among the ragged front lines of the Fourth, quite far ahead of the rest of the reserve cavalry and singulares who had ridden to the legion's defence. How had that happened in a few short clashes? He turned to glance over his shoulder, and could see other riders only a few ranks behind, one of them the proconsul in his rich panoply. As his gaze fell upon the army's commander, he realised that Julianus was shouting and pointing, apparently at Maximus.

He frowned. Yes, he was in more danger now than the others, but...

Then he realised that the proconsul *wasn't* pointing at him. He was pointing *past* him. With a sense of impending dread, Maximus turned.

The Fourth Flavia Felix were in trouble. Oh, not the rank and file. They were back to battling the enemy hard and gaining ground, their moment of wavering trouble over with the arrival of the cavalry at their back. But near the front, a new situation had developed. The senior tribune, Lappius Frontinus, a man Maximus knew to be solid and dependable, had led his mounted command party too close to the front line. With the proconsul serving as the legion's legatus, Lappius had taken command in the field, and now he and his colour party were just a falx-length from the Dacian warriors who, even being beaten back, were still fighting like mountain lions. Even as Maximus watched, two signifers were felled, along with a centurion. Several legionaries pushed through the press and managed to grab the standards, which were then manhandled back across the ranks, to safety.

But the vexillum was something different.

Maximus watched in horror as the flag-bearer, one of the legion's most important men, took a falx blow to the shoulder, expertly angled and placed such that the point managed to tear through the chain shirt, the curved blade punching into the meat beneath. The banner, bearing the golden winged victory above a "IV", symbols of the legion, disappeared beneath the press.

Maximus felt the chill of a hundred generations of Roman soldiers then, horror at the loss of a vexillum, almost as dangerous and ignominious as the loss of a legion's eagle.

He was halfway through the press before he knew what he was doing.

Stupid. He was the proconsul's guardsman now, a rider of the singulares, and may never go back to serving in the Fourth, and yet the sight of its vexillum falling had triggered in him something instinctive. He couldn't just let such a thing happen. It had to be stopped.

He pushed forward, guiding Celeris with his knees and heels, swinging his sword wildly every time a Dacian came within reach, even using his free hand to punch or push men away. Legionaries lurched out of his way, and Dacian warriors disappeared beneath his hooves to be broken and churned. One particularly large specimen loomed suddenly before him, a man clearly trying to get the flag for himself, a prize that he could hang in his hall for his neighbours to envy. Maximus snarled in defiance and threw himself forward, over his horse's neck, ignoring the pain the saddle horns drove into his middle, sword lancing out.

It was not an elegant blow. Driven by desperation, it was at the limit of his reach, and only just connected with the Dacian, carving a stripe along the top of his head. The man howled, and rose, angry and pained, but Maximus was in the grip of some sort of automatic drive to protect the flag, which he was not sure he could put into words if anyone asked. His sword swung wildly, and the Dacian's head came free, whirling through the air to be lost in the press. Even in the midst of it all, Maximus blinked. His training officer had told him that never happened. That a single blow beheading was a fiction from old tales, and that if a man wanted a head for a prize, he had to be prepared to hack and saw at it for a while.

Still, the headless body dropped to the ground, and somehow, through the agency of the gods, he presumed, Maximus could just see the fallen vexillum. He gritted his teeth, pushed on in the press, and began to lean. It was another thing his training officer had told him that was, apparently, not true. You couldn't lean low in a Roman saddle. Well, bollocks to that. Though he could feel the leather saddle jabbing and bruising, and his leg and hip almost disconnecting with the stretch, he leaned low to his left. His fingers closed on the shaft of the vexillum, and moments later, that glorious golden Victory was rising into the air once more, flapping and shaking, albeit muddy and bloodstained.

A roar around him told him that his action had gone neither unnoticed, nor unappreciated. The men of the Fourth Flavia Felix found new heart. Men who, a moment earlier, had been flagging, were suddenly the very embodiment of Mars, bringing death and mayhem to the Dacians at Tapae.

Revenge would be theirs after all.

Maximus fought the urge to struggle on and kill a few more. The vexillum was more important. Instead, he turned his horse with some difficulty in the press of men and started to make his way slowly back.

He stopped after a moment. A man stood in his way. He realised, with surprise, that it was the man who had almost finished him with a falx while he'd pushed forward. He had a wicked wound in his side from Maximus's own strike, and was holding it with one hand, falx drooping low in the other, lacking the energy to lift it.

'Pax,' the man said, with the hiss of a man in a lot of pain, dropping his weapon and raising both hands.

'This man is my slave,' Maximus found himself shouting, in a move that surprised him more than anyone. 'Kill him and you owe me a hundred sestertii.' Two legionaries suddenly grabbed the man, and Maximus thought for a moment they were going to dispatch him, but then they took him prisoner and turned, dragging him. Apparently, saving the vexillum had earned Maximus sufficient celebrity that no one was going to argue with him.

He pushed his way back through the ranks towards the proconsul, gripping the vexillum tight, his new slave being dragged along in his wake.

His heart leapt at the sight of Lucius Tettius Julianus, for the proconsul was nodding his appreciation at the sight of one of the day's heroes making their way towards him.

'I think today is won,' the governor said, as Maximus fell in close by, holding the vexillum high. 'And we have lost no standards or flags today, as Fuscus managed last year. No, I think the Dacians are beaten at Tapae, this time.'

Maximus turned and watched, as the Fourth, full of fresh vim, swept the beaten natives away ahead of them.

Revenge.

*

The camp fires guttered across the valley before the pass. Maximus stood at the entrance to the proconsul's command tent, straightening and smoothing his best parade kit. He turned, to where two helpful legionaries from the Fourth were watching his slave, a Dacian he now knew to be called Duras. He nodded to them, and they nodded back in kind.

Leaving the beaten warrior in their care, he pushed his way into the tent.

'Ah,' called Julianus, 'you see, this is the sort of man who will make Dacia a province. Not some wet junior tribune serving here because that will get him a pot of gold and a plump pillow in Rome. A man of steel and action. Claudius Maximus here pushed through the lines to save the legion's flag.' He turned to the new arrival. 'Maximus, I will be heading back to Rome in the spring, my job here complete, and will have no need of singulares.' He smirked. 'Although perhaps that is not true, given the current state of politics in

Rome. But my riders will be returning to their legions over the winter. You, on the other hand, I have other plans for. I think the legion needs a new vexillifer. Will you carry the flag on your magnificent horse for the Fourth? I do believe the pay is even higher than your current status, and you would not have to wear such a ridiculous helmet.'

Maximus blinked.

'Sir?'

'The Dacians are beaten, Maximus, but not destroyed. Enough got away to man the heights and stop any easy advance for us, and the season presses on. Winter knocks on our door, and I am told that winter is not a time to campaign in these mountains. We have done what we came to do. We kicked sand in the face of the smug king of the Dacians. And Rome is here to stay. We will occupy the lowlands by the river. Beyond that is the emperor's decision. And there is plenty of time for him to make it. Winter is upon us, and we will find a place for a seasonal garrison. So what say you to carrying the vexillum for the Fourth? It is a perilous job, I'm sure, but lucrative and glorious.'

Maximus could do nothing other than grin.

'It would be a privilege, sir.'

Chapter Two

Viminacium, Moesia, Spring AD 101

How little had changed, Maximus mused as he waited for the boat, one of the small but wide-bellied transports of the Danubian fleet, to touch the north bank. Oh, in some ways a *lot* had changed, of course. He supposed that if you were a man of influence back in Rome, it had all felt *tumultuous*, with the fall of Domitian and the end of a dynasty, the brief reign of the elderly and ineffectual Nerva, and now this new man on the throne, Trajan. But for a man like Maximus, born in Phillipi in Macedonia, who'd served only ever in the military in the East and had not set foot within half a thousand miles of the great city, the question of who sat on the throne rarely made much of a difference.

And nothing seemed to change in Moesia, really.

Thirteen years ago he'd crossed this same stretch of water, along with the army of the governor Julianus, to crush the power of the increasingly dangerous Dacian king Decebalus. They'd beaten the man and put to rest the phantom that was the First battle of Tapae. All had seemed so good in the immediate aftermath. But Decebalus was a wily bastard, and he had taken his remaining army and retreated into his mountainous heartland, knowing that winter was coming, and that therefore no real new Roman push would be possible. Instead, Rome had made peace with him, a rather *ignominious* peace that involved paying the cur a huge amount of gold annually, along with supplying Roman engineers and craftsmen to help him build up his kingdom as a client state, a buffer zone against the horse tribes of the steppe and the Germanics to the north. Maximus supposed that the thinking behind the move was to gradually Romanise the Dacians until they could simply be annexed peacefully. It was a nice theory, but after so many years of watching them and fighting against them, Maximus bore instead the private theory that all Rome was doing in Dacia was strengthening an enemy.

Trajan, it appeared, was of the same mind, for he'd ended the payments and support and begun to prepare for war. That, at least, was a good sign. No more appeasement.

The boat touched the bank and sailors threw out ropes, securing it, and then slipped the boarding ramp over, ready. Maximus gestured to his men as he led Celeris up and over the side of the vessel, then down the slippery planks to the grassy bank beyond.

He chided himself for such simplistic thinking. In many ways, *everything* was changing. Half the military of the East had been moved around and concentrated here in Upper Moesia. For two years, soldiers had been carving out new roads in the rocky bank of the Danubius, building forts and watchtowers, even creating a huge canal that bypassed the dangerous river rapids and made the great Danubius navigable from source to sea, allowing the two fleets to combine at last.

So yes, a lot was changing.

But not the Dacians and the threat they posed.

And not Tiberius Claudius Maximus…

Or was that untrue too?

He waited for his riders to join him on the shore, and then gave the order to mount up.

They were good men, these men, if a little odd. He was getting used to them after serving two years in the unit now. That had been change, too, of course. For almost a decade he'd carried the vexillum for the Fourth, but despite the good pay, he'd gradually become jaded with it all. It seemed there was really nowhere to go, career-wise, from vexillifer. Most men moved from that position to the centurionate in the infantry or decurionate in the cavalry, but with no war going on, there had been no "dead man's boots" to fill, and so promotions had looked less and less likely as he aged towards inevitable retirement.

He'd made the decision when word came of the reorganisation of the Moesian military by the new emperor, who'd been in the province at the time, planning it all. Trajan had brought in extra legions and a number of auxiliary units, specially chosen, for clearly there was going to be a campaign, and before this summer was out. Maximus had put in for a transfer to any unit where he could secure an officer posting.

Initially he'd been disappointed, even a little irked, that the emperor's staff had sent him such an offer. It seemed a step *down*, from the legions to the auxilia, for it had always been the view, among the legions at least, that they outclassed their lighter compatriots. But when he'd sat back and examined the situation, he'd had to admit that it made sense. If he'd stayed in the same role, carrying the flag, but moved to the auxilia, it would have meant a drop in pay, but he'd been offered the position of duplicarius, second in command to a decurion, in a turma of thirty riders. And that meant double pay, which then put him slightly up on his previous role, and with the added possibility of moving up into the decurion's position when Naevius Bibula retired, it was clearly the right decision.

But it took some getting used to, especially in the Ala II Pannoniorum. The unit may have been founded in the mists of time in dour, Danubian Pannonia, but they'd spent time after that out in Syria, acquiring swarthy recruits with an eastern twang and some truly peculiar gods, and then been reassigned to Moesia Inferior, down on the banks of the lower Danubius where, as a non-citizen unit, half the manpower they'd taken on were of Dacian or Sarmatian blood themselves. They were a weird mix, to say the least.

He looked around at the seven men with him, a detachment from the ala assigned under Maximus for this specific duty. They were all mounted now, the last man gripping the lead rein of the pack horse, laden under a heavy burden of bags.

'Abgar, is everything secure?'

The swarthy rider with the hook nose leaned across, tested the straps on the pack animal, then nodded and straightened once more.

'Alright, let's move out.'

He could feel eyes on him from the treeline as they moved. *Unfriendly* eyes, and guarded. Dacians, for though Rome nominally controlled the northern bank in this area, with no actual bridges across, proper control was more or less impossible, and the current governor tended to limit Roman activity across the river to occasional scout parties, apart from the ubiquitous traders and the odd returning soldier or civilian who'd been among the Dacians helping set up aqueducts and the like. There were few of them all the time now. Since Trajan had given the order to stop the gold trains, relations with the Dacian king had crumbled at an impressive rate. Most Romans in the territory had long since fled back to their own lands.

Those watchers in the woods would not attack, at least. Rome and Dacia were not at war… yet.

Peace remained, but that peace was like a damaged vase. If you looked close, you could see so many cracks, some huge, that there was no hope of repair, and it was simply a matter of waiting for it to fall apart, shattering into a hundred pieces.

Until then, guarded, unfriendly eyes was all they would find here.

Maximus nodded his approval. All was ready. They didn't need full packs for themselves, as they would not be staying out here, on the northern side of the river. That would be asking for trouble. They would be back by sunset, and the same boat had instructions to meet them at the shore then, ferrying them safely back over to Viminacium.

He turned his gaze north and west. They would not have to go far, and a decade of serving in the region meant that Maximus had more than a passing grip of local geography. They rode in silence for the next few hours, heading always in the same direction, northwest, away from the great river. Over to the east, the distant mountains of Dacia hung like a blue-grey threat on the horizon, but here, out in the great plain, all they could see both west and north was an endless stretch of grassland, flat and featureless.

They came across the first sign of life as noon approached. They saw the cattle first, ambling quietly across the wide grassland, lowing and eating their fill, happy to be back in such terrain now, brought south by their owners. Then they began to see the children on their horses, rounding up any animal that strayed too far from the herd, always on the lookout for predators, each boy or girl, even those just half a dozen summers of age, comfortable in the saddle, and each carrying a spear and a sling.

But it did not take too long to find the watcher.

There, on the hill above the animals and their mounted herdsmen, sat a warrior of the Iazyges. His horse was a powerful beast, considerably larger than the Roman animals, and he sat astride it on a very non-Roman saddle, his legs, arms and torso all clad in heavy furs and leather. His head was covered with a tall iron helm of impressive design, and a great lance the length of two men sat in his right hand, the butt resting on the top of his foot, point reaching into the sky. The man made no move to come against them, but he did turn his horse slowly as they passed, watching them to make sure they did nothing untoward.

Iazyges.

Much like the Roxolani on the other side of Dacia, down near the mouth of the Danubius, clans of horsemen from the great steppe, Sarmatians. Barbarians. Maximus was never sure what to make of these people. They were about as alien a people to him as barbarians could be. Semi-nomadic, they spent some time in settlements that could loosely be called towns, and the rest up in the higher slopes of the great plain, ever moving their cattle. One might think them a bucolic, pleasant people, farmers and nomadic traders, if one did not know that every child from the age of five could ride a horse and swing a sword. That every Iazyx, no matter what age, no matter whether man or woman, was a farmer second and a warrior first. That when the tribe went to war, the *whole tribe* went to war. That made it always a nervous thing to approach them.

Because you also never seemed to know where you stood with them. In years past they had been staunch allies of Rome, and Vespasian had considered them friends, yet under Domitian, they had crossed the river in force, killing and burning, and even annihilated a legion. Oh there had been a retaliatory war, but there seemed to be an endless supply of these deadly nomads.

Currently they were considered allies, and given that war with Dacia was coming again, it had been deemed important that relations with the Iazyges be strengthened. The new emperor wanted these fierce horsemen on his side, not on that of Decebalus.

Monthly, Roman parties had ridden out to one Iazyx tribe or another with gifts, tightening the ties between the two peoples. And in between these sporadic goodwill gestures, grain and salt went north in regular convoys at a discounted price.

The beast of burden at the rear of this column carried a small fortune. Bandits would not think twice about killing eight Romans for it, if they knew what it was, but that was no worry here. Bandits did not operate in the lands of the Iazyges, or at least, not for long. They were not tolerated. And what the horsemen did to bandits when they caught them was sufficiently eye-watering to put anyone else off having a go. Such captives were usually given to the tribe's women, who would bind them to a stake and then burn them. Charred posts with bones and ash had been found alarmingly often within their territory. And it was said that they... *did things...* to the prisoners before they were freed into death.

Definitely better to have them on your side...

Half an hour later they found the 'town.'

It was little more than a plethora of leather yurts, gathered around a single thatched timber hall in the centre, the whole thing surrounded by a palisade. Men and women went about their business inside, as well as children and dogs, horses penned to one side. It was lively and loud. Maximus had visited one of these towns when the Iazyges were in high lands for the season, and it had been eerie to be alone in a circular palisade with one deserted building.

Still, the tribe was here, today, and so were the riders, and this was a time and a mission of peace, in an attempt to secure that peace for years to come.

As they approached the gate, he waved over one of the other riders.

'Rigozus? You speak their tongue, yes?' After so many years of service here, Maximus had a good grasp of Dacian, but these horse tribes spoke a whole different, weird and eastern language.

'Close enough,' the soldier shrugged. 'Roxolani, at least. But they're all Sarmatian, aren't they.'

'Tell them we need to see the chief. We have gifts.'

He waited while there was a completely indecipherable exchange between the trooper and some locals, and then, after a pause, a warrior in a coat of bronzed scales gestured for them to follow. They dismounted at the gateway, out of politeness, and then walked their horses on between the yurts towards the wooden house at the centre. As they approached it, Maximus gestured for two of his men to join him. 'The rest of you stay here with the horses, and for the love of blessed Apollo, don't start anything. Don't insult anyone. Don't even *look* at someone funny, alright?'

Nods all round at that one. Everyone here knew the Iazyges, and no one wanted to be their next enemy.

'Good. Rigozus, get the pack horse. Abgar, try not to look threatening.'

The three Romans led the horse into the large building, where they had to pause to let their eyesight adjust to the dimness. The place was decked out across the floor, the ceiling and all the walls with mats and hangings, all showing strange symbols and designs. A horse's skull hung on one, wearing what looked worryingly like a crown. There were maybe two score people in here, and all of them, regardless of age or gender, wore armour and a sword. The head man of the tribe had no throne. He sat cross-legged on a pile of straw-stuffed cushions, draped with a rough blanket. Beside him sat a bowl of meat and bread, and on the other side a tankard of something, several small leather bottles nearby. The man was tall, even seated, and elderly, his beard long and grey, his hair mostly gone. But there was something damned impressive about the old man. Something in his eyes suggested to Maximus that they should be nicely polite and careful here, and not risk pissing the man off. His eyes said 'I may be old, but I could kill you with my little finger.'

Another tribesman came scurrying over and plonked himself down beside the chieftain.

'We bring you gifts,' Maximus announced, coming towards the chieftain and stopping a polite distance from him. He started to remove the bags from the pack horse, and the other two riders joined him. Each time one of the bags came free, Maximus would open it, displaying its contents to the chieftain before fastening them once more and stacking the packs in a pile. Once the pile was complete, a sizeable treasure given to a single tribe, Maximus walked forward and then sank, cross-legged, opposite the king, the other two troopers sitting flanking him.

'In addition to the usual monthly grant of salt and wheat, the emperor of Rome, Great Caesar Nerva Traianus Augustus himself, sends these gifts to your tribe in the hope that our current mutually beneficial peace can be maintained, even in the face of the coming war with your neighbour, Decebalus of Dacia.'

He could probably have been more impressive, or more gracious, but Maximus was no orator on the steps of the forum in Rome. A man of iron and action was all he could claim to be, but then that, he suspected, was what the Iazyges respected most anyway. They wouldn't care about flouncy language. Just a good pile of treasure and appropriate respect.

There was a spot of rumbling conversation, then, in their native tongue, and in low tones. The chief and half a dozen of his nearest warriors seemed to be discussing the gifts, and Maximus glanced across at Rigozus, a man who, though he served Rome as an auxiliary rider, still remembered his Roxolani grandfather bouncing him on his knee, horse-and-rider style. Rigozus did not reply, did not even move. Quite right. Better to stay quiet and respectful among the Iazyges. Maximus waited patiently. Finally, one of the warriors crossed and sat beside his chief. He cleared his throat

'Radamasis say gift good. Want more.'

Maximus frowned, pursed his lips. 'With respect, great chief, this is a *fortune*. More would have to be sanctioned by the governor, then the emperor. We don't just simply have more with us.'

The spokesman shook his head. He seemed to be trying to find the Latin words, and then wandered off into his own language again, talking to the king. Suddenly, Rigozus spoke again, in their tongue, or something close enough that they understood. There followed another intense discussion in the Sarmatian language, before the trooper nodded and turned back to Maximus.

'He couldn't explain it well enough, sir. They are more than happy with the trinkets.'

'*Trinkets?* There's enough gold there to buy a trireme.'

'His word, sir, not mine. Or that's more or less what it means. Precisely, I think the word translates as *decoration for a horse harness that is pretty but not really important*. Anyway, he wasn't saying he wanted more of it, but that he does want *something* more. He says that the lands to the east, as far as the hills, and I think that he means right the way across to the Iron Gates, are vital to his people for cattle grazing. All the low grassland of western Dacia. Apparently Decebalus first took those lands and settled them years ago, pushing the Iazyges out, and then we built a few camps up there too.'

Maximus nodded. He remembered them, as he'd been there when they were built, on the way to Tapae.

'And then after Domitian, when we pulled back to the river, Decebalus took control of them again. Radamasis here says that he and the other chiefs of his people are all of a mind. They will band together in support of Rome in its coming war, in return for the guarantee of all grasslands west of the Dacian hills being ceded back to the Iazyges.'

'Shit.' Maximus chewed on his lip. 'We both know that's not going to happen. Rome needs that route up into the Iron Gates. It's the main western passage into Dacia. We can put it to the big heads back in Viminacium, but I really doubt they'll go for it. They'll expect us just to buy these people off with gold.'

A tense silence descended, and then the chief spoke again. This time there was no need for the warrior beside him to become involved, for Rigozus translated directly.

'He would like to remind us that they are not Roman lands to give, any more than they are Dacian. Those lands belong to the Iazyges, and have done since his ancestors came here from the east. As such, he is not so much asking you to give him those lands, but rather telling you that those lands are his, and if we don't want war with his people, we'll renounce any claim to them.'

The tension ramped up once more. Maximus fretted. He doubted a senior officer back in Viminacium was going to respond any better against threats, either.

More native speech, and then Trooper Rigozus gestured to him. 'The chief says he will sweeten the deal with information.'

'Oh?'

'He has a warning for us.'

Maximus's spirits sank. *Great. Another threat.* 'Go on.'

'He says that representatives of Decebalus, king of the Dacians, have been at work in these lands. They have been seeking an alliance with the Iazyges. To this time, the tribes have not agreed to any such move. They have thus far remained impartial to any notion of a new war – uninvolved. They are disinclined to aid Decebalus, since he was the one who took their lands in the first place.'

Maximus sagged. 'But they might change their minds if Decebalus offers those lands back, and we refuse.'

'He didn't *say* that, sir.'

'He didn't have to. That's what he means.'

More speech, then more translation. 'Sir, he says the Iazyges are not alone in this. Beyond their lands, the Osii have also been approached by the Dacian king.'

Maximus straightened a little. The Osii were a little known people, far from Roman lands, beyond other neighbouring tribes. But if Decebalus was seeking allies there too, he was doing something more than simply strengthening his position in the south. 'What else can he tell us?'

'Nothing, sir. He suspects the Roxolani of being in league with Decebalus, but since the Iazyges and the Roxolani hate each other these days, they're hardly likely to chat about it.'

'Something is building,' Maximus muttered. 'I think Decebalus has seen the emperor's preparations and is making some of his own. And he's a devious bastard. Whatever he's planning will be more than just some extra bodies to block the passes with.' He took a deep breath. 'Tell him Rome agrees to his conditions.'

Rigozus turned, brows raised in surprise. 'Sir?'

'We agree. Tell him.'

'Sir, we don't have that authority. *You* don't have that authority.'

'Just fucking tell him,' hissed Maximus, glaring at the Moesian trooper. Rigozus held his gaze for a few moments, then swallowed nervously and turned back to the chief, rattling out a short speech in their language. Maximus glanced the other way at Abgar, who looked equally troubled, but blessedly remained silent. The chief seemed to sit quietly, waiting, until Rigozus finished, and then nodded once. He made a gesture, and the warrior by his side rose and crossed to

Maximus, where he held out his hands. In one sat one of those barrel-shaped leather flasks that had been near the chief, in the other an iron symbol the size of his palm that seemed to be all points with an incomplete curve at the centre. He turned a questioning gaze on Rigozus, who translated for the warrior.

'The symbol is the tamga of his tribe, sort of their standard or flag if you like. It's his symbol, which they use to mark their property and brand their animals. He gifts one to you as a sign of friendship. The flask is to drink now to seal the deal. And he says he gives us three good cows to take back with us, too.'

'Well I'm sure I'm bloody grateful,' Maximus grunted, eying the flask warily. He tucked the tamga away in his belt pouch, and then waited as the chief was passed another flask. Then, as the man pulled out the stopper and raised it to swig, Maximus followed suit.

Whatever it was in the flask, he simply could not find the words in his head to describe it. He very carefully held on to his blank expression, while inside every nerve that touched a tastebud screamed at him to pull a face. He coughed, once, and then turned to Rigozus. 'Tell him thank you, and that it's very nice,' he said in a slightly hoarse voice.

The rider grinned. 'And is it?'

'If you distilled feet for a year and added the scrapings from a leper's toenails, boiled it all up and then served it in a flask, I'd choose that over this.'

Rigozus chuckled, then turned back to the chief and translated, leading the man to nod appreciatively, then take another swig. He gestured for Maximus to do so. Bracing himself, the Roman took another mouthful from the flask. 'Shit, they could probably use *this* stuff to brand cattle.'

'Try and get accustomed, sir. I think he expects you to finish the flask.'

Spirits sinking, Maximus turned to the chief, who was grinning and taking another swig, lending weight to that expectation. Bracing once more, he took another pull from the flask. And so it went for at least half an hour. By the time he handed the empty flask back to the warrior, Maximus was not sure whether he had become used to the drink enough to even appreciate its burning acridness in a way, or perhaps he had just seared away all his tastebuds and numbed his body to an extent where he could have drunk cattle piss and not noticed. Either way, he'd managed it, without insulting their host.

'I should give him a gift,' he said, a little waveringly.

'Sir, we gave him a horse packed full of gifts.'

'I mean me personally, rather than Rome.' He started to check his person for anything appropriate, aware as he did so that his hands felt rather numb. He touched the torc around his neck, and the arm-ring, and even considered those for a moment, but decided against it. They had been his gifts from the proconsul after Second Tapae, for his bravery and action. He couldn't give them away. Smiling, he reached into a pouch at his belt, felt around, and produced a coin, a silver tetradrachm he'd had for years. A rare coin, it had a head on both sides, Vespasian and Titus, and Maximus had used it on more than one occasion to make a call when he wanted to be certain of winning. Sighing, he slid it back. These people didn't really use coins at all, so they probably had no idea about flipping one to make decisions. With the latest in a series of sighs, he undid his belt, slid his pugio dagger from it, still sheathed, and then refastened. He held it out. The warrior took it and passed it over to the chief, who held it up and examined it, nodding his appreciation.

And well he might, Maximus grumbled silently. It was an extremely expensive one he'd picked up in Serdica on leave, bearing the images of both Alexander and Philip of Macedon. It had cost him two months' pay.

He sat there, then, as pleasantries were exchanged, and then made to stand. It took three tries even just to get to his feet, as his legs seemed to have stopped working properly, and each seemed to have acquired at least two extra knees. A group of Iazyx warriors laughed loudly at this. Slightly embarrassed, Maximus bowed his head to the chief, and then made to leave. Behind him, as he staggered towards the open air, Rigozus closed matters for them, thanking the chief and making many, many hollow promises.

Maximus reached his horse with some difficulty. He didn't feel drunk, although he felt he should, after that. He did seem to have precious little control of any muscle or joint south of his hips, though. One of his men came to his aid and helped him up into the saddle.

'Thanks. Drank some awful shit in there that seems to have robbed me of my legs.'

The trooper chuckled, and climbed into his own saddle. Moments later, Rigozus re-emerged from the house with the other trooper, native warriors behind them. Another Iazyx appeared, leading three very slow-looking fat cows. As soon as everyone was on their horse, Maximus waved a hand in what he hoped was a south-easterly direction. 'Let's go home.'

A quarter of an hour later they were riding away from the town, across the sea of grass beneath the afternoon sunlight. He felt extremely odd. That drink should be used by medics when they wanted to do foot surgery. Maximus was beginning to doubt he'd ever feel his toes again, and was glad he was *riding* back, and not walking. As they rode, Maximus letting his men get ahead, since they knew where they were going anyway, Rigozus pulled in close.

'Was that wise?' he asked

'Most definitely not. I may never walk again.'

'I meant telling them we agreed to their territory complaint?'

Maximus shook his head. 'Also probably not. But I had to make a decision right there. I doubt anyone in Viminacium will agree to it, but if we refuse today, by tomorrow every Iazyx tribe from the Danube to the ice shelfs will be trying to decide whether they might perhaps get a better offer from Decebalus. We can't afford to have the Iazyges fighting for Decebalus, even if we string them along and then don't live up to our side of the bargain, as in the meantime we'll only face the Dacians.'

'I hope that doesn't come back to haunt us,' the trooper said quietly.

'Me too. For now, let's get back. War is coming, and soon. Oh, and cut those bloody cows loose. It'll take weeks to get back at their speed.'

Chapter Three

Viminacium, Moesia, early summer AD 101

'Run, man, run.'

Maximus balled his fists and planted them both on his hips, watching as the recruit raced after his horse, cheeks bulged, puffing and panting, sweat making his forehead glisten and sticking his tunic to chest and back. Rufus, the ala's custos armorum, often doubled as one of the unit's training officers, and was currently running ahead of the recruit, gripping the horse's reins as man and animal pounded across the packed earth of the training ground. Other trainees jeered at their friend as he raced comically in the wake of the horse, desperately trying to catch up with it.

Finally, exhausted, the trooper faltered in his run and collapsed to the ground, onto his knees, gasping for air. Twenty paces ahead, Rufus slowed the horse, and then came to a halt. He rolled his eyes at Maximus, who took a deep breath.

'Why do you think we're doing this?' he said to the exhausted, kneeling man. The recruit failed to reply, gasping for air, and Maximus plucked his spear from the ground and strode over, giving the man a prod with the weapon's shaft. 'Well?'

'So I can get on a horse, sir,' the young soldier replied between gasps. Maximus didn't need to look over to Rufus to know the man was rolling his eyes again.

'Picture this, soldier: you're in battle, in the middle of a fight. Your horse collides with another. Or it's spooked, or wounded, and rears. Whatever the cause, you find yourself thrown from the saddle, and even the saddle horns don't stop you. Now you're on foot in the middle of a cavalry fight. Your chances of survival have just halved at the very least.'

'Surely that doesn't happen, sir? That's just freak chance.'

Maximus did look across at the Custos Armorum now. 'How often have you been unhorsed in a fight, Rufus?'

'Four times,' the man replied casually.

'Three for me,' Maximus added, watching the recruit's reaction. The man was frowning in surprise, and Maximus sighed. 'When you're unhorsed, your animal is often in a panicked situation and moving away, trying to reach safety. It is paramount for both of you that you get back on that horse and get it under control before it bolts and before you get ridden down by friend and foe alike. You need to be able to chase a frightened horse and vault back into that saddle before the worst happens.'

'It's impossible, sir.'

Maximus looked up at Rufus again, who nodded, clicked his tongue and urged the animal to move once more. As soon as man and horse were running, Maximus jammed the spear back in the ground and started to sprint. By the count of four, he was starting to regret it. He wasn't a young recruit himself any more, and he'd had more wine last night than he'd meant to, for Anichses's birthday celebration. It would look really bad now if he failed in front of the recruit.

That knowledge lent him an extra burst of speed, and he picked up the pace. A few moments later he was racing alongside the horse's flank, puffing madly. Rufus had let go now that he was here and had veered off, slowing. Maximus lunged, throwing himself upwards, hands reaching. He grasped the tall leather horns at the front of the saddle, and now he was half-running, half-dragged. With immense effort, he brought to bear every ounce of strength in his arms and upper body, and pulled. His feet left the ground, and he was suddenly on the horse, if not in the saddle. An extra manoeuvre then, as he reached forward, pulled, and vaulted from behind the saddle, lancing squarely between the horns.

Gripping the reins now, he used his knees and feet to help guide the animal and his gentlest tones to urge the horse to slow. Finally, man and horse came to a halt at the far end of the open ground, and he turned, then, and trotted slowly back to the kneeling recruit.

'Now stop sitting in the dirt, get up, and catch a bloody horse.'

He dismounted and handed the reins to Rufus as the red-cheeked recruit climbed to his feet and hurried back to his starting marker. Rufus waited until the lad was a good distance away, and then turned to Maximus. 'That was fucking shoddy, and you know it.'

Maximus laughed. 'It was. But it proved the point.'

'I should have *you* chasing Harax here until you can vault into the saddle properly, in one go.'

Rufus took the horse back to the other start marker, and prepared for another go, and Maximus retrieved his spear and strolled over to the tribunal, a raised bank of earth with a rough timber floor that provided a good view over the training ground. He smiled at his own horse, Celeris, who stood calm and patient by the side of the tribunal in the morning sun, but then his gaze slid to the man who held the reins, and his expression soured. Duras was glowering at him, but then Duras seemed only to know how to glower. Naevius Bibula, his decurion, regularly advised beating the slave to remove that air of defiance that clung to him, but Maximus held off, as he always had. It was not that he didn't think Duras deserved the odd battering, mind. For a slave he was incredibly insolent and difficult, for sure, but while beating slaves tended to cow them into better submission, it also tended to injure them and put them out of commission for a time. Maximus could put up with the glowering and even the whispered curses from time to time, if it meant Duras was hale enough to polish his armour and weapons, and to tend to the horse daily.

But he did have to admit, over the thirteen years since he'd taken the man prisoner on the battlefield of Tapae, Duras had never lost that bitterness and spite. Early on, when Maximus had still had hopes of turning the captive Dacian into a compliant and Romanised slave, he'd started putting a few coins now and then in the man's purse when he did something useful. The problem was that such things happened so rarely that the money never really built up, and Duras would probably have been dead for a century before he could hope to afford his freedom, so that practice had soon ended. Now, the two of them had fallen into a limbo that contained no trust or hope, yet stopped short of anger and beatings.

He turned at the sound of heavy footsteps on the timber steps, to see Naevius Bibula climbing to join him. The decurion fell in beside him, hands clasped behind his back.

'Will they be ready, d'you think?'

Maximus snorted. 'By the time we've conquered half the world, and three emperors' backsides have polished the throne, these shitheads will just about have mastered falling off a horse. Where do we *get* these recruits?'

Bibula laughed. 'At times like this we don't get to be choosy. The emperor's staff send us lists and we do what we're told. At least this lot have ridden before. When we were down at Bononia, we got sent two Cretans. Turned out they were excellent huntsmen, great with a bow, but neither had ever ridden a horse. Took a year to get them even remotely proficient.'

'Wonderful.'

Bibula grinned. 'This lot will learn. They'll *have* to. Soon enough they'll be doing it all for real across the river, so they can learn on the job if nothing else.' The decurion straightened. 'Anyway, enough of the small talk. I came to get you. You're wanted in the headquarters building.'

Maximus shivered. 'Really?' Only very good things and very bad things came from visits with senior commanders, and he couldn't think of anything he'd done recently that might end up with praise.

'Really. Come on.'

Maximus turned and waved to Rufus. 'Keep going with this lot. I have to visit the big chief, but I'll be back.'

I hope, he added silently as Rufus nodded and turned away to continue the training.

With Naevius Bibula leading the way, he descended the tribunal and gestured to Duras. 'Take the horse back to the stables and then go see the cooks and sort me some lunch.'

Ignoring the slave's black look, he marched away.

'You need to sell that slave on, to field or quarry work or something.'

Maximus chuckled. 'After all the time I spent training him in horse grooming and armour maintenance?'

'Tiberius, if a slave is still looking at you like that after more than a decade, he's never going to be properly broken. That creature is a knife in the dark just waiting to happen to you.'

'What does the commander want?' Maximus asked, largely to change the subject.

'No idea. I was standing outside with the others, and the prefect dipped out and told me to fetch you. But be on your best behaviour. The imperial standards are on display.'

Maximus felt his blood chill for a moment. The *emperor* was in there. He'd heard that Trajan had arrived in camp yesterday evening, but hadn't imagined the man would be active yet. Surely after travelling all the way from Rome, he would need a day to recover? He felt the nerves building as they strode away from the open training area, past the edge of the burgeoning civilian town, and approached the heavy walls of the fortress of the Seventh Legion.

The legion was not the only unit in residence, of course, even ignoring Maximus's own ala. Multiple legions, numerous cavalry alae, and seemingly endless camps of auxiliary infantry and mixed units covered the landscape for several miles around Viminacium. Not since Domitian's war had Maximus seen so many troops gathered together, and he would say with confidence that this army was at least a third as large again as Domitian's had been.

Trajan meant business.

The legionaries of the Seventh Claudia at the fortress gate barely blinked at them passing through, let alone stepping forward to bar their path. The sheer volume of soldiers passing in and out of each of the great fort's gates on a daily basis made any kind of security measures a joke, and men who were clearly auxiliary officers were barely even acknowledged.

Inside the gate, the wide street led off to the grand, monumental headquarters building at the heart of the fortress, every square foot of space seemingly filled by a soldier of some description going about their business. The place was crawling with life, like an ant nest, and it was like this from before dawn until after curfew. War meant constant activity. Indeed, a guarded and fortified temporary enclosure almost the size of the legion's fortress had been constructed half a mile away just to store the supplies that were ferried in from all directions during every daylight hour.

Maximus had been to this headquarters only twice, once when they'd arrived at Viminacium, and that had been before half the army had descended on the place, and once when Domitian had been here, planning his own war. Now, as they came closer to the headquarters, striding between ordered rows of barracks, stores and workshops, they could see the distinctive white uniforms of Praetorians here and there, going about their own, probably more important, business.

Indeed, as they walked around to the great building's main front entrance, it was clear for all to see who was now in residence. A purple banner bearing the image of Demeter, the emperor's birth sign, and topped by a golden eagle, hung above the grand arch, to one side of it the crimson banner with the golden bull of the Seventh Claudia, and to the other the red banner with the golden scorpion of the Praetorian Guard. Other legions and units were represented with smaller pennants, too, but it was those three that really caught the eye, and which also caught Maximus's breath in his throat. Unlike the fortress's gate, the arch that led to the headquarters was sealed tight, two men of the Seventh joined by eight Praetorians, gleaming and dangerous, protecting the imperial person.

As they approached there was a brief conflab, but clearly Bibula was recognised and their presence was expected, for the soldiers stepped aside to allow them to enter without question. As they passed beneath the archway and entered the great courtyard, two Praetorians fell in alongside them, and matched their pace, as though escorting prisoners. Maximus looked around. The statues of Mars, Minerva and Jupiter were unchanged, although they had been freshly repainted. The first time he'd been here, a statue of Domitian stood proudly opposite. It had presumably been hastily recarved to represent Nerva after the change of regime, but that statue too had now gone, and a brand new one of Trajan stood in its place, larger than life. He took note of it, committing the details to memory. People often said that imperial statues were idealised to make their subjects look good, but Maximus had been impressed with how close to the real thing Domitian's had been. Would the new emperor's be quite so good? His stony face was odd, even painted up correctly. Not particularly handsome, yet imposing and impressive in some indefinable way. He looked calm and thoughtful, yet there was a steel about that expression, too.

He was still tearing his eyes from the freshly painted statue as they passed through a door into the massive basilica. A hall large enough for small-scale cavalry practice, the basilica was rarely occupied, and usually echoed as a man walked across its marble floor to the offices beyond. Not so today, as even the noise warned them.

Four more Praetorians nodded their consent as the two officers passed through into the shade, and inside, the room was full. Maximus was quite sure he'd never seen so many officers and nobles in one room. Almost everyone here was dressed like a prefect or a tribune or the like, others with the knotted ribbon denoting staff officers and generals. Only a dozen or so men were not so dressed, barring the Praetorians, of course, who stood around the room in small groups. A dozen men wore the broad-striped tunics of senators, presumably members of the court who had come east with the emperor. There was no throne, no chair high on a dais, and Maximus frowned, for Domitian had made sure that was the case wherever he was. His gaze fell back on the men in tunics, for there was no clear purple of imperial regalia. He could not see a man among them who resembled the statue outside...

Then he saw Trajan. He blinked, realising that the reason he'd missed the emperor was because Trajan was dressed as a military officer, like many of the others, and far from looking down on them from a raised throne, he was standing among them, as though one of them.

And he did look like his statue. The same intense, yet calm look. The painters outside had only got one thing wrong that Maximus could see, for the real man's eyes were hazel, not blue. He looked then at the men surrounding the emperor. He didn't recognise any of them, but they all looked like military men, not one with that out of place pallor of a courtier playing soldier. They were standing on a map of the region, made of marble – a damned expensive map, for sure. It covered everywhere from Carnuntum up in Pannonia down to the Euxine Sea, with Moesia, Dacia and other provinces and lands marked out in tiny black mosaic stones. Trajan was tapping with his foot, somewhere in the lower Danube.

'We won't have time to finish pulling all the units in,' a man with a pinched face and an even more pinched voice was saying. 'There are cohorts all the way down to Byzantium and back to Dalmatia who've been given the muster orders, but told not to come until their own replacements have arrived. You're too early, Marcus. We're not ready.'

Marcus? Who could be so familiar with an emperor as to call him by name? Maximus stared.

'Next summer would have been ideal,' Trajan nodded to the man. 'I would have liked nothing more, but events move faster than anticipated. I even laid down my consulship half way through the term for this. We must move fast and decisively.'

He turned and waved west across the map. 'Any unit not yet with us will have to move for Viminacium at the best speed they can. You and I both know, Sura, that this war is unlikely to be finished in a single season, and we will need to bolster the troops before any fresh push after winter. Late arrivals will serve as a reserve here.' He turned and waved the other way. 'Any troops coming from the east and south should be diverted to Novae and assigned to Laberius's force. We can tarry no more.'

A throat being cleared in the moment's silence drew everyone's attention. A swarthy man with curly black hair and a gold ear ring, wearing an ornate cuirass with white pteruges, lifted a hand. 'With respect, Imperator, many of us are still in the dark as to why the campaign has been brought forward, and what has brought you from Rome so early.'

Maximus almost jumped as the emperor turned and looked directly at him, as though expecting him to be standing where he was right now. Trajan nodded, not to Maximus, but clearly to himself. He straightened. 'I was waiting for another source of intelligence before explaining in too much detail, but I believe that source is now here.'

He stepped back and a space opened up before him. 'We are quite fortunate really to have the warnings we do. Sauromates, King of the Bosporan lands, remains loyal to Rome, thank the gods. Word arrived at the palace in Rome, by fast courier, that our good friend Sauromates has been approached by Decebalus of Dacia, seeking an alliance. From what we are given to understand, the embassy was clever and very carefully worded. There was no overt indicator that any such alliance would be formed with the objective of opposing Rome, but clearly sufficient inference was there for the king to immediately send warning to Rome. Sauromates has dissembled, in an attempt to keep the Dacian king off-balance and unprepared, but the longer we leave Decebalus in control, the more chance there is of either war or alliance in the east, neither of which suits our own goals. I decided, therefore, to abandon my consulship and march east with all haste, bringing forward the campaign so we can hit Decebalus before he can get his own plans in place.'

There were nods of approval at this, and then the emperor turned and gestured to one of the officers, Maximus glanced across and spotted the prefect of his own cavalry unit.

'This is the man?' the emperor said, pointing now at Maximus.

'That is him, Majesty.'

Trajan's brow creased for a moment, and then he beckoned to Maximus. 'Come.'

Nervous, shivering slightly, Maximus clacked across the marble map until he was a respectable twelve paces from the emperor. He couldn't help but notice how Praetorians had closed on him at the same time, making certain that he couldn't get to the emperor before they could get to him.

'I understand you have been in talks with the Iazyges, Duplicarius?'

Maximus bowed his head. He was trying not to look directly at the emperor. Domitian had hated that. Men had been blinded for meeting Domitian's gaze. Trajan was clearly different. 'Look at me,' he said, and Maximus's gaze rose to those pale brown eyes. 'Good,' Trajan said. The truth of a man's heart is visible in his eyes. I like to see whether I can trust a man when he talks. So...'

'Tiberius Claudius Maximus, Majesty,' the prefect prompted.

Trajan nodded. 'So, Claudius Maximus. You led a scouting mission into the lands of the horse people.'

Maximus flashed a panicked look across at the prefect, who nodded. He swallowed. Some emperors took exception to being spoken to directly at all, and *most* emperors, by all accounts, did not like to be corrected. Oddly, from the way Trajan was peering into his eyes, Maximus had a feeling that, again, *this* emperor was different.

'Not quite, your Majesty.'

'Oh?'

'We were neither diplomats nor scouts, Majesty. We were simply the cavalry unit given the task of escorting the latest gifts to the Iazyges' chieftains.'

'Yet you somehow managed to strike a deal with them?'

Maximus felt his heart lurch. The *emperor* had heard about that? How? Maximus had told no one about the escapade. He floundered for a moment, not quite sure what to say.

'Come on, man, spit it out,' Trajan said, sounding slightly irritated.

'Majesty, the chieftain we spoke to, one Radamasis, informed us that emissaries of Decebalus have been approaching various of the Iazyx clans, seeking alliances. Possibly worse still, Majesty, King Decebalus appears to have been similarly approaching the Germanic tribes *beyond* there.'

Trajan tapped his lips. 'Beyond the Iazyges. You mean the Carpi?'

'The Osii, Majesty.'

Trajan frowned, turned. A young officer with curly hair and a beard, something almost unheard of in noble circles, nodded. 'A tribe we've had little contact with, Marcus, but who could be influential. They're close enough to the curve of the Danubius up near Aquincum that they could capitalise on any attempt to draw troops away from the region for the war.'

Trajan gave a small smile. 'Good job I did no such thing, then.' He turned back to Maximus. 'You believe this chieftain?'

Maximus nodded. 'I do, Majesty. He had no reason to lie. He himself was in a position of making overtures to *us*.'

'Yes,' a sly smile crossed Trajan's face. 'So I understand. If the report on my desk is to be believed, you have promised part of Dacia to the Iazyges in return for their help in the coming conflict.'

His face was unreadable now. Maximus felt the ground opening up beneath him. 'Majesty, it was a moment's decision, and perhaps foolish, but to have denied him there and then would almost certainly have driven the Iazyges into the arms of the Dacian king.'

There was an uncomfortable quiet. Maximus found himself praying silently.

'*What* part of Dacia?' the bearded man asked quietly.

'I do believe,' the emperor replied, without taking those piercing eyes from Maximus, 'that our friend here promised to give to the Iazyges all the good agricultural land as far as the Dacian mountains.'

There was an explosion of disbelief and anger among the many officers in the room at this. Comments came thick and fast.

'That is the main western route into Dacia?'

'You mean right the way up to Tapae and the Iron Gates?'

'Such things are not his to *give*.'

'Perhaps we should be conquering the Iazyges *first*.'

'No ally is worth such a price.'

Maximus closed his eyes for a moment, weathering the storm, aware that his career seemed to be balanced on a knife edge right now. When he opened them, and the comments were still going, sporadically, he realised the emperor was still looking at him.

'*Are* they?' the bearded man asked.

'Are they what, Publius?' Trajan replied, still without taking his eyes off Maximus, who was starting to twitch.

'The Iazyges. *Are* they worth that price?'

Now complete silence fell for a moment. Trajan took a deep breath. 'No,' he said in the end, and Maximus felt that pit opening wider. 'No,' the emperor said again, 'they are not. But regardless, I would have made the same offer at the time. The Iazyges have a fearsome reputation, and it is far better to have them fighting for us, or even neutral and uninvolved, than fighting for Decebalus. And no, we cannot spare a year in a needless war against the horse clans first. As to whether we can make good on such a deal in the end? Clearly the answer is no. We cannot give away the main western route into Dacia.

But we can perhaps compromise and give them *some* of that land. Once we have beaten Decebalus, we will be in a position to negotiate with the horse clans. For now, we want them with us.'

Finally, he smiled at Maximus. 'Yes, I would have made precisely the same call, given the choices. Indeed, I think it shows remarkable foresight and political acumen for a man with no authority to grant anything to have made such a decision. And you are not a scout? Not an ambassador?'

'A soldier, Majesty.'

'And a good one, clearly,' the emperor added, pointing. After a moment, Maximus realised Trajan was indicating the gold torc around his neck and the arm-ring hanging from the bronze hook that connected the shoulder pieces of his chain shirt. 'Given by the Flavian who should not be named, I'd wager,' Trajan smiled. 'My own predecessor was not in much of a position to give out military decorations, and the last time they were handed out here would presumably be under Domitian.'

Maximus simply bowed his head in answer to that.

'Imperator, you surely don't mean to let this soldier off free, after having dared to make such an offer?' one of the officers asked incredulously.

The bearded one laughed. 'Watch this, Pompeius.'

Trajan flashed just a tiny grin then, and Maximus had an odd feeling that it was meant specifically for him and him alone. 'The talents of such a man are wasted on cavalry escort duties. Clearly he and his companions are more suited to clever work. What's his unit?'

'Second Pannonian, Majesty,' called the prefect.

'Yours?'

'Yes, Majesty. For over a year now.'

'Have this man's turma of riders reclassified. They are wasted in their current work. Assign them as exploratores. I want men like this moving ahead of the army, testing the waters, checking the land, making deals when they need making, and gathering information everywhere.'

Maximus blinked. Exploratores? Dangerous work, but respected, and it could be lucrative, too. Trajan seemed to be waiting. Maximus glanced about. The bearded officer was grinning, looking as though he might burst out laughing at any moment. The ala's prefect was looking at him, wide-eyed. He nodded slightly, and Maximus realised they were all waiting on him. He turned back to the emperor. 'I am honoured, Majesty. Thank you.'

The bearded fellow let that laugh out now. 'Don't thank him yet, soldier. The army moves north within the month, and now you'll be the first across the river, preparing the way.'

Trajan turned, flashing his grin at the bearded man, then turned back and nodded at Maximus. It was a polite dismissal, and he recognised it as such, thank the gods., without overstaying his welcome. He bowed and started to back from the room. After a moment, Naevius Bibula fell in beside him. The moment they left the great hall and stepped out into the courtyard, Maximus exploded with relief. 'Fuck me, but I'm a grizzled old bastard with two decades of war behind me, and I felt like a frightened recruit in there. Gods, but that man is clever. Decebalus has no idea what's coming, I think. Who was the one with the beard? I had the feeling he was playing with us.'

'That, I think, would be the emperor's new nephew, Hadrian. He's on the staff for the campaign.'

They strode through the outer gate and into the streets of the fortress, making for the next exit. 'I cannot thank you enough, Tiberius,' Bibula said, tone so heavy with sarcasm they almost fell over it.

'What?'

'The whole turma. Speculatores. My *whole* turma.'

'More interesting than guarding wagons, Naevius. And a bit of a pay rise. And excused duty for all camp work. And we ride at the front of the column, not in the dust cloud at the back.'

'Yes, about *ten miles* in front of the column,' Bibulus snorted. 'It's alright for you, Tiberius. You've got another ten years in you, climbing the ladder. Twenty probably, if you reenlist. Me? I'm forty-eight. I've a dodgy hip and arthritis, I have to get up three times a night to piss. I'm old, and I've seen *enough* bloody action. I don't *need* more excitement. I could happily have sat in garrison for the next four years and then retired.'

Maximus laughed. 'Bollocks. I know you, Naevius. You live for thrills.'

'At my age, a comfortable shit is a thrill.'

They left the fortress and strode back towards the training ground, climbing the tribunal. Maximus sighed. That same recruit was hopping madly across the dirt, having somehow contrived to snare his other foot in the haunch strap. The horse was merrily trotting away with the panicked trainee trying to free himself behind. Close by, Rufus stood with his hand over his eyes, shaking his head. Maximus turned a long-suffering look on his decurion.

'Perhaps we should show this to the emperor,' Bibulus snorted. 'He might change his mind quite quickly.'

Chapter Four

Danubius River, 10 miles downstream from Viminacium, high summer AD 101

Maximus was impressed with the bridge. Trajan's preparations for war were impressive, and had been underway for two years now, but they were still incomplete, the campaign having commenced a year early. A proper bridge had originally been planned in time for the campaigning season next year, but the river here was half a mile across, and any attempt at a full-scale structure would take far too long for a push this summer. As such, a pontoon bridge had been put in place by the hard work of three legions in just half a month.

Maximus had used pontoon bridges before, and always found them to be nerve-wracking, especially for a horseman. Even the sturdiest versions had a tendency to shift and undulate with the river's currents, and that made horses nervous, let alone their riders.

Not so this bridge. The military road to Dacia was carried across what appeared to be half the ships of the Danubian fleet sitting mid-flow, side by side, in a perfect line. Each was held to the next not only with enough rope to tether a Titan, but also with beams and planks nailed and pegged in place. Atop the boats ran a wooden bridge, bank to bank, that would not have looked out of place atop brick piles as a permanent thing. It was a marvel of engineering, really. Maximus had known plenty of engineers in his days in the legion, and even a professional architectus in the auxilia, and the way the minds of such men worked continued to baffle him. They were all geniuses, and they were all odd, something which suggested a correlation built into the human condition.

Despite a half mile width and a current that could pull the purse from an Aegyptian merchant, the ships remained in perfect place, and the boards remained sturdy and unmoving even beneath the hooves of thirty-two horses.

As promised, the turma of Naevius Bibula, freshly assigned scouts, were to be the first across the river. In a way, they were to be Rome's red spear, planted in Decebalus's lands and declaring war. Of course, they were not *entirely* unaccompanied. In this army alone there were a dozen units of scouts, though most would come across with the army and then disperse in due course. And then there was the *other* advance. Trajan himself would advance here, from Viminacium, taking a strong force across the river and along the same route as Domitian's war had taken. The renowned general Gnaeus Pompeius Longinus, along with a cadre of experienced officers, had led a force almost as large, a few days earlier, down the bank to Dierna, where they would cross on the other side of the Danube's fearsome gorges, and take a lesser pass to meet the main column far to the north. Then, of course, there was a third army down in the lower Danube with the general Laberius. The purpose of this third force had not been revealed to people as lowly as scout officers, and so they could only guess at Laberius's role in all of this.

Maximus's gaze rose from the timbers across which they pounded, and to the land beyond. It did not look entirely suited to the plan.

'A statement,' Trajan had said in his last address to the officers. 'We cross the river in force and then pause. I want a camp on the far bank, all our might gathered there before we move on, a standard planted in Decebalus's own back garden, to tell him that we are here and that this time there will be no humiliating Roman payments in gold. We will stay for a few days, seeking the blessings of the gods on this endeavour, and then move north.'

Maximus was sceptical. A camp large enough to hold so many legions and auxilia, let alone the endless stream of civilians and hangers-on, would spread across the landscape from horizon to horizon. The north bank here did not present appropriate space. To the left of the bridge, upstream, the River Nera poured into the great Danubius. They had to be east of the Nera as they headed north, but the land close to the lesser river was fairly densely wooded. Then, only a quarter of a mile east across good ground, the terrain rose into hills that then became cliffs further downstream. Essentially, only a quarter of a mile of good land stood before them.

He reached the end of the bridge and the clattering of hooves became the dull thud of horses on turf, and Maximus, with the rest of the turma, gathered on Bibula, who had his hand raised as he reined in.

'Alright, lads,' the decurion said, 'looks like we've got three areas of terrain. I'll take ten men and check out the woods. I want to be sure there's nothing lurking there and waiting for us. Maximus, you take ten up onto the hills. See if they get worse or perhaps flatten out beyond, suitable for an army. Rufus, you have the rest. Move up into the gap, but be sure to keep pace with the rest of us. I don't want anyone racing out halfway across Dacia before we know what's going on.'

At that, he gave the signal with a drop of his hand, and the unit split three ways, a third under the decurion, a third under Maximus and the rest under the nearest thing they had to a third officer, the dependable and experienced custos armorum.

Maximus watched the others go for a moment, then waved on his own men, taking the lead. The terrain was easy enough for horses, good moorland grass, with scattered rocks here and there and a small smattering of trees and scrub dotted across the landscape. He pounded across the gentle incline, and with the experienced eye of a lifelong horseman, guided Celeris towards the best route, a track that cut sideways and then doubled back as it climbed.

They rode easily, reaching that bend soon and then turning east, away from the other riders. In a matter of heartbeats they were moving into land that levelled slowly out, cresting the hill. As he reached the top and jerked the reins, Maximus looked ahead, then behind, at the Danubius, then ahead again. He was peering a little east of north, straight in the direction the army was to take. He smiled with relief. This stretch of hills was a spur that jutted out where the cliffs of the gorge dropped to the gentle valley of the Nera, and on the far side lay a huge stretch of plateaued flat land, perfect for a camp for an army of any size. All Trajan's force had to do was either crest this hill and cross it, or move along the plain between there and the river, then pass around the other end of the hills.

Perfect.

'Thank fuck for that, sir,' Rigozus said, reining in close. 'I thought we were going to be camping on top of one another for a while.'

'As long as I'm on top,' Arrianus shouted. 'You drool in your sleep, Flaccus.'

'Piss off.'

'Shut up the lot of you,' Maximus said, though not unkindly, for he too was relieved. Turning, he trotted along the ridge towards the Nera Valley, where the others were at work. As he reached the peak overlooking the river, the woods and the narrow flat approach, he reined in again, the others joining him.

He could see the middle group below him, moving at leisure across the grass. When the others stopped yapping for a moment, he could even hear them, laughing and shouting at one another, down the slope. They were moving with deliberate slowness to stay in line with Maximus. His gaze rose, past them and to the woodland bordering the river. He could just make out Bibula and his men moving through a clearing, in good formation. All was fine.

'Maximus!'

The call drew his attention, and he looked down again at the group in the middle. While his men probed the area ahead slowly and carefully, Rufus had stopped and turned to the hill, both hands cupped round his mouth.

'Yes?' Maximus called back as loud as he could, then turned to his men and waved them to quiet, since their conversation was making it hard to hear.

'What's it like ahead?' Rufus shouted.

Maximus smiled. 'Flat as Nero's singing,' he shouted back. 'Perfect ground.'

'Good. Should we go back?'

But before Maximus could answer, they were interrupted by a cry. His gaze snapped across the ground to the sound, and his pulse leapt as he saw a man and his horse from Rufus's party on the ground. He frowned, focused, trying to see what had happened, then his eyes widened as he realised. The rider had walked his mount straight into a concealed pit.

The man's horse was done for, legs broken and flailing in agony, but at least the rider had been thrown clear, and was now standing slowly, shaking his head to clear it.

Even as Rufus bellowed the order for his men to halt, another disappeared into a pit. The holes were maybe six feet in every dimension, covered somehow with a delicate lattice of wicker that held up a thin slice of turf rendering it invisible. From here, any of that ground could be another pit.

'Shit.' He turned, hoping that the unit's only musician was here with his horn. He wasn't. 'Shit,' he said again.

Down below, Rufus was gathering his men on his position, and carefully stepping back in the direction of the river. Maximus's gaze nipped up to the woods, wondering how he could get the decurion's attention, but at that moment he realised there was more trouble happening unseen in the trees, for he could hear very distant shouts and screams.

He bit his lip. After Bibula, he was the second in command, and already Rufus was looking up at him, expectantly.

'Down the slope. We grab the others and head into the woods to find out what's happening.'

'Down *there*?' Abgar asked, pointing down the relatively steep stretch towards the low ground where Rufus and his men were gathered.

'Got something better to do?' Maximus shouted, and then, with a silent prayer to Epona, kicked Celeris into life and turned her towards the slope. She had been with him now for so long that there was trust between them, and no room for indecision, and the moment he directed the animal, she obeyed. He reached the edge of the incline and tried not to swear again as they began to hurtle down the slope towards the others. Horses were not always good with slopes like this, and he could hear some of his men behind him having trouble controlling their mounts. He left them to it. Time was almost certainly of the essence here.

It seemed to take forever to reach the point where the slope evened out to the flat land, and Maximus's heart was pounding with exhilaration, and not a little trepidation, as he reached the good open turf once more. Aware that his men were close behind, he pelted over towards Rufus, hoping against hope that they were still south of the pit traps and that none waited to catch him on the way. As he reached the custos armorum, the two men who'd lost their horses to the pits were staggering to join him, one of them cradling what had to be a broken arm.

'I think I was getting cocky,' Rufus said. 'Should have realised it was all a little too inviting.'

'The clever bastards. They're so hard to see.' Maximus pointed to the two dismounted men. 'Have two riders take them back across the bridge and report. We have met resistance, and they have set traps. What we need now is a legion's engineer corps to check over the land and clear it to make way for the army.'

Rufus gestured to two of the riders, and the dismounted men clambered up behind saddles and were carried back towards the bridge.

'What now?'

Maximus pointed at the woods. 'Something's happening in there. Let's go help. Move carefully, though.'

Gathering the others around them, Maximus now led a force of sixteen men towards the trees. As they neared the forest's eaves, he fought down uncertainty and trepidation. Woodland was the worst of all terrain for horsemen. He aimed for the most open approach, aware that this had to have been the route Bibula took. As he, at the front, passed the first trees, he lowered his face a little and tucked in his arms and knees. Despite aiming for the clearest of paths, he felt small branches and foliage smacking into him as he rode, things ricocheting off his helmet. Something struck a cheek plate and for a moment he had the taste of forest in his mouth, before that became blood from the lip split by the whipping branch. Once upon a time, he had cursed having to wear a face mask with his cavalry helmet. Right now, it would have been bloody useful.

Snarling curses, he pressed on, the others at his back, many of them bellowing imprecations as they suffered pains and discomforts. Maximus tried to concentrate. Despite the noises all around, he could just make out a din ahead, and angled his approach towards the noise. He sucked the blood from his lip again, and blinked as something smacked across his face and almost took his eye out.

Then, suddenly, he was in the open. A clearing of some size.

A figure burst from the trees opposite, and Maximus peered, blinking at it.

He knew that look. A tall iron helmet with a peak that leaned forward, ornate cheek pieces below. Scale armour, an oval shield bearing ornate curved patterns, full trousers, and... a falx.

Dacians.

Roaring, aware that he might be being a little stupid before knowing what was going on, Maximus turned his horse with his knees and kicked her flanks, sending her into a gallop across the open space. The Dacian warrior, who had clearly stumbled out into the clearing alone, unaware of what was coming, saw him and turned, lurching back into the trees. The way he moved suggested he was suffering a mild injury. He disappeared into what looked to be a game trail made by deer, wide and high enough for a horseman, at least if he hunched down and ducked.

The man vanished from sight, and Maximus raced in after him.

What happened next should not have come as a surprise after what had happened to Rufus's riders. Just inside the gloom of the trees, he encountered the Dacian's trap. It felt as though someone had struck him in the chest with a great wooden mallet. He was torn from Celeris's back, plucked from the saddle, and thrown to the ground in that narrow trail. As he hit the rough forest floor, winded and bruised by the branches and rocks sticking up, he realised he had hit a rope stretched across the trail and tied between two trees. Celeris had gone beneath it, but it had swept him from the horse's back.

He struggled. His back hurt, and his head was fuzzy from the sudden fall. His left arm ached where it had landed awkwardly beneath him. He fought for breath, for sense, for urgency.

His rather random flailing saved his life.

The Dacian warrior's falx came down like the judgement of gods, three feet of curved steel with a razor sharp inner blade. Had Maximus happened to have been moving more to his left, the blade would have lodged in his brain, cutting right down from scalp to mouth. As it happened, his head had snapped right in panic. He felt the pain as the point of the falx punched through his cavalry helmet as though it were made of parchment, and left a scrape across his skull beneath.

A shard of bronzed helmet fell away with the light spray of blood, and on instinct alone, Maximus rolled away. That primeval will to survive took over, which, when added to a lifetime's experience in war, allowed him to overcome both the pain in his ear and the fuzziness of his mind, and he staggered upright, pushing back, behind a tree. As he did so, he reached up to his helmet and sent its rather sad remains off into the undergrowth.

That falx came round and lodged in the tree, a few inches from his face, and he ducked back in shock, but then realised the opportunity that had been granted him. The Dacian was pulling at his weapon, trying to free it from the tree, teeth bared and growling. Maximus's hand went to his sword hilt.

It wasn't there.

He stared down in horror. In his fall, the leather baldric had either snapped or come undone, and the sword had fallen away. Desperately, his hand reached down to the other side, where his pugio dagger sat above his hip on his belt.

He pulled the blade and leapt. The Dacian was so busy, trying to pull the falx free, that he was too late to stop the inevitable. Snarling curses, Maximus slammed the tip of the dagger into the Dacian's throat and, even as he did so, his other palm wrapped around the pommel and pushed, so that the pugio dug deeper and deeper into the neck with every tensing of muscle, grinding through bone and cartilage, scything through muscle and flesh.

Blood washed out of the man's neck, across Maximus's dagger and both hands, but he continued forcing the blade, jerking it this way and that for good measure, until the light left the man's eyes and he dropped, hands coming away from the lodged falx.

The cavalryman stared down at the twitching, dead form of the warrior, then to the falx. For a moment, he was tempted to take it, but common sense overrode the desire. If it was that well lodged it would take a while to free it, and he had a sword and a horse to find and a unit to help. Staggering this way and that, he found his sword entirely by accident, stepping on it in the undergrowth as he pushed his way back on to the track. He looked at it in irritation. The leather strap had come away at one of the rings that held it in place.

As he staggered out onto the path, looking this way and that, he undid his belt and threaded the scabbard onto it. A baldric was far more comfortable for a sword when riding, but a belt would do if needed. Fastening the buckle again, he stepped out into the clearing. There was no one here, but, much to his relief, Celeris was standing in the open, completely unconcerned, enjoying the lush grass. He approached carefully, in case she was nervous after the incident, but she remained calm and let him approach and climb into the saddle.

As he walked his horse back over to that deer trail, he cocked his head, listening carefully. He could still hear trouble, and it was coming from various sources, though all in the same rough direction. He carefully guided Celeris back into the trail, but even as he did so, a new noise drew his attention. Here, where there was still room, he turned the mount with a little trouble, in time to see a wounded Dacian stagger out into the clearing. The man had no idea Maximus was there, hidden in the trees, and looked this way and that, left hand clamped to his neck, where it was drenched red.

Maximus smiled viciously. The last Dacian may have surprised him, but it was going to be the other way round, this time.

He drew his sword slowly, trying to avoid too much noise. The wounded Dacian had stopped in the middle of the clearing, and turned, listening, trying to work out what was going on. Maximus turned Celeris directly towards the man, and then kicked her flanks. She reared a little for just a heartbeat, but the moment her hooves touched the ground again, she was off like a ballista bolt.

Maximus and his horse were halfway to the man before he'd registered what was happening, and turned, wide-eyed, to see the Roman riding at him. His left hand remained at his neck, trying to stem the flow of blood, and his right reached down for a sword at his side.

He'd drawn it maybe a hand-width from the sheath when Maximus hit him. The Roman's sword, pulled back to the right, swung in a horizontal arc, and slammed into the man's panicked face.

He was dead from that moment, even though it took a little while for his nerves and brain to catch up. The body fell to the grass, weapons released, blood free to flow from the wound he no longer held.

Two men downed with no real injury to himself was a win, Maximus acknowledged. In truth, any fight where he walked away would be a victory. But this one was a *proper* win. The only problem was that there were twenty-seven men from the ala in these woods, and though there could be half a dozen Dacians, there could equally be half a thousand. Best not to gloat and get complacent.

He shook the worst of the gore from his sword and rolled his shoulders, taking a deep breath. Then he paused, listening carefully. Readying himself for yet more traps and surprises, he angled Celeris towards the trees in the direction of the sounds. He found himself in a narrow trail through the woods, and as he moved slowly, carefully, towards the sounds, he could see the signs of what had happened along the way. More ropes, some still tied, others cut through. Pieces of armour and clothing, shields and weapons lying among the undergrowth. Here, a Dacian, head cleaved, arm broken impossibly behind his hip. There, a Roman horse lying, bloodied and silent.

He cursed and moved on, the sounds coming ever closer.

He met the next Dacian suddenly, and the man was as surprised as he was, running along a track he thought clear. He tried to bring his falx round to bear, but Maximus's sword slashed out and knocked it aside, and in the following heartbeats he was trampling his horse across the fallen man, hooves breaking bone and pulverising flesh.

He left the ruined body and emerged into another clearing to see Naevius Bibula wiping his forehead with his scarf, blood everywhere. Other cavalrymen were emerging from the woods now, gathering around their commander. The noise had changed from one of combat to one of recovery.

'Clearly you found a fight of your own,' the decurion said, noting Maximus's state.

'Rufus's men walked their horses into pit traps,' Maximus replied with a sigh as he reined in. 'He lost two horses. No men. At that point we heard the trouble you were in and raced to help.'

'Probably a good job.'

'Many losses?'

Bibula shrugged. 'A few. Not many, all things being equal. Could have been a lot worse. I don't think this was an intentional ambush. I think we walked into them unexpected.'

Maximus nodded. 'I think they were setting up traps in the night, and left a small group to watch and report back. They didn't expect you to go into the woods. They're dead?'

'Dead or fled. I think the moment they knew they were outclassed, they ran. They used the terrain to get away into places horses couldn't follow. I saw at least half a dozen escape, which means there were probably ten times that.'

'You realise what this means?' Maximus said.

Bibula nodded. 'If they're leaving traps for us from the outset, they're going to be ahead of us all the way.'

'Beating a fighting retreat,' Maximus sighed.

'Perhaps they're just leaving small irritating units to trap us and slow us, pick off whoever they can and buy them time.'

Maximus stretched, and then sagged. 'No. They're drawing us in. I've seen this before. *Twice* before.'

'Ah yes. You were with the last emperor.'

A nod. 'I was there at First Tapae when they ambushed us and kicked ten shades of shit out of us. I was a lucky survivor. And I was at Second Tapae, when they thought they were drawing us into an ambush, but the general turned it on them. Still, despite everything, we were lucky to win, and all it bought us was a decade of peace until here we are again.'

'But Rome learns from its mistakes.'

'Does it?' Maximus sighed. 'I'll grant you the new emperor and his generals seem clever, but what are we doing? We're marching along the same old roads with the same old units against the same old enemy. One loss, one costly win. What happens this time? They'll draw us to Tapae, but if Rome learns, so do the Dacians, and they won't make the same mistakes this time as they did last time. I think we're headed for the shit pit again, Naevius.'

'Shit, but you're a ray of bloody sunshine, you are, Maximus.'

The decurion straightened. 'This is a win. We've lost four riders and six horses, but we've killed half a damned cohort of Dacians, and identified the traps waiting for us. The emperor will be pleased with his new scouts, I'm sure.'

*

That night, Maximus changed into a fresh tunic and stood for a moment, breathing in the summer air gently, largely tainted with the tang of horse, and then gestured to Duras. The slave was busy cleaning his master's sword.

'Walk with me.'

The Dacian put the sword away carefully, then rose and crossed the room. In one way, Maximus was tempted to take it as a sign of acceptance that Duras could be trusted with his sword, but then they were in the middle of a camp of many thousands of Romans. Killing his master and trying to run would be a suicidal option. Still, Maximus felt again the need to make an effort.

He left his own room, Duras at his shoulder, and walked between the ordered lines of tents of the men of the Second Pannoniorum. Their horses were corralled off to one side, tended by the unit's livery slaves. They were more pliant, younger lads bought early and brought up enslaved, given a job, and the hope of a future in which they could be free, or even join up and serve in the unit with their own slaves one day. A long way removed from Duras.

He led the way, walking through the camp, nodding at various people, officers and men he knew, officers he didn't, guards who were content that he was no trouble. He strolled up the hillside. It took almost a quarter of an hour to reach the top of the nearest slope, and there he stopped and turned slowly, taking it all in.

The camp, a massive affair, full of legions, auxilia, a few groups from the fleet, officers, civilians, merchants and supply wagons, lay in that nice flat plateau area Maximus had located beyond the hills. On the far side, he could see across the black, glittering ribbon that was the Danubius, to the distant, twinkling lights of Viminacium, and the ships and bridge between. Small camps remained near the bank, mainly men of the Danubian fleet, and engineers were still hard at work from hill to river, unpicking Dacian traps of various types. The emperor would tarry here for a couple of days at the most before moving north, and he wanted the land free of surprises before he did so. Torches burned on every peak, where scouts from the army sat watching the area.

'Who *are* you?' Maximus said

Duras sat in silence.

'Alright, who *were* you?'

More silence.

Maximus dropped to a crouch. 'You are Duras. Of the who? There are so many Dacian tribes. Did you come from the area around Tapae, or from the northern mountains? Or from down near the river in lower Moesia. Duras the what?'

'You should never have let me keep my name.'

Maximus blinked. 'What?'

'Why do you think they give you a slave name? To remove that last bit of humanity from you. To make you something else. Something less. The day you took me, you asked my name, and you've used it. And it took you thirteen years to ask more?'

Maximus sighed. 'Oddly, it never seemed to matter until we came across the river together again. This is the first time we've both been north of the Danubius since Second Tapae.'

'I am Apuli, to answer your question. Are we done?'

Maximus breathed deep. 'I have never understood resistance.'

'What?'

'The Gauls fought back for seven years against Caesar's legions. In the end they lost millions of men, and ruined their land forever. Even now they are a shadow of what they were. Carthage fought back, and their own land was sown with salt to ruin it. The Jews? What did Vespasian and Titus do to them? When Rome seeks to expand, those who stand in resistance inevitably fail, and the result is near annihilation. But there are those who see the light. Aegyptus is prized and dear to the emperor. Galatia thrives, as its king embraced Rome. So does the king in Bosphorus. To work *with* Rome is to invite civilisation.'

He looked down at Duras. 'Well?'

The slave's lip twitched.

'Go on.'

Duras looked up, and there was no subservience in those eyes. 'I know my histories. When Rome was muddy farmers and spear-throwers, the states of Achaea were producing men like Herodotus and Aeschylus. Why did Rome not simply accept that they should be a Greek state?'

Maximus frowned. 'Because that's insane. I'm from Greek lands myself, but Rome is strong, and Greek states were weak.'

'Dacia is strong.'

'But...'

'And why should we accept Roman hegemony if we are strong enough to resist.'

Maximus rubbed his chin. 'Because you aren't.'

'That remains to be seen,' Duras replied, straight-faced. 'And when Decebalus sends your Spanish emperor back across the river with his tail between his legs, I shall skin you, tan your hide, and make a new shield out of Tiberius Claudius Maximus.'

Maximus's expression hardened. 'I think we are done for the night. Go see to my horse.'

Duras gave him an exaggerated bow, rose, and walked away down the slope.

As he went, Maximus spoke under his breath.

'Maybe I should have beaten you after all.'

Chapter Five

*Temporary Camp North of the Danubius,
High Summer AD 101*

'This is going to take weeks,' Arrianus muttered under his breath, earning a glare from their decurion. The emperor was officiating, and though there was little chance of the trooper being heard, it was still bad form.

Maximus tended to agree, though. According to ritual, the three sacrificial animals – the bull, the pig and the sheep – had to be led around the subject that was to be blessed. When that was a field, a chicken coop or a house, it was fine. When it was a quarry or a farm, it tended to take a little longer. When that meant leading them around in excess of fifty thousand men, plus horses, slaves, civilians, hangers-on, wagons of ammunition, artillery and supplies, and the endless stuff that went into forming an army on the march, that was a massive route to cover. Some *cities* had a shorter circumference than this camp.

He could see the animals coming now. They were being led by priestly helpers in plain tunics, and wherever they passed, a reverent silence fell.

The words of the emperor, opening the Suovetaurilia ritual, were still echoing across the camp, largely because they were relayed by carefully chosen men at strategic points so that the entire army could hear.

'That with the good help of the gods success may crown our work, I bid you, Mars, to care for and to purify the army of Rome with this suovetaurilia, in whatever manner you deem best.'

Maximus's gaze slid across the assembled masses, past auxiliary units, and then over legions in their gleaming ranks, past the Praetorians, assembled proudly beneath their standard, then the tribunal platform upon which Trajan stood with his officers and attendants, then *more* Praetorians, of course. And then, by strange chance, the gathered slaves, under the watchful eye of a detachment from the Seventh Claudia. Whoever planned the gathering so that the slaves were closer to the emperor than the legionaries would probably be sent back to Rome in disgrace. Especially, Maximus noted sourly, given that Duras was in the front rank of the cavalry slaves, holding Celeris and glaring with open malice at the emperor of Rome.

His attention was drawn back to the procession as the animals bumbled past the Second Pannonian. There was an uncomfortable moment as the bull stopped in front of the unit's vexillum. Every pair of eyes in the vicinity swivelled to the animal as the white-robed attendant leading it swore quietly and hauled hard on the tether, trying to get the bull moving again. It did so a few moments later, but only after leaving a huge, steaming pat right in front of the ala's officers and standards. Maximus tried not to see it as a comment or an omen. He failed.

The animals moved on, leaving the acrid smell of dung in the air. His eyes beginning to water, Maximus forced himself not to wipe them, and watched as the animals moved on. His legs were aching.

'Why couldn't we have been mounted for this?' he murmured very quietly.

Naevius Bibula replied without looking round. 'Because we'd be on a level or higher than the emperor, and that's not done.'

They fell silent again, watching the seemingly endless journey of the animals. Finally, they passed the slaves, and Maximus noted with irritation that Duras moved his angry glare to the animals, then back to the emperor. There was another momentary pause there, as the pig decided to urinate in torrents in front of the slaves. This, Maximus approved of, and had trouble forcing himself not to smile, although moments later there was a ripple of laughter, and he could see the distant figure of the emperor himself on his dais, chortling at the sight.

Things settled once more, and the animals were led to the sacrificial area in the open space before the raised platform. The emperor had pulled his cloak up over his head now in priestly fashion, and held up both arms, palms forward.

'Father Mars, I ask you, be gracious and merciful to this army, to which intent I have bidden this suovetaurilia be led around the legions, the auxilia, and all the forces of Rome; that you ward off disaster, sickness, ill-fortune and destruction; that you grant victory in battle and success in all our endeavours, and give good health and strength to these warriors. To this intent, to the intent of purifying the army, deign to accept the offering of these suckling victims.'

The oblation cakes were then held high by attendants so that all present could witness them, before being placed on the offering table. Still with his head covered, Trajan now descended the steps from the dais in a stately manner, his attendants following on, as well as Hadrian, who was serving in some capacity. Reaching the ground, the emperor strode across to the three animals, and then held up his hands once more.

'To this intent, Father Mars, deign to accept the offering of these victims.'

Hadrian's role became apparent, then, for the emperor's nephew stepped forth as an attendant handed him a heavy-headed axe, while another handed the ritual knife to Trajan. The bearded nobleman took the weapon reverently, turned it so that the heavy iron poll was ready, and stepped towards the bull.

Maximus held his breath. This could be a dreadful moment. He'd seen a sacrifice once at the consecration of a temple in Phillipi, when the attendant had not been strong enough. He'd hit the bull between the eyes, but all that had done was enrage the animal, which had pulled free of the others' grip and had maimed and gored the unfortunate priest before it could be brought down and restrained.

His breath came calm and slow as Hadrian raised the axe and brought the poll down hard. The bull gave a single groan as its legs gave way and it collapsed, and then Trajan stepped forth, and bent low, out of sight. Maximus couldn't see the action then, though he knew well what was happening, and after a few long moments of work, the emperor rose once more, his arms crimson to the elbows. An attendant then rose beside him with a bronze bowl, and proceeded to dip a cloth into the container and paint Trajan's face red with the blood, before tipping the rest onto the altars gathered in a trio behind them: Mars, Minerva and Jupiter.

The procedure was repeated then, with the pig and the sheep, one after the other, though without the face painting this time. The blood was drying on the emperor's face, turning dark, as the third animal was finished with. Now another man was brought forth, a second figure in priestly garb, and this one carried a bronze liver-shaped plaque, etched with mysterious symbols. The haruspex handed this to his helper and nodded to the emperor, who bent once more. When he rose again a while later, he was holding the bull's liver, an immense, glistening pile of offal. He turned, carefully, for the organ was slippery and dropping it would be a terrible omen, and held the thing out to the haruspex. Trajan was too far away for Maximus to make out such details, but he could well imagine the emperor trembling and sweating under the weight and the strain.

The priest examined the liver, consulted his plaque, repeated the process several times, then held up his hands.

'The gods give us the best of omens for this war. Rome shall triumph, and Mars, Minerva and mighty Jove will shelter and protect the army in the land of the barbarian. So be it said. Give thanks to the gods.'

With that, Trajan turned and walked over to the brazier, dropping the organ onto the iron grill, where it sizzled and spat, sending up a column of meaty smoke to please the gods. This done, the emperor returned to the dais, face now red-brown with dried blood, and washed his hands in a bowl of pure water brought by another attendant, drying them on a towel. Hadrian joined him moments later, as the other attendants busily removed the vital organs of all three animals and added them to other braziers, so that soon nine different columns of smoke rose to the watchers on Olympus.

The main ritual being complete, as Trajan stood, solemn and impressive, the various attendants went about the skinning and butchering of the three carcasses, carefully stacking the meat in trays that were carried away. Tonight, before the army departed on campaign proper, the senior officers would dine well. Maximus's lip wrinkled a little in irritation, remembering the three scrawny chickens hanging from the rail outside Azimus's cook tent back in camp. Stringy chicken cooked in a broth flavoured with the rider's native Syrian spices, mopped up with bread. His stomach gave an appreciative grumble, and he nodded slightly, deciding that perhaps it wasn't so bad after all, even if the emperor's cronies would dine on steak tonight.

There were ripples of slight movement among the front ranks around the ceremony, and Maximus smiled to himself, realising what that was. Three animals that size produced a lot of blood, even after three bowls full had been taken for the gods. The lines of legionaries and guardsmen were standing in a shallow lake of gore, which would be seeping into boots and socks, and that evening would involve a lot of cleaning and polishing. At least in being a lot further back from the action, the ala had been spared that.

There was a sudden squawk of shock across the crowd, and with all others, Maximus's eyes rose to the noise's source. For just a moment he couldn't see anything amiss among the slaves, but then, with a horrible sinking feeling, he realised he couldn't see Duras. The slave had gone, the beautiful form of Celeris standing peaceful and untended with the other cavalry mounts. Near panic gripped him. What had the idiot done?

This was a solemn religious ceremony, officiated by the emperor himself. He regretted not having left Duras in the tent and paid some kid to hold his horse instead. Then Duras reappeared, straightening, and as Maximus squinted, he realised there was blood on the slave's shoulder and tunic. He realised in that moment that Duras had slipped in the steadily growing lake of blood and gone down on his side. The fucking fool.

His gaze darted back past many soldiers and officers, some with furious looks, others clearly amused, to fall upon the emperor on his dais. The world went silent, tense. Trajan was frowning, peering off at the slaves, then he leaned over to the haruspex and the pair held a brief quiet exchange before the emperor nodded and straightened again.

'It would seem,' Trajan said loudly, and, given the silence, could be heard across the gathering without being relayed, 'that the gods favour us indeed. For what more could we ask than a Dacian falling for an omen of victory. Mars shows us the way with this fallen slave!'

At this, a massive cheer went up. Maximus hoped he was the only one that could spot the hint of outrage that passed across Duras's face before he became carefully neutral, knowing he would be scrutinised now by very important men.

Maximus felt the relief come like a tidal wave. This was not going to come back to bite him after all. He heard a chuckle and turned to look at Bibula, who was grinning.

'You are a lucky, lucky bastard, Maximus.'

*

The next day dawned clear and blue and warm, and the army of Imperator Caesar Nerva Traianus Augustus moved north in the best of moods, leaving the camp intact and with a small caretaker garrison to control the passage of supplies across the river.

The onus was taken from the Second Pannonian then, though, for the column boasted a number of scout units, and they were all deployed now, spread out up to ten miles in advance of the vanguard, and variously moved about so that no one unit was ever left in repeated peril or boredom. With their recent activity, roving around all over the place on various tasks, Maximus had grown used to the freedom and ease of cavalry service, and had had forgotten just how damn slow an army could be on the march. Any army moved at the speed of its slowest component, which was almost always the supply and artillery carts drawn by oxen. Given that and the need to carefully survey the surrounding landscape as they moved, the first day the army covered a grand twelve miles by two hours before sunset, a distance Maximus alone, on his horse, could easily cover in an hour.

Not that there was much of a landscape to survey. The land lying to the east of the Nera River consisted almost entirely of flat, featureless grassland. The river was kept in sight regularly by the exploratores, and they could see a few low hills beyond, in the lands of the Iazyges. In the other direction, the grey peaks of the Dacian heartland lay far enough distant that they created just a ribbon on the horizon at this range. Even the most distant scouting forays had only reached the forested foothills.

They found villages here and there, little more than shoddy collections of a dozen huts and a smithy by a stream or at a crossroads. They were all deserted, exhibiting signs that the occupants had departed mere days earlier. Meals left behind on tables had not yet gone rotten, the dung of livestock still soft. But no sign of people or their animals, vehicles, granaries or stores. Not that this should be surprising, of course. An army this size could hardly pass unnoticed, and there had been Dacian warriors by the river that would have carried north word of the approaching force. What fool would pull out a rake to defend his village in the face of that?

But it was still eerie.

An entire day of travel and the only signs of life had been occasional deer that raced away as they approached, or wheeling birds, high in the sky. No people, no pets, no livestock.

Just empty farms and villages.

A dead land.

Another thing that became evident was that the Dacians had not only pulled out ahead of them, leaving the landscape empty, but they had carefully made sure to take an early harvest before they left. No crops remained, all having been cut and taken. It was too early for a proper harvest, so it could only be a deliberate move to prevent forage for the army.

Maximus found himself musing about the terrain, and he could quite understand why the Iazyges wanted the place. The prevalence of deserted farms spoke of how lush and productive the region could be, even if right now it was empty.

Another scout unit identified the best site for the night's camp, although as far as Maximus could see, the entire region was suitable, being uniformly flat grassland. As such, they waited until first the cavalry vanguard arrived, and then the surveyor teams, who took poles and twine, gromas and measuring sticks, and marked out an area of camps. Soon after the pioneers began to arrive, marching at the front of the main column, where they could get to work straight away, and with them the senior officers, who always rode near the front where they were not in the cloud of dust created by an army this size. With the officers, of course, also came the Praetorians, far too noble and well-paid to do any actual work, and so stood around looking suspicious while the legions and auxilia began to dig ditches and raise ramparts.

It took, just as planned, two hours to form the defences for the various camps and compounds, and to raise all the tents and create the pens and corrals. Of course, the senior officers' tents went up straight away, so that the emperor and his top men could disappear into comfort and discuss progress while the camps were built.

That night Duras was even more taciturn than usual. He had been extremely quiet ever since the incident at the suovetaurilia, which had to be a blessing. He sat there, polishing and cleaning, after having fed and groomed Celeris, and then lay down and went to sleep. Maximus watched him for a while, still trying to unpick how he felt about the man. In an odd way, he admired Duras, for having clung to the ghost of his warrior past and his Dacian pride despite a decade of slavery. In another way, he didn't like Duras, nor trust him as far as he could spit a rat, and was fighting a regular urge to smack him and tell him to have a little humility. Still, he didn't, and eventually, Maximus, too, slept.

On the second morning of the campaign, they received word that there had been an accident on the pontoon bridge. A ship had come unfastened, causing havoc, and it had taken half a day to restore integrity, followed by a period of recovery as supplies were gathered from fallen carts and reloaded, and then the bridge safety-tested before the supply convoy could begin again. The emperor, with clear irritation, had announced that they would stay in camp here for an extra two days to allow the supply situation to return to full efficacy.

It was hard to see how the disaster back south could possibly be the work of the Dacians, but the interruption of the supply train, when combined with the harvesting and removal of all possible forage in their path suggested an organised campaign designed to starve the Roman invaders into failure. Maximus waited, tense, for any word that Dacian saboteurs had been apprehended near the river, though such word never came.

The next day, then, the majority of the army was at liberty in the camp, hunting in the surrounding land, and generally enjoying the rest. Not so the scouts, who were sent off further than usual to test out the region ahead of them. Through chance, the turma of Naevius Bibula drew the lot to scout out the direct road north, and so by late morning they were alone in the sea of grass.

Thirty-two men, including the officers, all horses resupplied after that initial clash near the river, and any injuries dealt with. Bibula pulled in close to Maximus as they rode.

'What's ahead, then? What can we expect? You've been this way before.'

Maximus frowned. 'I thought you'd been involved in the last war, Naevius?'

'We were, but not here. We were involved in cross-border action, down on the lower Danubius. We never got to Tapae, after all.'

Maximus nodded. He'd forgotten that. He, of course, had been serving with the legionary cavalry back then.

'This is only the start. Last time, Domitian didn't put so much emphasis on the army being well-supplied. We moved a little faster, although in truth, it was probably not such a good idea. Anyway, we reached Arcidava at the end of the first day, with just enough light to make a temporary camp.'

'Arcidava?'

'It's a native Dacian fortress. Not one of their big ones, but neither is it a wattle hut. We camped below it for a bit of a nervous night, and then had to take it off them in the morning. They fought like bastards. They were outnumbered horribly, but they fought to the very end. No surrender. Out of a couple of hundred defenders, by the time we secured the place there were maybe a dozen prisoners who'd lived, and they were generally wounded.'

'What did you do with them?'

'Domitian was emperor and commander. What do you *think* we did?'

Bibula nodded solemnly and drew a finger across his throat.

'Exactly. Every last one of them. I'm really hoping we don't have to do that again.'

Bibula simply nodded his agreement, and they rode on in silence. Maximus had carefully not mentioned his second visit. The first had been on the way to that awful defeat at Tapae. The second had been worse. Although ultimately they had won the battle, that had not taken the sting out of finding

Maximus's best mate Pansa at Arcidava's gate. Pansa had been one of six men who had vanished from camp the night before. What happened to his body, they never learned, but his head had been neatly displayed with the others above that gate.

He brought his thoughts back to the present.

Silence. Just the gentle breeze stirring the long grass, the sound of jingling armour and harnesses, the creak of leather and clonk of wood, the snorting of horses and the high crawing of birds above.

Arcidava came into sight towards noon.

Maximus tensed automatically. He didn't like this place.

They rode along the riverbank until they found the timber bridge the legions had built a over a decade ago, still standing strong and usable across the Nera. On the far bank, Maximus could imagine the camp as it was when he was last here, though they had efficiently torn down the ramparts and backfilled the ditches upon departure, leaving no direct evidence they had ever been there. Indeed, all that remained now was a grassy field on the edge of yet another ghost village. But two reminders of that year stood in plain sight, and Maximus shivered as he clopped across the timbers of the bridge.

A small grassy mound stood not far from the invisible site of the camp. To the casual visitor it could easily be a natural feature, or, if not, then perhaps a tribunal podium to overlook a parade ground. The knowledge that under that mound lay six heads, buried hastily but with reverence, lay in Maximus's heart alone of the men here.

Beyond that burial mound, and the camp site, and then the village, a wooded slope rose to a hill that overlooked the entire area, and atop that, even from here, he could see the earth banks of the Dacian fortress. It was said that deeper into the heart of Decebalus's lands, the fortresses were of stone, and powerful enough to withstand catapults. Not so the smaller, earth-banked forts on the periphery, yet the siege here had been brutal enough regardless.

'That's it?' Naevius Bibula asked, pointing up at the hill. Maximus nodded. 'Doesn't look much,' the decurion commented.

'Not any more, no.'

With Bibula and Maximus in the lead, the turma of riders passed through the deserted village and began to climb the slope on the rough track connecting it with the fortress.

'Can't see any sign of life,' the decurion said. 'Not that that is any guarantee of safety.'

They rode on in silence, climbing the hill. Deep in Maximus's memory, images were rising to the fore. On either side of the track, scrubby grass was suddenly populated with legionaries struggling, shouting, screaming, falling, shields above heads as rocks and arrows rained down from the heights. In front, the rough track was filled with sixteen men lugging a massive tree trunk on rope handles, a ram for the breaking of a gate, while other men held shields up around them to protect them, and every few steps a man fell away, letting go of the rope with a cry, his place taken instantly by another in an effort to get the great ram up to the hilltop fortress.

Of course, he'd watched most of it from a distance. There was not much use for cavalry in a siege like that, and the legion's horsemen had stayed at the lower slopes, watching the assault, waiting for the enemy to break, for that would be their time to act, chasing down fleeing survivors, mopping up panicked Dacians.

Oh, they'd had a little action, when the gates fell, racing up the slope and following their infantry counterparts into the place, killing anyone they could get to in the open ground within.

The images failed to dissipate as they crested the hill and approached the fortress.

The gate stood open, repaired since their last visit, but wide open. Not particularly inviting, though. The walls were unoccupied, the place silent. Peering through the opening, it was clear the fortress was deserted, but looking at the footprints in the gateway, it had not been so a day or two ago. That had been after they crossed the Danubius, surely? The Dacians, then, were pulling back away from them just ahead of the army.

'They're doing it again, luring us to Tapae.'

'There'll be no surprise for us this time, though,' Bibula said with a tone of quiet menace.

'I wouldn't be too sure about that. This isn't like rooting out a few Jewish rebels, or Berber raiders, or even British psychopaths. The Dacians are clever and dangerous.'

The decurion nodded. Of course, he may not have been here or at Tapae, but he'd faced the Dacians further along the river. Bibula turned in the saddle, waving to the riders behind them. 'Dismount and search the place. I seriously doubt you'll find anyone or anything of use, but we need to be sure before we report back.' He turned to Maximus. 'And I think we'll search the village thoroughly just in case before we leave.'

Maximus nodded, dismounting.

The turma left their horses to roam in the fortress, contained as they were and with good grass upon which to graze. Men moved hither and thither, leaving their shields with their horses but with swords bared. They pushed open doors to thatched, timber buildings, and here and there to stone towers of huge masonry blocks. He watched as he walked across the open enclosure, men emerging from buildings empty handed, shaking their heads. The Dacians had, once again, taken anything of use or value with them as they retreated out of the Romans' path.

He reached a door himself, and ducked inside. The squat building had just a single room, and he'd already known what he would find, from the empty wooden rack and the water barrel outside. The forge had been emptied, just like everything else at Arcidava, all that remained: the furnace, slag and ashes, and broken shards of discarded iron. Even the hammers had gone. They were nothing if not thorough.

He emerged from the place and surveyed the bailey once more. His eyes fell upon the well at the centre, and it took him a moment to notice the shapes beside it. A bucket lay on its side, where it had apparently fallen from the well's wall, and next to it lay the body of a dog, unmoving. Maximus frowned.

'At last,' a voice called, and he looked up at a man emerging from one of the doors. He'd sheathed his sword and was carrying what appeared to be a joint of salted meat on a wooden platter. As he walked, he plucked a piece free with two fingers and reached up.

'No,' Maximus yelled. 'Stop. Falco!'

The rider paused, meat hanging from fingers just in front of his face as he turned to the officer with a frown. Maximus pointed at the dog. 'One gets you ten that they poisoned the well before they left, and if they did that, what do you think they did to the meat?'

Falco dropped the platter in an instant, as though it might bite him, and hastily wiped his hands again and again on his tunic hem.

'Jove, but that's twisted,' Bibula breathed, walking over to him.

'Seemed unlikely they would go to the effort of taking even the hammers, but accidentally leave a tasty joint of meat.'

The decurion nodded, and turned, addressing everyone. 'Don't eat or drink anything. Anything at all.'

The men nodded, and went about their tasks once more. They searched for another quarter hour before declaring the place completely worthless, and then mounted once more and descended the hill to the village, which they similarly searched, and similarly pronounced worthless.

'Well, Arcidava seems to be safe enough for the next camp site,' Bibula said with a sigh.

Maximus opened his mouth to agree, when a shout drew his attention. One of the riders was pointing off to the trees that lay north of the hill, beyond the village. 'Movement.'

The two officers kicked their horses into action and cantered across the village to the northern edge, where the rider was sitting, staring off into the distance. Maximus looked past him. The treeline was quiet and still. As they fell silent, all they could hear was the wind, the distant chuckling of the river, and the calling of birds high above.

'I see nothing,' said Bibula.

'I swear there was someone there, just for a moment, then he disappeared.'

'Should we go check?' Maximus asked quietly.

The decurion shook his head. 'Priscus is always seeing things. Probably nothing there. And even if there was, he'll be gone into the woods now, and if coming north of the river the other day has taught me anything, it's not to follow Dacians into the woods.'

As Maximus nodded with a dry snort, Bibula straightened. 'Let's get back to camp and report in. The way ahead is clear but dead.'

As they turned, though, Maximus found his gaze drawn to that treeline.

'They're watching us,' he murmured under his breath, 'all the time.'

Chapter Six

Berzobis, Summer AD 101

'What are we to expect, then?'

Maximus chewed his lip as their horses plodded slowly on through the thick grass, made lush and deep green by the summer sun and a sprinkle of rain yesterday. It had been three days since they left Arcidava. Summer was wearing on rapidly, and at the pace the army was travelling, he was beginning to worry that they wouldn't meet any real resistance until winter. The truth was that he wasn't at all sure *what* to expect next. All he could do was tell the decurion what they'd found last time.

'We came to Berzobis about the same time of year, I reckon. It's not much, really, or it wasn't then. Not a stone fort, and there's no hill. The whole place is flat as an Amazon's tit. There was a stockaded settlement on an island formed by two channels of a small river, with a single tower and some timber buildings inside. A small, extra-mural village on the far bank, too. There were maybe a hundred warriors altogether, and twice that in ordinary folk.'

'Will it have changed much, you think?'

Maximus snorted. 'It changed straight away. We tore the whole damn place down. The timbers from everything were used for the pyres we made to burn Dacian bodies. I'm not even sure that all of them were dead. Domitian was not in a forgiving mood that year.'

Bibula shuddered. 'So there's a good chance the place won't exist any more.'

'I think it'll have been rebuilt. This is good land, and there's farms all over the place. There needs to be a market for them all, and that'll be Berzobis. It'll have been rebuilt. If we're lucky, the market will still be used, and there'll be granaries full of goods waiting for us.' He sighed. 'But I doubt we're lucky.'

They rode on, subdued. The feeling of anticipation and grandeur the army had enjoyed during their first few days across the river, with the magnificence of the bridge and the success of the emperor's sacrifices, had waned rapidly. That was partly due to the ongoing supply difficulties, which seemed to ebb and flow, so that every time one problem was solved, another reared up, but was also partly from the general and unavoidable ennui of travelling at ox-cart speed through featureless plains, with nothing to see or do except march and make camp.

From Arcidava, they had skirted some low hills for a time, first on their left, then their right, heading roughly northwest along the flat, and then turned north again. Last time the army had come this way, with Domitian, they had taken the shorter route, through the narrow hill-valley straight north, but then they had not been so carefully reliant on the supply wagons last time. This time the emperor was trying to keep the way as open and flat as possible.

'There,' he said eventually, pointing off ahead.

'Where?'

'You can see roofs behind those trees.'

It was not much, but the ground was so damn flat that it was hard to spot anything at a distance. Maybe a half a mile ahead, the next river, for they had left the one they'd been following at Arcidava, curved around and cut directly across in front of them, identifiable by the trees and undergrowth that marched across the landscape at its banks. Behind the line of green, rough timber and thatched roofs were just visible. No tower this time, he noted.

'Looks like they've rebuilt it, then.'

Maximus nodded. 'Mostly, but without the defences. Can't hear anything, but it's probably best to be alert just in case.'

As they closed on the location, Naevius Bibula threw out a few signals, and the unit split into three once more, with he, Maximus and Rufus each leading a section. The decurion took the central path, across the grass and towards those trees, while Rufus moved off to the left, flanking the village, and Maximus the same to the right.

He led his men to the treeline, the shapes of the houses becoming clearer here and there through the foliage, and then identified a point where the growth thinned sufficiently to allow the horsemen to pass through. He was the first to descend the bank into the river, a sluggish flow maybe twenty paces across, and shallow enough to traverse on horseback. Celeris stepped down into the water without pause, and Maximus sighed as he felt the river rise up over his boots and halfway up his calves as he moved into the deeper part at the centre.

His gaze rose to the far bank again then, as the men moved into the river behind him. He could see the houses now, all relatively new, built on the site of the village they had destroyed a decade ago. Once again, there was no sound, no sign of movement. The place was clearly deserted, but given the poison that had been left behind at Arcidava, it would be foolish in the extreme to presume no danger.

Rising at the far bank, his legs cold and sodden, he crested the slope and drew his sword just in case. Passing between two timber houses, one with a roof of wooden shingles, the other thatched, he peered at them. The windows were shuttered, but he was content they were empty anyway. There was an indefinable feeling that came from a deserted village, and he felt it strongly at Berzobis.

As he moved out into the open space at the centre of the village, he could see the other groups converging, Bibula from the left, Rufus ahead, and the thirty-two riders met once more in the heart of Berzobis.

'Best search the place,' the decurion said with a sigh, 'not that I expect to find anything.'

'Don't forget,' Maximus added, 'not to eat or drink anything.' As the men began to dismount and tether their horses in order to begin the search, Maximus turned to Bibula. 'Is it worth riding back?'

The decurion shook his head. 'The vanguard will be here in about two hours I reckon. I'll send Rufus and ten men back to report in. We might as well do some scouting around for a few miles just to be sure, and then we'll meet back here in an hour and wait for the army.'

Maximus nodded, and then turned to watch the men searching.

A rider across the square drew his sword and hefted it, then stepped to the closed door of one of the houses. He pushed the door open to reveal the interior, and after squinting into the darkness, stepped warily inside. He vanished from sight, and Maximus's gaze moved to the nearest shutters, waiting for the man to open them and let in some light to help his search.

He almost jumped in the saddle as there was a rumble and a crash, and the roof of the house collapsed in one large implosion, heavy wooden beams, rafters and shingles tumbling into the interior. The crash was, predictably, accompanied by a cry of pain, and two of the men nearby ran over to the doorway, from which clouds of dust and debris were billowing. Around the village, men with their hands on doors stopped dead.

'Shit,' was all Bibula said, and he and Maximus watched as the two men at the house waited for the dust to die down, and then very carefully picked their way inside. Three dozen heartbeats later, they re-emerged, half-walking, half-carrying their friend. The man's leg was dragging along the ground at an unhealthy angle, and the white of bone jutted from his elbow. Maximus shut his eyes. Poor bastard. He'd seen wounds like that before – breaks so bad that there was little hope of resetting them. Even the best medicus in the legions would give him a stick to bite on while they sawed off both limbs. And everyone knew the future of a crippled soldier.

'Get him somewhere away from the buildings and lie him down,' Maximus shouted, and then waved his hand in a circle. 'Everyone else, stay exactly where you are.'

He threw a questioning look at Bibula, and the decurion nodded, so Maximus slipped from the saddle and dropped to the ground, then walked across to where Abgar stood beside a house door, sword in hand. He passed the Syrian, gesturing him out of the way, then pulled up his knee and delivered a hefty kick to the door, instantly stepping two paces back. The door slammed inwards with a wrench of breaking wood, but nothing else happened. He stepped back again, looking up at the roof. Same timber construction. Crossing to one of the shuttered windows, he grabbed the twin wooden boards and pulled hard. The shutter catch broke, and they swung wide, then. He circled the house and did the same on the other side, then returned to the door. The interior was still dim, but was far brighter than it had been, and he could make out some of the details inside. He could see maybe five feet of clear floor inside the door, and moved into it, looking up warily, then all around.

He saw it straight away. A line of thin cord stretched across at knee height. His gaze followed the trap to both sides, each of which connected to what appeared to be a peg right up in the eaves of the roof. Devious bastards. He looked around. The interior was empty, barring poor furnishings and threadbare rugs and blankets, apart from a single pewter goblet standing on the table opposite the door. Clever. If whoever entered spotted that, they'd make straight for it and walk into the trap. Taking a deep breath, he stepped outside.

'Trapped,' he announced. 'The house is rigged to collapse when you trip a cord. I think we can safely assume they're all like that.'

'I'll check one of the thatched ones,' Flaccus called. 'I can cope with a bit of straw in my hair.'

'Stay right where you are, you daft prick,' Maximus snapped. 'How do you think thatched roofs stay up? There are still enough heavy timbers in there to smash that egg head of yours.'

Chagrined, the trooper stepped away from the door, lowering his hand.

'Right,' Bibula said. 'Force all the shutters from outside, carefully. Then look inside, but nobody *goes* in. Just look from the doorway once the light's up. If you see anything out of the ordinary or interesting, don't go look at it. Come back and report.'

Maximus returned to his horse and joined the decurion as men began to work. Before long the whole village was searched, and they'd confirmed every house trapped in the same manner, each with one small half-treasure left to entice the unwary. As the men gathered again, Bibula straightened. 'Alright. Rufus, take eight men and ride back to the column. Report in and give full details of what we've found, and of Statilius's injuries, so that the medics can be prepared for it when they arrive.' He turned to the others. 'Laenas,' he gestured to the unit's field-medic. 'Go to Statilius and see what you can do for him. Keep him comfortable and safe. I'm leaving three men with you as a guard, but you should be fine here now anyway, as long as no one goes into one of the houses.' He turned to Maximus, then. 'That leaves you and me with eight men each to do a few circuits of the area and then report back here. Let's make sure we're alone.'

Moments later they had divided up to go their separate ways, Rufus disappearing back south towards the approaching army, Laenas with his guards moving over to tend to the wounded rider, and the rest passing through the far side of the village. A second, smaller, branch of the river passed round that side, with another ribbon of trees and undergrowth, effectively forming an island upon which the deserted village sat, and they moved across the rough timber bridge warily, watching the land ahead as they passed through the treeline. When the village had been rebuilt, it had been without walls and all on the island, for the north bank was now clear.

'I'll head north, toward that – for want of a better word – hill,' the decurion said, 'then about three miles out we'll sweep out to the west and arc round back to the river and follow it into the village. You go east for three miles, sweep north to that hill, and then come straight back. That'll allow us to cover plenty of ground.'

Maximus nodded and, gesturing to his men, waved farewell to Bibula as the man rode off north, and then turned along the line of the river, heading east. He heard the ministrations of Laenas as they departed, in the form of a cry of pain from the patient, and he could imagine the capsarius making a spirited attempt to set either the arm or the leg, wincing as he pictured it. Then, soon, they were out of earshot of the cries, and out of sight of Berzobis, riding calmly along the northern bank of the small river, a good ten paces from the trees.

The view was excellent, and as they rode, Maximus continually shifted his gaze, peering back south across the river, between the trees where possible, and then out north, across a sea of flat grassland. He could see trees in the distance to the north, and it looked to be more than the thin line along a riverbank, but that had to be a good couple of miles away, and there was nothing to be seen in between but a lone deer at one point, watching them with interest.

After an uneventful half hour, Maximus reined in, pointing ahead to where a deserted farm sat silent in the morning sun. 'I reckon that's a good three miles. Let's follow the treeline back round to Bibula's favourite hill.'

The men nodded contentedly. An uneventful patrol was a boring thing, but an eventful one was usually worse. Just to be sure, they did a quick search of the farm, carefully, checking for traps. The place was as deserted as any other they'd found on their journey north. Happy that they'd missed nothing, and that the land was empty, they left the place and crossed the grassland towards that line of greenery. As they closed on it, Maximus reappraised. There was another river, or at least an overgrown stream, with a border of trees and vegetation, which gently arced back in their direct path towards that hill, but on the far side of the river were more trees. Not a thick forest, but scattered boles and occasional stands and copses of beech, oak and elm. Addressing the eight riders with him, he gave them a new plan, and they crossed that narrow flow with ease and began to spread out. Since they already knew there was nothing to be found in that sea of grass, for they'd looked across it from the other side already, they would ride between the small groups of trees and make sure this area was clear too.

By the time they were a quarter mile from their furthest extent, heading back towards the hill, such as it was, the nine of them had spread out to cover a reasonable area, each man keeping the next in view, so that there was no chance of anything untoward happening. Maximus rode easily, his horse on a loose rein, occasionally glancing this way and that, admiring the rich colours of the trees.

When he saw it, he had become so inattentive after the acres of empty green that he almost missed it. He reined in, frowning, turning. He shook his head, chiding himself for his overactive imagination, and almost rode on, but then he saw it again: something glinting among the leaves of a small copse of beech off to the north. Even as he turned Celeris to face it, there was a shaking of the foliage and the glinting stopped. Whatever it was – *whoever* it was – had realised he'd been seen and retreated.

Maximus turned and gestured to the next rider, who'd paused, noticing his commander had stopped. He hoped he'd relayed what he wanted in gestures, for he didn't want to shout, in case the man in the trees was not alone.

He kicked Celeris, and broke into a trot and then a gallop, pounding across the turf towards those trees. There was, of course, every reason a perfectly innocent farmer or loner could be here among the beech and oak, but somehow that was never going to be the case. Day after day they had moved north now, and had yet to come across a single living individual, barring those who'd attacked them near the

Danubius. That left the strong likelihood that anyone watching them from the undergrowth harboured only malicious intent.

As he closed on the trees, he kept his gaze on that spot, but nothing there moved, confirming that the watcher had gone. Though he could hardly ride Celeris straight into the trees, there was little to choose between left and right, and so he chose right entirely at random, skirting the edge of the small stand of beech. As he circled it, quickly finding himself at the rear, he peered off this way and that. It was too far to the next trees for the man to have covered the distance, which meant he was still in there. Just to be sure, he finished circling it, and was gratified to note that Rigozus and Flaccus had understood his signals and were now closing on the small knot of trees. The two men split off and moved to either side of the woods.

That was it. Between the three of them they had every side in sight, and the man had to still be in there. He took a deep breath and dredged his memory for the words. A while ago he'd been quite fluent in the Dacian tongue of the south-central region, but he'd not used it in a few years, and had become a little rusty.

'There is no escape,' he shouted. 'We surround you. Come out and surrender and you will not be injured.'

Yet, he added, silently.

He held his breath, listening for an answer. For a moment all he could hear was the wind among the leaves and the sounds of distant, high birds, and he certainly heard no reply echo forth, but after a few moments he did hear the crack of a twig, a thump, and a muffled curse in Dacian. He smiled grimly. Yes, the man was still in there, and close to this side.

He made the decision then and slipped from the horse, unslinging his shield from where it sat across his back on the strap, and gripping it tight, drawing his sword with the other hand. Dismounted, he was ready for trouble, although his long cavalry sword might be difficult to use in the close press of the trees. Spotting what looked like an old game trail, he made for that.

'Last chance,' he called, still using the man's own language.

Again there was no answer, and so he approached the trees and pushed his way into them along the overgrown track, using his shield to heave branches and greenery aside. He was starting to doubt his own judgement when finally he saw movement that wasn't green: the glint of a blade briefly. He pressed on, pushing harder, closing on his prey. The Dacian had seen him now, and was moving the other way, trying to escape pursuit, but Maximus was keeping pace with him through the undergrowth, and finally, as he moved into the deepest part of the wood, he heard a curse and smiled. The Dacian had got to the far side of the copse, and spotted the two horsemen watching for him from there. Indeed, a moment later, Maximus realised he could hear the man coming back towards him, probably reasoning that one man on foot was an easier proposition than two on horses.

Maximus moved into one of the few spaces that was a little more open and roomy and waited for the man. After a moment, he saw the Dacian coming, pushing through the woods, head covered only with a hat, bushy beard covering half his face. His shirt of chain glittered in the dappled sunlight. He had no shield, but in his hand he carried a falx of medium size. As the man spotted him, he let out a growl and ran for him, ignoring the whipping branches and undergrowth. He emerged into the more open space and gripped the falx in both hands, raising it, ready for that traditional Dacian combat manoeuvre all Romans feared. Maximus saw it coming, lifted his oval shield so that the greatest length between rim and boss was at the top, and prayed there was sufficient there to stop the blade cutting through both shield and owner like butter. Then he saw what was about to happen, and with a fierce smile, changed the shield's angle. Sure enough, the Dacian brought the blade down in a heavy, overhand chopping motion, but the falx had caught in the branches above the man's head, and stopped dead, mid-descent. The Dacian blinked in surprise, automatically looking up to see what had happened, and that was how he was when he became unconscious, the bronze edge of Maximus's shield slamming into his face. The Dacian fell like a sack of wheat, weapon released, where it simply hung there, still lodged in a branch.

Maximus sheathed his own sword and grabbed the Dacian by the belt. Grunting with the effort, and cursing the man's mother for having birthed such a heavy bastard, he dragged the unconscious Dacian along the trail, using his shield again to keep the branches out of the way. He emerged a short while later and threw the man over the back of the horse, hooking his belt over the rear saddle horns to keep him in place, and then mounted. Once he was round the copse, he met the other two, who wore wide grins.

'You got him.'

'I did. Let's get back to the village. I'll be interested to see what he's got to say when he wakes up.'

In actual fact, the Dacian woke only a half mile from the woodland. Draped over the back of Celeris, he came to suddenly and in a baffled panic. He started shouting, demanding to know where he was, and it took him a few moments to recall the fight and realise where he now was. He struggled then, and Maximus had to slow and then stop the horse. The man's speech was hard to follow, partly because he had a strong accent from, Maximus thought, the northern tribes, partly because he was jabbering so fast, but largely because of the broken nose and missing teeth and split lip from Maximus's shield. With only a little difficulty, he extricated the belt from his saddle horns and let the man fall to the grass.

Unarmed, aware that he was in trouble, and suffering from his injuries, the Dacian stood there for a moment, touching his face and glaring at Maximus. They had rejoined the others now, crossed the river and begun the straight line back to Berzobis, ignoring the wider route, and eight horsemen sat around the man in a circle. Maximus reached round to his saddle pack and removed from it his spare reins. In just a moment he fashioned one end into a noose.

'Hold your arms together, and upwards.'

The man didn't move. Maximus's eyes narrowed. 'You either do as your told, or I put it round your neck instead.'

This time the hands came together, arms raised, and with the practised skill of a man used to lassoing horses, Maximus cast the leather line over the arms and pulled so that the noose tightened on the wrists. He then pulled the cord tight and fastened the other end to his horse's harness.

'Come on.'

He didn't need to give the order to the others, for as he set off again, the Dacian staggering along, tethered, his riders spread out to make sure the man couldn't reasonably escape. Maximus walked his horse slow. He didn't want the man to fall and be dragged. This was capture, not torture.

They reached the village in another half hour, to find that the rest of the unit was already there, Bibula having returned only just now, and Rufus some time ago.

'You were quick,' Maximus said to the third in command.

Rufus shrugged. 'The vanguard were quite close. The lead elements will be here within the hour. There's a medicus among them who reckons he can mend any bone, so he's eager to get to work.'

Maximus glanced across at the still, blessedly unconscious figure of Statilius. He could imagine the pain in the lad's coming hours, and didn't envy him.

'You found a friend,' Bibula noted.

'We did. He was alone, watching us from the woods.' Maximus turned to the others. 'Tie him to a tree and keep an eye on him.'

As that was done, the three patrol leaders dismounted and met together, sitting on a large log in the open space at the centre of the village, where they discussed the results of their journeys. Then they rested, and drank from their canteens while they waited.

Scouts arrived just short of an hour later, then light auxiliary horsemen, legionary cavalry, engineers, and the officers. The three scouts shot to their feet finally as a small group of horsemen entered the square, each a powerful general or senior officer, and at the centre, the emperor, and his nephew Hadrian. Maximus dashed across to the tree and untied the prisoner, wrapping the bonds around the man's wrists behind his back. One of the lads had stripped him of his chain shirt and his hat, and as Maximus marched him out across the village square, his hair and beard streamed free in the breeze.

Trajan had dismounted now, along with Hadrian and the Praetorian Prefect, Claudius Livianus, and the three were muttering to one another and pointing at Maximus and his captive.

'What do we have here?' Trajan said with a smile.

The Dacian gabbled something quickly that Maximus didn't quite follow, but he heard words like 'arse' and 'shit', so he jerked on the cord and then slapped the prisoner round the back of the head.

'You speak his language?' Hadrian said in surprise.

'Some of it, sir.'

'Ask him where his people are.'

Maximus did just that, though he personally believed it to be a rather redundant question. The Dacian turned his head to look Maximus in the eye. 'Fucking your wife.'

'Not married,' Maximus replied calmly. 'Not allowed in the army. Give me something I can tell the nice officer there, or he'll give the command to have you peeled, from the feet up.'

'Go home, Roman.'

'Last chance.'

'Go home if you want to live.'

Maximus nodded, clouted the man again, just for good measure, and cleared his throat. 'Can we just say, sir, that the man is disinclined to answer the question.'

'Yes,' the emperor smiled, 'I may not speak the language, but I understand the *tone* very well. Tell him that for every useful answer he gives us, I will give him twenty heartbeats' head start. When I have finished questioning him, he will be released. If he can get away before I release the cavalry after him, he will live. His honesty and usefulness may buy him his life. I vow this in the sight of Apollo and Jove.'

Maximus winced. This emperor might not be cruel like Domitian, but neither was he soft, clearly. He relayed the emperor's words to the prisoner, who turned to look at Trajan. Perhaps something he saw there changed his mind, and the resistance he'd shown previously melted away. He nodded.

'Good,' Trajan said, clearly not needing an interpreter for that. 'Alright. Ask him this: Are the troops Decebalus is massing west of Tibiscum, or east?'

Maximus translated slowly and clearly, and then waited. He could see the deliberation in the man's expression. In the end he wasn't sure whether the man's instinct for survival overcame his Dacian pride, or perhaps whether he couldn't see any harm in the answer, but when he spoke, the Roman would have been willing to bet large sums that it was the truth.

'East,' he said.

Maximus relayed this to the emperor, who nodded slowly. 'East,' Trajan said. 'And I believe that to be the truth. His eyes hold no lie. Good. The man has bought himself a twenty heartbeat head start. Unfortunately that was my only question. Tell the prisoner he'd better run fast.'

As Maximus translated this to an increasingly panicked and wide-eyed Dacian, removing the tether, Trajan waved over six of the Praetorian cavalry, equipped for war.

'One,' the emperor called. The prisoner took one look at Maximus, then another at his free hands, and then ran. By ten heartbeats he wasn't even out of the village. By twenty, in Maximus's opinion, he might just have made it to the river.

Trajan nodded to the Praetorian Prefect, who took over the count, while he gestured to Hadrian. 'I thought that would be the case. The Dacians gather to hold us at Tapae once again, but it is valuable to know this, for it means that we should be able to recombine both columns at Tibiscum before we come close to engaging the enemy.'

He fell silent, and they all heard the scream then, as six Praetorian horsemen took turns sticking swords into the fleeing prisoner.

'Good,' the emperor said, clapping his hands together. 'We should have a free run to Tibiscum, now. Gentlemen, let us plan.'

CHAPTER SEVEN

TIBISCUM, LATE SUMMER AD 101

Maximus tensed on the reins, his hand going to his side, slowly, quietly drawing his sword. He looked left and right to confirm that the others were doing the same. The gates in the timber walls that surrounded the Dacian town of Tibiscum stood open, the wooden towers to either side empty. In almost every way, Tibiscum seemed as deserted as every other site they had found on the journey from the Danubius.

Almost.

Because, as the turma of scout cavalry had approached through the trees, there had been a loud bang from somewhere inside. It was not impossible, of course, that a stray deer or bear or suchlike had caused the noise, perhaps even by wandering into a Dacian trap meant for the Roman advance. But given the troubles they'd found so far, no one in the turma wanted to test their luck, and so they approached the gate cautiously, slowly, quietly, and armed. They were, at least, only one of three such turmae this time, each of them approaching the native town from a different direction.

Once again, Maximus found himself picturing the place as he'd seen it on his last visit, Roman heads on spikes above the walls, Dacian bodies everywhere, smoke rising from some of the houses within. He kept having to shake his head and clear it, concentrate on what he was facing now, rather than dwelling in the past. Last time, they'd had to fight to take Tibiscum off the Dacians. This time, it was *probably* abandoned.

Naevius Bibula led the way, sword out, shield in hand, guiding his horse with his knees into the gateway, head turning this way and that, covering all angles, watching for trouble. Maximus was close behind with the others, as they moved into the town. As with everywhere else they had been, every sign pointed to very recent abandonment, and there was no movement, and no sound since the echoes of that bang had died away.

As they moved into a square of some sort, a forge and what might be a market hall in pride of place, Bibula held up a hand and every rider stopped instantly and fell silent, stroking their horse's necks to prevent them making noise.

They could hear it, then. A distant murmur of conversation, though they couldn't hear anything other than the vague hum, no detail. Bibula's hand swept down once more, pointing towards that sound at the town's heart, and the turma began to move again, as quietly as they could. A few houses later, the decurion looked across at him, expression bearing a question. Maximus nodded. He heard it too. The murmur of conversation was louder, and was in Dacian. Knuckles whitened on sword grips as they spread out now, and approached the speakers from several angles, between the houses.

Maximus felt his skin prickle at the sight that awaited them. Five horses were tethered outside a hall, a timber and stone building larger than the others, and with the five horses, three riders. They were unarmoured, but each had a bow on their back and a sword at their hip, and each had the long hair and wild beard of the bulk of the Dacian populace as the men conversed in low tones. Maximus and Bibula shared a look. Five horses and three men suggested two others were inside the building.

At that moment, the Dacians realised they were not alone and turned, hands going instinctively to the swords at their sides.

'Hands away from the weapons,' Maximus shouted in their own tongue. 'Surrender and you'll not be harmed.'

Oddly, the three men just frowned at him. Then one started to laugh. Maximus looked across at Bibula, who was as surprised as he was. 'He seems to think it's a bloody joke,' the decurion snorted.

'And it most certainly is,' a new voice answered in clear Latin, as a figure stepped from the doorway of the big building.

The riders frowned at the man, but as he emerged into the light, their tension finally began to fade. The new arrival was dressed in Roman gear, and his hair was trimmed, his face shaved. He was no Dacian, certainly.

'Identify yourself,' Bibula said.

'Aulus Decius Bucco, decurion of cavalry, Fourth Macedonica. You?'

'Quintus Naevius Bibula, Second Pannonian ala. You're from Longinus's force?'

'Yes. And you're with the emperor?'

'We are. The front ranks are maybe three hours behind us.'

'Ours are a little further away, but should be here and settled by nightfall,' Bucco noted.

All around the square, men sheathed swords and relaxed. Not only had they not encountered the enemy as had been feared, in fact they had met the other column. By nightfall the army would have reunited.

'Have you met resistance?' Maximus asked.

'A little partisan activity in the hills, and a few traps left for us. The Dacians seem to have largely withdrawn north. The general thinks they're drawing us in to Tapae again.'

'The emperor is of the same opinion. Did you find anything inside?'

A second figure in cavalry gear appeared in the doorway now, shaking his head. 'Nothing of importance. They've cleared the place out. Nothing left for us. They've done that all the way north. Don't drink the water, by the way.'

'No,' Bibula said. 'We found that out, too.' Then he turned to his men. 'Rufus, take six men and ride back to the column. Inform them that we have made contact with the army of Longinus at Tibiscum, and encountered no resistance. Then find the supply column, commandeer a few hours' worth of wine, and bring it back here while we wait for everyone to catch up.'

Rufus did so, and the men of the Fourth with their native scouts joined Bibula and Maximus and the others in the sunlit open square, dragging stools or logs out to sit on. They checked a few of the nearest houses, but there did not seem to be traps in them, and by the time they had introduced one another, the other two units of speculatores from the emperor's army had joined them. Over the next few hours, they exchanged information and shared their experiences of Dacia north of the river, though the journey of the two armies seemed to have been quite similar in many ways. Bucco, like Maximus, had been here more than a decade ago with Domitian's army, and before long the pair were reliving past experiences, some humorous, others dark. Notably, no one mentioned Tapae, which Maximus knew to be no more than thirty miles east now. An hour or so later, Rufus returned with a pack horse loaded down with wine, and the gathering took on more of a social aspect.

Eventually the vanguards of the armies arrived. Bibula was called to the prefect, but in recognition of the fact that they had constantly moved ahead and prepared the way, putting themselves in danger, their commander graciously dismissed them from duty and gave them liberty for the evening. Other men from the ala came and collected their horses to take for stabling, and left them with little to do but socialise and relax. Thus it was that a gathering of cavalry drawn from four units and two armies sat quietly in the deserted Dacian town and drank toasts to one another and to past comrades, while legions and auxilia arrived and essentially deforested half the valley around the place, levelling the ground and forming huge camps for the combined army.

It was late evening, and already dark, when the gathering decided to call an end to their revels. They had lit a camp fire in the open square, using timber and thatch from the town, but even that was now burning down to embers. As the riders of the Second Pannonian emerged from the west gate of Tibiscum, the landscape beyond had changed wildly since their arrival. Gone were the trees through which they had wound on their approach, to be replaced by open land stretching into the distance, divided up into camps for the various units and groups of units. No one had gone to the trouble of digging ditches or raising ramparts, but fences of sudis stakes had been put in place, defining each area.

It took them a while to locate the camp of their ala, but Maximus smiled with relief to see that the others had been good enough to raise their tents for them. The other riders headed off to their own tents, four men to each structure. While the infantry were crammed in eight to a tent, the cavalry limited occupation to four, due to the need to store tack and saddle and the like for each man, as well as their own personal equipment. But just like the decurion, Maximus, as duplicarius, had his own tent, and he approached it with relish, looking forward to bed.

A dim light flickered inside, and he pulled aside the tent flap and entered, looking around with satisfaction. Duras had laid everything out as usual, his bedroll was ready, as well as everything he needed to wash, shave, and brush his teeth in the morning. The slave had lit the larger of his oil lamps, and the room was warm and comfortable.

He took it all in.

The horse gear was not here, and neither was the cleaning kit. Duras must be out at the corral with the others. Good. That meant a little peace and quiet, which Maximus felt he sorely needed. He unslung his sword and propped it with his shield against the wall, then unfastened his belt and bent over to peel off the chain shirt with a little difficulty, almost falling forward with the effect of excess wine. He removed the soft leather subarmalis that stopped the chain catching and chafing, and folded it carefully, placing it on his chest, then slipped off his boots, bunching and stretching his toes. Finally comfortable, he dropped to his bedroll and stretched out, lying on his back, staring up into the ceiling of the tent.

He must had drifted off like that, for the rap on the tent frame woke him suddenly from a dream about fishing. He sat up. 'Yes?'

Rufus pulled aside the tent flap, appearing in the doorway. 'We're having a sweepstake. Five denarii a piece, and first in the unit to bloody a Dacian takes it all. Could be a good haul. Want in?'

Maximus yawned. 'You know gambling's forbidden. Don't let the prefect know about this.'

Rufus grinned. 'Prefect was the third entry, mate. Do you want in or not?'

'Aye, go on then. Put me in. Get five denarii out of my arm purse.'

Rufus nodded. 'Where is it?'

'In the chest. Don't fuck up my nicely folded sub in the process.'

The custos armorum carefully lifted the garment aside and then pulled open the chest. 'What is that smell?' he complained.

'Foot powder. Get on with it. I was about to catch a trout.'

Rufus frowned in incomprehension, shrugged, and dug around in the container, nose wrinkling. '*Where* in the chest?' he grunted.

'Wrapped up in my spare scarf, with the arm-ring and the torc.' He leaned back again and closed his eyes, listening with irritation to Rufus rummaging, disturbing all his gear.

'Not here,' the man said, finally.

'What?'

'No purse. No scarf. No torc or arm-ring.'

'*What?*' Maximus said again, but this time he sat bolt upright. A horrible suspicion fell across him then. 'What time is it?'

'They blew third hour of the night not long ago. Why?'

'Shit.' Maximus was up in a heartbeat. He'd been asleep for over an hour. Just to confirm that, a glance across at the oil lamp told him it was guttering its last, almost empty.

And still no sign of Duras.

His heart started to pound. He looked around the tent, and now things stood out that hadn't earlier. Not only his saddle and riding kit gone, but Duras's meagre bag of stuff was absent, too. So was Maximus's spare sword, his good rain cloak with the hood, and now all his valuables.

'Oh, shit.'

'Have you seen Duras?'

Rufus frowned. 'Not for a while. He helped put up your tent, and brought everything in to set up. You don't think...'

Maximus bit his lip so hard he tasted blood. He'd been a little inebriated when he returned. He'd not needed to take his horse in for stabling, as it had been done for him earlier. He'd assumed Duras was tending to the horse, but then he'd had plenty of time for that before Maximus even came home.

'The bastard's done a runner. Grab my stuff.'

As he hurriedly donned his sub again, slipping into his boots, Rufus held things out for him. Chain shirt on, belt buckled, sword slung. 'Want some help?' the man asked, as Maximus was swiftly dressed and ready. He nodded. 'Go find the tesserarius for the camp and get him to change the passwords and report a potential breach to the other officers.'

Shit, shit, shit, he continued to mutter under his breath as he burst from the tent into the pleasant night air, looking this way and that. He'd not been to the corral tonight, and wasn't sure where it was. He stopped, listening, and it took only moments to pick up the sound of horses snorting and nickering not far away. He turned in that direction and hurried off, almost knocking over Priscus as he rounded a corner.

'Crap,' the trooper swore, then realised who it was. 'Sir?'

'Have you seen Duras?'

'Who?'

'My *slave*, man.'

'No, sir.'

'Oh, bollocks.' Ignoring Priscus further, he ran on. The gate of the camp stood nearby, a single guard from one of the other turmae sitting beside it, looking bored. Not much to do on duty here, for only an insane interloper would try to break into a camp of many thousands of his enemies. To break *out*, though...

'Did a man in a thick rain cloak and carrying a saddle come past you?'

The trooper thought about this for a moment. 'Sort of. A bit earlier. Didn't have the cloak on, but had it under his arm with a whole load of other stuff. I thought it a bit odd. Far too warm and dry for a cloak like that.'

Not if you wanted a disguise, though.

'He went to the corral?'

'Yes, sir. Maybe an hour ago.'

An hour. Apparently Maximus had only just missed him when he got back to the tent, but still the man could be almost at Tapae by now. He raced on, ignoring the man's call, demanding a password. That was a bloody joke. Duras, of course, had known the password, for he needed to be able to get to the horses.

His pulse quickened again. There was still a chance. Each camp and unit would have their own passwords, and while each camp was guarded individually, the whole mass of the army would have set a cordon of pickets round the edge, with their own specific password, to prevent anyone entering or leaving the place unannounced. Duras wouldn't know that password. That meant he was probably still somewhere in the camp.

Just to be sure, he ran first to the corral, where he confirmed his worst fears. Celeris was gone. Fuming, he turned away. When he caught Duras, he wouldn't stop at a beating. The man would pay dearly for this. Some coins, Maximus could live with. His cloak and sword were more important. His decorations, confirmed by the emperor Domitian and handed over personally by the propraetorian governor, were far too important to lose. But worst of all, Celeris. Fucking slave. Bibula had been right. He should have got rid of Duras long ago. Damn him, but Maximus was too soft sometimes.

He stood by the corral for a moment. Where would Duras go. He had to get out of the camp. The moment he'd stolen his master's goods, he knew he was a dead man if he stayed, so it would be paramount to the man to get out into the countryside. He tried to think of the topography of the area. Few Romans would have as good a mental map of it as he. He'd fought here a little over a decade ago, for the better part of a day, and only this afternoon had ranged all over it with his companions before entering Tibiscum. He closed his eyes. The camps' limit to the east would be the River Tibisis. The river was quite wide, and deep in places, but in others there were wide gravel or sand banks and low rapids. It was not hard to cross, which would make it attractive to Duras, who needed to go east, anyway. But that also meant that the pickets would be far more numerous and more alert there. Since it seemed no alarm had gone up yet, it was unlikely Duras had gone that way. The south and east approaches to the camp would be similarly dangerous, for supplies would continue to arrive throughout the night, along both the armies' routes, which meant the guards in those directions would also be busy and alert.

North, then. He tried to remember the northern aspect. There would be no roads or supply routes going out that way, just the river, gurgling off into the hills.

There was *another* river, though. A tributary of the Tibisis that came from the east, and the confluence would be away from this camp to the north. All Duras had to do was get between the northern pickets, and pick his way far enough out to get to that confluence, then he could cross on the other side, and follow the tributary halfway to Tapae, screened from the south by the trees.

It would have taken Duras at least a quarter of the last hour to tack and saddle Celeris, probably longer, if he was trying to do it quietly and unobtrusively. That gave him at most a three quarter hour lead. If he was going to the north of the camp, that would take another quarter, even if he moved brazenly. How long it would take him to find a gap, where the pickets had either dozed off, or were bored and inattentive, or even just placed a tiny bit too far apart, Maximus could only guess, but it would certainly be a careful, slow job.

A moment later, he was opening the corral gate, and waving to the strator – the groom – who was busy hanging harnesses in a shelter nearby. 'Get me one of the spare horses saddled, fast as you can.'

The groom did so with remarkable efficiency, and only moments later, Maximus was riding away from the corral at a trot, heading north. As he rode back past the camp of the Second Pannonian, he saw Rufus speaking to the ala's actarius, the chief clerk, who served directly under the prefect. He waved to them. 'I need the outer defence password.'

The actarius frowned for a moment, though he could hardly refuse to answer, given that Maximus was an officer and superior. 'Insidiae nefariae, sir,' the clerk said finally.

'Catchy,' Maximus grunted, then gestured to Rufus. 'I think I know where he'll be. If I'm not back in half an hour, you might need to come looking for me with the northern pickets.'

With that, he wheeled the horse and began to trot away through the camps. Already, even just one camp away from the corral, he was noting the difference in his steed. It was obedient enough, as it would have to be for a cavalryman, of course, but it just was not as clever, instinctive, or fast as Celeris. He'd had a bond with that horse for a long time now. Riding a new horse was like trying to walk in new boots, no matter how well behaved it might be. He passed the camps of legions and auxilia, even saw the standards of the Praetorians in the distance briefly.

A sense of impending dread fell across him then. There was a commotion up ahead, at the edge of the camps. As he neared, he could see a legionary centurion gesticulating angrily, surrounded by a dozen men, some of whom were from the legions, others from auxiliary units. Beyond them, maybe eighty paces from the edge of the camps, he could see the line of torches and fires that marked the pickets and the outer line of the army's defences.

'Oh, shit.'

He reined in close to the centurion, who finally noticed the new arrival and turned a puce-coloured face to him. 'What is it?'

'You've had a breach?'

'Yes. But going *out*, not in.'

'A rider in a winter cloak on a black horse.'

The centurion's eyes narrowed. 'Talk to me.'

'A thief. On my own horse.'

'Well he's out there in the night, now, only just out of sight, but I doubt you'll catch him.'

'Got to try,' Maximus grunted. 'Best double the pickets and change all the passwords.'

'Good luck,' the man said, then whistled and waved at the pickets out in the dark, telling them to let this rider past. Maximus nodded at the man and then urged his new horse into motion. He realised, as he grabbed the reins and kicked, racing out into the darkness, that he had no idea what this horse was called.

It was taking his eyes a while to adjust, having been in the brightly-lit camps and now out beyond them with only the wide-spaced picket fires and the moonlight above. He could see activity over by two of the fires, a clear sign of Duras's passage, but the men there had seen the centurion's gestures, and said nothing as Maximus raced past them at the speed of a chariot in the circus, break-neck and desperate to pass the leader.

As he passed, he squeezed his eyes shut, and waited until the dancing lights faded, then opened them again, beyond the influence of the flames and in the darkness. His eyes were adjusting, and the moon and starlight was adequate to make out all the detail he needed. There was nothing visible ahead, no shape of a rider, desperately hurtling away, but he did not pause in his pursuit anyway. He was convinced he knew where Duras had gone. Ahead and to the right, slightly east of northeast, he could see where that smaller tributary tumbled into the River Tibisis from the east, an area of thicker vegetation there. Beyond that, the escaped slave would stand a better chance of disappearing.

In a way, Duras had the edge, for he had Celeris, and there were few animals at Tibiscum who could match her for speed, endurance and agility, but equally, Maximus was not sure how much Duras had ever ridden, if at all, and he certainly hadn't over the past decade, so he was not likely to be at home in the saddle, which would give Maximus a different edge, perhaps even more of one.

He angled for that patch of thicker vegetation and pushed the animal as hard as he dared, racing for all he was worth. As he closed across the grass, he tried to peer ahead, in case there was any sign of his quarry. Nothing. He reached the treeline and angled for an area with a gap, urging every ounce of speed he could out of the mount. That was almost a mistake, for the river bank was steeper than he'd anticipated, and he swore, wide-eyed, as he pounded down it, almost unhorsed twice in the process, before he ploughed into the cold, black water, flecked with patches of white foam. He could see a sizeable bar of white sand that had grown up between the two flows, and there he found his first evidence. A line of churned sand, hoofprints betraying the passage of Duras.

Fresh hope and determination filling him, Maximus raced through the water, ignoring the cold as it enveloped his legs, and then up onto that sandbank, adding his own trail to that of the fugitive. A moment later, he was up and onto the grass above the river's far bank, a sense of triumph filling him. He was on it. He'd found Duras, and he'd catch him, and reclaim all his goods.

The arrow seemed to come out of nowhere. It thrummed from the darkness to the east and buried itself in the chest of the white horse beneath him. The unnamed animal shrieked, and reared. Maximus felt himself fall free of the saddle, and instinct kicked in. He'd had such things happen often enough over the years to know the drill. He tucked in his head and one arm, bringing his knees up, almost into a ball, while his other hand went to the sword at his side, gripping it, preventing it from becoming tangled in his legs where it could cause breaks. He hit the ground, mercifully soft turf, and rolled, far enough to be clear of the horse, as it too fell. The animal landed on the ground close by and began to whinny and flail, legs churning.

Maximus rose, then, pulling his sword free and peering into the darkness across the thrashing horse. He squinted, trying to make out shapes in the gloom, and saw the next arrow coming just in time to drop to the ground again as it whirred off into the night. He stayed low now, trying to decide what to do. He could hear the massive commotion back at the camps, as everything was reported in. Perhaps he could just hold Duras here long enough for others to come and help. The Dacian might not be an expert horseman, but he seemed to be able to handle a bow. It did occur to him for a moment to wonder where the slave had picked up the weapon, but then they would be in plentiful supply across the camps the man had just passed through, and he could easily have swiped one.

Another arrow came, then, thudding into the poor horse, who was still alive, and still crying out. Then the animal rolled, and the last thing Maximus remembered was a hoof coming towards him.

*

He awoke with the most shocking headache. He tried to move, and the whole world went swimmy and strange, and he felt distinctly sick, so he lay still and listened to the thumping in his skull. After a while, the nausea faded again, and he managed to turn his head, slowly. He was in his own tent, which was a blessing, as, if he was seriously injured, he'd have been in the hospital tent with all the other wounded.

'Ah, he's awake.'

He winced, which, it turned out, hurt quite a lot. Slowly, carefully, trying to avoid a repeat of the nausea, he turned to face the other way. A medicus was packing away his things, an attendant close by. Naevius Bibula stood by the door of his tent, but the most important figure was seated in a campaign chair near the flickering lamp: Gaius Julius Paullus, prefect of the Second Pannonian. Maximus swallowed nervously.

'Sir.'

'You have put me in an uncomfortable position, Maximus.'

'Sir?'

'A man who knows our strengths and weaknesses, plans and systems, supply routes and unit designations, has escaped your custody and undoubtedly kneels even now at the feet of the Dacian king, revealing everything he knows.'

Another wince. More regret. Maximus tried to marshal his arguments. The passwords were changed daily, and on discovery of his flight would have been changed straight away. Duras might have a little knowledge, but was not privy to much of importance, only what he could hear from other military slaves or as gossip among the men of the ala. Really, what he could tell Decebalus of Dacia would be of remarkably little use. What he did know, Decebalus probably already knew himself anyway. Yet, somehow, Maximus suspected pointing any of this out would only make things worse. To his mind, it was Maximus who'd really lost out. A slave, a horse, a sword, his military decorations, best cloak, and a purse full of three months' wages. Still, he remained silent, and tried to look contrite, without having to pull any facial expression that would hurt.

'In the grand scheme, it seems the emperor is not fazed,' the prefect went on. 'We had a visit from his nephew following the incident – Hadrian and about a thousand Praetorians, anyway. The emperor seems to be of the opinion that little of value can be gained from the man. Indeed, the emperor actually thinks this might work in our favour. It is one thing to hear of a huge army coming your way, but to see it in all its martial glory is different. Perhaps your slave will take worrying news of our strength to the Dacians.' He sighed and leaned back. 'Whatever the case, you seem to be off the hook with the commanders, and therefore I shall mete out no punishment for such carelessness myself. Although the cost of two horses, one stolen and one dead, will be deducted from your pay, of course.'

Wonderful.

'I suggest that in the coming days and months you work hard to regain that fame with which you came to our unit, and overcome the ignominy of this little mistake.'

He rose. 'The medicus tells me you will have a headache for a few days and he will change your dressing every morning for three days. After that, you're back on scout duty. Do *not* fuck it up again, Maximus.'

Chapter Eight

Tibiscum, late summer AD 101

Publius Claudius Arvina frowned and drummed his fingers on the leather saddle horns. 'I can't say I know a lot about the Dacians, to be honest, sir. You say they don't really do cavalry?'

Maximus nodded, eying the new man. 'They have a few, mostly nobles, but the heartlands of Dacia aren't really the sort of terrain cavalry thrive in. Mountains and forests, principally. When they need cavalry, they tend to pay mercenary bands of Sarmatian horsemen, either Roxolani in the east or Iazyges in the west, or any one of half a dozen subtribes of each. That's why we went to such pains to keep the Iazyges out of the war. That way we'll not encounter much in the way of cavalry.'

Arvina sat silently for a moment, digesting this, continuing to drum on the saddle. Maximus readied himself, recognising the buildup to another series of questions.

He wasn't sure about Arvina.

The man had been transferred in to replace Statilius, who spent all his days now with the medical section, praying his limbs would knit and he would be able to walk and fight again. He'd be out of the unit for at least the rest of the year, even if he ever recovered. Bibula had put in the request for a replacement, and they'd been sent Arvina yesterday. At first glance he was the most ill-fitting recruit possible. Oh, he seemed to be a more than capable horseman, and his sword and spear skills, as well as his bravery, seemed unquestionable. But everyone else in the Second Pannonian was either drawn from Pannonia or Moesia, the Danubian provinces, or from Syria, during their time stationed there. Arvina seemed to be from Rome itself. No one had asked him for details yet, but he had a similar accent to the senior officers from the city, and he was clearly a citizen, so everyone wondered what he was doing with the auxilia. That being said, Maximus, too was a citizen, having transferred in from the legions, so there were always possible reasons.

But Maximus just couldn't help feeling suspicious. Had Arvina been transferred in by the prefect to keep an eye on him? After the loss of Duras, several of the officers had given Maximus dark looks, maybe even a little distrustful. Was Arvina here to spy? To watch him?

He shook his head. Maybe someone who stood out as much as Arvina was too obvious to be a spy. It'd be like dropping an Aegyptian in a unit in Britannia and telling him to blend in.

'So they don't have an army as such, like us?' Arvina asked. 'More sort of warbands and rabble, like the Germanics.'

'Sort of. They're more organised than German forces, but they're still not a standing army. The nobles, the ones they call the 'cap-wearers', summon the warriors up when harvest is done. That means they're available to fight through autumn, winter and spring, and by summer they need to be back on their farms, planting.'

'Madness. Almost the opposite to *our* campaigning season.'

'You get used to it, serving on the Danubius.'

Silence descended again, and Maximus looked about. The men of the turma were gathered across the grassy slopes in small groups, talking, occasionally gazing out across the landscape, warily. At the centre of the gathering sat six carts, into which each of the forage units were supposed to be putting their findings every time they returned to this hub, before moving out in another direction. In theory all six carts should be full of forage before they returned to camp, though they could probably have fit everything they'd collected so far into two. The Dacians had been very thorough in not leaving anything behind for the advancing Romans. Here and there they found a field that had clearly not been ripe when the owners left, but had ripened since, and eagerly harvested it. And occasionally they would find a few scraggy farm animals too poor or lame to have been taken away.

Forage.

Because the supply situation was still touch-and-go. The pontoon bridge over the Danubius had been put back together, only for other issues to suddenly raise their heads. Supply ships seem to have become sporadic, though the reason for that was yet to become apparent. The number of ships docking at Viminacium from the west and Dierna from the east had almost halved since they'd entered Dacia. But more alarming was the fact that small problems kept arising along the supply route *this* side of the river. Roads flooding, bridges collapsing, embankments crumbling and the like. Every incident could clearly be explained away by natural means, or simply bad luck, but there was a growing tendency among the men to believe in sabotage of some sort. How the Dacians, who seemed to have retreated ahead of the Roman forces, could somehow cause trouble behind them remained to be seen, but it was happening often enough for it to be increasingly difficult to blame on luck. The daily offerings and prayers given to Ceres, Fortuna and Mercury in the wagon that carried the altars had grown exponentially recently.

His gaze rose to the eastern treeline, where the valley narrowed slightly, the hills rising to north and south. Tapae was not far. The Dacians would be waiting for them at Tapae. If only they could get there and bring the bastards to battle, maybe this could all be brought to a close.

'Why are the supplies so important, anyway, sir?' Arvina asked.

'What?'

'Well, we've got enough for a few days, and we're only a few days from Tapae, where everyone seems to think we'll win the war. So why is it so important to keep the supply route functioning.'

Maximus had been thinking on that, himself, and he believed he had the answer now. 'Long-term strategy.'

'Sir?'

'When we came with Domitian's army, we marched and rode hard to bring them to battle, and bloodied their nose, and we were not slowed by, or reliant on, the supplies. But I reckon that's because Domitian never intended us to stay any length of time. We were a punitive army, sent to teach Decebalus a lesson for crossing the river and attacking Roman lands. This time it's different.'

'Oh?'

'I don't think this new emperor will be happy forcing Decebalus to his knees. I think he means to stay.'

'Conquest?'

Maximus nodded. We're putting a full system in place as we go, for supplies, but also with regular fortified positions. Have you noticed that wherever a camp has been built on this march, where they raised and dug banks and ditches, we've moved on afterwards without backfilling it?'

Arvina nodded too then, thoughtfully. 'Because they will be used again.'

'The army's leaving caretaker units at them all. Ostensibly the reason is to guard the supply trains, but I reckon they'll become permanent. I don't think the new emperor wants to teach the Dacians a lesson. I think he means to turn Dacia into a full province.'

Arvina whistled through his teeth, and they turned to look back into the distance. Some way south, maybe a mile and a quarter away, they could see the legions at work all across Tibiscum. Among the temporary camps, a more permanent fort was being constructed, with banks and ditches and timber palisade, and nearby, solid bridges were reaching out across the rivers, connecting the world for Roman supplies and men to pass through at will.

A shout drew his attention, and he turned to see Naevius Bibula on a slight rise, waving at him. Leaving Arvina to his ever-present questions, Maximus trotted over to the decurion, as best he could with his new horse.

'What's up?'

'Sun's sliding away now, Maximus. Afternoon's wearing on and I reckon the recall will be sounded any time. We need to start gathering them in. I'll take half the men, go round up the hunters and get the wagons moving. You take the others and round up the three forage parties.'

Maximus nodded, turned, and rode over towards Proculus, the tubicen for the turma. 'Call groups one, three, five and seven, will you?'

The musician bowed his head, pulled his tuba from his side, and blasted one long call, then four short ones. Across the open ground, four of the tent parties kicked their horses into motion and rode over to join them. Once they were gathered, half the turma in one place, Maximus gestured east, across the slopes. 'Time to bring the foragers in. We're off to find them.'

With that, he turned his new horse, an animal he'd discovered was called Ferox, and which seemed to be horribly misnamed, for he was about as fierce as a sponge, and about as bright, too. As he rode away, leading half the turma on their latest duty, he tried to find some sort of parity with the animal. He couldn't remember his first days with Celeris in detail, but he did remember that she was trouble, and took a while to settle down, following which they became as close as horse and rider could be, a true team.

Ferox, on the other hand, was an idiot. Half the time he didn't do what you told him, and the other half, he did it wrong. On the two occasions Maximus had taken him into the practice ring and chased down the straw man to put a sword through his straw head, Ferox had sort of danced merrily towards the target, and on the second time had actually stepped away at the last moment as Maximus swung, so that his sword missed entirely.

It was not a good omen. He was on a friendly, stupid horse. That would not be good in a fight. In theory, Ferox should be as well trained as any spare cavalry mount, but he was just... thick. Maximus had been to see the equisio to change horses, but the man had told him flatly that the way he kept losing horses, he was not going to be given a high quality mount until he proved he could keep one for more than a few days. He'd contemplated taking the matter to the prefect, but couldn't see that going well. The prefect's last words to him – 'Do *not* fuck it up again, Maximus,' made him wince every time he thought about it.

Three parties of foragers, all legionaries, forty men split between the three, with one optio in charge. They couldn't be *too* far away. Up the slope, Maximus found the first marker. The forage parties had each taken coloured rags with them and tied them to obvious places to create a trail, so that they could be found, or could make their own way back if not, given that this was very unfamiliar territory. It took a while, following the trail of red wool scraps, to find the first forage party. They were some way back into the wooded hills, along what was probably a logging trail, and had found a small collection of buildings, a minor village. Their baskets were half-filled with what looked to Maximus a lot like the forest floor.

'What *is* it?' he asked the optio in charge, who looked into the basket, then up at him.

'Berries, wild garlic, some mint... that sort of thing. Mostly taken from the woods. Not a lot of value to be found here, but if you know what you're looking for, nature provides.'

'Frankly if that's what nature provides, I'll skip dinner.'

The optio's expression hardened. 'Can I help you, duplicarius?'

'You need to finish up and follow your trail back to the carts. This is the last search of the day and we're back down to camp, now.'

The optio nodded and turned, shouting to his men, who each hurried with whatever they were holding, and dropped them into baskets before running over to the stacks of weapons and equipment, finding their own helmet, shield and pilum from among the piles. Maxmus left them to it, gesturing onwards. In moments, they were heading back to where the trail of red scraps had started, seeking out the next marker. When they found it, they followed the line of rags again, which, after a while, led them to a shallow valley among the trees, along which a wide stream gurgled and whispered. Following that upstream for a while, they came across twenty or so men, some with baskets, standing gleefully on the edge of a pond, some waist-deep *in* the pond, laughing and telling jokes. Maximus smiled as one of them men gave a cry and suddenly wrenched his hands from the surface, throwing a heavy trout across the pond, where one of his mates almost fell headlong into the water, trying to catch it with a basket. As he did, there was a huge cheer from the others.

It took a while for the men to notice the riders watching them from the edge of the trees.

'Sir?'

'Having fun, soldier?'

'Quite a bit. Trout for dinner tonight, sir.'

Maximus chuckled. 'Hope you caught enough for everyone.' Given the size of Trajan's army, Maximus would be surprised if the contents of the soldiers' baskets would divide into more than a single fish-scale per man. Still, every little helped. 'Come on. Climb out and head back to the wagons. We're going home for the night.'

Again, they left the soldiers to it, then, turning and riding back through the valley and then along the trail of red markers until they reached the hillsides where the parties had all begun. The wagons were already moving off now, and Rufus had returned with a few men, Bibula still out there somewhere, trying to locate the pockets of hunters – those soldiers from the army good with spears and bows, tracking wild animals through the woods or bringing down birds to add to the meat stocks. Leaving them to it, Maximus and his men located the last of the three trails and began to follow it. It took a while, but the line of red cloths led them across a slight rise, crested with a line of silver fir trees, and down beyond into a shallow bowl.

Maximus smiled. Either the farmer here had been too late pulling out to save everything, or the place had somehow been forgotten. A cluster of rough buildings at the centre was surrounded by fields full of slightly overripe wheat, past harvest time but still good. A mule and cart sat near the farm buildings, half-loaded with supplies. Excellent. This lot would be a big help.

Waving on the others, he set off down the gentle slope at a trot, heading for the buildings at the heart of the place. As they neared, though, his smile began to falter. No one appeared from those buildings with a sack of grain over his shoulder, adding to the supplies in the cart. Indeed, he could see no activity at all.

His skin prickled, and he reached out and held up a warning hand to the others as he slowed. The fields were half-harvested, the cart half-loaded, yet there was no sign of anyone doing any of the work.

'Trouble?' Flaccus murmured.

'Where are they all?'

They fell silent, listening, then. Nothing. Wind through leaves causing them to rustle, and through the swathes of grain, making them hiss, and above them, the high cries of birds. Nothing else. Maximus gestured to the others, spreading his men out to search the farm. The riders began to disperse, fanning out through the fields to locate any of the men. Maximus himself headed for the farm buildings. There should be eight men here: a contubernium of legionaries. He resisted the urge to call out for them. If there was trouble here, then someone had *caused* that trouble, and he didn't want any enemy to be more prepared than they had to be. Clenching his teeth, he drew his sword as quietly as he could, and pulled the shield round from his back on its strap, to where he could grip it in his hand.

Four buildings, all very much alike, and more or less the same size, all poor, old, rural timber structures with thatched roofs. In reasonable condition, having been lived-in until quite recently, undamaged, unburned...

Silent.

He closed on the nearest, and as he approached, he slowed and then slipped from the horse with that litheness and skill that only a lifelong rider can claim. Landing light on his feet, he lifted the shield's carrying strap over his head and left it loose, gripping the painted boards tight, ready for trouble. The house's windows were open, the shutters pulled back against the stone to allow the light to enter. Leaving Ferox to wander, and hoping to the gods the animal wouldn't suddenly decide to run off like the prat he was, Maximus reached the window and peered in. The building seemed to be the farmer's house, and looked as though the family had just stepped outside for a moment. No sign of movement, though. He moved around the building to the door, sword and shield up and ready, paying attention to the other areas around him as he went. Still no noise or movement other than the sigh of wind through grain.

He tensed as he stepped to the door, half expecting someone to leap out at him.

Nothing.

His eyes sought anything of interest in the place, but picked out nothing. Certainly no Roman foragers. A sense of tension building, he quickly checked on Ferox and rolled his eyes as he spotted the horse, who'd walked over to the house's wall and was licking it enthusiastically. Arsehole. Gods, but how he missed Celeris.

The next house, and the same procedure, glancing first through an unshuttered window. An animal shed, he reckoned, or shepherd's hut. A few tools, a table and chair, some fleece lying in a pile in the corner. No Romans. Round to the door for a better view, to confirm. Nothing.

The third building was divided in two, part being a workshop, filled with tools, bench, water-butt and the like, the other half clearly the storage space for the cart that now stood out in the open. Once again, no soldiers in either side, and little of value.

Last building. No windows at all.

Approaching the door, he could already see that it was a barn, and that the soldiers had been working out of here, for sacks and baskets and chaff and stalks were everywhere. But still no soldiers. He was about to leave, when he caught sight of something gleaming among the crap on the ground, and stepped inside, closer. He had almost reached it when he stepped over a bulging wheat sack and his foot landed in something wet. He frowned, lifting his leg, and his own blood ran cold to see someone else's all over his boot.

Something dripped on the back of his neck.

Slowly, and with a sense of awful foreknowledge, he stepped back and looked up.

Eight bodies were hanging from the roof of the barn, their feet tied with rope, hands bound behind their backs. All eight were headless, but all eight were easily identifiable from their russet legionary tunics.

'Shit.'

He tottered backwards, out of the building. 'Shit, shit, shit, shit.'

All dead. All beheaded. No sign of the heads at first glance.

Shit.

'Found them, he shouted,' and instantly cursed himself for having done so. The blood was still wet and warm, still dripping from necks. That meant that this could only have happened shortly before Maximus and his men appeared through the trees, looking for them. The enemy could still be here, somewhere. Suddenly very alert, Maximus's gaze darted back and forth around the farm. He could see his men, all now turned and heading his way, having heard his call. The memory of being targeted with arrows in the night as he chased down Duras surfaced, and for a moment, he pictured Dacian archers in the trees around the periphery, picking his men off from the back, yet no arrow came.

'Bollocks.'

His gaze now fell upon the ground nearby and again he cursed himself. He was a scout. He was supposed to be alert and careful. Why hadn't he looked at the ground before he went to the huts. The dirt had been churned up by the hooves of at least a dozen horses, and neither he nor his men had been to that part yet. That mess could not possibly have been made by the hapless mule attached to the cart. He'd clearly been too quick to tell Arvina that Dacian cavalry was rare, since this seemed to be the work of those very men.

'Are they…?' Flaccus, the first to arrive, began.

Maximus nodded. 'Dead. Very. All of them.' Loud enough to be heard by the others. He gestured to eight of them. 'Get what can be easily and quickly gathered into that cart and get the animal moving back towards camp. I'm not wasting all this.'

'And what about us?' Flaccus asked.

'I want to see if they're still here. They can't have got far.'

It took only a few moments to locate the point at which the horses that had made the mess in the dirt had departed. Mounting, they began to move. With half the column at his back, Maximus spotted the line the enemy had cut through the crops, and urged Ferox on. The animal's top speed appeared to be about the same as Celeris's was when she was asleep, and no matter how much he heeled the animal, called encouragingly, squeezed his legs, leaned forward, it didn't seem to make much difference.

He started for a moment as Arvina fell in beside him.

'Slow?'

'Yes. Stupid and lazy too.'

'I know the sort. Where's he from?'

'Thracian stables, I think.'

Arvina grinned and spoke quietly then, almost conspiratorially. 'Try leaning forward to his ear and whispering "steiróno".'

Maximus frowned. 'Steiróno?' he replied, louder. 'As in "geld him"?'

He squawked with shock as Ferox suddenly started to properly run, and behind him could hear Arvina laughing. It took half the distance to the treeline before he realistically had any level of control over the animal again, guiding the horse towards any sign he could spot of the recent passage of other riders. He raced up the slope, the others close behind, aiming for a break in the trees that the Dacians seemed to have used, and as he reached the crest, he hauled on the reins, it still taking a moment for the damned beast to stop moving. His gaze passed across all the land ahead, and it didn't take long to see them.

A dozen or more riders in a small knot. They were visible for only a moment or so, almost a mile to the east, as they disappeared into another scattering of trees. As he watched them go, knowing damn well they'd got away, he tried to commit every detail to memory.

He turned to find Arvina and Rigozus close by.

'What did you see?'

'More than a dozen riders,' Arvina replied, 'less than a score.'

'Details.'

Rigozus closed his eyes and rubbed his forehead. 'I reckon they weren't Dacian.'

Maximus nodded. 'Me too. Too much armour for Dacians.'

Arvina frowned. 'What? Remember I'm new to all this.'

Maximus turned to him. 'The Dacians have horsemen, but they're nobles. They have chain shirts, they have helmets and shields, but no Dacian I've ever seen, in twenty years of service and three wars, armours their horse.'

Rigozus nodded this time. 'Sarmatians. Too far west to be Roxolani, I reckon. They're on the other side of all the mountains, hundreds of miles away. But then I thought the Iazyges were going to sit it out for now?'

Maximus shrugged. 'Evidence suggests that either the Iazyges are reneging on their deal, or the Roxolani have come west. One thing I'm sure of is that they were not Dacians.'

Rigozus sighed. 'Could be either tribe in small numbers, of course. You know how Decebalus works. A few coins here, a few coins there, and he has odd small tribes flocking to help him. Mercenaries. Doesn't mean *all* the Roxolani or Iazyges are involved.'

'Doesn't mean they *aren't*, either.' Deflating slightly, he looked around at the others. 'Alright. What's done is done. They're gone, and we're not going to catch them. Let's go back, meet up with the others, and then ride back to the decurion, then camp.'

'What about the legionaries you found?' Arvina asked with a frown.

'They stay where they are.'

'That's not how things are done. We should either bury them or take them back with us, sir.'

Maximus shook his head. 'Sun's on the way down already, and it'll be getting quite dim by the time we get back to camp. Stay here long enough to bury them and it'll be dark while we're still here. Don't know about you, but I don't fancy that at all.'

Rigozus was shaking his head avidly at that.

'And,' he went on,' there are eight bodies in that barn, but no heads. You ride into camp with eight headless legionaries over the back of a horse, and panic and rumour will pull half the bloody army apart. Better they were just "lost in action".'

'I don't think...'

'On the contrary, you think too *much*, Arvina. Come on.'

They rode back down through the trees, across the fields, past the farm buildings, and caught up with the others as they urged the mule and cart up the far slope. Half an hour later, they were emerging out into open ground once more, the lights of the massive camp at Tibiscum twinkling in the deepening gloom.

Most of the unit and the wagons had gone, now, and only Naevius Bibula and half a dozen of his men waited for them on the slope. As they appeared from the trees, the decurion spotted the cart they were accompanying and smiled for a few moments at the sight until he registered the fact that no foragers accompanied them.

'Trouble?'

Maximus nodded. 'They found an untouched farm. They'd worked on it for a while I reckon, when the enemy took them by surprise.'

'Shit. Prefect's going to want an explanation for this. Our remit was to watch over the foragers. We should have sent riders with each group.'

'Blame it on me,' Maximus grunted. 'I'm already deep enough in the shit I can't see daylight. Besides, there's nothing we could have done. If there'd been a rider or two at the farm, five gets you ten they'd both be dead now too.'

'Maybe. Still, the onus is on me. This is *my* command, Maximus. I'll talk my way out of it somehow. But how did the enemy get such a surprise over the foragers anyway?'

'They were horsemen.'

'Dacians?'

'I don't think so. Roxolani or Iazyges, probably. Sarmatians. Likely a small mercenary unit serving Decebalus.'

'That's worrying news. But it might be enough to buy sufficient goodwill from command to keep us out of the shit. Come on. I'll go face the shouting. When I'm done, I'm coming to your tent, and you're going to get me drunk.'

Maximus laughed quietly. 'Deal.'

Chapter Nine

AGNAVIAE, SEPTEMBER AD 101

'Bloody frustrating is what it is,' Maximus grunted, controlling the bored dancing of Ferox as they sat on the hillside.

'Better the army is rested and prepared, than walking blindly into something they can't handle,' Naevius Bibula countered, his own horse calm, and considerably less stupid.

They peered back down the slope and along the valley to the west. The latest camp was already more than half ready as the sun glimmered its last late afternoon light, beyond. A massive defended enclosure, with numerous subcamps, every unit in the army fortified against trouble.

They were less than fifteen miles from Tapae now, and the terrain was looking horribly familiar to Maximus. This close to where they were now sure Decebalus's army waited, no chances were to be taken. The army was now moving less than ten miles a day, by the emperor's command. It was slow going, but the change had several advantages. Firstly it meant the columns could stay tight in formation and close together, able to defend should they need to, and not strung out, as Varus's army had been in Germania, back when three legions had been massacred in the forests. Secondly, it meant that all units were relatively bright and well-rested at all times. There would be no marching into battle exhausted, and should the Dacians suddenly decide to pull some trick, they would be prepared. Thirdly, it meant the supplies could keep up, so everyone was well-fed and -equipped. And fourthly, it meant that from now on the scouts could occupy more or less every mile between the two armies, granting foreknowledge of what lay immediately ahead to the commanders.

But it was also frustrating to be so close to the enemy, yet crawling towards them so slowly.

The noise of the army making camp was immense, but even echoing along the valley as it was, it was distant enough to become a background tapestry and, without the confines of a helmet, Maximus was just listening to the cry of a bird of prey somewhere nearby and trying to work out what it was when a new noise broke across the hillside: the thunder of hooves.

He turned, peering back east, a moment's alarm at the possibility of a Dacian attack pushed aside as he spotted the Roman scout on a single horse, thundering along the treeline. Above, forests closed in across the peaks, while below only scattered trees interrupted the grass. The man was riding fast, but without that panicked feel that usually accompanied dire news. Still, Maximus straightened, alert, in his saddle as Bibula, next to him, similarly turned.

The turma was all off in the east this afternoon, with a limit of eight miles. This morning, when they'd reached Agnaviae, the scouts had gone as far as the edge of the Iron Gates, close enough to Tapae for Maximus to start having flashbacks. They'd confirmed the presence of a large force there purely by the smoke from many cook fires, and so they'd pulled back, and the limit had been imposed for the day. If the enemy remained more than eight miles away all day, then they were not likely to come in earnest.

'Report,' Bibula said, as the rider reined in.

'Enemy patrol, by the looks of it, sir. Three of us came across them, and they didn't attack us, but they also didn't go away. They seem to be waiting for something.'

'Where?'

'Bottom of the valley about a mile east, sir.'

'Show us.'

As the rider turned and led the way back along the valley towards Tapae, Maximus leaned a little closer to Bibula. 'Could be a trap. Should we not have sent word to camp first?'

'We're not at the top of the popularity list with the prefect at the moment. I'd rather know what we're reporting before we report it.'

There was a certain logic to that, and Maximus pulled a little apart again as they rode the short journey to the site of the incident. As the scene came into view ahead, it was clear that more and more of Bibula's turma had gathered from their patrols in the local area, converging on the visitation. Eleven cavalrymen now sat facing east, spears in hand, shields in place, helmets gleaming, ready to move to the offensive at a moment's notice.

Maximus tensed. A score of Dacians stood at the edge of a copse of trees, similarly all armed and ready for a fight. They were not mounted, so they probably *were* Dacian, rather than Sarmatian mercenaries, and at least it meant these were not the men who'd butchered the forage party a few days earlier.

The two officers reached the arc of riders, their guide falling in to give them a full dozen cavalry in support. Maximus found his confidence growing. With twelve of them, he was content that they could get the better of twenty infantry. The Dacians didn't seem to be worried, either, though. As the two groups settled in facing one another, one of the warriors, the only one in armour, a vest of bronze scales, stepped two paces forward, and rattled out something very imperious and confrontational sounding in the native tongue. The riders all looked at one another in confusion. Other than Maximus, only two men in the turma had a reasonable grasp of Dacian, and both were clearly still out scouting. Maximus had caught a few words, but the man had a thick, strange accent, and had spoken fast.

'What did he say?' Bibula asked.

'Don't know. Spoke too quickly, and he's not from round here. Strange accent. Hang on.' He dredged his memory, then gestured to the leader, and in Dacian, quite slowly and clearly, said 'Speak slower so we can understand.'

The Dacian frowned, clearly surprised that there was anyone among the Romans who spoke his tongue at all. He folded his arms, and when he next spoke, it was still in a horrendously thick accent, but was at least slow enough for Maximus to work on.

'This is a message,' he translated for the benefit of the others, 'for the emperor.'

'From Decebalus?' Bibula prompted. Maximus turned back to the Dacian and passed on the question. The man shook his head and spoke again, and after he'd finished, Maximus turned to the decurion. 'No. He says it's from the Buri and the Lacringi.'

'Who in Juno's name are they?'

Maximus was casting his mind back to the many briefings they'd had under Domitian. That emperor may have made a more direct and swift campaign in Dacia, but he definitely liked his briefings and information.

'The Buri are from up north, on the edge of Iazyges land, one of the most peripheral Dacian tribes, as much German as they are Dacian. The Lacringi, if I remember rightly, are from beyond them, right up above the mountains. Not even sure if they're Dacian at all. It explains the weird accents, though.'

'When they say "this is a message", what is "*this*"?'

Again, Maximus translated this to the deputation, and the leader nodded, turned, and gestured to his men. Two of them stepped forward with a large, hairy, grey bundle.

'What the fuck is that?' Bibula said under his breath.

'Looks like a pelt,' Maximus hazarded, 'or maybe a pile of them. A gift?'

The leader spoke again, and Maximus relayed it to Bibula. 'He wants us to bring the emperor.'

'Not going to happen,' the decurion said, flatly.

Maximus turned to the man and explained. 'The emperor is busy and will not walk out into danger and potential traps without good reason. Pass your message through us.'

The leader seemed to consider this for a while, then nodded. 'Done,' was all he said, as he stepped back. His men rather unceremoniously dropped the bundle on the ground and did the same. The Dacians glared at the cavalrymen in silence for a short while, and then turned and walked calmly away, back to the east.

'Do we follow, sir?' Flaccus asked.

Bibula shook his head. 'They'll just rejoin their force at Tapae. Nothing to gain there. Open that parcel.' He gestured to Azimus. 'Give him a hand.'

The two troopers dismounted, handing their reins to their nearest companion, and then walked over to the pile.

'Helios's balls, that's ripe,' Azimus gasped, reaching down and pulling his scarf up to cover his mouth and nose as they approached. Flaccus, nodding, followed suit as the pair bent over the pile. Maximus could see flies beginning to cloud above the thing, and was rather glad it wasn't him examining the gift in the late evening heat.

'It's a skin,' Flaccus announced. 'Wolf, I reckon.'

'Unfold it.'

The two men, faces creased with repugnance, reached down and grasped the pelt and began to open it. The flies massed even more now, and the grunts of effort were interspersed with swearing as the troopers unfolded the pelt, peering at it. Even from here, Maximus could see it was definitely a wolf pelt, dark grey. The head was still on, and fragments of the paws and tail. It had clearly not been tanned or prepared, merely pulled off its owner, which explained the smell and the flies.

The soldiers, happy they'd done the job, turned it over so that the inside faced up, dropped it on the ground and stepped away, only removing their scarves and gasping in clean air as they reached their horses.

Maximus peered at the pelt.

It *was* a message, just as the Buri chieftain had said. Whether for speed or for effect, the Dacians had left the skin raw and part bloody, and had scored the message into it by burning. It was one of the most unwholesome things Maximus had witnessed in all his years, yet he had to admit that he was impressed in a way. It was brutal, horrible, not particularly neat, but it was in Latin.

TRIBE KILL ROME
GO HOME FOR PEACE
NO WAR ROME LIVE

Maximus peered at it. 'Now the question, I'd say, is whether that's a warning, a plea or a threat.'

'What?' Flaccus asked.

'Well either it's blustering on behalf of Decebalus, telling us to fuck off or they'll kill us all, or it's meant more as a warning, reminding us that a lot of people are going to die if we don't back down and leave Dacian lands. For my money it's a plea, though.'

'Oh?' Bibula prompted.

Maximus scratched his chin. 'If this was a message coming from Decebalus himself, I reckon there would be more pomp to it. More nobles on horses, standards and music and the like. And it would have come probably with someone who could speak Latin directly to us. But this came specifically from the Buri and the Lacringi. It strikes me that the Buri are right on the edge of Decebalus's lands, closer to the Iazyges than they are to their cousins. And we know the Iazyges have rebuffed Decebalus's requests they join him, and sided with us. I think the Buri are in a precarious position. They can hardly refuse to fight for their king, yet their lands will be open to Iazyx invasions. Their best hope is that all this can be resolved without war.'

Bibula nodded. 'Makes sense. Can't see the emperor turning round and walking away, though.'

'No.'

The decurion waved to the two men who'd opened the pelt. 'That'll need folding again, and I'll let you two argue about which of you is going to transport it back to camp.'

Maximus smiled as the troopers bickered while they worked, and finally decided to share a horse on the way back, leaving the other to carry the pelt alone. While they worked, the tubicen blew the recall, and it did not take long for the rest of the scouts to form on their position. Once all was made ready, the entire turma gathered together, they turned and began to make their way back to the camps at Agnaviae. Pickets from the Thirteenth Gemina Legion met them at the edge of the works, and Maximus nodded with approval as the legionaries demanded the password before admitting them, despite the fact that they were so very clearly Roman riders. Once back within the Roman lines, they sought directions from a few men and managed eventually to fix on the grand tents of the officers at the camp's heart.

Approaching, it became clear that this close to the enemy, Trajan's guards were taking no chances. Even surrounded by a mile or more of legions and auxilia, the Praetorians had created a fortified camp *within* the main camp, using sudis stakes to form a fence of sharpened timber around the perimeter. Inside, the tents of the Praetorian cohorts and of the emperor's Horse Guard surrounded those of the emperor and his senior officers, leaving a muster ground before them. Praetorians in their crisp white tunics and gleaming steel were visible over every three paces of land around the inner camp, making sure the emperor was never in danger.

'Should we not go see the prefect first?' Maximus nudged.

'Might be considered time sensitive, this,' Bibula countered. 'Send Rufus to inform him what's happened, and to let him know where we are.'

Maximus did just that as they arrived at the cordon of Praetorians and Bibula began negotiations for admittance. As they conversed, two guardsmen walked through the line of horses until they came to the animal carrying the pelt.

'Shit, that smells like a corpse. You can't bring that near the emperor?'

'That's the *message*,' Bibula said. 'Unless you just want us to tell him about it.'

The Praetorians had a brief conflab, moving away from the pelt in the process. 'Can you not fumigate it somehow?'

'I'm a cavalryman, not a tanner,' the decurion said, pointedly. 'I don't know how to do shit like that. Just ask the emperor for permission to approach, will you?'

The Praetorians withdrew into their camp for a while, and found an officer, who they consulted. They then walked off and spoke with more Praetorians and officers, and the cavalrymen stood waiting, murmuring among themselves under the ever-watchful eye of the Praetorians on guard duty around the stake fence.

After a while, they reappeared, and Maximus was just chatting to Rigozus when he felt a sharp jab in the ribs and turned to find Bibula looking at him with a touch of warning. He turned back to the approaching Praetorians, and noted that the emperor was with them, as well as Hadrian and the Praetorian Prefect. Every man in the turma suddenly shot straight in the saddle, as though someone had shoved pila up their backsides.

As they neared, the decurion cleared his throat. 'Dismount!'

The men did so hurriedly, aware that it was standard procedure for no cavalryman to sit ahorse when the emperor was present on foot. In moments, each trooper was standing at attention beside his horse, Flaccus and Azimus together by one. Trajan peered out at the horses and riders and started to step forward. Praetorians dived in front of him and moved to push the cavalrymen out of the way, but the emperor snapped at them to back off, and strode from the gateway of the inner camp, out among the riders.

'I remember you,' the emperor said, almost conversationally, as he passed Maximus, then, to Bibula: 'you, I don't know.' He stopped, worryingly close to the stinking pelt. 'Show me.'

Flaccus and Azimus did not require the prompting of their commander, and immediately hurried over to the horse, pulling their scarves up over their lower faces once more. As they began to unfasten the pelt, Bibulus removed his own scarf and turned to the emperor, head bowed, and holding it out. Maximus could have laughed out loud at the horrified looks the Praetorians all threw at him, but the emperor simply nodded, reached out and took the scarf, fastening it in like manner around his lower face and thanking the decurion as he did so.

In a few moments, the two troopers had the wolf skin unfolded and were holding it up by the grotesque sticky paws without comment, while the emperor read the legend burned into it.

'Fascinating. Licinius tells me this came to you from a Dacian embassy.'

He turned to Bibula, who shook his head. 'Not quite, your Majesty.' He gestured to Maximus, and the emperor turned to him. 'Go on?'

'The Buri, Imperator. It was from the Buri, and the Lacringi, specifically. Delivered by them. I do not believe this was sanctioned by the Dacian king, Majesty. In fact, I suspect he would be rather angry if he knew.'

Trajan nodded. 'Quite. The Buri. I know the name.'

Hadrian, who had threaded his way out past the Praetorians subtly, unnoticed, nodded. 'The Buri act rather as a buffer between the Dacian Kingdom and the Iazyges. They are nominally a Dacian tribe, but through intermarriage with both their Sarmatian neighbours and the Lacringi, a Germanic group further north, they have become rather something else. It occurs to me that the Buri probably feel they have rather more at stake than the other Dacian tribes; more to lose.'

Trajan smiled. 'Yes, now I remember the name from the interminable briefings Pliny insisted on pressing on me before I left Rome.'

'I swear I thought he was going to insist on coming with you,' Hadrian chuckled. 'Imagine having him here on campaign. You'd have lists awaiting you every morning.'

Trajan rolled his eyes, though in a sympathetic manner. 'He tried, his consulship over. I set him instead to cataloguing the libraries in the palace. Domitian reorganised them in some arcane fashion, and no one can find anything. I told him if they were done when I got back from campaign, he could choose an imperial villa for his own.'

At this Hadrian laughed loud again. Maximus turned at footsteps, to see the prefect of the Second Pannonian approaching the meeting. He wisely said nothing, but bowed to the emperor and halted with the riders, Rufus at his back.

'So there may be division in the ranks. The Iazyges should not be there, although I gather you ran into a mercenary group that may have been Iazyx?'

Bibula nodded. 'We did, Majesty. Or they may have been Roxolani.'

The emperor tapped a finger to his lips. 'It is always good to know of fractures in enemy command and morale. Despite our preparedness, there can be no guarantee at Tapae, and every edge we can gain will be worth gold. If the Buri and their peripheral allies are less than keen on war, they will be easier to break, and when one part of an army breaks on the field of battle, it has stark effects on all the others. This could be very useful. I want to know more. Decurion?' Bibula bowed his head, and Trajan smiled. 'I want you to return the gesture. Take the Buri a message from me. Tell them that Rome comes for Decebalus, and we will leave Tapae victorious or not at all. Tell him that mighty Jupiter is with us and has given us favourable omens. The king of gods will watch over us at Tapae. Tell them all this, and make sure you emphasise that it is *Decebalus* we come for.'

The Praetorian Prefect, Claudius Livianus, who was now close by, frowned. 'They can't just walk into a Dacian camp and demand to see the Buri. They'll be butchered out of hand.'

Trajan gave the man a sly smile. 'I think not. I think the king will be sufficiently intrigued at the development to allow them past.'

Hadrian chuckled again. 'And he will start to ask the Buri difficult questions when they leave, driving the wedge between them ever deeper.'

'Quite,' the emperor said. 'Moreover, our scouts here can bring us back estimates of numbers, morale, and the composition of their forces in advance of the fight.'

Across the meeting, the prefect was glaring daggers at Bibula, presumably for having done all this without him and now committing his troops to a dangerous mission that he could do nothing about, for it was the emperor's own order. In turn, Bibula was giving Maximus a pointed look for something very similar. Maximus turned away and attended to his harness fastenings. He half-listened to the rest of it, as plans were laid, and then fell in at attention as matters were drawn to a close.

He stayed silent as they resupplied, and then began to move through the camp, and it was only once they were past the pickets and moving into the purple gloom of evening in the valley that Bibula turned to him. 'There are days when I curse the gods that you got assigned to the Second, Maximus. Two decades of service in a restive frontier province, and I very rarely found my life in actual danger or senior officers giving me a talking to. Then *you* turn up, and it happens roughly on the hour.'

'You know this isn't my doing. All I did was translate.'

Naevius Bibula sighed. 'Well as long as we make it back out, I suppose this will go a long way to making up for earlier cock-ups.'

By the time they had moved nine miles, an hour into their journey, the gloom was truly gathering, the clawed hands of darkness tearing shreds in the purple and gold of the dying day. The shadows among the trees of the Iron Gates pass deepened and became all the more oppressive. They were now beyond the scouting perimeter, and the closest they had come to Tapae since their arrival at Agnaviae.

Maximus was starting to feel uneasy. His gaze flitted from tree to tree, from shadow to shadow. Beside him, Bibula spoke in a low voice. 'You can feel it too, can't you?'

'We're being watched,' Maximus said. 'Dacian scouts or pickets, I don't know. But we've been watched for a mile or more now.'

His eyes searched out movement in the shadows that was almost certainly just leaves stirring in the light breeze... almost.

The decurion's voice was low. 'We're lucky they've not picked us off, I reckon.'

'Probably too curious. We're being fairly brazen and there aren't enough of us for this to be a proper attack.'

They rode on, thirty-two horsemen moving ever closer to the enemy camp. The landscape was becoming horribly familiar to Maximus now, from slopes to gulleys, and he could swear he even recognised certain trees. He kept looking down, half expecting to see mouldering corpses in rusty armour beneath his hooves, though, of course, there was nothing.

'You look nervous.'

'Not nervous, but definitely uncomfortable. This is Tapae. We're here.'

'It was bad?'

Maximus shivered in the saddle. 'First Tapae was the worst thing the gods ever delivered to man. I've never seen so much blood and so many body parts. There was a carpet of the dead. You sometimes couldn't tell where a dead Dacian ended and a dead Roman began. I hate to run away from a fight, and I'm no coward, Naevius, but from First Tapae, if it hadn't been for exhaustion, I may never have stopped running 'til I reached the encircling sea. Second Tapae we won, but it wasn't much better. Still a bloodbath. We won because of a couple of tricks and sheer bloody-mindedness. It could easily have gone the other way. And I can't say I felt much better even after it than the first time. Can't say I'm glad of a third visit. Just *looking* at this valley gives me fucking nightmares.'

'It was here you got your awards?'

Maximus nodded. 'And not far from here I lost them again,' he added, bitterly.

'You'll gain new ones this time, and they'll count for more given by Trajan than by that lunatic Domitian.'

Maximus's only response to that was a grunt.

They rode on.

'The Fourth were over there,' he said suddenly, pointing. 'I remember seeing them. The governor spotted that they were in trouble and personally led the reserves in to save their hides. It's where I took their vexillum when it fell. Shit, that was a hard day.'

'The difficulty of a battle makes the victory more worthwhile.'

'What happened to the moonlight?' Maximus grumbled, changing the subject. 'It was nice and bright the last few nights. Now the sun goes down and it's like being at the bottom of a bloody well.'

Bibula nodded. 'Heard some fellow from the Syrian archers last night managed to find a hen and did some divination by chicken – you know these weird Syrians. Said the weather was changing. Reckons we're in for storms.'

'Oh good. Critical battles in cursed passes, and now in pissing rain, too.'

'Just pray it hold off until *after* we've kicked Decebalus's arse.'

They wandered on into the valley, closer and closer. Every step was a memory, and none of them happy ones. 'Look there,' he said, pointing left, up the slope of the norther side of the ever-narrowing valley. They could see twinkling lights up there from the Dacian fortress, a heavy stone affair on the upper slopes, a silent sentinel, guarding the Iron Gates pass.

'Dacians?'

A nod. 'We had orders to pull the fortress down after Second Tapae, but Domitian had us pulling out and back to the Danube before we had the chance. Might have made today easier.'

The glow ahead was becoming clear now, marking out a massive camp.

'Stop,' barked a voice in the Dacian language.

They did so, sharply, as three men with spears stepped out, two archers behind them with arrows in their bows already half-drawing the string.

'We are here in peace,' Maximus said in his best Dacian. 'An embassy from Trajan, emperor of Rome, to the chieftains of the Buri.'

He winced. There, it was done.

The surprise among the pickets was clear. There was a sudden huddle.

'Wait,' one snapped, and the others levelled every weapon at them while the first ran off. Others drifted out of the darkness now, each with a weapon in hand, every expression one of belligerence.

'We're fucked,' Bibula hissed.

'Steady,' Maximus replied, keeping a neutral expression on the men before them. They sat in tense silence for what seemed an age before a nobleman on a horse appeared, with a small group of dangerous-looking armoured warriors in tow. He stopped close to them, an eyebrow arching.

'You want mouth Buri?' he asked in horrible Latin. Maximus looked to Bibula, who nodded, and then turned back to the man and spoke in Dacian. 'Please. In the coming days there will be enough butchery without you butchering my language first. Let us speak *your* tongue. Yes, we wish to speak with the Buri chieftains.'

'The king will see you,' the man replied, 'if you agree to surrender your weapons. We are not animals. We give you assurances that they will be returned and you will be permitted to leave, if no offence is given during your audience.'

Maximus braced himself. 'I think you misunderstand. We are not here to see Decebalus of Dacia or even Decebalus's own Apuli tribe. We are here to see the Buri.'

The man's eyes narrowed to slits. He was fighting an inner battle, and Maximus could see it. The man wanted nothing more than to give the order and have them all filled with arrows. He wanted to deny them their request, and had thrown that in about the king in an attempt to divert them. But it looked as though he had his orders, and finally they won out.

'I will take you to the Buri. You will be observed.'

Maximus turned to Bibula, who shrugged. 'In battle or camp, I command,' the decurion said, 'but out here, I think this is *your* command for now. *You're* the one who can speak to them.'

Maximus nodded as the Dacian turned and began to ride back towards the glow of camp fires. The men of Bibula's turma rode into the camp of the Dacian army, past their pickets and guards, with a heightened sense of tension, making sure to keep their fingers away from the hilts of their weapons, where they seemed to want to stray. Maximus took in everything he could as they passed tent after tent, subcamps within camps, stacks and stooks of weapons, campfires of natives who had been singing and whooping until the Romans came near, and then fell silent and watched them pass with an aura of malice.

He noted everything he could think of, presuming everyone else in the turma was doing precisely the same, and finally, their guide led them to a smaller sub-camp on the lower northern slope of the valley, where five huge fires seemed separate from the others. The tents of the Buri, he noted, were different, more like the yurts of the Sarmatian horse clans, whose territory they bordered. There was definitely a divide between the Buri and their other Dacian cousins.

As they were led to a place near a fire, the Buri appeared with weapons drawn, circling them, wary, their shields notable for their brightness. After a short time, noblemen appeared, and Maximus winced to see that one of them was the man who had approached them with the pelt in the woods, earlier. Behind them came two bannermen, one carrying a draco standard, the cloth tube drooping for want of a breeze, the other a crimson dagged banner on a pole, showing a stylised horse.

'The emperor Trajan greets the Buri, and sends them this reply,' Maximus called, emphasising the last word to make sure that the bitter nobleman who'd brought them from the valley caught the fact that the Buri had already opened these negotiations.

He waited a moment, let silence settle. 'Rome comes to Tapae, and nothing can stop that. Rome comes for Decebalus of Dacia, and will not leave until Decebalus is beaten and cowed. The emperor wishes you to know that Jupiter himself, great king of the gods of Olympus, who you and I know as Zeus, has given the greatest omens to Rome, and will shelter and aid the emperor's forces in the coming conflict. Only a fool stands against Rome, but only a *suicidal* fool stands against the father of the gods. Trajan of Rome therefore sends the Buri this message. Leave. Go home. You will not be pursued. The army is here for Decebalus.'

He fell silent.

He looked around, and noted, nervously, the expressions on the gathered faces. Such a variety. Some of the Buri were surprised, even hopeful. Here was an opportunity, given by the emperor, for them to leave, an 'out' from the coming nightmare. Others were glum, knowing they could not leave without turning on their own king. More, including the man who'd spoken to them earlier, were angry, for they knew that by sending such a reply, Trajan had just set them up as rebels in the eyes of the Dacian king, had dropped them deep in the shit. But the best look of all was the Dacian who had led them here, who was furious beyond belief, his face purple, but looking back and forth between Maximus and the Buri chieftains, not sure who he was *more* angry with.

'We are done here, I think,' Maximus announced, turning to that man. 'Please escort us back to the lines.'

The man struggled for a moment. His hand danced close to his sword hilt, but he managed to restrain himself, and nodded curtly, turning and riding away without a word, with just a last glance of malice at the Buri.

Once more, as they rode through the Dacian camp, Maximus took note of everything he could, and once they reached the pickets and moved out into the now-deep darkness of the valley, he let out a sigh of relief.

'Plenty to report, I'd say.'

Bibula made a similar noise, then chuckled. 'You clearly missed a career on the stage. That was like a *performance*.'

'I can tell you one thing in particular I noticed in their camp,' Maximus said.

'Oh?'

'Nowhere did I see cavalry, the only horse belonging to that bloke who escorted us. Those riders we met before must just be a small mercenary unit, as we thought.'

'Well that's something, at least,' Bibula snorted. 'Let's go home and report in. Then I am going to get so blind drunk I can persuade myself I didn't walk in and out of an enemy camp just to insult them.'

CHAPTER TEN

TAPAE, SEPTEMBER AD 101

'Wouldn't it just be easier to launch an attack?' Arvina murmured. 'Straight on. We have to outnumber them.'

Maximus didn't even turn to the man. 'Don't wish for things like that. I've done it twice and I'm in no hurry.'

'But if we outnumber them...'

'We outnumbered them the first time, and they chewed us up and spat us out. We outnumbered them the second time, and even with knowledge of the land and the enemy, we still only just won, by so little that we ended up in an uneasy peace. The emperor knows that. He's not about to risk making this the latest in a long line of fuck-ups.'

'Why are they so dangerous?' Falco asked, sitting on his other side.

'There are lessons you only learn in war, my friend,' Maximus sighed. 'No training centurion, and no academy teaches them. One of them is: try never to fight an enemy on ground of their choosing. There's a reason Tapae is called the Iron Gates. The Dacians have evolved over centuries to be the perfect force to fight in this sort of land. Never attack a Parthian force in the open desert. Never chase Germans into the forest. These are things we learn the hard way. And never take on Dacians in their hills unless you have a trick up your sleeve.'

'So what trick is this?' Arvina said.

Maximus turned and looked around him. They were three miles from the pickets of the Dacian camp, tantalisingly close, but still far enough not to engage. Around them, the landscape was changing by the hour.

Legions and auxiliaries at work by the thousand.

Trees were coming down, torn out by the roots. The branches and foliage were removed and taken to open sites, where they were burned in two score great fires that blazed every hour the gods sent, while the good, heavy wood was loaded into carts to be used for artillery, fortification and other construction. Like a tide, Rome was moving through the valley of the Iron Gates, as it got narrower and narrower, and where they passed, the tree-strewn landscape that favoured the Dacian war machine became open ground suited to ranks of legionaries. But deforestation was only part of the work. Other units toiled at the cliff faces up on the valley sides, churning out basket after basket of rock chippings, gravel, and stones, all ferried down constantly into the valley, where they were used to create good surfaces leading from the Roman camps all the way into the pass. When Maximus had ridden this way a few days earlier, the idea of bringing a huge train of carts and wagons with them seemed ridiculous. Now, the pass was starting to look like a Roman highway. Moreover, where the land became difficult, stones had been removed, small rises pared down to gentle slopes, gulleys filled to flat ground. As the hours went by, the Iron Gates became more and more manageable.

'Not a trick per se,' Maximus nodded. 'But as we move east, the ground is less and less suited to the Dacians and more and more suited to us. We could even field cavalry properly now. Trajan is cautious. Not overly-so, but sufficient that he is levelling the field before the fight. Quite literally, in fact.'

He looked up. 'My only worry is that if we don't engage them soon, we'll be doing it in a downpour.'

Certainly the sky looked threatening. For two days now, the clouds had been gathering. Balmy autumn evenings were already a thing of the past, and every soldier in camp huddled in his winter cloak, looking up in miserable anticipation. Now the morning rose as a lead-grey thing, threatening rain, and the sun put in only an occasional appearance between the dark blankets of cloud before surrendering to the inevitable and disappearing for the night, leaving the moon with much the same problem.

There was a storm coming, in more ways than one. That, Maximus suspected, was why the army had put so much effort into stone and gravel road surfaces. When it rained, men, animals and vehicles would need purchase.

In some ways, though, Maximus had to nod to Arvina's frustration. In spending all this time making the approach favourable to Rome, they may well be surrendering the last of the good weather and volunteering to fight in the bad. It was, he supposed, a play off between the two: terrain and weather.

'Movement,' a voice called.

Maximus looked up. One of the riders of the Ala Bosporanorum was racing back towards them from the eastern trees, ahead of the Roman work. Maximus looked around, and found Bibula riding towards them from where he'd been updating a legionary officer.

'How many?' he called back. 'Is the army on the move?'

'No. Cavalry only. Maybe a couple of hundred.'

As the man closed on their position, Maximus glanced a question at his decurion.

Naevius Bibula sucked on his lip for a moment. 'Either coming to test our forward units, or maybe hoping to disrupt the legions from their work. Can we take two hundred horse, you think?'

Maximus winced. Two alae were on duty guarding the work at the moment, but of those thousand riders, only five turma would currently be in reach in time to engage. They would be outnumbered, and if those riders were Sarmatians...

'Screw it. Of course we can.'

'Sound the muster and call to war,' Bibula told the tubicen nearby, who lifted the horn to his mouth and blew two sharp cadences. As Maximus counted off the heartbeats, he could see riders from the Second Pannonian and the First Bosporanorum racing across the works to join them.

'Here they come,' shouted a second voice.

Maximus looked up sharply to see another rider pelting their way. That was fast. The enemy were not being careful, then.

'Form,' Bibula bellowed, and the riders fell into rough lines, three deep across the grass. All around the valley the infantry faltered in their works, aware that something important was happening, but in moments their officers had them labouring again.

He saw them, then, ahead and between the sparse trees.

Roxolani.

When Dacians rode to war, they looked like they did as infantry, just on a horse. Not so the Sarmatian peoples – the Roxolani, the Iazyges, the Alani and their kin. They were born in the saddle, out on the grassy steppe, weaned on horse's milk and learning to ride and fight as they learned to walk and talk. A fierce people, whose life was so hard and martial that their women could often be found at war alongside the men, with no distinction in sexes.

And Romans had learned to be wary of the horse peoples for the same reason they'd learned to be wary of the Dacians. That dreaded curved falx blade that could cut through a helmet like paper made the people of Dacia dangerous, but the Sarmatians had their lances and armour, and were, if anything, *more* frightening.

Their armour was gleaming, even in the overcast, shirts of leather sewn with scales made of horses' hooves, hard and shiny, which covered the riders from neck to cuff and even formed trousers to the heel, the inner side left leather for ease of horsemanship. Their head was crowned with helmets of conical shape, sometimes ribbed, often embossed with legendary creatures and borrowed gods. And if that armour was not enough, many had gone to the extent of coating their horses with the same hard, yet flexible scale, making them difficult to damage with sword or spear.

They were thundering through the trees, and now he could hear them, whooping and ululating, and there, alongside the voices, that eerie wail of the dragon standard that was carried by their banner-bearer.

Instantly, Maximus found himself regretting saying they could handle this. It was, in fact, going to be a really hard fight. To his relief, other riders were hurrying over to bolster their numbers, and several of the nearest infantry work parties had now downed tools and collected their shields and weapons, their centurions falling them in.

'Open formation,' called Naevius Bibula, a command Maximus echoed a moment later as the Roman cavalry began to separate, leaving wide gaps in their lines. 'Remember,' he told them, 'let them come in the charge, but don't try and stop them. Move out of the way at the last moment, and try to take them down as they pass.'

It was a tried and sometimes-successful tactic, though every Sarmatian tribe fought slightly differently, and it didn't *always* work.

'Screw this,' shouted a rider he didn't know so well a little off to the right, and started to back his horse away.

'You move out of line, and I'll gut you myself,' Maximus bellowed at him, the sudden threat sufficient to bring the chagrined and nervous rider back into line.

'On the mark of two horse-lengths,' Bibula shouted, 'sidepass right, strike, then turn, repeat and reverse.'

Again, the command echoed down the line.

Behind them, the second and third lines had opened up to make space too, their own officers passing them commands.

'Fucking Tapae,' Maximus grumbled as he gripped his shield tight and circled his sword wrist a little, limbering up.

Then the enemy were out of the trees and among the scarred landscape the Romans had cleared, bearing down on the cavalry alae. Maximus had to trust each man to do his job now, and concentrated on the fierce monster racing towards him. The man was coated in scale the same as each of them, though this one's armour seemed to only reach down to the elbows, the forearms clad in leather, and the hands in gloves of the same material. The lance, an immense spike, so long and heavy that it had to be held in two hands, was levelled straight at him, and strung with red streamers that looked unnervingly like sprays of blood as they whipped through the air behind it.

He judged it, hoping he'd judged it right, and then nudged Ferox's right shoulder with his knee, urging him sideways, even as he tapped with his left heel. He prayed the animal had been taught the manoeuvre as well as any cavalry horse, and prayed even more so that he was bright enough to know what was expected of him.

Fortuna was clearly with him today. The stupid animal only moved one step, not the mandatory two of cavalry training, and so only brought him halfway out of the Roxolani warrior's path. But fortunately, Maximus had misjudged his timing, and begun his sidepass too early anyway, and so he deftly, at that last moment, nudged Ferox again, and the daft beast once again performed half the manoeuvre, clearing the path.

The Sarmatian knew he was going past, then, and realigned his lance accordingly. There was no way of avoiding the coming blow, and all Maximus could do was try and block it. His shield came up and across, praying with every inch of movement that at least *this* manoeuvre he had judged correctly. The lance struck the boss at the centre of his shield, though he did not have time for a sigh of relief. The heavy weapon dinged a dent in the boss, then tore a deep furrow across the board before sending shards of the bronze edging wheeling away through the air. The tip narrowly missed taking a piece out of Maximus's shoulder, but then the man was moving past. Like the focused warrior he was, the rider had already forgotten about Maximus, and was now watching the next man in the second rank, his new target.

Maximus swung. It was not an elegant attack, and had to be carried out instantly, and at full stretch across his horse. His right hand brought the blade across, narrowly missing the remains of his shield. He hit the Sarmatian as he passed, though not, as he'd hoped, in that less protected lower arm.

Instead, his sword slammed into the man's back, at one side, just below the lung. It could have been a brutal blow, possibly, shattering ribs and puncturing lungs without even breaking the armour, or it could be just bad bruising that the warrior would soon shrug off. With the armour remaining intact it was just impossible to tell. The man made no clear reaction to the blow, simply continuing on his charge, now intent on killing the man *behind* Maximus.

He turned, now, for the fight was far from over. The next Sarmatian had him already in sight, lance levelled ready. Maximus used his knee and heel again, this time stepping left and continuing to press Ferox, urging him to continue his move, stepping twice. This time, he almost came to grief, as the horse took a third pace without any urging, bringing him perilously close to being in the path of a *different* rider. He did all he could. Even as he sidepassed, he brought his shield over the horse's neck and put it in the way as best he could. The lance hit the boards first this time, punching through the already damaged shield, tearing the thing apart. Knowing it was of no use now, Maximus simply let go of the shield, which then clung to the lance that had impaled it, causing the long weapon to sag and droop. He swung his sword, and this time knew he'd achieved something, for he struck the Roxolani in the back of the neck. The worst of the blow would be taken by the scale guard that hung from the back of the helmet, but he saw from the way the man's head suddenly lolled to the side that he'd done something critical. Indeed, even as he pulled his gaze away from the rider, he noticed him slew out of line. Leaving him to it, Maximus turned again. Another rider was coming for him.

He had no shield this time.

He would have liked to perform some fancy manoeuvre, but there were two problems with that. Firstly, already, the other men in line were repeating their move, this time to the right once more, and if he did something different, he might screw it up for the men to either side, but secondly, he simply didn't trust Ferox to manage it. Had it been Celeris, he'd have been dancing about the field now.

Instead, he did all he could. He joined the line in sidepassing to the right, and in the absence of a shield, he tried to predict where the lance was coming and to not be there when it did.

He almost managed it, and was pleased with what he *did* achieve. The lance tip caught his bicep, a narrow, glancing blow that took a small piece of meat with it as it then caught in the chain of his shirt sleeve, tearing it to pieces and sending iron links out across the grass. Maximus grunted in pain, but he had already been beginning his counterstrike even as the lance connected, and the Sarmatian rider took his sword in the arm as he passed. The blow should have been good enough to break bone, and he followed the rider with his gaze long enough to see the lance droop and then fall from the damaged arm.

Behind him now was chaos, as Romans and Roxolani fought in close quarters. A number of the enemy riders had been brought down as they dropped their long lances and drew their swords, but many had lived through that, the sheer scale of their protection sufficient to turn many a blow.

There were still others coming yet, though not too many, and not the same as they'd been before, for they were slower, riding into the fight rather than charging. Indeed, many already had swords out instead of lances.

'Melee,' called a strained voice, and Maximus spared a moment to glance left. Naevius Bibula was swaying in the saddle, one hand clamped to his side, where red had blossomed on his tunic and chain shirt. He was gritting his teeth.

'Get back to the medicus,' Maximus shouted at him.

For a moment, the decurion looked as though he might argue, then he gave a curt nod. 'You have command.'

For what that was worth. Already the whole clash had broken down into individual close-quarter fights. He smiled to see that they were getting assistance now from the infantry.

Off to the left, a century of legionaries had formed a tight shield wall and were pushing into two Roxolani riders, and off to the right, an auxiliary unit of gaesati were sticking their spears into any part of the Roxolani they could find to attack.

The tide of victory was clearly with the Roman force now.

The remaining Roxolani who'd yet to commit could see how things were turning out, and were already turning, and riding away through the trees. Others were breaking from the fight and trying to follow, some successfully, others brought down even as they tried to pull back.

A Sarmatian suddenly appeared in his view, lurching in from the side so close they were almost in an embrace, sword coming round, and Maximus reacted in an instant. Knowing the effective range of the longswords of both Roman and Sarmatian, and seeing how close they were, he urged Ferox in even closer, inside the sword's arc, and, instead of bringing his weapon to bear, he lunged, headbutting the rider.

The man's helmet was the usual conical style, without a noseguard, and riveted around the base, tight with the man's head. Maximus, though, was wearing a new Roman cavalry helmet with a brow of double-thick bronze, the bowl of the helmet itself, and an embossed visor atop that, his replacement helmet for the one that had so recently been cleaved with a falx. It had cost him plenty, especially since Duras had done a runner with most of his savings, and even as the two helmets collided, he prayed his came away undamaged.

Certainly that could not be said for the man's head. The Roxolani rider's forehead smashed under the blow, the brow of his own helmet crushed inwards, into the skull. He howled in pain as his helmet was scrunched tight onto his ruined head. Knowing the man was in no state to react, and saved being dazed by the thickness of his own headgear, Maximus took a precious moment to back Ferox away, surprisingly successfully, aimed, and then swung his sword. He timed it so that the rider was looking up at the time, reaching up and trying to prise the metal from his forehead. His sword smashed into the Sarmatian's neck, crushing everything vital there, and killing him in moments.

The enemy rider toppled from his horse, and as Maximus recovered, he looked about. Riders were down all over the place, men of his own ala, and of others, but noticeably many more of the Sarmatians. He saw then a couple of troopers putting heel to flank in pursuit of the fleeing Roxolani, and turned and gestured to the tubicen. 'Ad signum. Fast!'

The musician blew out the call to fall in at the standards, and every man reacted to that, instinct taking over as each rider had had that particular call drilled into him from the first day of service. The last of the Roxolani were departing now. The legionaries who'd joined in were already moving back to their worksite, sheathing swords and removing helmets and shields. The centurion of the gaesati waved a greeting at him, thanked him for the chance to give his lads a break from sawing logs, and left with a smile.

Maximus breathed a sigh of relief. That could have been a disaster. He looked around and spotted a shield of the First Bosporanorum. 'Who's your officer on duty?'

'Leucon, sir, but he's over there.' He pointed to a human body beside that of a dappled grey mare. A lance still stuck out of his chest, rising into the air like a grisly banner.

Maximus nodded. 'Right, then, consider this a field promotion, duplicarius. Gather your unit to whatever standard you can find. Tell my tubicen your recall, and he'll blow it for you. Then get your wounded back to the medics and put the dead on horses for funerals tonight. Then get yourself back to camp and drink too much wine.'

'Yessir,' the soldier replied with a salute and no sign of humour at all. As he gathered the men of the Ala Bosporanorum, Maximus took stock of his own. He could count twenty-six of the ala on the ground, either dead or looking like it. Among them, he noted with some sadness, Abgar and Priscus. The camp fire would be subdued tonight. He heaved in a deep breath. But then it was going to get much worse in the coming days. He waited for Procullus to sound the other unit's call, and then gestured for him to do the same for the Second Pannonian. Anyone else out there, he wanted back safely with him. He turned to Falco. 'Ride for command. Tell them what happened and respectfully suggest they move a line of pickets out and assign more cavalry. We're spent for the afternoon, I think.'

Falco nodded, urged his horse into motion, and rode back towards the heart of the Roman force. Maximus sat, recovering for a time as his more scattered riders converged on the scene of the fight. A thought occurred to him, and he waved to Rigozus. The man rode over and reined in, and Maximus regarded him for a moment. A grizzled veteran of many years, the man was probably the same age as him, and had likely seen just as much shit. He was trustworthy, and sensible. But more importantly right now, he carried a small amount of Roxolani blood in his veins, and hailed from the lowest stretches of the Danubius, where you could skip stones on the water of the river and hit the bastards on the far side. He spoke their tongue, knew something of their customs, had fought alongside them once, and against them a dozen times, and his opinion counted.

'How many riders have you ever seen when Roxolani mercenaries fight?'

Rigozus shrugged. 'How long is a piece of twine. Depends on the tribe, the reason, the season.'

Maximus shook his head. 'No, not when a tribe goes to war. Just mercenaries. One warband at a time.'

'I dunno. Probably no more than fifty in a single warband.'

'And there were two hundred here today, give or take.'

Rigozus nodded. 'It's high, I admit. Maybe they were several mercenary units together?'

'I don't think so. They fought like one group, and you know the horse clans. They never really work together, just next to each other. This was all one group. I can see the tamga of their tribe here and there, and they all have the same one.'

'So it's a whole tribe?'

Maximus huffed. 'Maybe. But one Sarmatian tribe going to war without the others is rare, isn't it? I mean, when the Iazyges or the Roxolani decide to fight Rome, they tend to do it en masse.'

'True. So what's the answer? Too few to be the Roxolani on the move, too many for an ordinary mercenary unit.'

'I don't know, but I think something is happening. Decebalus is up to something, and I think the Roxolani are part of it. I think he wanted the Iazyges and the Osii involved too, and pretty much everyone in this part of the world. All I can say is that if a couple of hundred Roxolani are at work over here, I seriously doubt the rest are still in their tents and farms down near the sea. Something is happening.' Another thought occurred to him. 'We *are* sure these are Roxolani and not Iazyges, yes? I've been here for decades and sometimes *I* can't tell them apart.'

Rigozus shook his head. 'These are Roxolani, sure as shit.'

'And another thing occurs. A couple of nights ago we were walking merrily through their camp and there was no sign of Roxolani, or cavalry at all, to my mind. I mean, it's possible they were there and out of sight, but there was only so much grazing land, and it all seemed to be filled with infantry camp fires. Where were they then?'

'Maybe they just arrived?'

'I don't think so. I'd be willing to bet my left ball they're the same bunch who took the foragers' heads back near Tibiscum.'

'Just your *left* ball?'

'Yeah. The right one's bigger. As I say, there's something going on, and it involves the Sarmatians. I'll be glad when Tapae is done with.'

'Won't we all. For many reasons. You going to take this question to the bosses?'

Maximus frowned for a moment, then shook his head. 'Don't think so. All I've got at the moment is a bad feeling and some suspicions. Nothing concrete. Can't disturb the prefect, or the emperor, for that matter, with nothing to go on. I'd give good money to be able to poke around about ten or twenty miles past Tapae, though, in Decebalus's heartland, where he knows we can't see what's going on.'

*

Four hours later, Maximus was feeling tense, though for entirely different reasons. The fighting over, they had checked the ground behind the fleeing Roxolani and found that they'd left no trace. Then they had sent the wounded back to the medical section and began gathering up the dead, heaping men and horses – with some difficulty – into carts, where they were taken to a new mass grave that had been dug. There was not time for a pyre, a funeral and a burial for each man individually, and in the coming days they would be joined by many more. They would be honoured together, and their contributions to the funeral club, not needed for the funeral or memorial, would be sent back to their kin as some small consolation. At least Naevius Bibula's family would get no letter. He was wounded, and would not see any action at Tapae, but the medicus was content he would survive as long as infection kept away, and reckoned he would be back on light duties in a month. He was lying in the bed next to Statilius, who at least now had a dice partner each evening.

Thus it was that the men of the Second Pannonian, all together, stood before two of the altars taken from the unit's supply carts. Torches burned and braziers glowed in the shelter of the makeshift awning, adding an acrid, smoky, oily aspect to the evening.

Maximus's arms ached. In the absence of Duras, he'd spent an hour polishing his own kit, and resolved to buy a new slave as soon as he had the chance. His new helmet had survived the day, though there was a dent in the brow and one of the embossed gods was now misshapen, which irritated him.

He looked at the two altars, incense streaming up in very expensive smoky lines, two well-shaped altars, adorned with appropriate symbols and marked to their gods. To Jupiter, Greatest and Best, in a very traditional manner, and to Helios, the sun god, beloved of Syrians. The unit's de facto priest, Phillipos, was busy intoning the names of the lost as he held his hands up to the gods. They had sacrificed two chickens, all they could find and spare, and every man in the ala had put a little something on the altar of the god of their choice, sometimes both.

As the long service went on, a mass funeral, along with sacrifices to the gods, requests for aid, blessings for the unit and their animals and equipment, thanks for the day's victory, and then the obligatory poking and prodding of an animal's liver to see if the coming days would be beneficial, Maximus spent most of his time with his attention elsewhere, thinking.

The whole Sarmatian cavalry question was nagging at him. And it was as he was only half-listening, contemplating the possible motives of the Roxolani, that he heard the first spatter of rain. Not heavy at first, but steady, and increasingly so as the hour wore on. By the time Phillipos was holding up a sticky liver and trying to explain why it was full of good signs, Maximus was starting to worry. The rain had picked up to a steady drumming quite fast, and now, in places, their awning was sagging under the weight of gathered water.

He glanced around at the poles holding it up, and could swear they were starting to bow a little. He cleared his throat and pointed up. 'Maybe we should speed this up?'

The prefect glared at him, and Phillipos replied in an aloof voice. 'The gods will not be rushed.'

'The *gods* are not about to get drenched,' Rigozus whispered next to him.

Maximus winced at a nasty groaning sound. Now, as if on cue, every pair of eyes, including those of the prefect and the priest, turned upwards. The awning gave way in one huge burst, tearing and falling apart, gallons of water cascading down on the men below, all gathered in their best for the funeral.

Maximus cursed, as he shook his arms and legs and head, wiping his brow. The rain was beating down on them properly now.

'Bloody wonderful.'

'Behold,' called Phillipos in his best 'I am a priest so I am more interesting than you' voice.

Everyone turned to where he was looking, and a silence fell. By sheer chance – or *was* it by sheer chance – the one place the water had not fallen in great torrents, where it was propped up by two poles that had stayed the test, was right above the two altars. Every single man in the unit may have been drenched, but somehow the two altars had avoided it.

'Behold a sign from the gods,' Phillipos announced. 'Jove and Helios are too powerful even for weather to touch.'

Some consolation, Maximus thought bitterly as he shook yet more rain from his soaked apparel.

Chapter Eleven

'I've noticed that when you're in camp, among the ala, you all seem to speak Greek. Same for a lot of the units here,' Claudius Arvina said, almost conversationally.

Maximus turned in the saddle, though he did not slow his steady pace. 'It's natural. I'm from Phillipi, Rigozus from Troesmis in Lower Moesia, Azimus from Emesa in Syria. Bibula is from Athens, and we've even got men in other turma of the ala that came from Judea and Aegyptus. All of them speak Greek fluently, not all of them speak as good Latin, beyond what they need for military life. You speak Greek? You're not from the East.'

Arvina nodded. 'Standard education, I suppose. Greek included.'

'Why are you here?' Maximus said at last. It was seemingly less likely as time went on that Arvina was some sort of spy for command, since they had rather redeemed their earlier failings, and the prefect was happy, as he was starting to look good now. Everyone sort of danced around the subject, but no one had asked directly. Perhaps it was time.

Arvina looked a little embarrassed for a moment. 'I probably shouldn't have been. We were quite wealthy and influential a few years back. Then my father went and said something stupid in front of the emperor – Domitian, that is. He took offence first, then Father's fortune second. Stripped him of everything, houses, villas, treasury, even heirlooms. We had nothing. Dad went off and drowned himself twice. First in wine, then in a bath house. Bit of a scandal that. There were three of us kids left with nothing. Me and Julius could have got some sort of job, but there's no high income guarantee there, and we have a sister to support. If we can't keep her funds healthy, you know damn well where *she's* going to end up, and we're not going to let that happen.'

'So you and your brother joined the army?'

'I did. Julius sold himself to a lanista. Now he's fighting in the arenas in Rome. Makes good money, but we worry about him.'

'And why didn't you join the legions? You're a citizen. Could probably have been an officer.'

Arvina's blush came back. 'I hear you were in the legions, sir.'

'I was.'

'Can you imagine how life would be for a nobleman fallen on hard times and having to slog for a wage with everyone else. I can guarantee some officer would find out about my family, and things would get difficult. Here in the auxilia, I can get a bit of anonymity. It's just easier, and the wage isn't much of a drop.'

Maximus nodded. 'I suspect you did the right thing. And I suppose you ended up here because you were a good rider, and educated.'

'I think I ended up here because command weren't sure what else to do with me.'

That made Maximus smile. He was warming to the man. That was good. They'd lost some good men, and the turma needed a bit of unity. He looked up. There were the others. They'd caught up with the rest of the turma. A number of them turned to nod at the new arrivals, and, as they did, Maximus waved at Rigozus, who turned his horse and walked over to meet him. As he neared, Maximus reached down to his belt and pulled from it a yellow crest, which he then tossed over to the veteran. Rigozus caught it with ease, frowning.

'I'm acting decurion until Bibula's back up, which means I need an acting duplicarius.'

Rigozus simply nodded, took the crest and removed his helmet, attaching it. Maximus put his own helmet back on and fastened it.

'Alright, we're all here,' Maximus said, loud enough to catch the attention of the entire twenty-seven surviving men of the turma. They'd actually lost a few more in the fight, but the three new recruits that had been training at Viminacium and who'd been on duty looking after horses had been promoted to full trooper status now.

'I'm sure the emperor has orders, and so will his generals, and our own beloved prefect, but before that, here's my own comments.' He straightened in the saddle, and looked to the pass ahead. 'Tapae will be a bloodbath. It always is. I was at the first and second one, and they were the stuff of nightmares. Most of you have been in battle, and some of you were even at Tapae once or twice, so you'll know what I mean now. Obey orders. Keep formation and *do not* engage in melee unless specifically commanded. If an enemy runs, you do not follow. As light cavalry, we'll probably be posted to one of the wings in an attempt to make them break, and my guess is the left wing, on the valley's northern side. We have more experience in Dacia as a whole, and here in particular, than any of the other alae, and that means they'll probably want us to be the ones taking the position below the Dacian citadel on that slope.'

He paused to let that sink in.

'Yes, that means we'll be in the thick of it, in one of the most dangerous positions on the field. So you know what to expect from the force in front of us. Whether they be Apuli or Buri or any other Dacian tribe, the bulk of them will be bearded and bare headed, lightly armoured at best, with a shield and weapon or, gods help us, with a two-handed falx. Be prepared. Be inventive. Listen to orders. There is a possibility we will face cavalry. Something seems to be going on with cavalry at the moment, and we cannot say for sure whether they will even be fielded and, if they are, in what strength, or whether they'll be light Dacian horse, or heavy Sarmatians. That we'll have to work out when the time comes. Be prepared for missiles. A favourite tactic of these bastards at the Iron Gates is to keep us engaged in the lower valley while their mates send sling bullets and arrows down from the heights, and that will include from the fortification. Be aware of that and make sure you keep your eye out and your shield up when you're not engaged.'

He looked around the pass, much of which had now been deforested and flattened, made easy for the approaching Romans. Only half a mile of trees now separated Rome from her enemy, and that had been where work had stopped, for trying to fell trees and build roads right underneath the eyes of Decebalus would have been ridiculous.

'We have a clear run almost to their camp, with plenty of space to deploy. No tactics have been handed down to unit level yet, but the general feeling is that the emperor has something up his sleeve and intends to draw the Dacians out of the woods and into the open, where we can fight them cleanly. Take it from me, the last thing we want this time is to be drawn into that narrow gap in the trees between his fortifications. Alright, the rest of the cavalry are coming up now. We need to show them all up. Who are we?'

'Second Pannonian, sons of Jove and Helios,' bellowed the men of the turma.

'And more?'

'The turma of Claudius Maximus, bane of Dacia,' more shouted.

He almost corrected them, for really they were still the turma of Naevius Bibula, but somehow it felt good to claim the title today. 'Fall in with the rest of the ala.'

His men manoeuvred with the approaching horsemen, moving into lines as commanded by the prefect's messengers. The rumble and the cloud of dust from behind, back west, told them clearly the Roman army was almost with them, almost in the field. Tapae would see bloodshed again, and it would see it today. Gods willing, this would be the last time Rome had to fight for the Iron Gates.

The first figures to emerge from the west were the couriers, each carrying orders. A rider hurtled over to Gaius Julius Paullus, prefect of the Second Pannonian, bowing his head respectfully and proffering a sealed epistle from command. Paullus cracked the wax and opened the orders, running his gaze down them even as his men finished falling to their ordered lines. When he had read the last, he tucked it away and then rode around to the front of the unit, where he sat tall in the saddle.

'We are to be given the honour of the left flank, accompanied by the Ala Bosporanorum and the Gallorum Flaviana. The centre of the field will be held by the auxilia, both infantry cohorts and mixed units, with three more alae on the right flank. The legions are being held in reserve.'

There was a stifled groan from among the men. It was, Maximus knew, an old story. Legions and auxilia fielded for battle, and the legions were kept in reserve while the auxilia did the fighting and dying. Popular military subject. But having served in both, he also knew there was always a reason for it, usually down to the suitability of the troops being brought to battle.

'Before you feel hard done by, be aware that the legions are fielding their artillery from the outset, which means three hundred cart-mounted ballistae, and fifty onagers. More than a tenth of their manpower will be occupied with the artillery, and so they will not be fielded as infantry until the barrage is finished, the artillery withdrawn and the legions re-formed.'

Always a reason. Perhaps a particularly good one this time.

'The ballistae and onagri are to be brought up into position, indeed, they are already primed and loaded and on their way. They will pound the Dacians until Decebalus has no choice but to flee his position or to commit. Each ala deployed is to stay close to these weapons and be prepared. The moment the Dacians emerge from the trees, the artillery will cease and withdraw, and we are expected to cover their retreat until they are safely far enough back to be out of danger. Then we commit on the third signal from command. Follow orders, stand fast, and neither pursue a fleeing enemy, nor flee the field yourself, and the Second Pannonian will leave Tapae with honours. For Jupiter, the emperor, and Rome!'

That last cry was picked up by every rider in the ala, and similar calls were echoing out across the valley from all the others. The prefect saluted them all, and then turned and rode his horse back to the rear of the unit.

'For coins, for wine, and for women,' someone shouted in the middle of the unit, and fully half the ala echoed this call as well, the whole unit exploding into guffaws. Maximus could imagine the prefect's face as he rode away, but he had to smile himself. It was small things like this that lifted the spirits of soldiers at war.

'Will the artillery be able to *reach* the Dacians,' Falco asked. 'I've seen them in action. Their range isn't that long, and the enemy are half a mile away.'

Maximus nodded. 'Normally. The machines can be tightened such that they're overwound, and that gives them extra range, at the cost of accuracy, and increased danger of the weapon snapping mid-shot. But at full strength, they could get over a quarter of a mile, maybe a third. They won't be able to drop shots into Decebalus's lunch bowl, but with the sheer number of weapons, the ammunition will fall all among his pickets, scouts and forward parties. He'll lose men repeatedly, and the barrage will mean he can't replace them without risking the replacements too.'

'So won't he just sit back and wait?'

'I doubt it. They're not in a fortress, just a big open camp. If they don't have eyes on us from the woods, they don't know what we're up to. We could already be on the march and heading for their camp. He'll have to put men in danger to know what we're doing, until he decides either to commit or to withdraw and give us the Iron Gates.'

A distant rumble suggested the bad weather was coming back with a vengeance. The rain had stopped early in the night, leaving the land soggy, but there had been another shower at dawn, and the colour of the sky had darkened all morning, suggesting worse was on the way. Falco looked up and blinked as a spot of rain slapped him in the face.

'Will rain cause trouble for the artillery?'

Maximus shook his head. 'Archers will have trouble keeping their strings tight, but the torsion on the artillery is so powerful that the rain won't make much difference. In fact, it might even help ease it a little.' He looked up too, then. What he'd said was certainly true, but the rain would also make fighting any battle much more unpleasant.

It was only as the cloud of dust and dirt to the west started to dissipate, and units to emerge, that Maximus realised that the rumble he'd been hearing was not the weather after all, but the approach of the artillery. They arrived at Tapae in droves, each weapon on a cart drawn by two oxen, each with eight men in control, one hundred and seventy-five carts on each side of the valley. It was one of the most immense shows of strength Maximus had ever seen, for each cart also carried sufficient ammunition to keep up a barrage for hours. It was moments like this that justified the attention the emperor had paid to having his supply system in place.

Behind them came more soldiers, the infantry and part-mounted auxiliary cohorts that were to take the centre of the field when the barrage ended, as well as a huge variety of numeri, irregular units of troops, drawn usually from the periphery of the Roman world. He could see Syrian archers among them, in their long, flowing robes and pointed helmets, scale armour gleaming, short, curved bows in hand; he could see Raetian gaesati with their iconic long spears; he could see a force of German tribesmen, hair and beards wild or braided, stripped bare to the waist, their chests painted with wild designs, shield in one hand, brutal club in the other.

The ala separated into narrow columns to allow the carts through, where they moved forward as far as the myriad of flat platforms that had been engineered by the legions over the previous day, each perfectly sized and levelled for an artillery wagon. Now, half the preparations were making sense. Each wagon was manoeuvred into place and then turned so that the vehicle's rear faced the east, the weapon pointing that way, so that when the time came to withdraw, it would be a swift and efficient operation.

Once every cart was in place, and the riders sent by command were in position ready to relay any news or orders, the Second Pannonian, and the other two alae who'd come to join them now, moved into well-organised places where they were *between* wagons and at their rear, and carefully not between the artillery and their forest target.

Still the weapons did not loose. The crews loaded, winched and prepared, moving their machines to a ready state. Somewhere near Maximus, one of the legionaries warned a cavalryman that he was too close.

'I'm not in your way,' the trooper said defensively in reply.

'It's for your benefit, not mine,' the artillerist explained quietly. 'If she winds too far and the spar breaks, anyone within six feet is likely to be picking foot-long pieces of iron and wood out of their body.'

At this, the rider gave the soldier a startled nod, and obediently sidepassed by two more steps. Every rider in the area estimated his distance from the nearest machine and moved a little if they felt the need.

Nothing moved among the artillery, ballistae primed with bolts, wound and ratcheted back, ready for their first shot. Onagers were pulled back as far as possible and loaded with rocks. Every time there was the slightest groaning noise, soldiers leapt out of the way just in case. And as they waited, the auxilia and their irregular support fell into position at the valley bottom below, ready for the fight.

'Great Jupiter,' Maximus said quietly, under his breath, 'I beg your watchful eye, your favour and your protection for me and for my men. Let the Dacians fail and fall, and Rome claim victory this day.'

He looked up, to see the dark clouds racing past at high speed. How odd, given that there was barely a breath of wind down here in the pass. With luck it would blow the clouds away into the hills and leave them with dry long enough to fight.

As if to ruin his day, another heavy droplet of rain splashed off his arm, heralding the very opening of the storm. Just let it hold off long enough.

Everything was in place. The dispatch riders, given the nod by the forward officers, raced back towards the commanders and the legions that were now moving into reserve position, and a matter of heartbeats later, signals began to ring out all across the valley. They ended, echoing away into the pass, slowly iterating back into silence.

Nothing. Not a breath of wind. Clouds racing overhead, but no other movement. No sound.

THUD.

It began with a single onager, its arm snapping upwards in answer to the release of the trigger. The rock it hurled made it perhaps three quarters of the way to the treeline, and the artillerists swore and began to make adjustments. Before their curses had even died away, the valley came alive to the sound of weapons discharging. The thuds of onager arms were intermingled with the snap of ballistas releasing, their cross-arms flattened, the bolt shot from its runner at immense speed.

No one in the world could match the Roman army for its artillery.

Initially, many of the shots went wild or fell short as the artillerists slowly found their range, but in a hundred heartbeats, the first rock disappeared deep into the trees. In moments, others joined it, and then finally the iron bolts began to strike their target too. Shot after shot vanished into the trees. It was not long at all before the first blood-curdling scream came in answer, and only moments before another joined it.

Maximus sat quietly, waiting, feeling the odd drop of rain but nothing more, listening to the groaning of wood and the huffing of oxen, the crack and thud of the artillery releasing, the occasional curse of the artillerists when something did not go quite according to plan, and the screams and hollers of men in the woods, Dacians standing forward of their lines to watch the Romans, repeatedly impaled with bolts or smashed to pieces by falling stones.

It was not long before the first accident. One of the artillery teams over-tightened their ballista just a little too much, and even as the trigger-man went to release, the spar snapped. The result was both impressive and horrifying. A cloud of flying debris, from foot-long timber splinters to twisted shards of metal, went in every direction, an expanding circle of death and dismemberment. Of the eight men at the ballista, three survived the explosion, two because they were down below the level of the cart, and the timber sides protected them, and one because he was a short distance back, collecting another box of bolts. Annoyingly, the explosion also took out two of the riders nearby, two men from the Second Pannonian, but from another turma, one of them suffering a lacerated leg and a horse that was rearing wildly, bleeding profusely from a wound in its flank, and the other down in an instant and crushed beneath his horse as it writhed in pain at the wooden shards that had ripped all the way along its right side.

Time for another quick prayer.

'Mighty Jove, brave Fortuna and powerful Mars,' Maximus said very quietly, 'let the machine close to me survive the barrage without breaking, and I vow a full jar of wine on the altar of each of you.'

He was going to have to stop spending money on divine bribes and replacement equipment soon. Since Duras took his purse, he seemed to be spending almost his entire wage just keeping things going, let alone spending it on nice or new things. He then chided himself for pondering such matters when he was sat waiting for a battle that he very well might not survive, and concentrated once more.

An hour passed, accompanied by the thuds and bangs, the distant screams, the sporadic individual drops of rain, and the murmured prayers of men all along the lines. As noon approached, though only the timekeeping call of the musicians made it clear, since the sun had yet to put in an appearance, the second ballista exploded. This one was some distance away, and all Maximus knew of it was the sound of the machine breaking and the screams of pain and dismay. Others went, though, as the afternoon rolled forwards, here and there a ballista or an onager.

Then, finally, someone along the line shouted 'listen!'

They did so, and Maximus was aware then of a strange, low rumble, not unlike the one that had accompanied the arrival of the artillery carts. But this was different. It was a constant drone rather than a single noise or sporadic sound. Some along the line were questioning what it was, asking one another, but not those like Maximus, who had been through this before, even in this very valley. It was the Dacians' greeting to the spirits of war.

Someone clearly anticipated what was happening now, and an order was sent out. Moments later, the artillery stopped loosing their bolts and stones, though the crews reloaded them ready, regardless.

'Hoooooooooom,' went the sound, inside the woodland, a deep tone formed by thousands of voices. 'Hoooooo……oooOOM!'

As the noise stopped, it ended with a crash that made many a man in the Roman lines jump, as every Dacian in there with a sword and shield or two weapons smacked them together in unison. It was deafening, and nerve-wracking. Maximus could see men already visibly shaking.

'Hoooo….OOOOMM!'

crash

'What the fuck is that?' a rider nearby said.

'Dacian warcry. Like the Barritus of the Germans.

'I nearly shat myself.'

'Save that for when he's coming at you with a falx,' Maximus advised with a wry smile.

'Hoom… hoom… HOOM… HOOM… HOOOOOM!'

crash

That was, to Maximus's mind, not only louder, but noticeably nearer. The army was moving towards them through the woods. Trajan's plan seemed to have worked. He had needled Decebalus with his artillery until the Dacian king snapped and sent his army forth. Maximus watched the treeline, tense with anticipation.

A single figure emerged a few moments later, from the narrow road that passed through the woods and formed the pass itself. One man on a horse, wearing a gleaming cuirass of bronze or gold, and an ornate helmet. He carried in one hand a spear decorated with coloured streamers, and in the other a draco. Maximus listened to that eerie sound. The dragon standard was used by both Dacian warlords and by Sarmatian riders, and it was just as unnerving whoever bore it. A metal dragon's head on a staff, hollow from mouth to back, and with a great long red tube of material extending from there, when held high on a moving horse, the tail streamed proud behind it, and the air, as it passed through the thing, made the weirdest, creepiest noise that echoed out across the valley, seemingly overriding all other noises.

The rider kicked his horse and raced towards the Romans, almost as though he intended to charge their lines. Indeed, some of the auxilia readied themselves to meet him, surprised at this bizarre audacity, but they did not have the chance. The rider hurtled forward until he was perhaps a bowshot away, and then drew his animal to a sharp halt, and used that momentum, in addition to his own, not unimpressive, overarm throw, to cast his streamered spear at the Roman lines. Before it even landed, he'd turned, bellowing a curse in his own tongue, and rode back towards the east.

Maximus was impressed. The spear struck one of the front auxiliary infantrymen in the leg, impaling him. He screamed and collapsed as his mates pulled him back up and ripped the weapon from his leg before helping him limp back through their lines, his place taken by another soldier.

'A bag of coins to the artilleryman who brings him down,' shouted a centurion from that unit, presumably the man's commander.

The men on the carts did not need telling twice. No senior officer had given the order to resume the barrage, but scores of ballistae and onagers released the shots they'd already primed, and a whole valley full of ammunition poured down on the lone rider as he cantered back towards the trees.

Maximus winced. Less than a quarter of the shot found their home, but that alone was enough to kill the man a hundred times over. He and his horse were peppered with iron bolts and pounded with rocks. A wild cheer went up all along the Roman lines, and the artillerists reloaded just in case.

'How many bags of coins have you got sir?' shouted a soldier down in the valley bottom, raising a round of laughter from the men around him.

The single heap of man and horse lay still on the turf, three quarters of the way from the Roman lines to the trees. Another single raindrop hit Maximus. The clouds had slowed, but they had darkened, and it almost looked like night in the valley now. Silence fell on the army once more, but the valley was not quiet for long.

'Hoooooom... HOO HOO HOO HOOOM!'

crash

The volume was far louder now, much closer.

Then the Dacians arrived. They began to emerge from the trees by the hundred, men of dozens of different tribes, nobles in their gleaming armour and peasants with a spear, warriors with falx and oval shield. No horsemen as yet, that Maximus could see anyway. He tried to get a good look at the men directly opposite, on their own flank, but he couldn't identify anything specific about them. They were Dacian, like the others.

He had to fight down the nerves, then. He was no coward, and certainly he would never back down from a fight like this, but at the sight of those men coming out of the trees, every blow, every struggle, every scream and every corpse from two other days in this valley, rose into the eye of his mind, bringing with them that terror and despair that always threatened to unman a warrior before battle. That was the thing. The politicians back in Rome who had never stood in a line like this thought that a man who did so and quailed was a coward; that a man who stood in the face of the enemy and shook, or whimpered, or even pissed himself... was a coward. Maximus, like all soldiers, knew the truth. Every man felt that fear. Every man, from a champion gladiator to the raw recruit of a new auxilia unit, felt terror in that moment before the action started. *Every* man. That was not cowardice. It was human nature. But when that man trembled, pissed himself, whimpered, and yet stood his ground, *that* was *bravery*. A man conquering his own fear and gritting his teeth as he fought, iron on iron, for survival, that was bravery.

Bravery asserted itself with Maximus, even as the next call went out. The artillery loosed a last volley, and then, their torsion spent, the oxen were urged forward, and the legionaries led their weapons back away from the forefront of the field of battle. All along the lines of the advancing Dacians, men fell to that final volley, but the lines did not stop, marching over the top of the dead. The wagons were out of the way efficiently, quickly, and the artillery were gone, safe. New calls went out, and the auxilia moved forward, forming their lines, both infantry and cavalry, in the wake of the retreating artillery.

Maximus edged his horse into place, sitting between Flaccus and Arvina, with Rigozus just three men along in his new crest, identifying him as an interim officer. The riders shuffled into position, readying themselves. Another movement caught Maximus's eye now, and he turned to look up the slope. They were not obvious, but every now and then he saw brief movement among the trees on the heights. The enemy archers and slingers were moving into position. They would not find it as easy as in previous years, for the legions had cleared the trees from the slopes as high as they reasonably could, and so now the Dacian missile troops were further away from the main fight in the valley bottom than they would like to be, but they would still be close enough to pour down shots at the flanks of the advancing Romans.

He made a decision there and then. Probably a stupid one, but a decision, nonetheless. He leaned forward and gestured to Rigozus. 'Pass the word. I need everyone in the turma to move to the rear. The other turmae can fill the gap.'

The man nodded professionally, which made Maximus smile. The day Bibula retired, this was the command dream team. Turning his horse, he looked at the ranks of riders behind him.

'Muster at the rear. I have a plan.'

Chapter Twelve

Maximus gripped his spear and shield tight, knuckles white. He held Ferox's reins in his left hand, sharing the grip with the shield, and cursed every time he tugged it and almost dropped one or the other. Normally he would rely on guiding with his knees, but the stupid horse had something of a tendency to drift. He looked over his shoulder, blinking away the rain. The other twenty-seven riders in his turma were right behind him, all armed and ready, and guiding their animals with considerably greater ease, by the look of it.

The slope was easy enough here, grassy and clear, with small knots of trees dotted about, though the ground was becoming a little slippery with the increasing wet. This high up the valley side, the legions had only removed trees they specifically needed, and a little higher up the incline that the trees began to form a true forest. As his gaze moved back to his right, and then ahead, he could see the battlefield laid out before him. Some of the troops were already engaged, and the fighting had begun, particularly in the middle, where the elite troops of both armies contested for the heart of the pass. But even on the near flank, the prefect would probably be cursing his absence now, as the Second Pannonian closed the last few paces with their enemy.

He could still see the prefect's expression in his mind's eye, passing through anger at his troops pulling out of the line, through denial and shock at Maximus's suggestion, and finally a grudging acceptance of it.

It did make sense, and it would make a difference.

Judging that they were at the right height now, he motioned with his spear and turned to the right, now facing east and riding *along* the valley side, rather than *up* it. Ahead, the trees still grew, where the legions had not reached with their deforestation, and amid them lay the ancient Dacian defences of the Iron Gates, leading from the valley bottom all the way to the peak.

The archers and slingers in those trees needed to be stopped. From their position, they were at liberty to send their missiles down into the battle at will, and given their height and the press of numbers below, they didn't even need to aim that hard. Send an arrow towards the huddled Roman forces and they were likely to find a target. Plus, the shelter of the trees would be keeping their bowstrings dry so far. There wouldn't be many more than a hundred of them, if he was any judge. There were comparatively few missile troops in the Dacian force anyway, and on both previous occasions at this pass, there had been fewer than two hundred archers and slingers in the heights on each side, though Rome had learned to its cost how much damage a hundred archers could do in half an hour, left unchecked. Decebalus would not want to put *all* his precious archers out on the wings ahead of his main army, in case what was about to happen happened, so many would still be held in reserve in the east.

Every rider knew his duty now, and every rider knew what they were up against, and should be prepared. No more orders. Just their execution.

This was the side of the valley with the main Dacian fortification. On the south, it was just a ditch and wall that protected the heights, no towers or enclosures. Here, though, the Dacians had built a citadel with three towers, the shape of a half moon, with a ditch and rampart running from there up the slope to the highest peak, in the forest, and another facing the valley outside the main fortress, like the lid beneath an eye, with another line stretching off down to the valley floor, behind the Dacian advance.

The archers and slingers would be at that lower rampart in the woods, and in front of it too, not up at the main fortress, from which their shots would not reach the field of battle. And that made a cavalry action possible, for they had no need to break into the fortress. They rode faster now, he setting the pace, for they were almost upon the Dacians. He could identify the shapes of towers among the trees in the distance, and finally spotted the lower rampart, hard to see though it was, through the rain and in the gloom of an almost night-time sky. He gave a tight smile, for he'd judged their height perfectly. They were riding at the level of the top end of that external rampart.

'Serpent tongue,' he called, the ala's code for a two pronged attack, and in response, Rigozus peeled off to the right, dropping down the slope just ten paces or so, half the riders following him, the rest staying behind Maximus. Perfect.

There it was. The outer rampart of the system was a simpler affair than the great defences of the citadel above, whose walls were formed of great square stones, built to more than twice the height of a man. This lower defence was only a preliminary obstacle, an outer face of ashlar blocks like the citadel, but only seven or eight feet high, backed by an earth bank with a flat wall walk above, and fronted by a narrow ditch. And it was open at the top and bottom, for its sole purpose was to pour missiles down on anyone attempting to seize the pass.

Into the trees, blessedly spaced sufficiently to ride between with relative ease, and even more so where the rampart arose.

As they closed, he began to see the shapes of archers and slingers, their arrows and stones whirring between the trees to fall upon the army below. Only when the danger was upon them did those scattered warriors begin to notice the thunder of hooves approaching from the other side, above them on the slope. Men began to turn then, to face the new danger. Some nocked arrows or placed fresh bullets in slings and began to whirl them, others cast aside their missile weapons and reached for their swords instead.

Maximus prayed to Mars and Jupiter again as he led the charge around the top end of the outer rampart. Here, they were within range of both the men they faced, and anyone standing on the walls of the citadel. He had taken the risk, presuming that missile troops and most warriors from up there would have been fielded in the battle, only a caretaker garrison left in the fortress, and he seemed to be correct, for as he bore down on the bank, no missiles came from the walls further up the slope. From the cavalry's high approach, it was a simple thing to canter up the bank behind the wall and to the walk where the archers and slingers stood.

The first archer was not ready for the attack, and hurriedly nocked an arrow, pulling his string back and raising the bow even as Maximus reached him, slamming out with his spear, punching it through the man's midriff so hard that it emerged from his back. The arrow left the bow at a low angle, thudding into the ground nearby.

The warrior screamed, but Maximus ignored him now, out of the fight as he was, and moved on, letting go of the spear and ripping free his sword with practised ease. The second archer had been more prepared and had that little bit more time, and managed to bring his bow up and loose an arrow before Maximus hit him. Fortunately, the Roman was prepared, and the shield dropped to the correct point, taking the arrow with a thud, the point driving through the board, worryingly close to his arm. He didn't bother with the sword this time, and simply rode the man down, bones crunching under Ferox's hooves as he moved on to his next target. His blade was red as he hefted it, though the rain was now penetrating the canopy of trees and had the red turning pink and streaming down the steel in trickles.

His men were with him now, catching up as he slowed with each engagement, and some raced past him to hit other archers and slingers. A Dacian ahead, unarmoured and bare headed, had dropped his leather sling and drawn an axe from his side, and as he bore down on the man, Maximus leaned forward and left in the saddle, throwing his shield in the way of the axe swing, protecting Ferox's neck from the blow. The blade bit deep into the wood, but while it was lodged there, Maximus brought his sword round and down, slamming it into the man's head. The bone cracked loudly under the blow, and blood sprayed out, fortunately kept from soaking Maximus by the ravaged shield.

The slinger fell away, and for a moment the Roman was free of opponents. He spared a breath to take stock, manoeuvring Ferox better onto the flat walkway, as the slope was becoming slippery now with the rain.

Left, he could see the fortress up the slope, a heavy shape looming in the stormy gloom with just a few figures on its walls, watching impotently. Ahead, his men were cutting down archers and slingers atop the rampart. Right, and he could see past the wall and the ditch to where Rigozus led the other half of the unit, racing between the trees and cutting down those Dacians who'd taken up position on the slope in front of the wall. And beyond that, through the sparse trees and under the dark clouds, he could see battle raging. At least it would be raging easier now, for the fall of rain might be increasing all the time, but the hail of arrows and bullets would have stopped. He urged Ferox into movement again now, dropping a little down the bank, to ride past where two of his men were busy hammering at one of the few Dacians who had a shield and wore a chain shirt.

He chose another target, but even as he did so, one of his men veered towards the archer. Maximus was about to find another victim when that archer let his arrow fly and the trooper, Vedius, took the missile to the throat, misfortune guiding it to the unprotected span between helmet and chain shirt. Vedius lolled in the saddle, choking his last, his horse veering wildly and then racing off down the slope, and so Maximus pressed on, hard. The archer tried to nock another arrow to bring down his next attacker, but there was insufficient time now, and once again, Maximus hit him hard and rode him down, churning the body beneath Ferox's hooves.

It was about to get all the more dangerous. Looking ahead, the archers and slingers were better prepared now, with more time to sort themselves out, and arrows were turning their way, slings whirling. He blinked away rain and urged

Ferox on hard, racing towards them, half a dozen other riders of the turma beside him. The cloud of missiles came, and Maximus hunched down behind shield, heavy with the axe still wedged there, and horse's neck. He felt something graze his thigh just above the knee, and the familiar white hot pain as the blood flowed free, heard and felt missile after missile thump into his shield, and then his world inverted as Ferox took a sling bullet to the forehead and died in an instant. The animal simply stopped moving while at a run and collapsed in a whirling leggy heap.

Maximus did all he could, throwing himself free as they hit the ground, and curling as tight as possible in an effort not to be ridden down by his own men as they passed. He held his sword out to the side and let go of his ruined shield, though not before it hit the ground and wrenched his shoulder painfully. He lay there for precious moments, waiting for death from one of the many sources. If a flying arrow or shot didn't do for him, then undoubtedly one of his troopers would accidentally ride him down, or perhaps the shuddering shape of Ferox would roll onto him and crush him.

Hooves thundered past, missiles cracked into trees or hit the body of Ferox with dull thumps, horses whinnied, men shouted and screamed, and all the time, beneath it, that insidious hiss of rain falling through leaves.

Maximus opened an eye.

He was alive.

His other eye flickered wide, and he moved his head, looking around. Ferox was still, and close by lay his shredded shield. He allowed himself just a moment of grief for the fallen beast. He'd been nothing but a pain in the arse from the start, but oddly, Maximus had discovered he'd grown quite fond of the idiot. The prefect wasn't going to be pleased at yet another horse chalked up to Maximus's carelessness.

He scanned the area. The ground all around him was churned by hooves into a parody of a furrowed field, this one sown with the dead. Bodies lay around here and there in rictus poses of agony, mostly Dacians, though with one or two bodies of cavalrymen among them, as well as the shapes of other horses, dead or dying. Slowly, still not trusting his body to be whole, Maximus rose to his feet and checked each limb and joint. He was not only alive, but mercifully unbroken, apart from a left shoulder that was excruciating if he moved his arm several ways. He twirled his sword, testing the movement, and discovered it was fine, and his mind was clear and regaining focus by the heartbeat. When he adjusted his helmet, it hurt, and so he removed it and peered at the outer. Not every horse had missed him, for a hoof had knocked a hefty dent into the thing. Great. Rufus was going to charge him an arm and a leg to hammer and polish that out. It seemed he was starting to have as much luck with helmets as with horses.

Ahead, the fight was still on, men of the Second Pannonian ploughing into the archers and slingers, mostly still on horseback, but two of them, like him, now on foot. Their swords rose and fell, the few still with spears lodging them in bodies and moving on, drawing blades. He was losing men in a slow but steady stream, but they were cutting down the Dacian missile troops in droves.

He spotted one archer, left for dead on the walkway near the wall and rising with a bloodied scalp, picking up his bow and looking around for an arrow. In a heartbeat Maximus was running, clambering up the slope with his sword ready, wincing with every judder in his other shoulder. To prevent too much unnecessary pain, he tucked his left hand into his belt as he ran, reducing the shoulder's movement. The archer saw him just as he nocked the arrow, and turned. Maximus panicked in that moment, realising that he was still too far away to take the man down before the arrow was released. He threw himself desperately to the left even as he ran, in the hope of dodging the missile, but Fortuna was with him, and there turned out to be no need. The archer pulled back the string, but the rain and the mud where bow and arrow had fallen had made them slippery, and as he let the string go, they slid, the arrow jerking upwards so that as the string snapped tight, the shaft went off almost vertically.

Praying that it didn't hit him when it came back down, point first, Maximus closed the last few paces and swung. His sword cut through the bow string and shattered the bow itself before lodging in the archer's upper arm. The man screamed and fell sideways, and the Roman almost left him then, for as an archer, he was done. But the man had already seemingly risen from the dead once to become a threat behind the turma's back, and it would be foolish to tempt fate and leave him to do the same again. Maximus took another step, pulled his sword back to the right, high, and then swung across and down. The blade slammed into the man's neck above the shoulder, cutting deep, a killing blow. As he pulled the sword free, blood fountained up, some of it splashing across Maximus's legs and boot. Ah well, there was nothing so sure as rain would clean them soon enough.

Stepping past the stricken, dying man, he reached the parapet once more and looked around. The fight on the wall top was almost over, most of the enemy lying bloodied and torn, but there had been a price, for bodies in red tunics lay here and there among the Dacians, and the men who were still fighting were as often on foot now as mounted. He looked out across the trees below, and Rigozus was having much the same fight. He and his riders had cleared out most of the archers on the slope, but again had lost a few men, though more of his remained mounted.

Maximus jogged along the wall walk, to where it turned and began to descend the slope towards the heart of the Dacian forces, and there stopped.

'No further,' he bellowed to his men. The last thing he wanted was for them to find themselves surrounded by angry Dacians at the bottom of the slope. They had neutralised the archers, and that was what they'd come for. Now they had to regroup and return to their lines. For a moment, he feared that Procullus was among the fallen, but then he spotted the musician, still mounted and holding his sword out so that the rain could clean it for him.

'Get back to the start of the rampart where we separated and sound the recall. Fast.'

Procullus nodded and started to ride, still gripping his half-clean sword. 'Back to open ground,' Maximus shouted to the other men who were still finishing off the last few missile troopers who'd stayed. A number had managed to flee, back into the Dacian lines, but they would not return here, after this slaughter, so they were of little concern now. He certainly wasn't going to chase them back to Decebalus's side. As his men turned and began to pull back, he leaned over the parapet and repeated the call, aiming it at the riders below, and then turned and began to run that way himself, still with one hand tucked into his belt and his sword in the other. His shoulder ached with every heavy footstep, but he ran on. They really could not afford to delay now, in case those men in the citadel decided to stream forth and join the fight.

By the time he was only a third of the way back, he could hear Procullus blowing the recall on his tuba, and already riders were pounding past him, those men on foot running to keep up. Reaching the end of the wall, breathing heavily, tired and achy, Maximus turned to see his men converging on him. He did a quick headcount as the last arrived. Nineteen. By gods that had been costly, and only twelve of those men had horses. One was Rigozus, and he waved to his second in command. 'Take all the mounted men and race back to the rear echelons. Find us eight replacement horses and then bring them back to the rear of the Second Pannonian's position on the wing. We'll meet you there.'

Rigozus nodded and called out, and he and the other eleven mounted troopers turned and raced away across the grass. Maximus turned to the other seven. 'We have a little time before he brings the horses, so let's make our way back down to the wing slowly and get our breath back.'

With that, they set off back down the slope at a steady pace, staying close together. Men cleaned swords and sheathed them, and those without helmets pulled up their scarves to keep the increasingly heavy rain from their scalps. Maximus just let the rain slick down his hair. His scarf was soaked with rain and blood, and the helmet he carried would not sit comfortably on his head now. The grass underfoot was treacherous, between the slope and the rain, and men kept slipping and staggering in the descent. He himself slid a short way at one point, and hissed in pain as his shoulder jerked when he stopped.

'Let me look at that,' Laenas said, suddenly next to him.

'It'll be alright.'

'I'll be the judge of that,' the capsarius said. 'Pull your hand free.'

He did so, and as they walked, the medic began to poke, prod, manipulate and examine his shoulder, without removing chain shirt or tunic. Maximus did his best not to yelp repeatedly, and succeeded some of the time. Finally, Laenas nodded. 'A sprain. Probably only a mild one, and certainly not a full tear. Hold your arm out.'

Maximus did so, wincing with the effort and the pain. Laenas untied his own scarf and pulled it free from his neck. He unfolded it to its full extent, and then pulled it round Maximus's shoulder. Once it was in place, he pulled it tight, which made the officer grunt, and then tied it. 'The rain will soak it through, so by the time we get back halfway down, I'll re-tie it tighter. Reach your arm up in the air, bend your elbow and put your palm on the back of your head.'

'What?'

'Just do it.'

He did so, and even in the first few moments marvelled that the pain lessened noticeably. 'Feels good.'

'Keep it like that whenever you can. That's the best I can do for now. When the fighting's over, shout me and we'll remove your armour, apply some raw onion and cold water for a time, and then bind it properly. Ten days, fifteen at the most, and it should be back to normal.'

'Thanks.'

The capsarius moved on, looking for his next patient among the dismounted riders. Maximus peered out into the deluge, trying to take stock. Rome certainly had the numerical advantage, and he could see that straight away. The far wing seemed to be faltering a little, probably because the enemy archers and slingers were still active on the slope at that side of the field, while at this side, the three alae were pushing hard, suffering no assault from above. In the centre, the fighting had already become truly fierce, the infantry of both sides busily hacking and smashing at one another in the press, auxiliaries and German clubmen battering at warriors of a dozen different Dacian tribes, who battered them in return.

There was a very distant rumble. The rain they were suffering right now was little more than a preamble, for the main storm was on the way. As they descended, they began to angle a little westwards, away from the Dacian forces. They would have to meet Rigozus and collect the spare horses behind the main lines of combat before they thought about more action, for the last place they wanted to be found dismounted was between Dacian warriors and Roman cavalry.

He looked at the clash while he still had the height advantage. It was hard to make out much detail, especially in the downpour, but the fighting was fierce, and the cavalry were being seriously put to the test. The Ala Bosporanorum had tried to flank the Dacians, as planned, where they could use the skirmishing skills of light cavalry to pare away the lines of the enemy, but those lines were dense and had been sent out at precisely the correct position to block access, for the bottom end of that same rampart where Maximus had just been fighting reached down to connect with the Dacian forces. The valley was too narrow. There would be no flanking. Just like last time, and the time before, this would come down to simply pushing forward and carving meat, and hoping *you* were doing it faster, harder and more efficiently than *they* were.

There was no such thing as a shieldwall when cavalry fought, and the Dacians were no proponent of the tactic, and so what was happening on the wing was best described as a brawl or a melee. The two armies had met and merged, pushing into one another so that now Dacians were visible in numbers among the horsemen, laying about themselves brutally with falx and spear, axe and sword, behind the nominal front line, while Roman horsemen were clearly visible among the press of Dacians, behind their own front line, too. No tactics, no organisation, just killing.

His gaze swept across the mess, and he paused, brow furrowed.

'Flaccus?'

'Sir?'

'Do you remember the Buri, and the wolf pelt?'

'Vividly, sir.'

'When we visited them in their camp, I got a fairly good look at everything – we were supposed to be gathering information, after all – but in this bloody rain it's quite hard to see. Look at the Dacians on this flank, fighting our ala.'

'Yes?'

'There are a couple of banners waving around there. Look a bit like a Roman vexillum, but with a dagged edge at the bottom. Can you see them?'

'Yes sir. Red, sir. Some sort of symbol on them.'

'Does it look like a badly-drawn horse, in gold?'

'I'd say it does, yes, sir.'

Maximus allowed an entirely unfriendly smile to slide across his face. 'I think we're facing the Buri. Well, well, what a coincidence.'

'I thought the Buri didn't want to fight, sir?'

'Look at where they are. On the flank, a distance away from Decebalus's important troops at the centre, where they can do the least harm. And facing cavalry who the Dacian king will expect to brutalise them. And they're jammed between his more trusted troops and the fortifications that lead up the hill to the citadel, where the garrison and the archers could keep an eye on them, and where if any arrows fall on their own side, it's only the Buri. I don't think they wanted to be involved in this at all, but Decebalus doesn't trust them now, so he compelled them to fight and put them in a position where they were going to get battered. But because of that, I reckon they feel they have a lot to prove. So in some ways, because they don't want to fight at all, they're having to fight harder than anyone else.'

'Gods, sir, but your brain works in spirals. Is that how they choose officers, sir? Thinking like that?'

'That, and a blind willingness to do stupidly dangerous things, yes.'

Another rumble, this time louder, drew his attention and he turned. The thunder told him the storm was behind the hills, slightly north of west. 'Sounds to me like Jupiter himself is coming to join the fight,' he murmured with that same martial smile.

'No one down there seems to have noticed,' Flaccus replied.

'That's because they're busy making a lot of noise themselves and the thunder's still distant. Once we get involved, we won't hear it either, but pretty soon *everyone* will hear it. That's breaking our way.'

'I fucking hope there's no lightning,' Flaccus muttered. 'I'm not feeling very divine, and I've no seal skin to protect me.'

Maximus's gaze slid from those dark hills beneath the grey, roiling sky, across to the Roman forces, gradually filtering forward where they could, the legions moving into position, ready to commit to the fight the moment their generals gave the order. A familiar group of figures were moving along the lowest slope of the valley, heading for the fight and leading a number of spare horses in their wake.

'Rigozus is on the way,' Maximus announced. 'Come on, lads, let's pick up the pace, now.'

As he did so, Laenas was at his side again, pulling his arm painfully down, untying and retying the scarf tightly enough to make him wince. When he was done, Maximus went to raise his arm again, but decided against it. He was coming back down among the legions and auxilia now and didn't want to look either like an idiot or like he was trying to ask a question. They met with Rigozus and the others just a hundred paces behind the fighting alae on the flank, and as Maximus mounted once more, praying that his new steed would last longer than his predecessors, he caught a flash in the sky, barely visible over the northwest slope. As he climbed into the saddle, he counted a number of heartbeats. Ten beats later there came a rumble of thunder that he could only just hear over the din of battle.

'Two miles away,' he said.

'What's that?' Rigozus asked.

'The storm. Two miles away now, and getting closer all the time.'

'How can you tell?'

'Did your father never tell you anything? Count the heartbeats between the flash and the crack, and divide it by five. That's how many miles away Jupiter's dropping his thunderbolts.'

Rigozus shrugged. 'We're going to get caught in it, then. No way this fight's finishing before nightfall.'

But an idea was creeping into Maximus's mind, and his grin returned. 'I'm not so sure. I think there might be a way to finish this earlier, especially now that mighty Jupiter himself has come to give us a hand.'

Chapter Thirteen

Maximus rode steadily alongside Rigozus, Arvina on the far side. The rest of the turma rode behind, rain lashing down, hammering off their weapons and armour, soaking their clothes. Maximus would have liked to have been the focus of this little display himself, really, especially since it was his idea in the first place, but he had to admit that he was not the most imposing of men, being a little over five feet and of a small, wiry build. His Moesian friend, on the other hand, was a strapping six and a half feet, with a chest wider than a hand cart, a colossus of a man. But it had been the garb that clinched it. Maximus rode in drenched clothing with a sodden binding around his shoulder, while Rigozus had somehow managed to get himself so soaked in blood during the encounter in the trees that he was more red than flesh, and though the rain was slowly working on that, so far all it was doing was making the crusty crimson run in rivulets which was, if anything, *more* horrible.

Not that such things mattered anyway, face-wise at least. As they'd hurried back towards the lines of battle, those riders who had them had fished out their steel face masks, and the three riders at the front had borrowed them from the others. The masks were usually donned only for show – for parades and ceremonies, for the cavalry sports events and the like. There was something eerie and austere about a gleaming steel face with a set expression. Children tended to flinch and run away when they saw them. To add to the image, they had draped a red wool scarf over the man's helmet in the manner of a priest, a symbol even the Dacians would recognise. To complete the image, Rigozus had been handed a spear, and, taking their cue from the enemy, they had torn strips of red wool from tunics and scarves and tied them to the spear so that they streamed from it as he rode.

Twenty bloodstained riders, many wearing facemasks, the three at the fore implacable and proud, riding in a truncated diamond formation. Now it was all about timing and the impression they gave off. This was a show. Their hooved churned already muddy wet ground as the advanced. They were approaching the lines of the cavalry now, and could hear the front rows already screaming and shouting, the whinnying of horses, the clash of iron and bronze. From the rear of their formation, Flaccus's voice led them.

'Jove!' he shouted.

In response, the entire twenty-man unit counted five heartbeats under their breath, and then bellowed in unison at the top of their voice.

'JUPITER... OPTIMUS... MAXIMUS...'

And on cue, the next crack of thunder broke across the valley. This time it was close enough and loud enough that a sizeable part of the Roman force, those a little back from the action, heard it.

Men at the rear of the cavalry alae turned, white faced.

As the rumbles still echoed among the hills, Rigozus bellowed on his own, his voice powerful, added an eerie otherworldliness by the steel mask from which it emerged.

'JUPITER TONANS!'

Tonans. The 'thunderer.' Jupiter in his aspect as lord of storms and caster of lightning bolts.

Maximus had been prepared to force a path to the front with sound alone. He was ready to shout an order for the riders to move aside for them, and even had Procullus with his tuba out ready, but it turned out there was no need. As they approached the alae, those awe-struck riders at the rear simply peeled aside like the tide ebbing from a causeway, away from these riders of Jupiter.

They trotted forward at a steady pace, keeping formation, almost like some sort of parade, solemn, silent, implacable as the rain bounced from them endlessly, and the riders of the

Second Pannonian melted out of their way as they approached. Maximus briefly caught sight of the prefect, safely off with a group of other senior officers behind the next ala, and the man's face was a picture. If this went badly, it would probably be the end of Maximus's career, or so that expression suggested. On the other hand, if it went well, the prefect would claim the credit, and all would be fine.

'Jove.'

Flaccus's voice. The thunder was coming fast now, with not much pause between strikes.

Four seconds, hoping the timing was still good.

'JUPITER... OPTIMUS... MAXIMUS...'

This time, the crash was much closer, seemingly coming from the baggage train just behind the army. It was, Maximus had to admit, truly unnerving. The way the black and grey clouds boiled and churned in the sky suggested the god was just above them, stirring to life. And when the thunder boomed, it was not one simple bang, but because of the nature of valleys, the sound bounced from slope to slope, echoing off into the distance. It put the shits up Maximus, and *he* knew that it was he and his men putting on the show, almost as much as nature and the god himself. He could only imagine how it felt to other people, especially the more pious or superstitious among them.

'JUPITER TONANS!'

The metallic hollow voice of their front rider.

The last echoes of thunder died away, and Rigozus's voice followed them, bouncing around the valley, for the din of battle had ebbed a little, so many men now paying attention to the small unit of riders in their midst. They were halfway to the front of the Roman lines now. Men were still peeling out of the way, though with more difficulty as the press became thicker. Behind, he knew, they would be closing ranks once more, so that the twenty men formed a small clearing that moved with them through the army.

This time, Maximus didn't need the warning. In fact, he saw the flash of the lightning before Flaccus warned them, for it reflected off helmets and armour, spears and swords, standards and shield bosses. The flash was almost dazzling even in a thousand small reflections. The sky boiled and churned. The army parted. The twenty men rode on, counting to three now.

'JUPITER... OPTIMUS... MAXIMUS...'
Pause.
'JUPITER TONANS!'

He could see the fighting now. One more crash. That was all they needed.

The front ranks pulled apart with a little more difficulty. Inside his mask, Maximus grinned maniacally. The timing was perfect. It couldn't have been better if he'd been able to give the lord of thunder the cue himself.

Flash.

The last of the Romans pulled out of the way, leaving Dacian warriors, confused, nervous and uncertain, looking into a clearing with the masked and bloodstained Roman riders bearing down on them in formation.

'JUPITER... OPTIMUS... MAXIMUS...'
The shortest of pauses.
'JUPITER TONANS!'

Even though Rigozus had been bellowing this at the top of his voice throughout, somehow he managed to find extra volume now, knowing this was their moment, and left that last syllable hanging in the air as he thrust that red-streamered spear towards the enemy lines, then lowered it to a killing angle, and charged. They were all ready for it. The men of the Turma of Tiberius Claudius Maximus each put heels to flanks and commanded their horses to run.

They charged across that last open stretch and into the ranks of the Buri, the lines of Roman cavalry closing up behind them once more, presenting an indomitable front. The only one with a spear, Rigozus made it count, identifying a noble among the enemy by his high quality armour and helmet, and he planted the spear in the man's chest at full tilt, impaling him and letting go of the spear the moment it punched through, to draw his sword like the rest of the unit and go to work, the fury of Jupiter made manifest.

This was no careful, organised conflict. What happened among the Buri, then, was the chaos of battle, Mars laughing madly in a hail of blood and mighty Jove casting his bolts as they rode their horses in among the infantry, swords rising and falling, blood spraying up into the air, men falling in droves. Maximus saw the world through watering eyes as the continual pains with every jerk to his left shoulder sent waves to his brain. Yet he clenched his teeth and ignored the aches, putting his active mind on hold as the instinct of war took over.

Because he'd been here before.

Tapae: the place of blood and horror and death. A third time now, sitting ahorse in this valley, carving men to meat and hoping his steed didn't fail beneath him. It was all so horribly familiar. Every blow brought back those earlier times. A sword strike down at a terrified Buri warrior with a blue shield, cleaving his shoulder, and suddenly it was a bright spring morning fifteen years ago, fighting desperately for survival, knowing they'd lost and just hoping someone had the sense to sound the retreat. A slash out at a wide-eyed face, and now it was high summer, sizzling hot, thirteen years ago, bringing vengeance to the Iron Gates for that ignominious defeat.

And now it was autumn again, and the rain hammered down so hard it felt like sword blows to a man's helmet and armour, the ground already churned to thick mud, the hiss of rain through leaves nearby almost as loud as the fight.

The flash and crash of Jupiter's ire was upon them now, above them and all around them, bouncing from the valley sides, flashing from armour and blades, and amid the seemingly endless killing, Maximus became dimly aware that the entire army behind them were continuing the bellowed chant to the king of the gods.

'JUPITER... OPTIMUS... MAXIMUS...'

A blade caught him in the leg, but like the last time it was a flesh wound, just a little cut that could be stitched. He felt the hot pain, then the pummelling cold as the rain battered the open wound, oddly calming it. Something else caught his other knee, but did not draw blood. His horse was injured now, but only a scratch on his shoulder. He prayed the animal made it through, partially for the good of the beast itself, but also because he'd lost three horses now in a matter of months, and that was the sort of thing that earned a man a reputation, or worse: a nickname. Losing a fourth would clinch it. It was, perhaps, telling about his expectations that he'd not even bothered learning this one's name. He was still distressed over the loss of Celeris, and had been more saddened than he had expected when Ferox died. To become familiar with a horse was to care, and to care was to set himself up for loss and sadness. He may never learn the name of a horse again.

Still, they fought on. It was automatic at this point. Mechanical butchery, sword up, sword down, sword out, sword back, feel pain, ignore pain, find target, identify weakness, and then back to sword up, sword down. Once upon a time, a lifetime ago, he'd decided to try and count the souls he took on the battlefield, but he'd given up such a notion at First Tapae, and now he couldn't have said how many he'd killed just in the last hundred heartbeats.

Something thumped into his side, and he knew it would bruise, but by the time he turned, sword raised, the man who must have been responsible was falling, a Roman spear in his chest. And then, oddly, no one was hitting him. He swung his sword and caught a man, and as he fell there was no one behind him. He paused, and let that red fog of war start to clear from his mind and vision, focusing once more, bringing his conscious mind back from where he'd put it aside in order to kill without mercy.

The Buri were running.

Over the ongoing sounds of battle and the batter and hiss of rain, the rumble of thunder and the sound of desperate horses, he could hear the chanting to Jupiter from behind, and a slow smile reached his lips. Mighty Jupiter had been with them throughout. Trajan had told the Buri that the god would be here in his message. At that time, riding into the enemy camp as an embassy, Maximus had thought it mere rhetoric, but it seemed it had been true. The emperor had seen it on that day of the sacrifices near the Danubius. He had seen it in the favour of the gods, and he had even seen it in Duras falling in the blood amid the reverent silence. And while Maximus had capitalised on it with his little show, bringing Jupiter's might directly into the face of the Buri, it had to be true. The greatest god in all the world had been with them this time at Tapae.

Decebalus was no fool, though. The Buri may have been put to flight, but the king of Dacia had already been prepared for either treachery or cowardice on their part, and that had been the reason for their placement in the field. Even as the three alae on the left flank whooped and moved forward to take advantage of the gap, Dacians from another tribe were moving out and forward from the centre rear to block the way.

Through the eyeholes of his silvered mask, Maximus could see them, strong warriors running to face the riders. They were fearsome, these Dacians, as he knew of old. The wealthy were there, the nobles in their peaked bronze helmets and chain or scale shirts, wielding powerful swords. So were the bearded, wild-haired warriors of the mountains, their locks loose or held back with thongs or headscarves, garbed in tunic and trousers, their axes and swords accompanied by brightly coloured shields with intricate floral designs. Or, perhaps worst of all, those broad-chested killers stripped to the waist, hair and beard wild, with a great two-handed falx held high, ready to cut a man in half.

But for all their power and fearsome appearance, a closer look showed the crack in their armour, the loose mortar in the wall of their strength. Even as they ran, screaming war cries, Maximus could see uncertainty in their faces. They may not have fled like the Buri, but they too feared Jupiter's wrath, and they too recognised that they were now fighting more than just Romans in the pass of the Iron Gates.

Publius Claudius Arvina was next to him, suddenly, the strange young Roman already now fully part of the turma. His left arm hung limp at his side, blood coating the limb below the elbow, but his right gripped his sword tight, ready to fight on.

'Force the flank,' someone shouted from behind, an officer, clearly. 'Widen the breach!'

That was what they needed to do. The Buri had fled, but Decebalus was trying to fill the gap with his warriors. The army of Rome needed to prevent them doing so effectively, keep a breach in the enemy lines. Bellowing Jupiter's name once again, the turma joined the other alae on the left flank in pressing their advantage. Heedless of the danger, they charged once more into the Dacian ranks, the third time that day. Maximus swept his sword out at a warrior with a yellow shield. His blow was powerful enough, given the momentum of the horse, that it sheared through the hide edging and shattered the boards, taking a large piece from the warrior's bicep in its passage. The man howled, and swung his axe even as he staggered. For a few moments as the warrior fell away, Maximus thought the man had missed. Then his horse faltered.

With a sinking feeling, Maximus took a deep breath and adjusted his posture. Sure enough, a moment later, the animal slumped forwards, and Maximus, prepared, threw himself from the saddle. At least he'd been ready for it this time, and instead of rolling into a ball to protect himself, he landed on his feet, staggering for a moment, and then righting himself as the horse lurched and fell onto its side, that axe still buried deep in its chest.

He heard his name bellowed, and turned at the warning, in time to see a bare-chested Dacian leaping at him, a horrifying two-handed falx raised for a killing blow. Panic gripped him for a moment. There was nothing that could protect him from that thing right now. A one-handed falx could punch through iron and cleave wood. The *two*-handed variety was a nightmare. Even if he'd had a shield and a working arm with which to use it, the falx would simply slice through it, arm and all, probably. His helmet might not save him, either. The infantry had begun to adopt a reinforcing cross-piece of iron or bronze atop their headgear to help rob a falx blow of its strength, but they were not yet common on cavalry helmets, for few riders would be close enough to the ground to suffer such a strike. He knew first-hand what a falx could do to a helmet. Knowing he couldn't *stop* the blade, and so all there was left was to *avoid* it, he threw himself to the left, while he lifted his sword to parry.

The falx struck with the power of a falling wall, and knocked Maximus's blade to the side easily, actually shearing some of the razor edging away in a cloud of sparks. But it was enough. The parry had been sufficient to prevent the dreaded weapon robbing him of his life, by razor edge or deadly point. Glancing from his cavalry sword, the weapon thudded down to the ground, point sinking deep into the soft, wet earth.

Maximus, now on his knees, reacted on instinct, throwing himself forward and swinging his sword in the only direction it would go after the parry. It swept out a hand-breadth from the ground, and sank into the Dacian's ankle with a distinct crunch. The man howled, and let go of his falx, leaving it protruding from the ground as he fell back, his leg ruined. There was no time to breathe, though, for two men took his place in an instant, one hammering down at Maximus with a shorter, one-handed falx, shield held protectively in front of him, while a second man leapt forward axe in one hand a sword in the other, bringing the former back ready to swing. There was a horrible moment, then, when Maximus knew he could only defend against one of the men, for both were coming at once, and it seemed little more than a choice of how he preferred to die.

Arvina, now also unhorsed, saved him, the man's sword catching the two-weaponed Dacian in the side even as he leapt to attack, sending him spinning and flailing away. Saved having to make the decision, Maximus blocked the falling curved falx with his sword, twisting his wrist and sending that man's blade aside, and then stepped forward to counterattack. The man brought his shield up to protect his body, and Maximus took advantage of that, slamming his boot down on top of the man's foot, hard enough to break every bone in it.

The Dacian howled and wobbled, head tilting forward as he looked down at his broken appendage, and as he did so, Maximus lashed out with a headbutt, catching the man squarely on the scalp. The warrior made a strange squawking sound and collapsed like a badly-mortared pillar. Maximus turned, to see that Arvina had taken down the other man, but was panting with pain, blood running in a gentle trickle from the dangling arm.

'Get to the medics, man, and have that seen to, before you bleed out.'

Arvina paused for only a moment, then nodded and turned, limping away and cradling his wounded arm. In the momentary lull, Maximus looked around. It was getting distinctly hard to see, between the restriction of the cavalry mask's eye holes, the sweat inside and the torrential rain outside. With a little difficulty, still gripping his sword, he pulled the mask free of its catches and lifted it away. He tried to think of somewhere to secure it for now, and then gave up and simply dropped it into the mud. He seemed to be riding a new horse every couple of days and buying replacement equipment more often than he ate meals anyway. What was one more face mask? Damnit, but he'd lost a fourth horse, after all.

Freed of the steel confines, he allowed the rain to slap him repeatedly in the face, while breathing deeply of the open air, which, even though it smelled of blood and shit and death, was still a relief after his own stifled breath inside that mask for half an hour or more.

He looked around. His turma seemed to be faring pretty well, all things considered. He could see Arvina, wounded but alive, lurching back towards the medics. Rigozus was still mounted and laying about himself with wild abandon, felling Dacians. Arrianus and Azimus, the two Syrians, stood back to back, each still fighting hard. Rufus was trying to back away from the fight, apparently with a leg wound, for a man from another turma with a broken arm was trying to help him, dragging his foot as he was. There were losses evident, too, though. The body of Macula lay carved and broken, and Procullus lay in a bloodied heap next to his horse, tuba fallen away and crushed by a passing hoof. The unit was going to need a new musician, and good musicians were hard to come by. The others all seemed to be up and struggling, some of them bloodied and limping, but alive. He could hope for little more on a day like this.

His attention then went from the men to the weather and to the landscape.

The storm was already moving on, heading southeast across the hills. Just a count of the latest flash and rumble confirmed that the heart of the storm was already half a mile away, and moving fast. The rain was still here, though, settled in for the day and lashing down in torrents. The ground underfoot was becoming increasingly boggy, churned by feet and hooves from turf to soupy, clinging mud.

But he could see the Iron Gates pass, to the east!

Between the mass of Dacians, who continued to fight hard, and that rampart and ditch that climbed the northern slope to the citadel, there was actually a gap. He frowned. There should still be enough Dacians to close that gap, so why was it open? Blinking into the downpour, he followed his instincts. With a little squinting and searching he found them. Myriad figures on the northern slope, men having left the battlefield, scrambling up to the relative safety of the hilltop fortress. And then, looking in the other direction, to the east through that gap, he could see them. Distant figures moving away along the pass, just small shapes already, for they had been departing from the moment the Buri had broken, if not before.

The Dacians were pulling out.

He took a deep breath. It was far from over, for Decebalus had covered the retreat of the bulk of his surviving forces by sending men in to die, just to distract the Romans. He was a wily bastard, the king of Dacia.

Then war came back to Maximus, for those brave and doomed Dacian warriors, who had stood their ground to save their departing comrades, bellowed their war cries and curses, and threw themselves at their foe to the last.

Maximus found that his men, injured and exhausted as they were, were equal to the task, for even as the Dacians came on with renewed fury, the men of his turma fell in beside him. Only Rigozus and Falco were still mounted, and they took the flanks, where the other turmae of the Second Pannonian, and men of other alae too, joined them now, unit cohesion more or less forgotten in the chaos. He saw Laenas the medic, his helmet gone and a red line carved down cheek and jaw, settling into a warlike stance, sword at the ready. Maximus took a deep breath, and then the Dacians hit them again.

An axe struck the right shoulder of his chain shirt, where it still bore the gleaming signs of recent repair from that engagement with the Roxolani. The links compacted, the shirt robbing the blow of its strength, leaving just enough impact to bruise. Maximus cursed. He could rather do without losing the ready use of *both* shoulders.

As the axe continued outwards on its path, Maximus cut with his sword in a backhand, up and right, catching the warrior in the midriff, just above the hip, and cutting through shirt and flesh together until it hit the ribs and grated free, sending blood and entrails flying in scattered gore. The man fell back, his cry lost amid the din of battle. Again, the mechanics of war took over, and Maximus found himself stepping back and to the side when there was room, swinging and chopping, parrying and cursing. Another piece taken out of his left forearm, another thump to his side that would bruise. A falx coming from an unexpected direction almost finished him, and only an instinct to lean back saved him as that brutal curved tip took a tiny nick out of his chin in its passage. The falx wielder joined his fellows on the ground a moment later, Maximus's sword in his chest, and the Roman discovered to his surprise that he was weary enough that he simply couldn't pull the sword free. He hadn't the strength. He placed a boot on the Dacian's body and gripped his sword hilt with both hands and pulled. The blade came free with a horrible sucking sound, and blood fountained up in its wake. He lifted it with both hands in time to parry another blow and just managed to swing it enough to catch the man on the arm, sending him spiralling away.

There were no more.

Maximus staggered, sword dropping in tired arms, and he watched the last survivors of that wave of warriors leaving the field. He turned. His men were still with him, though they'd lost at least one more, he suspected. He couldn't be sure. He was too tired, and his mind spinning, and he simply couldn't keep count right now. He let go of his sword with one hand, allowing it to fall to his side, and stood there, breathing deeply, trembling in the rain.

Someone from another unit a few paces away shouted 'after them,' but no one responded. The fool. No one was going to chase the Dacians down. Not now. Decebalus had been careful today, and clever. He'd fought hard, but the moment he knew it was over, even before the Romans had realised that, he'd begun the process of pulling back, sending his reserves and rear ranks away, probably even before the Buri had fled. Then he'd continued to abandon the field, sending a veneer of warriors to keep the battle going, to allow them time to pull back.

'It's over,' a man said, his voice a thing of wonder. 'It's fucking *over*.'

It wasn't. Not quite.

'It's over,' Flaccus breathed nearby, echoing the man.

Maximus shook his head, wearily.

'What?'

He took a deep breath. 'It's just beginning. We beat Decebalus here. *This* fight is won, but many of them got away. He'll pull back into his mountains now. You've no idea, my friend. I've *seen* their mountain fortresses, years ago. We've just committed to a long war, I fear.'

'But at least we won *here*,' a man from another turma interrupted. 'I mean, the Iron Gates are ours. The road into Dacia is open.'

Maximus's gaze rose to the left, up to that towered fortress on the valley's northern slope. He'd seen hundreds of figures swarming up that hill from the battlefield, running to take shelter in the Iron Gates' citadel.

'It's not open yet.' He pointed upwards. 'We have to take *that* before we can claim the pass.'

Around him, every pair of eyes lifted to fall upon the hilltop fortress.

'Bollocks,' said Rigozus, with feeling, then turned a weary smile on Maximus. 'By the way, I see you lost another horse.'

Chapter Fourteen

Tapae, September AD 101

'Why are we here?' Rigozus grumbled.

Maximus looked around the hillside. At least the rain had stopped, so visibility was easier. 'They like to have cavalry around to run down escapees,' he said.

The Dacian fortress stood stocky and defiant on the hillside amid the trees. There could be as many as a thousand Dacians in there, and almost certainly they included many archers and slingers who'd either fled Maximus's lightning attack or had been held in reserve, where they could easily retreat to the safety of the walls. There was no sense of urgency in the assault. Rome had won the field of Tapae, and the pass was more or less theirs, with just this pimple to squeeze. Decebalus had taken the bulk of his surviving forces east, at that speed only practised by a loser with the victor at his heel.

He would fortify the mountains at the heart of his kingdom, and digging him out from there would be like opening a recalcitrant oyster with a sponge. And it was September, too. The whole army knew what that meant. There might be a little more action, on a smaller scale, consolidating a position of control over the region, but the campaign season ended any time now, and no Roman general, no matter how hungry for glory, would take an army into the mountains of central Dacia in winter. Small actions, small sieges, building forts and roads. Control.

So the cavalry alae who had so valiantly held the left flank had been sent up to the Dacian citadel on the northern slope, to keep it penned while they waited for the assault force, and they had split into the three separate alae. The First Bosporanorum had taken the eastern side, the most likely angle from which the fortress's occupants could flee, heading to join their departing army. The Gallorum Flaviana had moved up into the most difficult area, the northern slopes above the fortress, where the trees were thicker and cavalry action more difficult. Since the southern approach was the pass itself, which was filled with the armies of Rome, that left only the west, to which the Second Pannonian had been assigned, due to their familiarity with the outer defences there. It was considered the least likely position from which the enemy might leave, given that it would be heading further and further away from the Dacian heartland if they did.

But no one had tried to leave anyway, which was foolish, really. They should never have shut themselves up in there in the first place, for they had then merely delayed the inevitable. Rome was hardly going to walk off and leave them in there. The moment the battle was lost and Decebalus had taken his survivors east, these men should have realised the futility of manning the fortress and fled east before the cavalry cordon could be established.

But they had not. The panic and dismay at having failed to hold the critical Iron Gates had gripped them, and they had shut up tight and set their own fate, essentially sealing themselves in a battlemented tomb.

His gaze slid down the slope.

A tomb about to be opened and plundered.

The legions were on the way. The auxilia were too busy back down the hill, for the cost to Rome had been high, and the medical sections would be working well into the night. The legions, who had been kept out of it in reserve, were fresh and untouched, and now stomped up the hill, either in their eight-man tent parties, or carrying equipment, including one massive battering ram formed from a tree trunk and ropes. Maximus did not envy them carrying that thing even a hundred paces up this slope. Not a pleasant task, that.

The fortress was formed of heavy stone walls in the shape of a D, with the curve facing west. A tower sat at the lower corner, overlooking the pass, and another at the upper corner, from which another wall and ditch ran up the slope. There were two gates, one to the east, as one would expect from a fortification protecting against attack from the west, but also one in that curved western approach, in order to provide access to those exterior ramparts from which they had earlier cleared the archers.

Indeed, as the ala sat, spread out across the slope to the west, they could see the bodies of fallen comrades and Dacians alike amid the trees, evidence of the first action they had seen at Tapae.

'They're not going to come this way,' Rigozus shrugged. 'That would be stupid.'

'I think you might be surprised. The legions are going to try and force the gate on the far side. The approach is easier, for one thing, and it is the main gate. And they, like you, think the Dacians won't come this way. But they're wily people, my friend. It's my thinking that the moment it looks like the fortress will fall, they're going to try and break out here, where the legions will be less concentrated.'

'Makes sense,' Rigozus nodded. 'As much sense as anything they do now makes, anyway. The fools.'

'It *would* be considerably better for everyone if they surrendered,' Arvina noted, wincing as he moved his bandaged and splinted arm in its sling.

'They'll not surrender unless they have no other choice,' Maximus said. 'Decebalus will have drilled into all his people the worst possible outcomes of failure. They will believe that their best ending if they surrender will be a short life in chains down a mine or in a quarry, and the worst: torture and death, probably by crucifixion. Of course, that's not far from the truth. I doubt this new emperor is going to give them the favourable deal Domitian did. No, they'll not surrender. They'll fight to the end.'

The legions were moving in now, crashing through the trees. The ram had gone round to the east, out of sight on the far side of the fortress. Siege ladders were being brought up too, as well as grapples on ropes.

'I don't recognise their shields,' Rigozus muttered, watching the legions as they settled into units ready to begin the assault, scorpion bolt-throwers placed on the best ground possible, ready to try and pin any figures on the wall and tower tops.

'They'll be the new legions. The emperor raised two new ones for the war, the Second Traiana and the Thirtieth Ulpia. I suspect he's giving them a chance to prove themselves to the other veteran legions in the army. It may be a foregone conclusion, given they have a ten to one advantage, but it'll still be a fight.'

They watched, then, as a horn call rang out from the valley below, and the legions started to move, centurions' whistles accompanied by their shouts, and those of the optios, the dipping of standard joining in, all directing the assault.

It began with the scorpions, with the clack and thud of bolts being released, then the clatter and ratchet of the weapons being hurriedly reset and reloaded. The first volley was, perhaps, unexpected by the enemy. The legions may be new, but they had not wanted for training, and twenty bolts slammed up at the wall tops, few aimed poorly. Maximus could only see the seven scorpions aimed around this curved wall, but, of those, three took figures on the parapet, sending them back with shrieks, to fall inside the walls. The figures tried to drop out of sight when the second volley came, but some misjudged, and once again one of the bolts took a warrior on the curved wall in the face.

By the third volley, the defenders had learned the signs, the sounds, and the routine, and ducked behind their parapet to avoid the bolts. Still, the artillery kept up the barrage, and to the watching riders, the reason was clear. Even as bolt after bolt swept over the wall top or clattered against the defences, the infantry were on the move. Split into centuries, they were advancing. The strongest attack would be at the main gate on the far side, but even here, at the curved wall, centuries were approaching in testudo formation, shields held up in a roof, while others carried ladders and ropes, ready to attempt the walls.

The enemy began to see the danger, then, noting the legions creeping into position, and in no time, they reacted. Archers and slingers appeared on the walls, along with men ready to drop rocks and tiles and the like. The barrage began from above then – missiles, both manufactured and makeshift, pouring down on the approaching units, but with less result than they perhaps expected, for the men below were protected by their roof of shields. And even as they launched those clouds of missiles, the enemy on the walls fell foul once more of the scorpions, men dying, punched through with a foot-long shaft in the neck or chest, even as they drew back bowstrings or whirled slings.

The carnage began in earnest, then, men climbing ladders, attempting to gain the wall top, only to have the ladders pushed away and fall, or to be hit by rocks as they climbed, and sent tumbling back, screaming, to the earth below. Men with ropes managed to get the grapples over the walls and climbed, trying to reach the top before the defenders could manage to cut through the thick cord with their swords. Artillerists aimed carefully, trying to help by picking off the men above the ladders and rope carriers, buying them time. And in between, legionaries formed into testudos reached the walls and slammed against them, providing a platform for their friends. Other legionaries ran, then, jumping onto the shield-roof and skittering up it in their hobnailed boots to reach the walls, where they were tantalisingly close to the defenders and began to stab upwards with their pila, attempting to hit the men above them, sometimes with great success.

It was hard and brutal work, and there was clearly going to be a significant rate of attrition. Maximus watched men falling all around the curved wall, and the number of Romans staggering away to seek a medic, or simply falling to the ground to lie still, was larger than the number of men falling atop the walls. But still the result was inevitable. And even if by some miracle the defenders managed to fight off the legions assaulting them, there were many more legions below waiting for their turn. Rome would never relent, and no people within the encircling sea had the manpower to throw into a war like the empire.

On it went: butchery and struggle. But it was a *finite* wait for an end, and the turning point could come at any time. All it would take was one man to gain the wall top, and the enemy would spend time trying to remove him, which would distract them from their other work, and allow more Romans to reach the parapet. And the unwritten rule was that once there were three men on a wall top, that wall was doomed, for three men could generally hold off enemies on the wall long enough to allow the rest of their mates access. Soon enough, the wall would be flooded with legionaries, and from there the whole fortress would fall in short order. And throughout all of this, they could hear the steady, repetitive thump of the ram against the gate at the far side. If that gate caved, and it inevitably must in the end, the fortress was done. Soon, one way or another, Tapae's citadel would be theirs, either by cresting the wall or by breaching the gate.

Maximus switched his attention to his own unit. The men of the Second Pannonian waited a safe distance back, where the trees were thinner, allowing the legions room to work.

'Be prepared,' he told the men to either side, who passed on the warning, the word spreading across the cavalry.

He could feel it coming. They were almost into the citadel, and that meant that anyone in there with an ounce of sense would try and escape. And when they did, it would be swift, unexpected, and chaotic.

Tapae broke, in the end, at both sides almost simultaneously. As the sun dropped below the trees to the west, behind Maximus, and the light immediately began to fade, finally they heard a great crack and a cheer from the east of the fort. The ram had broken the gate. They may not yet have full access, but once the bar had cracked, it was just a matter of a few more blows to see the gates burst asunder. The sound also drew the attention of the defenders on the curved wall top, who turned in dismay, allowing the assaulting legionaries a moment of grace with their enemy's distraction to clamber up and over the parapet. Legionaries had the walls, and the gate was breaking.

The citadel was falling.

With a roar, the legions pressed all the harder, sensing victory at hand, but, recovering from their distraction, the Dacians were far from finished. Rather than embrace failure, they fought back harder than ever, each struggle between men a contest of Titans. Maximus watched from a distance as men killed each other in brutal and inventive manners. The number of Romans on the wall increased every moment, and it was not long before he saw a legionary standard raised above the southern tower. A tremendous noise and a roar of victory announced the final end of the east gate, and that was it. Rome was in the fortress, on every side and at every level.

Maximus braced himself. The prefect had given no warning, but it had to be coming...

The west gate opened suddenly, and men poured from it like a pent up dam breaking, flooding out into the open. The legionaries outside were not prepared for it, though they recovered quickly from their surprise and formed into lines, preventing the Dacians getting away, driving forward at them, swords and shields to the fore.

But the surprise had been sufficient for a few of them to make it past. Cavalry officers bellowed orders, setting their men to containing the escapees, and Maximus joined in, sending his own men in to pen in the fleeing warriors.

That was when he saw the three riders.

Three Dacians burst from the gate in the wake of their pedestrian warriors, each on a strong horse, leaping over obstacles, already at a gallop as they reached the archway in their bid for freedom.

Maximus shouted orders to stop them, though with the sounds of battle and the shouts and screams all around now, he wasn't at all sure whether anyone even heard him. The three riders raced for liberty, allowing the warriors all around them to keep the attackers busy as they did so.

Then they were through the legionaries...

Although one fell.

A legionary had turned and cast his pilum, which caught the horse in the rear and sent it into an agonised panic, rearing and throwing its rider, clearly a nobleman of some importance, as all three had to be, purely from the fact that they were on horses. The legions fell on the man in droves, each desperate to be the one to either capture or kill the first chieftain of the war.

The world slowed.

Maximus blinked. As everything crawled past in slow motion, his gaze fixed on the two remaining riders. His jaw twitched. His hand gripped his sword, knuckles whitening.

The middle of the three horses was Celeris.

He would know her anywhere, after so many years of the two of them serving all over the east, riding together as a team, in both war and peace. He could almost *feel* her, almost hear her thoughts. He couldn't identify the rider, head down and tucked into Dacian tunic and trousers, with a chain shirt, a bright shield and a black felt hat with the peak pulled forward, Dacian-style. It could be any native nobleman. Yet Maximus was sure... it had to be Duras. *His* slave, on *his* horse, facing *his* unit.

Men moved to intercept, but the two riders were fast, already at full speed. Maximus turned his horse, foreseeing the inevitable. Duras was clever and determined, and Celeris was fast and as well trained as a Roman cavalry horse could be. Sure enough, moments later the two Dacian riders burst through the lines of the cavalry, Romans swinging at them as best they could. The second rider faltered for a moment, a blade having nicked him in passing, but he rode on, and Rigozus and Arvina were both moving to intercept.

Maximus was already racing, though. He'd anticipated Duras making it past their lines before they could stop him, and even as the escaped slave charged through the sparse trees, heading for freedom, already Maximus had turned and kicked his new mount into life – his fifth in a month or so, ridiculously.

This horse, though, at least felt fast and confident, and had none of the dithery idiocy Ferox had enjoyed. If there was a horse on this hillside that could catch the slave, it was this one.

He had a moment, then, as they rode, in which he worried that the man would get away, for no matter how hard Maximus pressed, he did not seem to be able to gain ground, Duras staying just as far ahead. But he shook that thought from his head. Celeris might be the faster horse, but she would be tiring already, while Maximus's horse was fresh.

Determined, furious, he put his heels to the horse once more, squeezing with his thighs and leaning forward into its mane, urging it to run, run, run. He saw Duras break out into open ground, and by the time Maximus did the same, his prey had turned and raced uphill towards the thicker trees. Perhaps the other directions led a little too much towards the Roman lines and gathered legions, or perhaps the higher northern slopes offered more chance to slip away and use mountain trails to find the army of Decebalus. Whatever the case, Maximus was determined that it would not happen. The bastard had stolen from him everything he cared about, and he was so close... so close!

That closeness spurred him on ever more, and he pounded up the hillside. He was getting even nearer now. He could see the distance between them closing, even as his quarry approached the next treeline. He turned, acutely aware that he was far from his own lines. He'd almost hoped to see Rigozus and Arvina close behind, knowing the two men had been on the trail of the other enemy rider, but there was no sign of either, just the distant shapes of legions and auxilia massed in the valley bottom some distance away.

Just he and Duras, then.

A little more speed. The gap closer.

Celeris was tiring, just as he'd expected, while his own steed was still good and fresh. He was going to get the man. Blood pounding in his ears, he raced on. He had his helmet on now, but no face mask, and sword in hand, reins in the shield hand, though still his shoulder hurt with every jerk. And though he had aches and pains, cuts and bruises, and an arm that sent shockwaves through him every time there was a lurch or bump, he gritted his teeth, determined.

Duras and Celeris disappeared into the trees, following some hunter's path, and Maximus followed, a grim smile across his face. Not only was Celeris slowing, while his own mount raced on, but the man had a shield that would catch on branches in the tight confines of woodland, and he was protected only by a felt hat. Maximus similarly had a chain shirt, but he could pull his body in tight, and was largely protected facially from narrow, whipping branches by his helmet.

Sure enough, as he reached the treeline and pounded into that same game trail, he could hear Duras only a short distance ahead. He listened carefully as he rode – half of being prepared for a fight was being aware, of knowing what was coming against you. And that was how he realised that Duras had stopped. The noise of the man had been getting just a touch louder all the time as they closed, but suddenly he had become *much* louder, which meant he was close, and must have stopped.

Maximus made a decision, for good or for worse. He kicked his new horse into extra speed, racing along the narrow trail, but even as the animal picked up speed, he pushed himself from the saddle and allowed himself to fall sideways into the woodland. It was painful, for he rolled into sticks and rocks and undergrowth until he hit the bole of a tree, but there was too much at stake now. Ignoring all the pain and trouble, he rose like the ire of gods, sword out, and started to run, leaping back onto the game trail and in the wake of his horse.

He hit the clearing after twenty heartbeats, and knew in an instant he had made the right decision. Duras had stopped at the edge of the clearing and put a rope across between trees at rider-chest height. He'd not had time to tie it off, and so he held on to the end to keep it taut, but had blinked in surprise as Maximus's horse had appeared in the clearing riderless, and had raced under it. He'd not yet let go.

The horse slowed as it crossed the clearing, and stopped near Celeris, but Maximus was less inclined to slow as his animal had. He spotted Duras holding the rope, and turned, racing for the ex-slave, roaring. Duras had made the mistake of sheathing his sword – *Maximus's spare sword* – in order to deal with the rope. Now, seeing the Roman burst from the trees behind his horse, he let go of the rope and drew the blade.

Maximus hit the man like the hammer of Vulcan. He slammed into Duras, and the two men stumbled into a tree trunk, the Dacian letting forth a massive rush of air, winded by the collision, yet never stopping drawing that blade. Maximus snarled, yelled, invoked half a dozen war gods, and suddenly he was brawling. It was not that he didn't want to use his sword to put the bastard down for good, but the two of them were too close for that sort of fight. Even as Duras drew the spatha and both men had sword in hand, neither could bring them to bear, for they were just too close. Instead, Maximus slammed his sword pommel into the man's breastbone, hoping to hear a crack. The man's chain shirt robbed the blow of enough force that the strike broke nothing, but it clearly hurt and further winded Duras. The man gasped, and his foot stamped again and again, trying to find Maximus's own foot to break. The Roman found himself dancing, moving his feet repeatedly, keeping them out of danger. Rarely could he concentrate on anything else, and he realised very quickly that, unless he could use his left arm, he was in trouble.

His shoulder hurt like a bastard, even when he just slightly moved it, and when they'd last changed the dressing, the capsarius had warned him that if he did it much more damage, he could finish tearing the partly-broken cord in his shoulder, putting him out of action for months. Still, he didn't have a lot of choice, right now.

He elbowed Duras with his bad arm. The pain was excruciating, but clearly it hurt the man at least as much, for the Dacian cried out, loud, bellowing in a cry that descended into a cough as he doubled over. Unfortunately, Maximus was in too much pain for a moment to capitalise on that, and while he recovered, Duras slipped away from the tree, out into the open where his sword would be more effective.

The Dacian swung the weapon back and forth. He was not so familiar with the Roman cavalry longsword, for Dacian blades tended to be shorter and generally curved. Still, he handled it well enough, suggesting he was serious. Maximus straightened, tested the grip on his own sword, and stepped out into the clearing.

Duras did not come for him. The man was brighter than that, for he knew Maximus's abilities, and would be weighing him up, working out a way to win, despite his disadvantages. The Roman stepped slowly closer and closer, pulling back his sword as he did so. The moment he was within range he swung, a powerful cut across, at hip height. Duras dropped his own sword into the path and deflected it. It was not an expert parry, but sufficient to keep the blade from cutting into him. The man tried to turn the parry into a counterattack, but he was too slow, too unfamiliar with the weapon's weight and balance, and by the time he was lunging with it, Maximus knocked it aside with his own blade.

He spun, bringing the sword out for another strike, and this time only a combination of leaping out of the way and dropping the sword to parry saved him. His blade swept out to the side, knocked away by Maximus's, and he took advantage of that, stepping in and cutting his own sword back across, his control over the blade far better than the slave's. Again, Duras leapt back out of the way, giving ground, and in doing so he saved himself. The Roman's sword cut a line up his forearm, but failed to deliver the crippling blow it could have done.

Maximus pressed the attack, stepping heavily forward, but his foot found a dip in the grass he hadn't noticed, and he jerked to a stop, hissing in pain at his arm. He steadied himself, and looked up at Duras. The slave's eyes were narrowed. The man swung the sword again, but again Maximus caught it, knocked it away, turned his own blade and came back for a counterstrike. Duras leapt away, another gash opened up on his bicep. He could not win this fight, and his expression suggested that he knew that. Armed with a familiar weapon, a sica or falx, or Dacian blade of some sort, he could perhaps hold his own, even after a decade of servitude with no practice, but with an unfamiliar and unwieldy blade too? No, Maximus had him, and they both knew it.

The Roman struck again. This time, he made an unexpected move, lunging, attempting to put the point of his blade into the unprotected thigh of the slave. Duras's gods were clearly watching over him, for he ducked to the side, and managed to sidestep the attack, though the tip of the blade glanced from the hem of his chain shirt.

Then Duras struck.

Knowing the sword was not going to be a deadly force in his hand, instead he leapt at Maximus, taking advantage of their current proximity, and hit him hard. The two men fell backwards, the Roman landing on his back in the grass, Duras atop him, and as they struck the ground, Maximus let out a yelp of pain from his shoulder wound. He knew in an instant that had been a mistake, and could be his downfall. The former slave's eyes narrowed again, as he recognised the weakness, understanding Maximus's cry.

Before the Roman could do anything, Duras reached up, letting the sword fall away, balled his fist, and brought it down in a punch, hard, into Maximus's shoulder. This time he screamed, for the pain was truly intense. His eyes screwed shut automatically, his jaw clenched against the agony. He lay there, unable to move, unable to do anything but try to master his body, fight the pain down and regain control. The end would come any moment. Duras would stick him through with a sword and finish him. That this never happened came as a great surprise, and when he finally unclenched his teeth, gasping, and opened his blurry, tear-filled eyes, it was a shock that he was still alive. He blinked away the tears and focused in time to see Duras slipping into the saddle of Maximus's new horse.

The former slave gave him one glance, then turned, and pelted off into the woods.

Maximus gasped again, and managed to sit upright. His shoulder was throbbing powerfully, and he worried that Duras had done just what the medic feared and finished the job on the joint. He would have to visit the makeshift hospital the moment he got back and have his shoulder checked out.

But why had Duras run and not finished him? Certainly not from any sense of loyalty or fairness. The answer came a moment later, as hands reached down to him, helping him up. He looked around, sharply. Rigozus and Arvina were with him, dismounted.

'Don't tell me, he got you in the shoulder.'

Maximus just nodded, which hurt surprisingly badly. He didn't quite trust himself to talk yet.

'Who was it?' Arvina asked. 'You knew him?'

'His ex-slave,' Rigozus replied, saving him the effort. 'He stole the duplicarius's horse and most of his valuables at Tibiscum and ran away. Seems he's making a habit of that.'

'Thank you,' Maximus managed, realising now that he could at least talk. 'If you hadn't turned up, he would have finished me, for sure.' Maximus's spare sword lay in the grass nearby, along with his own, for Duras had seen the Romans coming and run while he could.

As Arvina gathered up Maximus's swords and helped him upright, Rigozus wandered across the clearing and took Celeris by the rein, walking her back across the grass to her master. 'At least you got your horse back. Maybe that'll be the end of you losing a horse every four days,' the man grinned.

'Look in the saddle bags,' Maximus said, and then gasped again as he reached an upright position and his shoulder once again sent a symphony of pain to his brain. As he gently reached up and tested the tender shoulder, Rigozus did as he was asked. He turned with a smile. 'He kept your stuff. Your torc and arm-ring are here, and your arm purse. Not so many coins in it now, mind.'

'Coins, I can replace,' Maximus sighed with relief. The bastard may have got away again, but at least Maximus had retrieved his horse and his valuables. In some ways that meant more to him than winning the Iron Gates pass and putting to bed the ghost of Tapae.

He smiled. 'Let's get back down to the valley and find out what's happening.'

Chapter Fifteen

Tapae, September AD 101

The Iron Gates pass was a scene of tightly-controlled chaos, and had been for three days.

There had been so many Dacian dead that the idea of burying them had seemed ridiculous, and so instead all their weapons, armour and valuables were gathered as trophies or loot, and the bodies were loaded into carts and driven half a mile up one of the more gentle slopes, where they were gathered in huge heaps and burned, far enough away that the stinking smoke didn't bother the imperial force, down in the valley.

The Roman dead, on the other hand, were dealt with more honourably. It had seemed wrong to bury them at Tapae, given its history, but the emperor had paid such attention to the supply line of the army this summer, and left garrisoned forts, that it was no great difficulty to take the supply carts as they arrived, empty them, then stack them with Roman bodies, liberally sprinkled with fragrant flowers, and send them back. Despite the months it had taken the army to reach Tapae, moving slowly and putting the infrastructure in place, in fact the route back to Viminacium would not be much more than a hundred miles, and now that the roads and bridges, cuttings and depots were all in place and functioning, it would not take the wagons more than five days to reach the great staging centre of Moesia, where the bodies could be buried appropriately and have monuments raised to them with the funds from their burial clubs.

A marble altar had been brought from one of the wagons – a high quality item, one of five that had been brought all the way from Rome – and was carved by one of the legionary experts to display the names of the units that had lost men at

Tapae, a memorial to the men, which was placed at the very centre of the valley, where the worst of the action had taken place. In some ways it was a seal, forever pushing down and containing the memory of the defeat and ignominy of Tapae. But it was also a memorial to the fallen, and, devoted as it was to Jupiter Tonans, it was also a homage to the god who had made it happen.

That, of course, left the wounded and the captives.

Maximus had actually blinked in surprise when he'd heard the figures. Of course, there may have been the same *proportion* of wounded at both previous Tapae engagements, but there had simply been more men present at this one, and so the figures were high enough that it astonished him. Fully a third of the auxilia present had either died or been wounded, and the two legions who had taken the citadel had suffered significant losses too.

'You'll like this new emperor,' Bibula had said on one of his visits, for now the medicus was allowing the decurion short walks to help improve his strength and speed his recovery. 'You know what they say in the hospital? There were so many wounds in the battle that the capsarii and medicii ran out of dressings. I can quite imagine it. I watched them come in, and they were stacked three deep for a while. The medical staff are still working on the lesser wounds, three days on. But anyway, the chief medicus visited command and asked what to do about bandages, and the emperor grabbed a pair of shears and cut his purple cloak into strips. He dropped them in the medicus's hands, and then told his officers to do the same. In an hour or so, every officer with a good wool cloak had given it up for bandages. The wounded love him already.'

Maximus nodded at that. He'd got that sort of impression from Trajan. A proper 'hands-on' emperor, who'd cut his teeth on war commanding the border legions in Germania.

So the wounded were still being dealt with, the Roman dead had now all been shipped out, and the Dacian dead burned on the hills. The Dacian wounded and prisoners were all under guard in a temporary stockade. About three or four hundred of them was the word in the camp. There was some speculation about what would happen with them. Slavery was the likelihood, though Maximus could personally attest how bad a slave a Dacian made. Execution, perhaps. The decision would undoubtedly be made by the emperor, and that would not happen until he decided whether he needed any kind of leverage.

Maximus leaned back, winced, and then adjusted his position to put his shoulder under less pressure. He'd tried to get in to see a medicus, but they were all too busy, and he was apparently not wounded enough to be a priority, which annoyed him. But he'd seen the capsarius, who had checked him over. The man had confirmed that he'd done a little extra damage to the shoulder, but it still was not fully torn, and would heal in time if he took care of it. He'd seen the prefect about that and, given that there was no fighting expected in the coming days, the officer had told him to stay in command, since Bibula was also still in recovery, but to take on only light duties. That suited Maximus. He'd managed to palm his polishing and cleaning off on one of the lads in return for an increased wine ration, which made things easier. And he himself had doubled his wine ration, which helped soothe the shoulder pain.

Of course, the unit was in favour with the prefect now, and with *all* of command, in fact. The actions of the Second Pannonian early on in the battle, when they had taken the archers out of the fight, had been noted, but then their part in bringing the power of Jupiter Tonans to the battlefield and routing the enemy was clear to all, and word of it had even reached the ear of the emperor, who had vowed to honour the great god for his part in the victory, *beyond* the simple Tapae commemorative altar. And if those two actions had not been enough, that they had chased down and stopped the escaping survivors from the fortress had clinched the matter. Not one Dacian was recorded escaping the field. Of course, neither Maximus nor his companions had mentioned the escape of

Duras. The matter had been glossed over, focusing instead on the recovery of Maximus's horse and goods, and the demise of two Dacian leaders. The prefect had clearly presumed that Duras had died during the recovery, and had taken great pride when the heads of the two nobles had been displayed before the emperor by Arvina and Rigozus on behalf of the unit. To have killed two of the leaders of the enemy was important, after all.

'You know,' Maximus said conversationally, as they sat in his tent with a bottle of wine, 'I think Duras has risen in the world.'

'What do you mean?' Rigozus said.

'When I captured him at Second Tapae, he was just a Dacian warrior, one of many. A soldier in the mass, wounded and angry. Since then, he's spent years as my slave. You saw him the other day, even if only briefly. Tell me what you saw?'

'He was on a horse,' Arvina noted. 'So far only nobles and Sarmatian mercenaries have had horses, and he's neither.'

'Quite. And he had a chain shirt, which only the wealthy own. Of course, he *was* wealthy, since he stole all my money, and the horse was free too, so that's no surprise. But two things make me think there's more to it than that.'

'The hat,' Rigozus said.

'Hat?' Arvina looked across, frowning.

'Only nobles wear the Phrygian cap,' Rigozus explained. 'The Dacians have two castes in their society: the cap-wearers and the bearded ones. Bit of a misnomer really, as the cap-wearers generally have beards too. But you get the point.'

'So somehow he's gone from warrior to slave and now to nobleman.'

Maximus nodded. 'And when he escaped the fortress, he was in the company of two chieftains. He's definitely risen in their ranks. I take it they found nothing useful in the fortress?'

Arvina shook his head. Over the past three days, the fortress that had been guarding the Iron Gates for the Dacian kings for generations had been systematically emptied of all goods until it was little more than an empty shell. Then the legions had moved in and proved that they were as adept at demolition as construction, as they removed the walls and towers of Tapae citadel from the battlements down. The stonework had been stacked neatly and was now being moved to wagons to help construct new sites down the line, leaving the great fortification that protected Dacia as little more than ankle-high foundations. They had even largely removed and backfilled the outer ramparts and ditches.

'The answer is fairly clear,' Naevius Bibula put in, visiting on another of his recovery walks.

'Oh?'

'There can be few men with as good a knowledge of our army as him. I know,' he said holding up his hands. 'I know, he was never privy to grand plans and the like, but he's spent over a decade in your service, and he's seen all these units at work time and again. He knows nothing critically important, but his knowledge of small things will be immense. I'll bet he knows how often our passwords are set and who sets them, the standing order of march, the deployment of scouts, the supply system and so on. I suspect any man who brings that sort of information to Decebalus and his people would find himself at the top of the heap pretty quick.'

Maximus winced. That sort of thing would not go down well with the prefect.

Bibula grinned. 'So it's a damn good job that no one outside this tent knows he's still alive? And now, Maximus, you'll be supplying me with plentiful wine to buy my continued silence, eh?'

'Great.'

'Think of it as staying in my good books.'

Maximus tried to think of something pithy to say in reply, but drew a blank, so he simply topped up everyone's wine, then wandered over to the corner and found the other jar. At least now that he had his purse back, half full, he could afford more drink without panicking over the cost. He wandered back with the jar and left it on the table, then fell into listening to a tale Rigozus was telling, about a Thracian giant from his hometown, who knocked out an ox with one punch. It was almost certainly a fictional tale, but the man was good at telling stories, and it was entertaining regardless. This led to an anecdote from Arvina about the late emperor Domitian, who had apparently turned up at a senator's party in Rome, where Arvina's father had been part of the gathering, wearing a hairpiece so unconvincing that one of the wags had come in from the garden halfway through the evening wearing a bird's nest on his head. Of course, the man had paid a heavy price for his humour, but it was still a good story.

It made Maximus smile to see the burgeoning friendship between these two riders. Rigozus had been one of his most trusted men since he had first been moved into the unit, but Arvina was a relatively recent addition. The two men could hardly be any more different in personality or background, one being a hard-worn provincial veteran, the other a well-bred Roman gentleman fallen on hard times, yet they were fast becoming close friends.

There came a rapping on the tent door just as Arvina was about to break out his usual story about the German whore who turned out to be a man, and as he stopped abruptly, Maximus bade the visitor enter. He blinked as a man in the uniform of the Praetorian Guard strode in. He had the sudden urge to stand and snap to attention, and fought it down. The man may be Praetorian, but he was a guardsman, while Maximus was an officer.

'Can I help you?'

The guardsman straightened, and clasped his hands behind his back.

'Your presence has been requested at the command tent, acting decurion Tiberius Claudius Maximus. Promptly.'

Maximus frowned, jumped up, regretted that as his shoulder shot pain at him, and nodded. I'll follow. I must change a few things.'

'No. Now.'

Maximus turned to Bibula, who shrugged, and he told his superior: 'Don't drink all my wine. Save me some.'

Then he turned and gestured at the door, and the Praetorian marched out. As he followed, the guardsman started striding through the camp that occupied much of the wide valley approaching the pass. He hurried forward to fall in beside the man.

'What can you tell me?'

The Praetorian turned a frown on him.

'Well, what's happening for a start? Who's there?'

The guardsman huffed. 'Strategy meeting for the autumn, I think. And all the staff officers and legates, prefects and tribunes.'

'Shit.'

'Quite.'

In the silence that followed as they walked, Maximus weighed it up and decided not to bring up the fact that he was an officer and should be addressed appropriately by the common soldier, no matter what force he was from. The Praetorians always considered themselves above any other unit, and it was not unknown for a common guardsman to speak to an auxiliary prefect as though they were equals. People tended to make exceptions for the Praetorians. They did have the emperor's ear, after all. And sometimes his head, if they didn't like him...

The unfairness of that gnawed at him as he walked beside the supercilious Praetorian all the way to the command tent. They were let through by the Guard, and then by the second line of them at the headquarters, and as he was about to enter, and the Praetorian turned to walk away, Maximus couldn't resist a jibe.

'Don't worry. They won't make the Guard fight, like real soldiers.'

The Praetorian snapped round to glare angrily at him, but he'd already slipped into the command tent. The huge marquee was full of men of rank and privilege, but two imperial slaves, each wearing a tunic of a quality that few auxiliary soldiers could afford, checked him over, took his sword, and bade him wait, while they fetched Gaius Julius Paullus, the prefect of the Second Pannonian.

He snapped to attention as the prefect approached. The man chewed his lip. While deliberation went on behind him, Paullus spoke quietly.

'You trouble me, Maximus. You are at one and the same time useful and troublesome. But currently you seem to be riding a wave of success, and so your activities have drawn the imperial eye again. You have been requested by imperial command. Why, I cannot say, but be careful how you respond, and do not speak until you are spoken to. Now go and stand with the lower officers.'

Maximus bowed his head, and then slipped between members of the gathering, whispering apologies as he moved past people, before finding a small group of men in ordinary uniforms, rather than the cuirasses of the great and powerful.

'Ah, the scout,' murmured a man next to him, dressed similarly, giving him the side-eye. 'Word has it you're one to watch.'

Maximus frowned at the man. He was wearing no insignia of rank and could very easily be an ordinary trooper, but the way he spoke suggested otherwise.

'*You're* the one to watch,' snorted another man quietly nearby, addressing the short, dark soldier. Maximus had no chance to pry further, though, for at that moment, a commanding voice called for Decurion Claudius Maximus, and he straightened, stepped forward from the line into the open space at the tent's centre, and bowed his head. Then, remembering the last time he had been in this emperor's presence, he lifted his eyes so that they met Trajan's. The emperor gave an oddly knowing smile, as though he knew precisely what was going on in Maximus's head.

'I have been informed of the part you and your men played in our victory at Tapae,' the emperor said. 'It is in my mind to reward you for your service, but Hadrian here reminds me that there are others who deserve as much, and some are not currently present. Besides, such awards are yet to reach us via the baggage train, and so I must delay such gifts. Believe, though, that an award will come in due course, perhaps when the current season is over. And that brings me to the reason I called for you.'

The emperor took a few steps forward. 'Our army relies heavily upon the information and activity of our advance scouts. I have increased the use of such men over the past months, and the success of the initiative shows that it was the correct decision. As such, I intend to do much the same again.'

He gestured, with a sweep of the hand, to the tent's other occupants. 'I was, in fact, in the process of discussing the next steps of campaign. Clearly, we cannot hope to press into the central highlands, with winter coming. I am given to understand that winters can be extremely hard there, and I have no wish to subject my army to such conditions. As such, we will move forth through the Iron Gates, and there consolidate for the winter. Legionary camps will be established at various sites, and campaign camps for other units, but we will remove all the smaller fortresses around the plains beyond the gate and make sure the entire area is subjugated, leaving only the mountains for now in enemy hands. That will be our work. I will extend the campaigning season by one month, and we will spend the rest of autumn securing our hold on western Dacia.'

Now he turned back to Maximus. 'The army will be split, dealing with a number of locations for speed. However, we will still be as reliant as ever upon the information of the scouts. While your prefect will retain *nominal* command of your unit, I am placing you in *temporary* command of fully half the ala. You will select appropriate personnel, and liaise with other scout officers and appropriate persons, and will move throughout the freshly occupied zone, making sure that we are fully informed of everything that is happening, so that we can maintain control. You retain the pay rank of duplicarius, but I appoint you praepositus of this extended scout unit for the winter. Do you have any questions?'

Maximus, stunned into silence, shook his head.

'Good. Then I suggest you remain, and take in anything else that is discussed in this briefing before you return to your unit and start appointing men. Any officer you do not require will be reassigned with a pay increase to counter the inconvenience. I want only the most ingenious and competent of scouts leading these units.'

Maximus bowed and stepped back into line.

He stood then, for a while, listening, as the plans were discussed, and often related to a great map that hung on the wall. He noted that the sphere of planned operations for the next month spilled out from the pass and into the plains that lay between there and the mountains where Decebalus held court. Sites were indicated that reached perhaps thirty or forty miles north, and others that connected through other mountain passes to the south, including one that led down to a place called Buridava, on the road back to Danubian Oescus, where a small cluster of flags suggested that the Roman force of the general Laberius was currently in occupation. It was a lot of territory to cover. Maximus half-listened to the vast slew of details, but spent most of his time thinking on how half an ala of cavalry could be best utilised across that region. Finally, the meeting broke up, and Maximus made sure to stick with that group of lesser officers as they left, so that he didn't tread on the toes of the great and the good, quite literally.

However, as he left the tent and started to walk towards the gateway in the Praetorian defences, that same fellow he had been standing beside in the briefing reached out and grabbed his shoulder. He turned in surprise.

'Stick around,' the man said.

'Sorry?'

'Trust me.'

He frowned at the man, but came to a stop, stepping out of the way of the other departing officers. Another man, dressed in the tunic and cloak of an officer, wandered over and fell in beside them. Maximus frowned, his confusion deepening as this new officer and the ordinary soldier nodded at one another, as though they were equals and old acquaintances. The rest of the officers were gone and out of sight when an imperial slave walked over and stopped beside them.

'The emperor is ready for you.'

Maximus stared, then, as the two men with him nodded and followed the slave, beckoning to him as they went. He followed, his sense of trepidation increasing all the time, and it shot up once more as he realised they were not returning to the command tent, but making instead for the emperor's own accommodation, which lay close by. The tent was purple, with gold décor, and two Praetorians stood outside, holding the imperial banners. They did not move as the men approached, and did not attempt to question or intercept them. The slave led them on into the tent, where he bowed and did not raise his eyes to the emperor as Maximus had.

He felt the chill of nerves as he entered the imperial presence. This was not the same as standing near the emperor at a sacrifice, or attending a meeting in the command tent. At almost all times Trajan was accompanied either by his court or by his staff. Not so, here. The tent was large, very organised, and surprisingly Spartan. It was not full of comforts, but more the home of a military officer. Trajan had removed his cuirass, and sat on a bed with one leg raised and across his knee, massaging his foot. He looked up as they entered, nodded at them, and then went on with his work. The only other occupant of the tent was Livianus, the Praetorian Prefect, who similarly sat in just his tunic and boots now, having discarded his helmet and cuirass. He too looked at the men, though there was just a hint of distaste to *this* man's face. *Who at*, Maximus wondered?

Trajan leaned back, letting his foot go, and rubbed his hands together. 'Three of you know one another, and all three of you know Maximus, even if just by his repeated presence in our briefings. Claudius Maximus, however, you may not know these men?'

Silence fell. Maximus felt a moment of worry. Was he supposed to speak? It generally wasn't done to address an emperor unless directly questioned, and that sounded like a question, but it might not be considered one. As the silence strung out, though, he decided they were waiting on an answer. He cleared his throat.

'I am, of course, aware of the noble Livianus, Imperator, but no, not the others.'

Trajan nodded. 'Good. If you knew them, then they probably wouldn't be doing their jobs properly. Ulpius Denter here,' he indicated the man in the officer's uniform, 'runs the frumentarii in the war zone for me. It is his duty, and that of his men, to keep me informed about everything that happens in the army, of all moods and theories, as well as any potential problems.' He then gestured to the other man. 'Curtius Cilo leads the arcani, who move unnoticed among the tribes beyond the border and bring back information on a political and military level. His men have been embedded within the Dacian and Sarmatian territories for several years, and it is he who provided much of the information that led to our current campaign. To some extent, Maximus, your speculatores form the third such force, filling in the missing part, the knowledge of what lies between those tribes and our army, the frontier, the danger zone.'

The emperor leaned back. 'What is your biggest worry, Claudius Maximus?'

Right now, his biggest worry was saying the wrong thing to an emperor, though he suspected that was not what Trajan was referring to. He thought hard.

'Imperator, I had worried that we might be committing to a winter campaign in the mountains, though that worry is now allayed. Clearly the plans have been carefully considered, and Dacia should be settled and safe for the winter.' He took a deep breath. 'But I fear there is something else going on.'

Trajan looked across to the others. The short man in the rider's uniform nodded. 'I am of a similar opinion. My men among the Dacian tribes have been unable to unearth anything concrete. Such men were inserted during the times over the years when Romans were sent into Dacia by imperial command to help Romanise the locals, but now that Decebalus is at war once again, such men are not trusted, and are kept largely in the dark. We hear a few things, some tantalising titbits, but nothing detailed. We were aware of the king's attempts to ally with the Sarmatian and German tribes, and with the Bosporan kingdom. And, though you may not know this, he has even been in touch with Parthia, seeking to form an alliance against Rome. But there is much that we do not get to hear.'

'So,' Trajan said, gesturing at Maximus, 'tell us your suspicions.'

He realised, then, that somehow Ulpius Denter, the head of the frumentarii must have heard something through his troops, hidden as they were throughout the legions and auxilia. He took a breath again. 'Majesty, I cannot be sure. I encountered riders near Tibiscum who bore all the hallmarks of Sarmatians, and then again just before Tapae. By the second time, we were sure they were Roxolani.'

'Roxolani are regularly employed as mercenaries by Decebalus,' the arcani noted.

'True,' Maximus replied, 'but we concluded that the group we fought there were too large to be a single warband, but too small for a whole tribe. That opens up a large number of questions. It suggests that there are more Roxolani in the area yet. And the strange thing is that we saw no sign of a Sarmatian camp when we were among the Dacians, delivering the emperor's reply, and no sign of Sarmatians during the battle itself. There was no trace of them even riding away. They simply weren't at Tapae, though they had been present days before. I fear that there is something else going on. Decebalus was all too ready to pull back to his mountains.'

'Nonsense,' the Praetorian Prefect scoffed. 'He left because we beat him. To stay would have been disastrous.'

'Yes, sir,' Maximus replied, turning to him, 'but the king's retreat was too neat and organised. He was ready for it even before it happened.'

'You are suggesting that we are walking into a trap?'

'I don't know,' Maximus admitted. 'But something about all this does not add up properly. When the Buri broke, Decebalus could have held against the alae with sufficient Roxolani at his command. There is something at work here that we are only on the edge of.'

At this, Trajan leaned forward. 'See, Livianus? I told you. I've felt this since the start, and the evidence continues to build.' He turned to Maximus again. 'I *do* value the use of scouts, and you and your men *have* been of great importance. None of that was untrue. But that is also not the principle reason I want you, and an extended force, out in the plains as we prepare for winter. I want you to investigate wherever you can. Unearth more signs of this suspicion of yours. If something is going to happen that is outside our preparations, I want knowledge of it before it is too late. That is your goal. That is your mission from here onwards, Claudius Maximus. Find out what is going on and make sure that I know before it is too late. As such, I give you freedom of command. Go where you need to and do what you need to. Requisition whatever you require, and refill your ranks from the rest of the ala. New recruits are already on the way from Viminacium. And before you move out, make sure to speak to these gentlemen here,' he added, gesturing to the two men who'd come with him. 'Curtius Cilo will have useful knowledge from within the heartland of the king, and may have access to more, and Ulpius Denter will be able to make sure that no matter where you are, there will be a friendly ear within the nearest unit.'

The discussion continued for a while, but Maximus only listened to important and pertinent moments, and when the four men were dismissed by the emperor, he could only marvel that he, Maximus of Phillipi, duplicarius and scout, found himself in the company of three of the most important men in the Dacian theatre of operations as they left the tent.

On the slow stroll back to his own quarters, oddly, he found himself fixating on how he was going to break the news to Naevius Bibula that his second in command was about to take control of half the entire ala for the autumn.

Chapter Sixteen

Dacian plains, east of the Iron Gates, late September AD 101

A legion's winter camp was an immense and impressive affair, even when only part-built, and this was only one of several. Another was under construction back across the Iron Gates, just west of Tapae, those two controlling the western approach to Dacia. And there would be others too, for Trajan had either full compliments or vexillations from eleven different legions in Dacia. The Fifth Macedonica were already camped in tents within the earth banks of the huge fort, but that was only a temporary affair. Once the wooden palisade and the gates went up around the circuit, timber buildings would replace the tents. The place might not be intended as a permanent garrison, but the Fifth would likely be here for a number of months, and needed more than just tents.

On the hillside overlooking the ongoing construction, Maximus turned in the saddle. Three turmae of cavalry sat around in their ordered groups. The others he had already assigned. Three of the twelve thirty-man units now under his command were already heading east and south, skirting the southern fringe of Decebalus's mountainous heartland, heading along the extended plain there, scouting the region towards the Vulcan Pass that would lead back down towards the Danubius, a potential future route for Roman troops and supplies. If all was good there, and there was nothing to report, they would escort a legion thence, to build a winter camp to control southern access to the region. Three more turmae were heading northeast, moving around the other edge of the king's defended region, to where the great Dacian plateau opened out for countless miles. There, again, if they encountered no trouble, they would escort another legion and form another base. The third group of three turmae, he had assigned here, remaining with this site, for they were within reach of Decebalus's forces here, too, and having scouts out to provide advance warning of any movement would be invaluable. All nine of those units were providing a solid scouting service for the army, helping secure Dacia for the winter and supporting the legions and auxilia. But all nine of those units were also carrying out a second duty, looking for anything out of the ordinary. Anything that did not seem to fit.

Decebalus had taken seemingly all his forces into those mountains, defended by numerous stone citadels that made the one they had taken at Tapae look like a child's toy. As such, no one expected those Dacian forces to foray from the mountains. It would be nonsensical, tactically, and Decebalus was too clever to simply waste his army on fruitless attacks of that sort when he could rely upon the terrain and the weather to keep him secure until the spring. Thus, any sign of Dacian military activity outside those mountains would count as unusual and suspicious, and would be reported back to the various contacts Maximus now had among the more clandestine sectors of the military.

And while one group went southeast, another northeast and the third remained where they were, Maximus would take the remaining three turmae north from here, along the edge of the western hills, towards another pass that led back towards Iazyx and Osii lands.

Rigozus had questioned that, when he'd laid out the initial plans. At first glance, it seemed as though two groups had been sent out into the more dangerous and unknown eastern regions, the third guarding the army, while they themselves would simply be scouting relatively harmless lands north of Tapae. But there was method to his plan. The Buri, who had already been a shaky part of Decebalus's alliance before the battle, and who would now likely be shunned as deserters, would probably not be part of that army the king had taken into his mountains. And their lands extended into the very mountains Maximus would take his men along the edge of.

The Buri remained an unknown quantity now. To their west lay the Iazyges, who had made a pact with Rome and would not be part of Decebalus's war, but to their east lay the lands of the other Dacian tribes, loyal to the king. They had broken and fled in the battle, and were largely to blame for the swift collapse of the Dacian forces and their retreat from the Iron Gates. As such they would not be popular with Decebalus. But how they would react to that remained the question. They may have decided that Rome was unstoppable now, and the future of the region was in the emperor's hands, in which case, they may be preparing to make peace with Rome and join the Iazyges as allies. Or they may be shamed at their flight from the battle, and be driven to seek redemption with Decebalus, which would make them all the more dangerous. Or, of course, they may decide to take the shakiest but least costly path and seek neutrality, retreating into their hills to lick their wounds and wait to see which force came out of the war on top.

Whatever the case, Rome needed more of an idea what was going on among the Buri, and that, then, was what Maximus was concentrating on.

Three turmae... almost a hundred riders.

And because they would be out far ahead of the Roman forces, they had with them six pack horses that carried tents and supplies, and could serve as spare mounts if required. It was quite a force, and some serious responsibility.

He turned to look back, down at the wide, flat land swarming with Roman troops settling in for the winter. This might be the last they saw of other Romans for many days. He turned and looked at Rigozus, who nodded, confirming their readiness, and then raised his hand and waved it in a northerly direction, urging Celeris onwards.

He smiled at that, at least, as they descended the slope, crossed the wide open grasslands and fields of the Dacian plain, and made for the green forested hills that formed the western edge of the region. No matter what else happened now, he had managed to get Celeris back.

Just below the slope, as they lost sight of the Roman works behind them, they found a river, or rather an overgrown stream, some eight or ten feet across, not deep enough to constitute an obstacle to infantry, let alone cavalry, but useful for scouts. Where there were rivers, there were inevitably settlements, for towns and villages grew up there, where the waters needed to be crossed and bridges or fords were constructed, where water was available to support their life. The river flowed in a northerly direction, sourced somewhere in the peaks around Tapae, and meandering along the edge of the hills out towards the plains. As it flowed, it would likely pass any habitation, and so they would follow it.

The hours passed, riding along the eastern bank of the stream, and by noon they had moved northeast and then north again, the stream having flowed into a larger river. They passed their first proper settlement around then, though just as they had found all the way to Tapae, this one had been abandoned recently, anything of value removed in advance of the Roman forces. Presumably the village's occupants had either fled into the hills towards Buri lands, or retreated with their king into his ring of mountain fortresses.

They stopped in the deserted village for a meal, corralling their horses in a fenced enclosure only recently abandoned. Maximus sat on a rough bench formed from logs, and dug salted pork and bread from his pack, softening the food with a little olive oil from his stoppered jar. As he, Rigozus and Arvina sat together, a trio fast becoming close, Maximus raised his gaze to the lands around.

A shiver ran up his spine.

'Can you feel anything?'

'Only aches,' Rigozus grumbled. 'My arse seems to have been in the saddle more or less non-stop for months, and now we stop for lunch, I'm sat on a rock that's even worse.'

Arvina, though, ignored the man's complaints and frowned at Maximus. 'You mean, sort of sense something around us?'

Maximus nodded. Once, years ago, he'd been involved in a punch up at a bar in Naissus between the off-duty men of two legions. He and the lads from the Fourth Flavia Felix had come off as the victors, while the men of the visiting Seventh Claudia limped off, hissing hatred into a damp and miserable night. The lads of the Fourth had celebrated with a lot more drink than was strictly sensible, and had finally gone their own ways when the caupona closed, some to find a comfortable bed, others a comfortable woman, and more to find somewhere else that served drink. Maximus had found himself wandering along an alley between warehouses, completely lost. Despite the wine, somehow his senses still seemed to be working, and he knew he was being watched and followed for some time before the two lads from the Seventh jumped him. He'd probably only survived the encounter because before they could beat him to death, a unit of local vigiles stumbled across the scene and chased the attackers off.

That was the feeling he had now. Not just of being watched, and not even of being followed, but of a malicious spirit tracking them, as though the vanquished from Tapae were in the hills above, waiting to seek revenge. And to some extent, if it were the Buri, that might actually be the case.

'Not noticed it until just now, but I could swear someone's watching us, and they have no love for us, either.'

Arvina nodded. 'To be honest, I've been feeling that for the past mile or two before we stopped, though I didn't want to say anything. I thought it was just my imagination, 'coz I never actually saw or heard anything, just sort of *felt* it.'

'You've got sharper senses than me, then, if you felt it earlier.'

He focused on that hillside. The weather was dry and relatively mild, and only a light breeze stirred the leaves, not enough to cause movement visible up the slopes, and so everything, all the way along the hillside, was still and silent.

Someone was there, though, even if he could neither see nor hear them. He spoke without taking his eyes from those hills. 'Don't give anything away. Act normal. Let's just finish our meal and move out as if nothing happened.'

'Why?' Arvina asked.

'Because it's better that we know they're there, but that they *don't* know that we know,' Rigozus said.

'Let them think they have the edge,' Maximus said quietly, 'because then they can be over-confident and walk into trouble.'

'Some of the Buri speak Latin,' Rigozus noted. 'Remember the writing on the wolf pelt? They'll speak a Dacian dialect and some sort of Suebian German, but clearly some of them have at least a little Latin. If they've got any sense they'll try and listen in.'

Maximus frowned. 'I think we'd have heard or seen something if they got close enough for that, but you may be right. I bet they don't know Greek, though, given how far north the Buri are of the Danubius.'

He turned and waved in a casual, familiar manner to one of the riders nearby, and spoke in quiet, calm Greek. 'We're being watched, probably followed, too, by someone in the hills. Act as though nothing's wrong, go about your normal business, but everyone speaks Greek from now on. Pass the word.'

The rider nodded, and moments later he was wandering over to a small group sitting together. He joined them and passed on the information. Maximus nodded. He'd been careful in selecting his men. Every one of the riders among his three turmae spoke both Latin and Greek, and a number of them had a smattering of Dacian too.

He sat and finished the meal, talking to the others and keeping his gaze back among them, forcing himself not to look up at the hills. Lunch seemed to take forever, and he could feel the tension among the men by the end of it, each of them now aware of the situation, all making sure it appeared as though nothing had changed. Finally, he gave the order, and the three turmae of riders moved over to the corral and gathered their horses, loading and mounting. Then they were off once more.

From here, the valley widened continually, and the river meandered gently along the centre, so the Roman horsemen departed from the river course now, and moved along the foot of the hills still, continuing their path north. Maximus breathed shallow, tension gripping him, the knowledge they were in constant danger preying on him. The lads were doing extremely well. Some of them were even managing chatter and carefree laughter. Occasionally a hand strayed to a sword hilt, but even if the enemy could see that from the hills, they would think nothing of it. All appeared normal.

But the feeling of being watched never once diminished. He could sense them. The men occasionally peered up at the hills, but that was perfectly natural, of course. They rode for a time then, along the eaves of a forest that rose thick and impenetrable up the hills. That they could still feel that uneasiness, still sense that they were being watched, despite the slopes becoming thick with trees, suggested that the unseen people responsible were on foot rather than on horseback. Either that or they were extremely familiar with the region and capable of finding suitable paths through the woods navigable on horseback.

Then the landscape opened up once more, and the hills returned to swathes of grass. Still, there was no sign of the watchers. They were good, he decided. But if they were capable of moving through the forest, and also of keeping themselves from prying eyes in open ground, there couldn't be that many of them. That perhaps explained why they had not as yet made any move to intercept or attack the Roman cavalry. They were greatly outnumbered.

A grim smile arose at that reasoning. If the watchers believed they were too few to face the Romans, then the turmae gained another advantage. Not only were they aware of the followers, but also they could be reasonably confident that they outnumbered them. At some point shortly, it seemed possible that the hunted might become the hunters. He leaned back and spoke quietly to Rigozus.

'We outnumber them, I reckon, and by a good margin. That's why they only watch us. So the first time we get the chance, I want to turn off our path, ride them down and try and find out who they are.'

'Bloody right,' the other officer said, quietly, but with determination. 'You stay out of it, though.'

'Is that any way to talk to your boss?'

Rigozus snorted. 'I heard the capsarius. Your arm might as well be hanging on by a thread. One bad knock and you'll be out of it for months.' He paused, and then a slow, malicious grin passed across his face. 'And then I'll be *decurion* Rigozus. On second thoughts, go get a few knocks.'

'Isn't it nice to know your friends have your back,' Maximus grunted.

'You might get another medal.'

'Oh piss off.'

They rode on, then, Rigozus occasionally needling him whenever a pithy comment leapt to mind. They'd lost the river now, which was way out of sight to the east, in the middle of the wide plain, while they continued along the edge of the hills.

'Do you see what I see coming up?' he said, gaze straying ahead and left.

'A fight.'

'Oh give it a rest. There's a spur on the left, then a wide valley.'

The low hills on their left seemed to drop sharply, and ahead they could see hills rising again in a new range.

'Looks wide and low. Big valley.'

'But the hillside on the left drops away sharply. If they want to keep pace with us, they're going to have to cross the open valley. Whether they're on horse or foot, we could catch them.'

'The horses *are* pretty well-rested,' Rigozus noted. 'As long as theirs aren't too good, yes.'

'Tell the lads to be ready. On my signal, they race in for the kill.'

The second in command nodded and allowed himself to slow slightly, dropping back to the next man. Maximus permitted himself a casual glance around, making sure that it appeared he was looking everywhere, not just up at the hill.

Quite by chance, he saw the slightest movement maybe half a mile back. Realistically, it could have been deer, or even a bear, but somehow he knew it was them. That was how they had stayed hidden on the open hill – they had dropped back to a position less noticeable. Maximus smiled to himself. That bought him all the time he needed.

They had to be horsemen. He'd probably not have noticed movement if they'd been on foot. And unless they were Sarmatians, then they would be only few. The Dacian tribes did not generally field cavalry, and there couldn't be many anyway, given that they'd been through the woods. Only meeting them face to face would answer his questions.

He could see that spur of land closing on the left, and, given that they were riding across open grassland and not along a marked road, he began to edge closer and closer to the hill, the rest of the column following suit. He controlled his breathing. He was ready. They could do this.

It took only a hundred heartbeats to pass that steeper slope. As he looked left, a wide depression opened up, leading deep into the range of gentle hills, but the left hand side, where the enemy were moving, steepened here. The gods were with them, and looking after them, for just a few hundred paces along that wide valley there was a stand of trees on the left, gleaming bronze and yellow in their autumn panoply. It was large enough to cover their presence from the hillside.

As he passed that corner, and judged that he must be out of sight of the pursuers for just a moment, he waved the others on, and rode swiftly for those trees, where he reined in and patted Celeris on the neck. The others played it perfectly, passing the spur, moving out of sight of the watchers, and then swiftly putting heels to flanks to race over and join him. Slowly the three turmae gathered at the trees. As the last men drifted into the cover of the copse, Maximus moved to the far edge, and peered through the sparser trees there, watching that steep slope.

He was just in time. As his men settled into their hiding place and he stopped and peered between the trees, a mounted figure reached the top of the steep slope and reined in there. Maximus grinned. The poor bastard would be flummoxed, wondering where they'd gone, and how he'd managed to lose them in such a short time, and he had no reason to believe the Romans knew about their pursuers.

Sure enough, after a few moments, another figure joined the first, and the two argued, both waving hands, pointing around the landscape. There was a push, a shove, further argument, and then more riders joined them. Maximus tried to count. They kept moving around and were clustered together, so it was hard to keep track, but he estimated them at a dozen. They did not seem to be armoured, for nothing glinted among them. That was a relief, because it meant they were almost certainly not Sarmatians. This being the edge of Buri lands, they were probably scouts for the local tribes, keeping tabs on the Romans moving along their border. Still, while that meant Maximus could really leave them alone, a little extra pummelling would only help to keep them afraid of Rome, and the great god Jupiter who joined them in battle.

He turned and gestured to the others, marking twelve in number, and tugging at his tunic, tapping his chain shirt and shaking his head. The other riders nodded their understanding. He turned back and watched again as the enemy began to pick their way down the slope with less care than they should. It was quite steep, but they had lost sight of their quarry, and so they were in a hurry.

He waited until they were almost at the bottom of the hill, and drew his sword. He heard the hiss of many blades leaving scabbards behind him, and smiled viciously. Here goes.

The very moment the first rider reached the flat land of the valley bottom, Maximus kicked Celeris into action and burst from the shelter of the trees. It was so nice to be back with a horse who understood and reacted instinctively. Horse and rider were in harmony, and picked up the pace from a trot to a full speed gallop in only moments. Behind him, the others followed suit, and ninety-six riders burst from the trees and hurtled towards the dozen or so native horsemen.

Such was the surprise of the move that the enemy wasted precious moments first looking around at the sudden sound, trying to work out what was happening, then in heated discussion, trying to decide what to do about it. Indeed, even as Maximus and his men rode them down, half the dozen decided that flight was the sensible option, while the other half drew swords and prepared to fight.

Maximus turned, and his faith in his men swelled as Rigozus nodded without even being asked the question. He simply pointed at the fleeing men and took half the riders after the fugitives, leaving Maximus with a solidly outnumbering force to face the others.

'Try not to kill them all,' he shouted in Greek as they rode. 'I want answers.'

Then battle was joined. In truth, Maximus might have been in the forefront of it, but he was happy enough when his men pushed to race past him and engage. Despite his blasé response to Rigozus's comments, he *had* been worrying a little about what might happen in his next fight if his shoulder took any damage.

His men hit the half dozen like wolves on unprepared sheep, yet even as swords rose and fell, men screaming, one of the enemy riders spotted a gap in the press, and his gaze fell upon Maximus, identifiable as an officer by his plume if nothing else. The man started towards him through that gap, and Maximus had a moment of doubt and indecision. If he were a sensible man, he would make sure his men dealt with the rider. The problem was that he knew deep down he was *not* a sensible man, and that was why, when Azimus made to intercept the enemy, Maximus found himself barking 'No, he's mine,' in Greek.

As the Syrian nodded, and moved aside, allowing the rider to close on him, Maximus noted oddly the narrowing of eyes as the enemy rider registered what he'd said. He let the man come, and as the Dacian reached attacking distance and lashed out with his spear, Maximus easily danced out of the way, Celeris taking the initiative without even the need for rider control. As the horse stepped easily aside, Maximus brought his sword down heavily, smashing that spear mid-shaft, leaving the man holding a short, splintered stick. Barely had the man even pulled back his useless weapon and been struck with panic when Maximus's sword came round in a circle and then swung again, this time hammering into the man's side. The rider cried out and slumped in the saddle, lolling low. Maximus cursed. He'd meant to leave the man alive to interrogate, but even as he watched, the rider tumbled from his horse to be broken and churned beneath the various animals, screaming to the last.

He stopped, breathing deeply, looking around.

The fight here was over. All six enemy riders were down, and it looked distinctly as though none of them had lived. He grunted his irritation as he rode among them, looking this way and that to confirm as much. He had just finished and given the order to have them searched, when Rigozus and his men reappeared, hurtling towards them.

'Report.'

The man reined in beside him. 'They only ran for a bit, until they knew we had them, then they turned and fought. Not particularly *well*, but they fought to the last. I tried to take prisoners, but they fought to the death and it was not possible.'

Maximus nodded. 'We had a similar problem here. I think they deliberately let themselves die rather than be captured. That tells me one thing about them, other than that they clearly aren't Sarmatian.'

'Oh?'

'At least some of them speak Greek. I reckon they heard the command to take prisoners. When I told this lot to leave one of them for me, the man looked up at that. He understood. He spoke Greek.'

'Not expected.'

'Quite. Oh, don't get me wrong. It's not impossible that some of the Buri speak Greek, especially their scouts, but they're from up around the Germans and the Sarmatians. I doubt they get to hear Greek much, so you wouldn't expect many of them to speak it.'

'Sir,' one of the riders said, and walked over towards him.

'Yes?'

'Found this on one of them.' He approached Maximus and held up his hand. In it was a silvered disc the size of a man's palm, embossed with an image of medusa and the legend COH I UBI.

'And?'

'The First Ubiorum were one of the units holding the centre at Tapae, sir, and they'd just been brought to the region last year. If this man took this phalera off a centurion of the First Ubiorum, he did it at Tapae, a few days ago.'

Maximus nodded. 'And if he was at the centre, he was not Buri. He was one of Decebalus's veterans. Daci, pure and simple. These men are not just not Sarmatian, but they're not local either. They're Decebalus's men. What are they doing out here?'

'I don't know,' Rigozus put in, 'but when they rode away, they didn't go into the hills, toward the Buri. They went north, I reckon along the edge of the hills, the way *we* were going.'

'They were going somewhere safe. Somewhere north there's somewhere held for Decebalus that's not part of his central ring of citadels. Why? If he has a solid fortress of mountains, why would he risk men to control somewhere distant? This is important, Rigozus. Wherever they were going, I want to find it. I want to see it for myself.'

The second nodded, and in short order the entire unit was gathered together, mounted, and riding north once more. Though the feeling of being watched and shadowed was now gone, Maximus and his men rode on with ever increasing wariness, the tension high. Whatever was happening around here, they were almost in the middle of it now. They rode at a steady walking pace, around another forested hilly area, and into a region where the flat land branched off like a valley northwest among the hills. They'd been about to pass that side valley once more when they found themselves riding along the eastern bank of a small river that meandered the same direction as they rode. Then, surprisingly, a bridge. The track that crossed the rough timbers showed signs of having been churned up by horses and men during the recent wet weather, having dried into chaos. He and Rigozus stopped and shared a look.

'West it is,' the second in command noted.

They crossed the river using the bridge, and rode then, heading into that wide vale in the hills, with a mounting sense that they were coming close to their goal.

Some seven or eight miles from the bridge, Maximus's searching gaze found something. He held up his hand and reined in, the others coming to a halt behind him, Rigozus and Arvina coming alongside.

'Now *that's* a fortress,' Arvina murmured.

Ahead, a small village sat in the low land of the valley, but at the far side rose a single high peak, and atop it a Dacian fortress, walls of pale grey stone the height of two men, towers all around the edge, looming over the slope. The low hills to the left were forested once more, and Maximus pointed to them and gestured to his friends. 'The others can stay here. You two with me. I want a closer look.'

The commands given, the three Roman riders hurried over to the side of the valley and there looked for a forest track until they found one, then hurried in. Within the safety of the woods, they moved from trail to trail, occasionally pausing anywhere there was a clearing or high view to gain their bearings. It did not take too long to close on that hill with its great citadel. Perhaps half a mile from the walls, they settled onto a ridge with a view between the trees, and took the place in.

'Tell me what you see,' Maximus said quietly.

'Strong fortress,' Arvina said. 'Well manned. Solidly defended. I can't quite be sure, but I think there are heads standing on spears above the gate.'

Maximus nodded. 'Eight heads, in fact. Can't be sure without getting much closer, but I'll bet you everything I have in my purse that's an eight-man forage party who died near Tibiscum a number of days ago. It seems more than a little odd that we were there when they were taken, and here we are finding them again. Almost as if they're expecting us.'

'Maybe there were other riders watching us and they went ahead.'

'Maybe,' Maximus agreed.

'It's the valley itself that worries me,' Rigozus put in, confirming what else Maximus had noted.

'Why?' Arvina asked.

'Because that amount of mess made of good turf in late summer and early autumn can only be made by an active army camp. And look at the fences down there. Corrals, at least seven of them. This was a camp for a large force, and they were at least mostly cavalry.'

Maximus felt a chill return then. The questions he'd been asking since they first saw the Roxolani seemed to be being answered at last, and he wasn't sure he liked the answers.

'I think we need to take this fortress. I'm going to keep half the lads here and make camp in the woods, make sure no one comes or goes without us seeing it. Rigozus, you need to take the rest and ride back for the main army as fast as you can. Ride into the night. Report in, and come back with a legion or two.'

Rigozus nodded, and the three men turned, hurrying back towards the others to split up and go about their tasks.

Whatever was happening, it was looking more and more worrying all the time.

Chapter Seventeen

Dava Fortress, late September AD 101

The Second Adiutrix Legion, supported by a vexillation of the Sixth Ferrata, began the assault.

Maximus heaved a sigh of relief at the sight. He'd worried throughout the wait that the enemy would move away before the army of Rome arrived. If that had happened, he'd have had to leave a messenger here for Rigozus and move off to trail them and then everything could very easily have gone wrong. Fortunately, over the two and a half days following his friend's departure, no one had arrived at this place, and no one had left. Not knowing the name of the place, they had labelled it Dava, the word meaning more or less 'fortress' in Dacian. It seemed appropriate.

During the previous day, one of the lads had slipped close to the walls, moving slowly from tree to tree and using undergrowth for cover, a single man moving at dusk, unarmoured and in a dark cloak, hard to see. He had taken stock of the place from a much closer position. The fortress had just one gate, reachable only via a single road that wound back and forth up the steep slope. All other approaches were little more than scree and grass inclines, each cripplingly steep and ending only in one of those Dacian walls formed of huge stone blocks. There was no real chance of the place falling other than by direct assault of the gate, and many men would die on the approach.

The man who'd scouted close had been one of those with them on that day near Tibiscum, and confirmed that the eight heads on stakes above the gate could only be the mouldering remains of the men of that lost contubernium, which had further incensed the men and made them all the more determined that Dava would fall and those heads be retrieved and buried.

Maximus had then waited for the return of the rest of his men with the legion reinforcements, tense and expectant. There was no way to be sure, of course, but certain connections were suggested by all of this. Apart from those few Dacian horsemen they had killed on the way north the other day, every group of cavalry they had met so far seemed to have been Roxolani. It had been Roxolani riders who had taken those eight heads at Tibiscum, and now here, at Dava, down on that churned-then-dried valley floor, there were signs of many cavalry being quartered, and now those heads in evidence once again. That meant that it was very likely Roxolani who had been here, and far more of them than the Romans had previously encountered.

But more than that, it seemed oddly personal. The fact that it had been Maximus in command when the heads were taken, and then Maximus in command again when they were rediscovered, it just felt too much for coincidence. And the only person who really knew him, and certainly who knew him so well, was Duras. Could the bastard be up there in that fortress?

'Be ready,' he said. 'The moment the gate falls, we go in.'

The others nodded. They would probably prefer to leave it to the legions, and in truth they had already done far more than their share in one campaigning season. But if Duras was up there, Maximus wanted him, and *personally*, not just butchered out of hand in passing by a legionary. Until the walls fell, cavalry were of little use in a siege, but the moment the gate was open, the interior became a killing zone for horsemen too.

He turned his attention to the assault. No one from Dava had escaped – anyone who'd been in the fortress when the Second Pannonian had arrived was still inside now, trapped. And though the assault was focused in only one place, moving up the winding road to the gate, still the entire hill was surrounded by men and no one could escape, even by slipping unnoticed over the back walls.

The legions moved up that snake-like road a century at a time, The front one moved into testudo formation some two thirds of the way up the slope, in a fluid, well-practised move lifting their shields into a solid, interlocked roof, the front and sides protected by walls of the same. It was well timed, for not long afterwards, stones and arrows and slingshots began to rain down from the wall tops above, crashing, thumping and rattling against the roof of shields. The beleaguered front unit had made it all the way to the next turn when a particularly large rock landed in the centre of the testudo roof and smashed through the shields and the men beneath it. As the roof's cohesion collapsed, shields tipped this way and that, and falling arrows and other missiles found targets, men screaming out in agony and falling. The unit's centurion, recognising that his unit had lost its chance, gave an order, and the century broke up in a heartbeat, each man helping tip the dead off the road, to roll down the slope, then ducking off the road themselves, raising their own shield as a single roof and crouching behind rocks or trees.

Maximus's gaze moved down the line of centuries. Every third one carried a battering ram within the confines of the testudo, hidden from above, but visible from behind if you knew what to look for. A tree trunk planed to smoothness and fitted with rope handles.

It was a war of attrition, this approach, but Rome was prepared to lose a lot of men to take a valuable target. The second century of men reached that corner, passing their fallen mates, and turned to double back, missiles pounding against them, arrows thudding into shields. The poor bastards managed almost the entire next length of road before Fortuna averted her gaze once again. One of the cloud of falling arrows happened by chance to strike the narrow gap between shield wall and shield roof, where the front rank could look out and see where they were going. The man hit died instantly, and the entire front rank of the testudo collapsed in an instant, men falling over one another, the whole protective shell coming apart, which, again, allowed other missiles from above to do their work.

Maximus ground his teeth. If only there were a clever, subtle way to take the fortress – another trick like the one they'd pulled at Tapae – but there wasn't. Sometimes there was nothing for it but to stomp up a slope with a shield above you and hope to Hades you made it as far as the wall. Once again, the broken second testudo dissolved at a centurion's whistle, and the men scattered, clearing their dead out of the way and falling into any defensive location they could find, using their shields as roofs. The survivors of the first attempt were now sliding back down the hill, shields still held up, to regroup as they could at the bottom, the attention of the defenders drawn by fresh meat.

The third testudo moved through the remains of the first and then of the second. One more turn and they would reach the gate. Unfortunately they too fell foul of a lucky shot, and the men in the centre of the formation let go of the ram in the chaos, which rolled, knocking men aside. Another collapse, another whistle, another run.

But each time, the units were getting closer and closer to their target. Attrition. If Rome couldn't win a war with ingenuity, it would win it with stamina. Sure enough, more and more men were approaching the top. The next testudo faltered around where the second had, and failed to dissolve and move out of the way, yet the following one simply barged them aside and continued their own climb. Men were now skittering back down all over the slope, the survivors of various attacking centuries, but up at the crest, the next group was on the final straight. Even as the defenders redoubled their efforts, pouring down their missiles like rain, hammering, battering and punching the shields. The centurion of that unit clearly decided his men didn't have much left, but he was not going to be the next transverse crest slipping down the hill on his arse, red-faced. Whatever he said to his men in the confines of that shield-box, the century broke into a run, still in formation. Impressive. They reached the gate, and there did something Maximus had never seen before, and had never even thought of. They split into two smaller testudos. A relatively simple process, yet one he'd never seen done, the two forty-men shield boxes pushing up against the fortress wall on either side of the gate, where they braced against the ever-increasing hail of destruction.

Maximus whistled his awe at the move, and watched with a slow, determined smile as the next century, the second one to be hiding a ram, somehow managed to pick up speed and moved fast up those last paces, rounding the final corner. The defenders on the parapet, their attention divided between the split testudo either side of the gate and the next one on the approach, divided their efforts, and therefore reduced their effectiveness against either.

The ram party reached the gate, and began to work. Even half a mile away, at the valley floor, Maximus could hear the thuds as the barrage began, that great trunk, bearing a riveted iron head in the shape of an animal or a god, hammering into the timber, every blow bringing them closer to victory.

The enemy were doomed from the first crash. They once more stepped up their own barrage, bringing every man they could fit up onto the walls, along with every piece of ammunition that could be gathered together. But it would not be enough. Now, more centuries of men were making it to the top of the slope, their approach made easy as the defenders concentrated on the ones already there. Here and there, a shot hit home at the testudos outside the gate, and a man fell. But now there were sufficient men and adequate officers up there that every time a man fell, someone else moved out of their own place and replaced him.

The thudding continued, again and again.

'Time to go,' Maximus said.

'They're not in yet,' Rufus noted.

'No, but it'd take us a quarter of an hour to get up there even without having to take our place in the queue of infantry using the road. Come on.'

In response, the various officers serving under him gathered their men, and the riders of the Second Pannonian began to canter through the camp, drawing surprised looks from the legionaries settling in for the night. They burst out into the staging area, racing past the gathered centuries awaiting their turn, and the medical corps, already working hard at the many injuries, large and small, that had made it back down the slope to safety.

They hit the slope just as a century from the Sixth was moving into position, forming up, and the unit's optio called them a number of unkind names as they raced past, raising dust in clouds, and pushed ahead of the infantry. Then they reached the rear ranks of another climbing century. They slowed to a walk, following them for a time. Along the first straight they rode slowly on the heels of the infantry, but as they hit the next corner and turned, the centurion of the unit seemed to decide he didn't like the cavalry a few feet behind his men, and broke up his formation, pulling them from four abreast, which filled the road, to two, so that the riders could hurtle past once at a time. This they did, albeit a slow job, and it frustrated Maximus immensely when they finally passed that unit, only to find themselves almost immediately at the rear of another century.

This time, he deliberately rode too close to the rear of the legionaries, pushing the matter. He knew he was being an arse, but there might be a man up there he needed to find and punch in the face more than any other human on Earth. Besides, given that he'd found them this place and identified its importance, he felt that he was owed it. He could *afford* to be an arse every now and then, surely?

Sure enough, after a while, the centurion re-formed his men to allow Maximus and his riders past. They did so, soon finding themselves behind the next century, now half way up the slope to the gate. This time, Maximus met his match in the world of arse-dom, for no matter what he did, the centurion ignored him and continued to move his men up at a steady pace, blocking the entire road with their formation, now in a testudo.

Maximus followed with his riders, aware that they were getting close to the danger area, while they could not form a protective shield like the infantry, and that they could soon be battered by falling ammunition. More than that, they were moving at a slow, plodding pace, and above, the gate had not yet fallen, judging by the rhythmic thuds. Had he misjudged it all?

In position in the mobile queue of infantry, Maximus led his men slowly, inexorably, up that slope to the fortress gate. His immense relief when he heard a ligneous explosion and a cheer, laced with invocations of Jupiter's name, was palpable. The gate had broken.

Indeed, everything changed in that moment. The number of falling missiles halved, as the men throwing them were called down to the gateway to help defend it, and every century on the approach picked up the pace, racing upwards, despite the incline, to get through that gate and be present at the fall of Dava.

The line of units climbing the zig-zag road moved on with fresh vigour, and Maximus and his horsemen climbed along with them. By the time they reached the last two turns and entered that stretch where so many centuries had fallen to missile attacks, hardly anything was coming down from the walls, for legionaries had surged in through the gate and, while they were engaged in bitter fighting just inside, men had slipped past and raced up onto the walls, cutting down archers, slingers, and various warriors throwing masonry down on the approach. The enemy barrage had stopped. Dava was falling.

Impatiently, wanting nothing more than to be the first into that fortress, and wondering how he would find and identify Duras if he was there, Maximus moved in line, ever closer to the gate. By the time he reached the wall, and the century in front pushed through, no longer in testudo formation, but simply charging forward and roaring their legion's name, he was forming a plan.

Dacian fortresses were not like Roman ones. While a Roman fort was more or less the same wherever you went, with similar layouts of buildings, and each identifiable for what it was, Dacian strongholds were largely designed with a view to the terrain upon which they sat, for they were almost always on defensible rocky peaks, and therefore of different shape and design each time. But Maximus had been in a few over the years for one reason or another, and he knew one thing that seemed to be the case in every one. The place may have interior walls, separating off part of the enclosure that belonged to the nobleman in residence, and would be scattered with buildings of stone and wood, from barracks to workshops to temples, but there would also be great, rectangular stone towers inside, not part of the defences, and the largest and most impressive of those would be held by the leader of the place. While they had no idea who commanded at Dava, it seemed certain that if Duras was here, he would be found with the nobles and commanders, as he had been at Tapae.

Thus, as they passed through the gate in the wake of the century, he had one eye on the fighting and how to get through it, and one on the fortress interior beyond, trying to identify where the noblemen would be.

A gap opened up among the lines of legionaries in front, almost as if the gods had gifted him a way in, and Maximus kicked Celeris to speed, charging into the space, sword raised. A Dacian warrior came at him with a shield of elongated hexagon shape and a single handed falx. He recognised the danger instantly, for that weapon could maim the horse very easily, and so he adjusted his swing even as it began. The falx came forward for Celeris's throat, but met Maximus's sword before it could get there. The momentum of a swing from horseback, combined with the length and weight of a Roman cavalry sword, was sufficient to smash the man's hand and send the curved nightmare weapon spinning back into the crowd behind.

Maximus did not stop.

The Dacians were crowded six deep trying to block access to the fort, but they had been pushed back inside by the legions and were being forced into an ever expanding and retreating arc. Yet they were still trying to stay massed close together. That suited Maximus. Where the legions were still having to butcher their way systematically through rank after rank of defenders, the cavalry, once they had taken down the front line, could simply push forward. The Dacians were too closely packed to be able to get a good swing at them, and Maximus prayed, offering devotions to both Jupiter and Mars if they broke through without losing Celeris. He couldn't change horses again.

The gods were kind. Maximus simply trampled the packed ranks of Dacians. He felt a light glancing blow here and there as he pushed forwards, but once he was in among them, the others were following, and they simply carved a path of churning hooves and falling blades through the mass of men.

And then they were through. Maximus raced forwards into the open space beyond the warriors, confident that Duras would not be among them. He had already, even as they fought, spotted what had to be the leader's residence, for one particular tower stood on the highest point of the peak, walled off from the lower housing area by a smaller internal wall. More warriors stood in a gateway in that inner wall, though as yet it remained open, presumably to allow warriors to withdraw through it in time.

'Don't let them close that gate,' he shouted to his men, and pushed Celeris on.

Rigozus was by his side a moment later, and more men pushing past, the faster horses among the unit, and the more determined men, pushing forth, desperately trying to reach that gate. The defenders saw the danger now, as the Roman cavalry broke through en masse into the heart of the citadel, and rushed to get the gate shut, forgetting about their doomed fellows outside it.

Rigozus and Falco reached them first, vying each to be in front. Falco never let them forget that his horse was of Arab descent, bred from racing stock, and had won prizes at inter-unit competitions. The two were in front of Maximus, and currently, given his worries over the efficacy of his left arm, that suited him well. Rigozus and Falco ploughed into the crowd of warriors trying to push the gate shut, the defenders getting in each other's way as they did so, and the Romans' swords went to work, cutting down Dacians and forcing a path through them. Before Maximus could reach them to join in, two more riders had passed him and begun the work of capturing the inner gate, but then he was there with them, and found a man unoccupied, trying to pull at the great wooden portal. His sword fell hard, and the man screamed as it bit into his shoulder, letting go of the gate and falling away. Maximus walked Celeris across the fallen man, to be sure, and looked for another target. He spotted Calpurnius, lolling back in his saddle, a native spear having jammed into his nethers, by fluke or by masterful design having been jabbed between the hem of his chain shirt and the leather horn of the saddle. As Calpurnius's horse turned, the spear snapped, but the damage was done. The cavalryman was done for, blood sheeting down the side of his animal. Maximus pushed in, found another man, delivered another sword blow, felt something slam into the chain at his left side, and the throb and flash of pain in his shoulder as he jerked away. But the defenders had lost. They had abandoned any attempt to force the gate closed now, and were scattering, trying to get away from the riders.

As Maximus moved into the open ground of the inner compound, he looked about. His heart broke as he spotted Falco standing in the grass, sword lowered, the body of his prized Arab stallion lying on the ground in front of him, neck sheathed in crimson. Maximus tore his gaze away to concentrate on more pressing matters.

He didn't care about the various warriors racing to find cover or a hiding place, or the ones kneeling and raising their hands in surrender. Let the others have them. He was looking for one man. He rode across to that huge, square tower, formed of the same great stone blocks as the citadel's walls, and found, to his relief, that the door was open. It was not manned as a last defence, for they had expected to be able to hold the gate in the inner wall.

He vaulted from the saddle, wincing at the shoulder pain as he landed, and prayed that Celeris would not be targeted by some random warrior, leaving her to graze near the door.

He pushed inside, narrowing his eyes to slits as he did so, in order to prevent the change in light affecting him too much. The tower's lower interior was Spartan, just a large table and a couple of stools, patterned woven hangings around the walls, narrow slit windows admitting just enough light to see by. In the corner, a ladder climbed to the second floor, and Maximus crossed to it with a sense of trepidation. Two problems presented themselves here. If there was anyone up there, not just Duras, he would be putting himself in dreadful danger climbing it, and secondly, with his shoulder as it was, he had only one usable arm, which made a ladder a daunting prospect at the best of times.

He breathed something of a sigh of relief as Arvina suddenly appeared next to him, bloodied sword bared. 'Need a hand, sir?' he asked.

'Someone with two would be very useful, yes. Just to get up there first.'

Arvina nodded and crossed to the ladder. He'd had his shield with him thus far, but dropped it near the ladder and began to climb, managing the rungs even with his sword still in his hand. He climbed easily, pausing as he neared the top. Then, taking a breath, launched himself the last couple of rungs and disappeared into the darkness. Maximus approached the bottom of the ladder, waiting for either Arvina's scream, or the clash of blades, and as the moments strung out and nothing happened, he frowned. He'd expected *something*, at least.

'Clear… sort of,' came Arvina's call.

Still with a frown, Maximus gripped the ladder and began to climb, jerkily and with difficulty using just one hand. Damn it, but he couldn't wait for this shoulder to get better. It took a deal of discomfort, and quite some time, to reach the top, and Maximus was just wondering how he was going to pull himself up when Arvina's hand appeared, offering help. He gripped it, and climbed the last few rungs, emerging into the upper floor. He looked around in the gloom, the light similarly dim to the floor below, admitted only by the same, narrow slit windows.

A small group of figures sat huddled in the corner, and he started for a moment before he realised it was a woman and her children. Whoever they were, they weren't Duras, and he felt at one and the same time relieved and disappointed. Despite his hopes, the former slave was seemingly not at Dava, and had therefore escaped his grasp again. But, on the other hand, they had taken the tower without a fight, and the woman and her children had to be important to be so protected.

He spotted a large oil lamp of Roman design on the table at the room's centre, and gestured to Arvina and then the lamp. The trooper crossed to it and drew his multi-tool from his belt pouch, using the flint and steel striker to light the lamp, something Maximus could not currently do, for the jerky movement on his left arm would hurt too much.

The lamp guttered into life, and the room slowly filled with the golden glow of light. Maximus turned. The woman was dressed in very rich clothes, and adorned with golden and silver jewellery. A noblewoman, perhaps the wife of a chieftain, and presumably her children. Probably the wife of the man who lived at Dava, who was likely a chieftain of the Buri. He turned, spotting Dacian dagged banners on the wall near the woman, and then saw Arvina staring, wide-eyed. He spun again, to find what the trooper had seen, and his own eyes widened.

A collection of Roman standards and vexillum flags were displayed proudly on a wall, along with embossed cuirass plates and swords in expensive, decorative sheathes.

'What *is* this?' Arvina breathed.

But Maximus had already identified some of the unit names on the flags and standards, and a fierce smile was breaking out across his face.

'These are the standards and banners of the units lost in that disaster at Tapae under Fuscus fifteen years ago. Decebalus has had these prizes for a generation. The emperor is going to be rather happy at their return. Arvina, my friend, we just won big.'

He walked over to one of the narrow windows and looked out. Below, he could see the last fighting in the fortress enclosures as the remaining defenders were either killed or captured, Dava falling to Roman control. He could see the main gate, piled with dead, most of them Dacian. And beyond that he could see the plain, stretching out between hills, back towards the Dacian heartland, below them the village and the camp of the army.

And that churned ground, where a mass of horsemen had stayed for some time.

He turned back to the room. His gaze slipped past the Roman standards, and the proud noblewoman and her cowering children, and fell upon the Dacian flags. The crimson banner with the horse of the Buri, whose lands this fortress likely protected, and close by, the black wolf banner of Decebalus and his tribe. And between them, hanging on the wall, a bronze symbol of intricate design. A tamga. He crossed to the ladder.

'Rigozus?'

Moments later, the man appeared below. 'Sir?'

'Come up here.'

The rider clambered out onto the upper floor a moment later, and looked around, gaze falling with surprise on the

Roman standards, but Maximus walked over, pointing, drawing his attention to the Dacian flags and the tamga. 'Tell me what you think that is.'

Rigozus frowned, studying the symbol. 'Unless I am very much mistaken, that is the personal tamga of the Roxolani king.'

Maximus nodded. That was what he thought. The Roxolani had many tribal chieftains, but in times of war they could come together as one nation under a single leader, and that appeared to have happened here.

'The Buri, Decebalus, and the Roxolani. And looking down in the valley, I would say *several tribes* of Roxolani were based here for a while. One wonders where they are now, given that they're clearly allied with Decebalus, but in those mountain fortresses he's retreated to, there's no real room for a lot of horsemen.'

'And if they weren't at Tapae,' Rigozus murmured, 'then where are they, and what are they up to.'

A very good question, and a rather unsettling one.

Chapter Eighteen

Camp of the Fifth Macedonica, October AD 101

'How were we to know?' Rigozus grumbled.

'The clues were there,' Maximus answered, watching the gathering all around them in its pomp and glory. 'We were distracted by the lost standards and the hints of mass cavalry. Should have paid more attention to the woman.'

It *had* come as a surprise. The Second Pannonian had jealously claimed the tower as their own, moving the three turmae in to raid it of all things important. The standards and banners and other Roman prizes were all claimed and loaded on horses for delivery to the emperor, and then the woman and the children were taken prisoner, mounted on the spare horses with hands bound. The woman had snapped angrily at the men who'd taken her, but Maximus and Rigozus had been away, stowing standards and deploying riders, and the people she had shouted at had no command of Dacian, and simply ignored her, unaware of what she was saying.

She'd then fallen silent throughout the day-long journey south. Undoubtedly she had assumed that since the men who took her captive spoke no Dacian, then neither did the others. And so they had returned to that great new camp to the east of the Iron Gates, full of pride and positivity.

Upon delivery of the standards and war booty, and of the prisoners, the truth had come out. When presented to one of the senior officers, the woman had begun her harangue again, and this time there were people around her who understood.

Any favour they hoped to enjoy from the capture of the standards evaporated at the discovery that they had roughly manhandled Cotatia, sister of Decebalus of Dacia, and her children, treating them as ordinary slaves and captives.

As he'd said, the clues were there. She had been extremely well dressed and adorned in gold. She had been protected above anything else in the fortress. And perhaps most telling of all had been the banners that hung nearby in that room, displaying the horse of the Buri and the wolf of Dacia. The king's sister had apparently been married off to the head chieftain of the Buri, bringing them into the war on Dacia's side. That was why there had been men from Decebalus's own tribe at Dava and in the hills nearby, and not just Buri. Of course, that didn't explain the cavalry, but *that* was a question that remained to be answered.

The annoying thing was that Maximus had a suspicion that the emperor would have been a lot more supportive of their position. They had achieved a *major* victory for Rome at Dava, after all. But with the way command worked, it had been the Praetorian Prefect, Livianus, who had been the senior officer on site when they returned, and it was fast becoming clear that the man did not like scouts, spies, and any sort of subterfuge. He had congratulated them on the standards, and then immediately given them a dressing down for their treatment of the king's sister.

For a moment, Maximus had wondered how word of the woman's capture managed to get back to her brother in that mountain fastness in the Dacian heartland, but he quickly decided that the arcani, that secretive group of paramilitary scouts that moved and worked among the tribes beyond the frontier, gathering information for the empire, must have passed the information deliberately.

Whatever the case, word had clearly reached Decebalus, for four days after their semi-triumphant return from Dava, the turmae assigned to this locale reported the approach of a column of Dacian riders.

And here they were, now, making their way into the camp, escorted by Praetorians and legionaries. The emperor himself, as well as several of his most senior officers, sat in curule chairs atop a dais constructed in the past hour and draped with crimson hangings, the eagle of Rome displayed behind them on banners, standards and vexilla all around. And the cream of the region's military were present in serried ranks, partially to provide protection for the emperor and his people, but also as a show of strength to the visitors, for a column of riders meant discussion, not war.

Maximus was not entirely sure why his turma was among the front lines of the soldiers. Arvina had assumed the position of honour was because of their part in the recent victories, but Maximus rather doubted that. Yet here they were, spitting distance from the First Cohort of Praetorians, the Imperial Horse Guard, and the First Cohort of the Fifth Macedonica: a war-weary, slightly battered group of auxiliary cavalrymen. But Maximus felt he was coming to know how this new emperor worked, and he was damn well sure there was a good reason.

The riders were approaching, now, and he turned to examine them. Ten noblemen, easily identifiable as such from the quality of their garb, the richness of their jewellery, the Phrygian caps they wore, but most of all from the simple fact that they rode horses. Behind them – *some good distance* behind them, in fact – came their guard, a mass of maybe a hundred of the most fearsome warriors the Dacians could muster. But they had been separated from their masters at the edge of the camp, the nobles escorted separately, ahead.

The riders were brought forward, and Maximus noted, not at all surprised, that the dais had been constructed at sufficient height that the visitors still had to look up at the emperor, even though they were in the saddle. Nothing escaped Trajan.

They stopped where the Praetorian tribune indicated with a rather perfunctory gesture, and guardsmen moved into ordered lines, boxing them in on three sides. Silence reigned for a moment, and then a man stepped forward on the dais, drawing his breath and holding out his arm in an oratorical manner.

'Behold, his radiant and imperial majesty, pater patriae, pontifex maximus, emperor of eternal Rome and son of the deified Nerva, Caesar Nerva Traianus.'

Maximus could have laughed at the bored look the emperor threw the announcer. He waved the man away and then turned the gesture on the riders. 'I am a busy man. Get to the point.'

This clearly threw the visitors, and there was a huddled discussion now, quite loud enough for Maximus to hear, before one of them straightened in the saddle, and began to speak in good Latin, if with a strong accent.

'By the grace of wise Zalmoxis, His Majesty, Decebalus, King of the peoples of the mountains and the plains, defender of the northlands, son of gods and master of the world, bids welcome to his brother, the noble Trajan.'

Maximus was impressed. He was fairly sure all that was drivel, dredged up out of the speaker's imagination as a counter to the impressive titles Trajan could claim, but it was expertly done, nonetheless, and that last bit was superb, stating that the king and the emperor were perfectly on a level with one another and suggesting far more understanding and amity than one might expect from men who had so recently stood on opposite sides of a bloody battle. Maximus knew the Dacians to be wily, and their king even more so, but this was still impressive.

'Brother?' Trajan said, a wide smile crossing his face. 'My sister Marciana *will* be surprised.'

There were a few chuckles across the dais at this.

The emperor's smile vanished as quickly as it had appeared. 'The point?' he reiterated.

'The king wishes to engage in a treaty with Rome. He is willing to meet with the emperor on neutral ground to discuss how to end this conflict and bring peace to the region.'

'No.'

The man blinked at Trajan's rather blunt reply. 'I'm sorry?'

'I told you, I'm a busy man. I do not have time to go wandering off into the wilds of Dacia to argue semantics that will inevitably lead to nothing, with a man I can trust as far as I can a Parthian in a game of latrunculi. So, no, I will not meet with your king.'

'This is a matter of great importance for *all* of us,' the emissary said, aghast. 'Surely the emperor can see the benefit to Rome of ending this costly war?'

Trajan leaned forward in his chair. 'What I see is a man who realises he has trapped himself in his own mountain prison, who lost the most important battle fought in a decade, who watched his own allies flee, and who has now lost his precious prizes that he had kept to gloat over Domitian. A man who also now knows that his sister is in our custody and that without her to connect him to the Buri, it is likely they will step out of the war like their neighbours the Iazyges. I see a man who knows he is in trouble, trying to save *what* he can, *while* he can. No. There will be a cessation of hostilities only when *I* decide as much, which will be when any such end is favourable to Rome rather than to your king. For now, Dacia lies open before us, and I am not of a mind to turn my back and walk away, because of the honeyed words of a few diplomats.'

'Emperor, I *beg* of you to accept the king's offer of parley.'

'Very well,' Trajan said, suddenly, and spun in his chair, looking this way and that. 'Sura? If any man in Rome could be said to be able to speak for me, then it is you, old friend. Until we face the man across the field of battle again, you will just become bored. Will you go and find out what the king of Dacia has to say?'

Sura, a middle-aged man with clever eyes and a strong chin, smiled. 'Of course, Imperator. You never know. It might turn into a battle anyway.'

Trajan chuckled. 'Try not to start a second war in the middle of the first, Sura. Take Livianus and his Praetorians with you. Best to make a good show of it. Try not to get yourself killed. I would miss your anecdotes at meals.'

Again, Sura smiled. Then he turned to the riders. 'Return to your king and tell him that the emperor's emissaries will meet him at...' he paused and frowned. Curtius Cilo, leader of the arcani, leaned a little closer to him and murmured something. Sura nodded, then turned back to the riders. 'We will meet your king at the Raven Peak, on the Ides of this month.'

There was a little more discussion between the Dacian noblemen, and Maximus strained, trying to hear what they were saying. As he watched, listening intently, he noted one of the men narrowing his eyes in thought. The rider leaned closer to another, and the way the pair spoke just drew Maximus's attention. There was something suspicious about it. As such, he stopped paying attention to the exchange between the embassies as the details were hammered out, and tried to focus on the two riders.

It was by pure chance, still, that he heard it, in a momentary lull in the discussion.

'It was supposed to be the emperor.'

'You heard him. The pale one is his old friend. The other leads the Praetorians. That is enough.'

The exchange went on a little longer, but then the conclusion of the main discussion became too loud and overrode it, as the matter was finalised. The Dacians, not entirely pleased with the result of their mission, presumably hoping to return with the king's sister, turned and began to ride away, still under Praetorian escort. It was only once they were little more than dots on the horizon, far from audible distance, and the area was secure again, that Sura turned to him. 'A busy man? Signing a few requisitions and sacrificing the odd pig? I think that could probably wait.'

Trajan laughed aloud. 'I cannot decide whether they are being desperate or duplicitous, or both. They want this meeting either because they know they are beaten and are trying to save what's left, or because they want to try and end the war fast by putting an arrow through my neck during a parley. Either way, I am not greatly inclined to go along with them. I meant what I said. I would consider accepting Decebalus's surrender and even letting him live, if the result was advantageous to Rome. As we currently stand, though, we have every advantage, and he has none, so there will be no peace for now. And I also meant the other thing I said. Try not to get yourself killed.'

Then, in a moment Maximus had already half expected, the emperor looked up and pointed at him. 'Attend.'

Ignoring the surprise and shock among his men, Maximus urged Celeris out and rode over towards the podium, keeping his head lowered. He was not sure whether he was expected to dismount, but he knew from watching the Dacians that he would be below the emperor anyway, even in the saddle, so that should be fine.

'Your Majesty?'

'What did you hear?'

Of course. That was why he'd been placed where he was.

'There was a level of disappointment. They were expecting you to agree. One of them said something along the lines of your 'old friend' and the commander of the Praetorians being enough.'

Trajan nodded. 'I suspect they were hoping for some sort of ambush that would remove me and bring the campaign to a premature end. In the absence of that, they will settle for taking Sura and Livianus captive. And I do not think they intend to kill them – maybe Livianus, I suppose, but not Sura. He will be captured. They will have my friend, and I will have the king's sister. At that point an exchange would put everything back to rights. Until then, Decebalus knows that any action he takes will put his sister in danger. Not that such a thing will necessarily stop him, but it will certainly make him think twice.' He gestured to Maximus. 'Get your riders ready. My ambassadors will be protected by a cohort of Praetorians, but they will need to know what they are riding into, and that is *your* job.'

*

And that was how Maximus found himself once more riding into the enemy's arms, far ahead of the army. He was starting to wonder which god he had offended in the past to the extent that he kept getting personally selected to walk into the wolf's maw with a smile and a jaunty step.

He looked round. The two important noblemen, Livianus and Sura, rode in the midst of a column of Praetorians, clerks, slaves and other attendants, perhaps a mile further back. The men of the Second Pannonian, once more the three turmae Maximus had taken north, had ridden, accompanying them, for the two days since leaving the camp, but now, with the mountains closing in, and their destination but a few miles away, the scouts would move ahead, testing the water.

They had crossed a narrow and high saddle between peaks, and then dipped down once more into a valley that was becoming increasingly oppressive, the hills to either side higher with every few paces. They had yet to see another human, but Maximus could once again sense the presence of watchers somewhere on the hills around them. They began to move a little slower, now. They'd not been here before, but the land conformed to the descriptions they'd been given.

Raven Peak was the westernmost of Decebalus's mountain fortresses, the one that guarded the main valley that led into the region. Cilo had told them to expect a small civilian village in the valley bottom, with a solid Dacian stronghold towering over it from the hilltop. He had described the route and the approach, to the extent that Maximus had almost felt he knew the place as they rode. Even now he could see how every undulation and rock conformed with Cilo's descriptions. They were almost there.

He heard the call in the tense silence, and it was so well done that he almost missed it. He cast his mind back to the preparations before they left.

'You can recognise the call of a swan, yes?' Cilo had said.

'Of course.'

'You hear a swan at Raven's Peak, then it is my man, making contact.'

Maximus frowned. 'Or, presumably, just a swan?'

The arcani leader had rolled his eyes. 'Not enough water up there for swans generally. That's why we use it. If it's a swan, then it's either lost or desperate, or it's my man, making contact.'

And it really *did* sound like a swan, which was why he almost missed it.

He looked around, this time paying attention, and when he heard the next call, a dozen heartbeats later, he caught its general direction and waved Rigozus forward.

'See that little side valley up ahead? Take the others and move into it, out of sight of the main run. I'm going to see whether one of the arcani has a message for us, or whether Cilo is just peculiar and there are swans up in these mountains after all.'

Leaving the others to go about their work, Maximus turned up the slope, a forested affair, though patchy, and with odd areas of grass and scree. He passed a few haystacks that should probably have long since been moved into granaries, and reached the trees, then began to climb, carefully. The next swan call sounded a little irritated, and that at least made him content that it was actually a Roman spy and not some stranded bird wondering where his favourite pond was.

He followed the sound, and emerged into a small clearing in the woodland. A man stood by a fallen tree, his woodcutter's axe still wedged in the trunk. He was wearing the clothes of a Dacian peasant, and his beard and hair were long and straggly, the latter bound with a leather thong around his brow. He leaned back, rubbing his sides, then folded his arms.

'Exploratores are supposed to be able to move into the wilds quietly and subtly,' the man said. 'Not like a parade, with musical accompaniment.'

Maximus bridled. 'We are not truly scouting right now, just riding ahead of the column. You have something useful to say?'

'Stop short of Raven's Peak. Once you reach the village, it will be too late. Near a thousand warriors have been brought in from the next fortress and scattered in hidden places around the valley, as well as a significant number of archers, including mercenary Thracians. The moment your column passes through the edge of the village, they will be in a trap sufficient to butcher the lot of them.'

'A thousand warriors wouldn't be enough,' Maximus replied, coldly. 'We have the First Cohort of Praetorians as well as my three turmae of the Second Pannonian.'

'Ah, so you're loud and clumsy and you don't listen *too*? Excellent. I said an *extra* thousand. Don't forget to add to that the garrison of the Raven's Peak fortress. And that garrison is one of the largest in the mountains, as it's the first gateway to Decebalus's domain. You're going to be outnumbered at least ten to one.'

Maximus shivered. 'Sorry. Rather missed the point of that.'

'Exactly. You're the one the emperor has out looking for signs of unexpected activity, yes?'

Maximus nodded.

'Then when you leave here, assuming you *manage* to leave here, get yourself down towards the Vulcan Pass. General rumour among the ordinary villagers of the mountains suggests there's something happening down near the Bolia's Rock fortress near there. I can't get specific details, but it sounds big. For now, though, just make sure you don't get as far as the next village, avoid the trap, and then piss off and leave me alone before someone hears this and realises I'm not just Tanos the lonely woodsman.'

He turned away, then, and pulled the axe free of the trunk, spat on his hand and gripped the thing, then went back to work. Maximus watched for just a moment, then turned and began to pick his way down the slope. Reaching the bottom, he cantered on towards that defile leading off into the hills to the right, and soon found Rigozus and the others.

'We're riding into a trap.'

'I think we all *assumed* that,' the man replied.

'Well, it's confirmed now. We should be alright as long as we don't quite get as far as the village below the fortress. At that point we'll still be outside the trap. Come on. Let's go escort the embassy.'

With that, the three turmae turned and rode back along the valley until they saw the white and gleaming silver of the Praetorian cohorts, then rode forward until Maximus could fall in alongside the two commanders.

'You have news?' Sura asked.

'Very much so, sir. It would appear that Decebalus has set a trap for you at Raven's Peak. Extra warriors have been brought in to bolster the garrison and then distributed around the valley, such that we can be attacked from all sides at once. In addition they have a number of archers, and I can attest to the extreme danger of letting the Dacians get archers on the high ground above you. As such, riding into their trap would be effective suicide.'

'I think you underestimate the Guard,' Livianus said coldly.

'Perhaps, sir, but I never risk underestimating the *Dacians*, and that is a lesson worth learning. I am given to understand that the trap is ready to be sprung on our arrival at the village. If we stop short of the houses, we should be sufficiently outside the trap that we can survive any attempt to close it.'

'You learned this from whom?' Sura asked. 'You have not had time to search the hills with your men.'

'One of the arcani made contact, sir.'

While Sura nodded at that, Livianus sneered. 'The arcani. A bunch of criminals and madmen, often gone native beyond help. And you are convinced that he tells the truth?'

'Enough to not bet my life on it, sir,' Maximus said, pointedly, and even Livianus nodded at that.

'Very well. We shall stop a half mile short of the village, announce our arrival there and draw them to our location, rather than walking into a trap.'

And they did just that. Walking their horses, the Second Pannonian led the deputation from the emperor slowly towards the houses below Raven's Peak. They stopped about half a mile before the edge of the village, Praetorians and auxiliaries formed up into their ranks. The deputation of Rome sat there for a while, in ordered lines, watching the village ahead, knowing the Dacians controlled every inch of land from there onward. Silence reigned, and then finally Sura rode to the fore and cleared his throat.

'Men of Dacia, subjects of Decebalus, we are here as agreed, to talk peace deals with your leaders. If you have any desire for peace, now is your time.'

Silence greeted this. The world's weirdest, tensest silence. Maximus knew damn well that scores of Dacian killers were waiting across the valley, and kept quiet, waiting for their quarry to come to them, something that was not going to happen.

As the pause grew, Sura straightened. 'Let it be known that Rome offered the olive branch of peace, but it was swatted aside by Decebalus, your king.'

Clever. Maximus had assumed the man was yet another of those senate-appointed rich boys who gained military position simply through family ties. Having now decided he knew how Trajan worked, Maximus should clearly have measured the emperor's friends with the same ruler.

Silence continued to blanket the valley. Most likely Sura and Livianus had no idea, where they were, surrounded by Praetorians, but Maximus could feel it. The whole trap, laid by Dacians, was ready to spring, even though the Romans remained just outside it. One move too far and they would end up fighting, struggling, desperate to return to Roman lines. Indeed, in a heart-stopping moment, he saw Livianus give the Praetorians the order to march on, into the village. But then Sura countered the order. The Roman embassy actually contrived to move a few paces back. And then Trajan's great friend spoke again.

'Then talk, such as it is, is done. We were drawn here by the possibility of peace, but with no answer, peace will not be found in this land. Decebalus and his nobles will bow to Rome, and that is where it all ends.'

With that, Sura turned his horse and began to lead the deputation back west, towards the Roman forces. Maximus could almost feel the frustration and disappointment of the Dacian warriors as their trap remained unsprung, and the Romans left, moving back up the valley. Still, Maximus and his men brought up the rearguard, keeping the ambassadors safe as they moved out of the mountains.

The hours passed with the sluggishness of seasons, but finally they reached the plains once more, and then Maximus rode ahead to join the commanders, bowing his head in deference.

'Am I right,' Sura said, 'that there was never any intention or hope of peace there?'

Maximus nodded. 'I think that was the fact of the matter, sir.'

'In which case we have lost nothing, but we may even have *won* something.'

'Sir?'

'We continue to surprise them, in this case by avoiding their trap.'

They rode north and west out of the Dacian heartland, and the further they went, the easier each step became, taking them back to safety. As they reached that great plain once more, and the main column began to head west towards the winter quarters of the Fifth and the advance camp of the emperor, Maximus pulled alongside the great general Sura.

'What is it?' the man said.

'I'm afraid that here, we must depart, sir?'

'Oh?'

'With a cohort of Praetorians, you will be quite safe crossing the open plain to reach the legions. But matters are afoot in the south, and the armies of Rome may be taken by surprise if her scouts are not aware of what those movements mean.'

Sura nodded. 'Go with Jove at your back, Decurion.'

Chapter Nineteen

The Fourth Flavia Felix had been hard at work in this region, kept informed by three other turmae of the Second Pannonian. As Maximus and his men passed small settlements on their way south and east, they found them depopulated and burned, piles of blackened bones all that remained of the occupants. Why these people had stayed, Maximus couldn't decide. Perhaps they thought themselves safe this far southeast into Decebalus's domain, presuming the legions to have gone as far as they would, knowing the Roman campaigning season to be over. Or perhaps they had simply become trapped, the Roman army of Laberius having marched from the Danubius into the mountains southeast of here, while the legions of Trajan's own column lay between here and the valley that led into the king's heartland. Quite possibly these locals had been informed there was simply not enough room for so many ordinary folk in the fortresses and citadels of the mountains.

Whatever the case, they had not lived to regret their decision.

The first day, after departing the column of Praetorians, they had travelled three hours until the sun began to sink into a sky beginning to cluster with clouds, and had already found their first such signs of Roman work. They'd moved on half an hour into the darkness to be sufficient distance from the ruins that the stink of charred corpses did not reach them, and had there set watches and camped for the night, a short shower of cold rain welcoming them to the south.

The next morning, they had moved on in increasingly dull weather, cold and with a world that felt damp, and soon found legionaries at work. Not killing, this time, but carrying baskets of stones to a narrow river to create a ford through which Roman wagons could pass with ease. Maximus had reined in beside the centurion in charge of the work.

'What's up ahead, Centurion?'

The man had shrugged. 'You'll be safe enough. The Fourth has dealt with most of the valley now. We've got six days left before recall for winter quarters, and the legate is determined to depopulate the valley and prevent any agriculture or industry benefiting the king's fortresses. There's another bunch of your lot up ahead somewhere, at the valley head, from what I hear.'

'Have you come across enemy forces?'

A snort. 'What do you think? We're pioneer corps. We wander along behind the legion cutting rock and building bridges.'

Maximus nodded. 'Have you heard anything, though? And do you know where the fortress called Bolia's Rock is? And the Vulcan Pass?'

The centurion gave him a scathing look. 'You're scouts. Aren't *you* supposed to be the ones finding this sort of thing out for *us*?'

'Oh, for Jove's sake. Do you know or not?'

'Bolia's Peak is right at the top end of the valley, where the gorges start, and then the pass. That's where you'll probably find the rest of the Fourth, as well as your lot.'

Maximus had given the man a rather perfunctory thank you, and led his men away, leaving the grumpy centurion to his labours.

They had ridden on, then. The valley became narrower and narrower as they travelled, all the time moving a little south of east, into the highlands of Dacia. As they moved, they came across more and more signs of the Fourth's activities, in the form of burned farms and hastily-constructed crossings. Finally, as the hills to either side closed in more and more, the camp of the Fourth came into view. The legion had constructed a temporary fortress where the valley floor was still wide enough to accommodate it, just a simple low earthwork crowned with a fence of entwined sudis stakes, filled with ordered rows of leather tents, larger officers' quarters at the centre. Ahead, the valley closed in to a narrow defile.

Approaching the gate, Maximus reined in, his unit slowing behind him, a solid mass of cavalry, travel-worn, and drab. The officer on guard was clearly surprised to see them, and frowned.

'Where have you been?' the man asked, but before Maximus could answer the cryptic question, he shook his head. 'Never mind. Here to see the legate?'

'Yes,' Maximus answered, with a frown of his own.

The officer waved over one of his legionaries. 'Show the rider here to the legate's tent.'

Maximus gestured to Rigozus. 'Keep the men mustered here, outside the gate. I don't expect to be long, and we won't be settling in.' It was yet early afternoon, and he was determined to find out what it was the arcani woodsman had heard to be going on in this area before dark. Leaving his men to it, Maximus followed the legionary along the central road towards the command quarters. As they walked, he took the opportunity to engage the soldier in conversation.

'Have you lads seen any sign of major enemy activity around here?'

The legionary glanced at him and shrugged. 'Thought you'd know more of that than me.'

Once again, the man fell silent, leaving Maximus frowning as they approached the headquarters. At the legate's grand tent, he was left standing for a time while the soldier disappeared inside, and then finally reappeared and gestured at the door with a thumb before turning and walking away, leaving him to it.

Still a little baffled with all this, Maximus stepped within, stopping just inside the door and bowing his head. 'Sir.'

'Ah, good. What news?'

Maximus's creased brow deepened. 'Sir?'

'You've been a while. We were starting to become concerned. But now you're back. What did you find?'

'I think you are mistaken, sir,' Maximus said, quietly and carefully. 'We have just arrived from the east, from the imperial camp.'

Now, the legate took a turn to look confused. 'You're not the Second Pannonian?'

Realisation dawned. 'Ah, I see. You refer to the three turmae assigned to this region. No, we're from the same ala, but just arrived from the west. Do I understand those turmae are missing?'

The legate leaned back in his chair. 'Hmm. More scouts? What do you know of our situation, then?'

'Not a lot, sir. We knew our lads were scouting out here, and that the Fourth were following up to secure the valley. One of the Arcani working in Dacian territory told me that he'd heard "something big" was happening down here, and we have seen signs of large-scale cavalry operations in other areas. I know one of the Dacian mountain fortresses is nearby, a place called Bolia's Rock, and a crossing called the Vulcan Pass that leads back down to the Danubius.'

The legate nodded. 'We had planned on attempting to take Bolia's Rock off the Dacians before we were recalled, but the more we looked at it, the more it became clear that no one was going to take that place in a few days. It's a big fortress, right on the top of a massive peak. The only way up is a narrow path through the hills to the north that turns into steps halfway. And the moment the storm breaks, which seems likely any time now, that approach will be treacherous to say the least. Quite simply, I'm not wasting good men sending them up there.'

Maximus nodded. That didn't really answer his questions, though. He stood silent, waiting, and the legate picked up his story again.

'I think there *may* have been "something big", as you say. When we arrived here, the area was already disturbed, used as a staging ground by a sizeable force, I think. We presumed they had retreated up to the fortress before we arrived.'

'Might I ask, sir, were they cavalry, or infantry, or both?'

'No idea. It was raining when we got here. We just took advantage of the fact they had already cleared out and set up a space for us. We fortified it and settled in. But if it's cavalry you're after, then you need to find your other turmae. When we sent a cohort to Bolia's Rock to weigh up the chances of taking it a few days ago, one century ran into enemy horse, and were rather battered. Your fellow auxilia chased them off, and then went in pursuit. Two days ago, that was, and we've heard nothing from them since then.'

Maximus felt a chill at that. They should have at least checked in by the end of that first day. The only reasons they might not have done so would be inability, through capture or destruction, or because they had found something far too important to leave alone, and could not afford to send anyone back. Either way boded ill for the rest of them.

'You'll follow them?' the legate said.

Maximus nodded. 'I have to, sir. They're my men.'

'I feared as much. I might suggest that to do so is rather foolhardy. If one man enters a dark cave and never returns, the man who follows him in is asking for trouble. At other times, as the region's senior officer, I would command you to stand down and stay in camp, but I am aware of the value the emperor places on his speculatores, and it is not my place to get in the way. Just be careful, and try not to bring the whole weight of Dacia crashing down on the Fourth.'

'Thank you, sir. I will endeavour not to. Can I ask where my riders were last seen?'

The legate nodded. 'Bolia's Rock stands at the entrance to the Vulcan Pass, and the valley runs east from the fortress. I'm given to understand that it turns south before long, but it was in that narrow eastern valley that my men were attacked, and where they last saw your turmae.'

'Thank you again, sir. We must find out what happened to them. I will try and send a messenger either before nightfall or with first light tomorrow, to keep you appraised of what we have found. I might suggest that if you have not heard from us by tomorrow noon, you begin a careful withdrawal from the pass, and back to winter quarters, for if we cannot contact you, then the matter is serious.'

'I will consider as much. I am not averse to the notion, as we were intending to withdraw in five days anyway, back to imperial lines near the pass, and it is increasingly clear that we will not take the local fortress while we are here. Fortuna go with you, soldier. Try and come back alive, and I pray you find your men safe.'

With a last bow, Maximus backed from the tent. The legionary who had escorted him here had gone now, and so he simply strode back along the main thoroughfare towards the gate, outside which his riders were waiting. As he walked, his thoughts raced. He was on the cusp of enlightenment, he was sure. *Something big*, and it was almost certainly the culmination of everything they had seen so far. Big enough to wipe out three turmae of veteran cavalry? Almost a hundred riders, all experienced, hardened by war, and chosen specifically for their knowledge and abilities? That was more than a little worrying, as thoughts went.

With a nod of thanks to the men at the gate, Maximus crossed to where Rigozus held Celeris's reins, and climbed into the saddle.

'What's the plan?' the man asked. Others turned at this, eager to hear.

'Sounds like the other three turmae might have got themselves into trouble in the pass. We need to go and find out what we can, and carefully. I don't want another three turmae to vanish looking for the first three. Come on.'

With that, he urged Celeris on, and they rode around the northern boundary of the huge legionary camp, heading east once more, into the narrower part of the valley. As they moved, the legion fading from sight in the distance behind them, Maximus could feel his tension rising. They were outside all Roman influence again, now, as they had been on the way to Dava, but then they had been in an area of little true danger, close enough to pull back to Roman lines in short order, and out in wide open country suitable for cavalry. Here, they were moving into a narrow, forested defile in the mountains, close to the centre of Decebalus's power, and into an area where they expected danger, where Romans had already disappeared. Every step east made those hills looming to either side all the more dark and threatening, the land ahead less welcoming.

Worse, the clouds that had been rolling in to fill the sky all day were lower and greyer than ever, presaging cold weather and heavy rain in the coming hours. Maximus was acutely aware that they could only afford to go so far along the valley and into the pass without becoming stranded for the night. If they wanted to return to the legion, they could only go until the sun started to close on the mountainous western horizon.

Bolia's Rock was impossible to mistake, when they found it. Much as the legate had described, an almost sheer rock jabbed up into the sky on the northern side of the pass, and they could see the signs of strong walls and towers on the top. From this angle, not even a giant ballista would stand a chance of reaching the place. Unless it was an awful lot gentler on the far side, no commander in his right mind would want to try besieging that citadel. Where the impressive Dava fortress had made Tapae look like a child's toy, this place did the same to Dava. Maximus actually found himself whistling through his teeth.

'Good job they don't want cavalry in sieges, eh?' Arvina murmured, looking up.

'Yes. Let's move on past quite quickly before they spot us and decide to start dropping rocks.'

They did just that, picking up the pace, most of the men looking up nervously as they passed. Only when the rear riders were safely out of the way of it did anyone start to breathe easier.

Half a mile east of the fortress, the rain began. Their spirits steadily sinking as the weather did its worst, soaking them to the skin, the three turmae of men rode on for another hour, heading along the valley to the east. The light was starting to fade, but it was quite possible that was more the fault of the clouds than the sunset. Still, the valley was becoming extremely dark and gloomy, trees closing in close on both sides, peaks above now dark green, dark grey, and very threatening.

'Fuck,' said Rigozus suddenly, and tugged on his reins. Maximus turned in surprise and did the same, the others following suit. The man was glancing off to the right, where the treeline ran parallel, some twenty paces away. Then Maximus saw it too. A small pile of armoured men lay in a jumble just beneath the eaves of the forest. Even from here, their colours and armament made it painfully obvious that they were auxiliary cavalry, and since the only such men anywhere out here were the Second Pannonian, that made it clear that these were riders from the missing turmae.

Maximus waved to his men to hold their position and walked his horse across to the bodies, the rain making a deafening hissing noise as it pounded the foliage above. His heart sank as he approached, for, as he closed, he could see more and more bodies among the trees, and soon could count sufficient to suggest that this was where all three turmae had met their end.

He dismounted, tying Celeris to a tree, and then moved in among the bodies, taking a closer look. He climbed the slope among the dead, some of them men he recognised and knew, examining them. Many of them had died from single wounds, some of which still bore pieces of the weapons responsible, making it clear who had dealt the blows: the contus, the long lance of the Sarmatian warriors. Others had been wounded with sword blows, which could be of any reasonable long, straight variety, but that again fitted with Sarmatian weapons. By the time he'd moved up the hill just a little, he was no longer in any doubt. The three turmae had been killed by Sarmatians, who had probably also taken their horses. That almost certainly meant Roxolani, which might explain where the gathering from Dava had gone.

Somewhere amid the dripping rain and on the endless tree-ridden slope, he found the message. One of the men, a duplicarius, with the same plume and uniform as Maximus, had been separated from the others and laid out on his back, spreadeagled. It should have been easy to miss, and almost anyone else would, but Maximus knew his own cloak, the one Duras had escaped with. It even still had the little tear at the hem and the slight discolouration where a tramp had once pissed on him when he was asleep.

Maximus leaned down and lifted the cloak aside. Sure enough, there, around the soldier's neck, was the chain and tag that identified Duras as Maximus's slave.

The bastard was still out there somewhere, and taunting him, now.

It was only when trouble struck that Maximus realised he had strayed too far up the hill, and could no longer see the others. His only warning was the thunder of hooves. He managed to pull his sword free just as the rider crashed through the branches towards him, heedless of the difficulty this might cause, for both horse and rider were armoured in coats of scales formed from horses' hooves. The man had his lance lowered and aimed straight for Maximus, and came so fast, especially with the additional momentum of a downhill slope, that the Roman had only a moment to react. He dropped to the ground, rolling off to one side and then sweeping back with his sword as hard as he could, just above ground level.

It was well done, if costly. Such Sarmatian riders were hard to injure, so heavily protected were they, but Maximus knew them of old. His sword connected with the horse's front legs below the knees, breaking one and scraping a line across the other. His sword was knocked back out of the way, but the surprised rider suddenly found his horse collapsing in a heap, still sliding forwards down the hill, and was forced to let go of his lance and leap none-too-gracefully from the animal's back.

Maximus missed whatever happened in the next few moments, for, having landed on his bad shoulder, he was cursing and hissing as pain flooded his mind. Blinking it away with gritted teeth, he forced himself to focus and attempted to stand, which took him a moment and a little leaning against the nearest tree, shaking his head.

When he was finally almost compos mentis, he looked around, realising in a panic that the Sarmatian could easily be right behind him now, preparing to run him through. Then he saw the man. The rider had lost his helmet and was already twenty paces away, climbing the hill, limping heavily. Another shout drew Maximus's attention above the drum and hiss of rain, and he turned back to see Rigozus, Arvina and Flaccus stomping up the hill as fast as they could, swords out, towards them.

They may well lose the Sarmatian among the trees by the time they got near him. Grunting, Maximus drew his own sword and gave chase, staggering up the hill behind the rider. It was hard work. The trees were thin enough to allow space, but the slope was steep, the ground uneven, and Maximus winded and still aching badly. Yet he was slowly gaining on the Sarmatian.

He could see the top of the slope, now, and a quick glance over his shoulder told him they had climbed some way, for he could no longer see a sign of the Roman bodies, though the shapes of his three friends were all catching up, clambering through the woods.

He was so close now. Taking a deep breath, and summoning up the very last reserve of energy he had, he sprinted, and threw himself at the Sarmatian. He hit the rider hard, in the back, just as they crested the slope, and the two went down, the enemy rider beneath Maximus. The Roman had little time to think. Before the Sarmatian could recover, he lifted his sword, and brought it down pommel-first on the only unprotected part of the rider's body, the back of his skull.

There was a nasty crack, and the body beneath Maximus shook and trembled for long moments before falling still. Just in case, the Roman gave him another clout, and felt the bone of the man's skull cave in this time. There was no coming back from that.

Panting, wincing, and in a surprising amount of pain, Maximus rose, wobbling, to his feet.

'Shit, but that was impressive,' Rigozus said, rapidly catching up with the others.

Maximus said nothing. He had no reply. All he could do was stare as the rain battered him, running down his face.

From the peak of the hill, through the grey sheet of falling water, he could see the pass as it turned south, opening into a wide bowl of grassland, and beyond that: grey peaks marching away towards the Danubius. The Vulcan Pass, one of the southern approaches to Dacia. But there was hardly any grass to be seen in that wide valley, for it seemed filled from side to side and from end to end with warriors, and largely cavalry.

'Oh, shit,' Flaccus whispered as he came to a halt beside them.

'I think we found the Roxolani,' Maximus said.

'That has to be *half their entire* warrior population,' Rigozus said, quietly. 'Dozens of full tribes. Enough to take on legions at a time. And if *half* the Roxolani are ready for war…'

'Then so are the rest,' Maximus finished for him. 'Half here, the other half presumably still in their lands in the east. And there are infantry down there too. Dacians. Decebalus's men. The emperor has a huge army up in the west, and Laberius has another force in the mountains at Buridava, but neither is anywhere near here. That means that if the Roxolani decide to pour down the pass here, and cross the Danubius back at home, Rome is totally unprepared for them. There's no one in the way to stop them. The wily Dacian bastard has outmanoeuvred the emperor.'

'I think we'd better go while we can,' Rigozus said.

'Yes. And get word to the commanders. Let's just hope there's time to do something about it.'

Winter had come.

But the war would go on.

THE END.

Historical Note

There are, in fact, *two* fascinating real-life characters involved in Trajan's Dacian wars: Tiberius Claudius Maximus, and Lusius Quietus. I originally envisaged this series as a tale told by the two men, and even went so far as to approach other authors with the idea of a joint work, along the lines of what Gordon Doherty and I did with the Rise of Emperors series. As time went by, though, I became more and more possessive of the idea, being a great lover not only of Rome, but of Romania too. I began to see it more as a solo project, and then, when I finally got round to starting to plan it out, I also decided that, although both characters are fascinating, the story was better told through the eyes of just one protagonist. As such, Maximus became my sole hero. Perhaps Quietus, who does appear in this book briefly, will be the protagonist in something else I write in the future.

The Dacian Wars of Trajan, surprisingly, are covered very sparsely in history. Cassius Dio tells us the whole six years of war in just over two thousand words, with only two paragraphs to cover the entire two years of the first Dacian war. Trajan, like all great generals, wrote a record of his campaigns, but unfortunately all that has survived is five words, which at least tell us something useful: *"Inde Berzobim, deinde Aizi processimus"* (We then advanced to Berzobim, and next to Aizi.) Fortunately, as well as these two sparse sources, and a smattering of archaeological evidence, we have the one great record that wows viewers every day: Trajan's column.

The art in trying to trace what actually happened at any given point during the wars lies in trying to match the accounts of both Trajan and Cassius Dio with the scenes from the column, and then both of these with the evidence on the ground. It sounds horrendous, and it does require some serious work, a few leaps of faith, and a lot of tearing out of hair, and yet, having biographised emperors and generals, it's still far from the worst research I've had to do.

Trajan's renowned work on the Danube, at least that which remains and is world famous, actually has an at-best peripheral connection with this book. The bridge he and Apollodorus built at Drobeta, which is remembered as one of the greatest architectural works of the age, was actually built later, and the Danube canal and the carved road, which have now sadly been lost to view thanks to rising water levels following the damming of the river, served to bring troops and goods to the area for the campaign, but have no place actually during it. In fact, of the recorded works of Trajan in this campaign season, all we have is two great pontoon bridges.

On the bright side, they are wonderfully rendered on the column, showing legions and Praetorians marching across them. The column shows two bridges, some way apart, and since there would be no point in them being built close together, we can assume this is a stylistic approach to two entirely separate pontoon bridges. One was clearly constructed near Viminacium (modern Kostolac in Serbia) which was a legionary fortress, a city, and the perfect base for the campaign. Trajan himself gave us the route, via Berzobis and Aizoi, to Tapae, where the battle would be fought… yet again. This indicates a bridge crossing just downstream of Viminacium, on the eastern side of the Nera River. The second bridge is generally believed to have crossed from Transdierna, some way downstream, to Dierna on the north bank, the route following a much narrower and more troublesome valley that would eventually reunite the armies at Tibiscum.

Perhaps I am getting somewhat ahead of myself here. After all, I begin the book eleven years earlier than this. Partly that is the fault of Maximus, who left us a full list of his military career!

I shy away from describing that career in full, and the text of the tombstone, for fear it will act as spoilers for further volumes in this series. Suffice it to say that what he tells us is precisely what happens in this text. Under Domitian, he received decorations in Dacia, and was promoted to the legate's bodyguard and to the flag-bearer of the legion. Then Trajan moved him into an auxiliary unit, made him a scout and a duplicarius. In fairness, that is the bulk of the tombstone's text, anyway. Try not to look him up, or you'll ruin the ending! Tiberius Claudius Maximus, then, is a veteran cavalry officer, having served in both legions and auxilia, as a commander's bodyguard, a flag-bearer and a scout. No wonder he was proud of his career on his tombstone. I have made him a little grizzled and jaded, perhaps because I miss writing Fronto from my Marius' Mules series, but somehow the attitude seems to be a natural fit to the character.

Most of the 'ordinary' characters in this book are my own fictional additions. Maximus, of course, is not, and nor, obviously, are Trajan and Hadrian. Sura, Quietus, Longinus, Livianus, and, in fact, the prefect of the Second Pannonian, are all historically attested characters. But the troopers of the unit are generally my own creations.

We know very little about the campaign that summer, as you might expect, given the meagreness of sources. We know the route that Trajan's own force takes, courtesy of his writings, though not the route of any other advance, and we know they fought the Third Battle of Tapae at the end. In between, we have a few odd glimpses, mainly from the column, such as the army crossing the pontoon bridges (scene V), or Trajan giving out speeches and performing the three-animal sacrifice (scene VIII).

In that same sacrificial scene on the column is an event that continues to have historians arguing. A man, apparently dressed as a slave, falls from a horse, seemingly during that rite. He is also gripping something that looks like a sieve, and is often thought to represent just that, either used in divination, or for gold extraction, for Dacia was rich in gold. Making the slave part of the cast so that I could justify including that scene is what initially brought Duras into this tale, though he quickly grew to be more than a clumsy holder of sieves. I pondered for quite a while on what that object was, and decided in the end not to include it. From Maximus's viewpoint he cannot see it anyway, so that's fine. Look for the scene (scene IX) on the column, and debate it yourself – a brief search on Google for "Trajan's Column scene of falling man" does it nicely. The slave's fall has been accepted by some as an omen of victory, and so that is precisely what I portrayed. Some have noted that the slave does not appear to be Dacian, although this is moot, for a Dacian who had served as a slave for a decade was hardly likely to be bearded and dressed traditionally by that time.

Given that on the column we are treated to no scene of trouble until Tapae, it seems that the army moved through western Dacia unopposed. The reason for that seems clear. Decebalus knew the value of the Iron Gates, and had won one battle there, and only just lost the other. If he *was* prepared and the Romans *weren't*, then he should be able to do it again. The idea that he withdrew all his might to that point is born of the fact that after that battle he did exactly the same again to defend the Dacian heartland. As such, it seems the most plausible approach. And if he is pulling his warriors out ahead of Rome's advance, what would a sensible king do, but remove all possible forage, and everything of use, in the process. Vercingetorix had done much the same to Caesar in Gaul. This, then, is precisely what I have portrayed. We know little of the Dacian settlements in this region, for they were not the massive stone affairs the Romans would later come across, and little has survived. What I have shown you in this tale is based on the topography of the region and known reconstructions of Dacian settlements. As such, there is no need to look for specifics.

Maximus captures a Dacian, north of Berzobis, and this is lifted directly from a scene on the column, where a Dacian prisoner is brought before Trajan, who appears to be accompanied by Hadrian and another officer. So there you go. If you look for that image (scene XVIII), early on in the column's story, you will find a picture of not only the prisoner, but of Maximus himself.

The following few chapters of activity are all born of standard Roman campaign fare – foraging, building and skirmishes. The column continues to show images of road building, forest clearance and the like, and nothing particularly stands out, with the exception of the embassy from the Buri. The second half of the chapter, Trajan's sending of a reply to the Dacian camp, is my own addition, but the embassy of the Buri comes from Cassius Dio's rather sparse account:

"*When Trajan in his campaign against the Dacians had drawn near Tapae, where the barbarians were encamped, a large mushroom was brought to him on which was written in Latin characters a message to the effect that the Buri and other allies advised Trajan to turn back and keep the peace."*

This, I feel, needs some explanation. Firstly, given that this scene occupies about a seventh of Dio's account of the entire first year of the war, it seems very odd that he attaches such importance to what seems a peripheral event, but before we explore further, I will clear up the 'mushroom problem.' Yes, it seems peculiar and extremely unlikely that a Dacian tribe would bring a message for the emperor carved on a mushroom. I sought an answer to this, and the most logical one I came across is the suggestion that there was a transcription error in Dio's account somewhere along the line, and the Greek word 'lykos' became 'mykos'. Mykos would denote a mushroom, but lykos would indicate a wolf, and a message written on a wolf skin seems rather more in keeping, as I'm sure you agree. But despite the fascination of the mushroom account, the actual important thing here, I would say, is that it is the Buri approaching Trajan.

The Dacians were actually made up of several tribes. At times they had been separate, but had combined into one nation under powerful kings such as the earlier Burebista, and now Decebalus. I found myself, therefore, wondering why one tribe, and their neighbours, might tell Trajan to go home, when the whole Dacian army is camped together. The notion that perhaps there was a rift among the Dacian tribes was born from this. Unfortunately, without Trajan's own account surviving, the only information we have on Tapae is Dio's rather brief *"Nevertheless he engaged the foe, and saw many wounded on his own side and killed many of the enemy,"* along with the images from the column. How the battle actually went is unrecorded in literature. As such, building on the rift with the Buri gave me some inkling of how the Romans may have won Third Tapae.

As an aside here, it may also be worth paying some attention to the identity of the Buri. A search will swiftly turn up a tribe of Buri in south-central Dacia, with a capital presumed to be at the site of Buridava. However, in his excellent work on the war (see the later bibliography) Radu Oltean discards the common assumption that it is this tribe who send the embassy before Tapae. If other theories hold, then at the time general Manius

Laberius Maximus, with the third Roman column, would be at Buridava, and so it seems likely that the Buri based in that region would have their hands full there. Another Buri tribe is noted, however, somewhere in the western mountains, north of Tapae and bordering the Iazyges. They are often considered Germans, related to the Suebi, but they are also on the border of Dacia, and so I have portrayed them as something of a mix.

There is, of course, some preamble to the battle itself. I return for a time to the Romans deforesting Dacia, and building roads and camps. I add my own cavalry action scene here, and, having reached the end of the book, you now know why I was placing emphasis throughout the work, on the movements of Sarmatian tribes like the Roxolani. Similarly, at the time you may have wondered about the emphasis I was putting on the weather. Then, the 'Trajan's message that Jupiter protected the Romans,' the onset of storms, the rain not hitting the altar and so on, should become clear with the pivotal moment of the battle. That Trajan might have seen the weather changing and cleverly implanted in the divisive Buri the idea that this was part of Roman power just seemed perfectly logical.

The following chapters, from the first engagements at Tapae right to the aftermath, are my own interpretation of the scenes on Trajan's column. The foraging scene, where the contubernium have their heads taken, is my own invention, but is based upon scene XXV of the column, where the Dacian fortress in the background is decorated with heads on spears.

Incidentally, another of the many contested questions about the Dacian wars is the site of Tapae. Various locations for the Iron Gates pass and the site of Tapae have been proposed. The one that I have used is simply the most commonly accepted among them, being the forested pass between Bucova and Sarmizegetusa, which fits Trajan's noted path, the terrain, and the archaeological evidence best. No sign of the actual battle has turned up, but the remains of presumed ancient Dacian fortifications have been located and mapped on both sides of the pass. My descriptions and the map I include are, once again, based on Radu Oltean's account.

Of Third Tapae, we have ridiculously little information. Above, we saw Dio's only line about the battle itself, and of its aftermath he tells us *"And when the bandages gave out, he is said not to have spared even his own clothing, but to have cut it up into strips. In honour of the soldiers who had died in the battle he ordered an altar to be erected and funeral rites to be performed annually."* And only two scenes on the column show us Tapae and the immediate lead up: Scene XXIII, in which the forest is cleared, and scene XXIV, the battle itself. What the battle scene does show us, though, is what I have included in my telling. Auxiliaries are the ones actually engaging, not legionaries, including cavalry and Germanic clubmen. The legions are shown to the rear with the emperor, in reserve. Men are fighting hard, one with a Dacian head hanging from his teeth by the hair. Two men show severed heads to the emperor, and above the whole battle, we see Jupiter Tonans in his cloud, in a pose ready to throw a thunderbolt. I may have embellished a little, but my telling is directly drawn from the column as the only surviving source of information on the battle.

All we can really infer about the battle and its ending is that the Dacians, seemingly panicked by the thunderbolts of Jupiter, broke and retreated. This being the case, Decebalus has little option but to abandon his defence of the pass and withdraw his army in the best order he can to retreat to the Orăştie Mountains, where he will be safe for the winter. That it is the Buri who break and lose him the battle is my own interpretation, but fits with my own account. The taking and demolishing of the Tapae fortress is, again, my own scene.

Cassius Dio and the scenes of the column seem to agree on the events that followed the battle. We are treated to images on the column of fortresses with severed heads and Dacian buildings being burned. The location of the head-adorned fortress on the column may never be confirmed, but one location suggested for it is that of modern Deva (to which I have assigned the contemporary name of Dava, meaning 'fortress'), where a Dacian citadel was noted on the hill in the Renaissance, later completely destroyed and now underneath the later fortress. I have chosen Deva as my site. Dio tells us why this event is so important:

"Trajan seized some fortified mountains and on them found the arms and the capture engines, as well as the standard which

had been taken in the time of Fuscus." He goes on to tell us that one of the reasons for Decebalus suing for peace was "*the fact that Maximus had at this same time captured his sister and also a strong position.*" It is generally assumed that this is a reference to the general Manius Laberius Maximus down at Buridava. I found myself not only imagining that it was Maximus the cavalryman and not Maximus the general who captured Decebalus's sister, and so I simply portrayed that. If Cassius Dio knocks on my door in the coming days and tells me off, then I shall be contrite. Otherwise, I am happy with my portrayal. The idea that Decebalus had married his sister off to the Buri chieftain to keep them tied to him fit well with my development of the political situation.

We are told that the Dacian king sends a deputation to Trajan, who refuses to meet with Decebalus, but who sends Sura and the Praetorian Prefect. We do not know where the two officers met with the Dacian envoys, not what was said. Cassius Dio tells us of the embassy: "*Those sent were Sura and Claudius Livianus, the prefect; but nothing was accomplished, since Decebalus did not dare to meet them either, but sent envoys also on this occasion.*" I chose to make it a trap they did not trigger, but the fact remains that 'nothing was accomplished.'

We do not know what activity the Roman forces in the area carried out after Tapae in the closing months of the season, but the column does show burning buildings and fleeing Dacians, and so a campaign of terror and depopulation fits with the theme. The massacre of cavalry near Banita fortress, and the mustering of the Roxolani in the pass are my own spin on the unrecorded events that lead us from the summer campaigns of Trajan to the extremely violent and unexpected winter campaigns that will follow in book 2.

As such, then, we have reached the end of the story for now. I hope you've enjoyed Maximus's story and a little tour around early second century Romania. See you in book 2.

Simon Turney

July 2024

Printed in Great Britain
by Amazon